The Heart of the Sun

and sundry other tales

by
Steve Leighton

with pen-and-ink drawings by the author

THE HEART OF THE SUN

and sundry other tales

ISBN 978-0-9926086-2-0

Published by
Dancing Mountain, Glastonbury
email: dancingmountain@outlook.com

British Library Cataloguing-in-Publication Data
A catalogue record for this book is available from the British Library

Typesetting and layout by Red Dog Books
(www.reddogbooks.com)
Printed and bound in Great Britain
by imprint*digital*.net

To order more copies of "The Heart of the Sun" or "Tales of Kaph" (postage free), or to communicate with the author or publisher, email:
dancingmountain@outlook.com
or write to:
Dancing Mountain, 1 Richmond Villas, Chilkwell Street,
Glastonbury, Somerset, BA6 8DF

"You never enjoy the world aright till the sea itself floweth in your veins, till you are clothed with the heavens and crowned with the stars: and perceive yourself to be the sole heir of the whole world, and more than so, because men are in it who are every one sole heirs as well as you."

Thomas Traherne (1636-1674)
Centuries of Meditations I, 29

"Hey man, take a look out the window, see what's happening."
Jimi Hendrix
Electric Ladyland, 1968

"I write for myself and for my friends, and I write to ease the passing of time."
Jorge Luis Borges
Author's note, The Book of Sand, 1975

I add, "...and I write for the joy of writing."

CONTENTS

Author's note: The reader is free, of course, to read these stories in any order he or she chooses. However, some of the stories share common characters and themes. I recommend that stories 1, 4, 5 and 7 are read prior to the final four stories.

1
The Heart of the Sun

"The Sun is God"

reputed last words of
J M W Turner, 1851

I knew, right from the beginning, that something was wrong. By nature I'm an optimist, but in this case I had a feeling - a strange, inexplicable but undeniable intuition - that what we were doing was doomed to failure. And I think I sensed, even then, that the consequences of that failure might change forever the way man considered his place in the Universe. Despite the hopes and fantasies of billions, perhaps we are constitutionally tied to this blue and green planet of ours. Okay, messing around in orbiting space stations or shooting off to the moon may be acceptable. But travelling to distant planets, leaving the Solar System, interstellar flight - it looks like that fantasy is over. For a hundred years or more, the popular assumption has been that it's only a matter of time before we're all zapping off to other stars, exploring the far reaches of the galaxy, "boldly going where no man has gone before" and all that ancient *Star Trek* stuff. Scientists, of course, have always been a bit more conservative in their dreams, what with the speed of light problem to overcome, but even most of them have been tempted by the idea that we just need one good paradigm shift and we'll have cracked it. I was always dubious. Somehow I just sensed that the dream bubble was about to burst.

I kept these thoughts to myself. I'm not stupid. Being head-hunted for "The Great Endeavour", as it came to be called, was the best and most lucrative career move I'd ever made. I became involved at the very heart of the project. It changed my life. It's probably fair to say that it could change the lives of all humanity.

The Great Endeavour to send men into the depths of the Solar System - and perhaps beyond - wasn't exactly secret, but neither was it public knowledge. Interest in space travel had waned in the early decades of the century, relegated to the realm of sci-fi movies. The age of fuel powered rockets was dying. They were simply too big, too cumbersome, too expensive, too dangerous and, frankly, too slow. The theory behind the new technology had been around for a while, although it was claimed that no more than a handful of physicists truly understood it, which is perhaps why it never really captured the public imagination. The mathematics involved was staggering. The smaller the particles, the bigger the sums, or so it seems. Converting the science into workable technology was a slow process: the birth of a radically new generation of space craft. Quantum Transmission, they called it, or QT - inevitably dubbed "Cutie". The motive power comes not from burning fuel but from light, derived, according to Einstein's old $e=mc^2$, from just a tiny amount of water. I don't know how. I'm just a psychologist. Like most people, I'm totally baffled by the weird and wonderful world of quantum physics.

The US government, even the United Nations, weren't interested. Far too costly a business. Far too speculative. Twenty-first Century Earth had more pressing problems to deal with than the sci-fi dreams and arcane equations of a bunch of boffins.

A man of vision was needed. In fact, two men emerged. One was Joseph Fairfield, the computer tycoon, reputedly one of the three wealthiest men in the world. He'd once taken an extra-terrestrial vacation on a Shuttle, and after that there was no stopping him. He dreamed of cruising through the Solar System, like so many others have dreamed. Unlike so many others, however, he was prepared to chuck a few hundred billion dollars at his dream. And then a few hundred billion more. A good bloke, Fairfield. I'd back him for world president, any day. Not that he needs anyone's backing. These days, it's money, not votes, that brings power. Actually, it's probably always been that way.

The second visionary was Dancing Mountain, a vast bulk of a man of Native American stock, a brilliant manager of people and machines who'd cut his teeth on projects in the final years of NASA. He was a no-nonsense, down-to-earth, natural leader, known by all of us simply as "Boss". Fairfield trusted him to lead The Great Endeavour, and so did the rest of us.

As for me, I was brought in on the medical team during the second, manned phase of the project. My expertise was the psychology of deliberately altered states of consciousness - sensory deprivation, deep meditation, hallucinogenic drugs and so on. Consequently, it never surprised me that I acquired the epithet "Dr Psycho" or "The English Shrink" - these Americans love snappy nicknames - and was never treated with the respect I fancied I deserved - except by Dancing Mountain, that is, who treated everyone with respect, from the top astronauts to the office cleaner. Psychology was considered to be the poor relation of Science, with a capital S, by all the physicists, astronomers, engineers, metallurgists, physiologists and computer whizz-kids on the payroll. How could psychology call itself a science, said the scientists, when it had absolutely no mathematical basis? We psychologists get used to such jibes. And I got used to my tiny office, well removed from the dynamic hub of the project. Besides, I was a mere doctor amongst a bunch of professors. My one claim to fame - or notoriety, as it happened - was to have written a book about my experiments with psychedelics that played some small part in the relaxation of the British drug laws, back in the 2020s.

It's generally supposed that I indulge regularly in recreational chemicals, but the truth is I haven't touched a thing for years. The greatest "high" I ever experienced, over a decade ago, came after a few years of complete abstinence - including alcohol and coffee - half way up a mountainside in Wales during a Zen Buddhist retreat. Suddenly, and quite spontaneously, I was aware of my consciousness expanding to encompass the heather-clad hills, the dark mountain tops, even the sky itself. At the same time, my ego and my thoughts were shrinking into silence. "I am everything and nothing," was the single thought that remained, drifting quietly through the vast bowl of awareness that was both me and the world. I felt so indescribably ecstatic that I stripped off my clothes and lay naked in the heather, soaking up the summer sunshine, simply being.

It was then that my fateful intuition first dawned - an unquestionable, tacit understanding, although I have since clothed it in many words. This is where mankind is meant to be, I realised. This is our natural home, our birthright. Right here, ninety-three million miles from the Sun, on this beautiful planet called Earth. Here, conditions are perfect, not just for man's body but his entire being. Our psyches are precisely attuned to this one, unique place in the Universe. Maybe the reason that we've never been visited by intelligent alien life is not because they're not intelligent enough, elsewhere in the galaxy, but because they're wiser than us. They understand that our life is intimately bound to our home planet, not simply physically, but in the depths of our souls.

It's taken a long time for any of my colleagues to regard this idea as anything other than pseudo-religious claptrap. I've even been tempted, myself, to dismiss it as wild fantasy. But then I found myself working for The Great Endeavour, and now I'm convinced.

Of course I kept quiet about all this. I was enjoying myself. This was the biggest thing in human history. The most expensive, anyway.

Most of the hard work had been completed by the time I came on board in 2035, some five years after the birth of the project. The infrastructure was well in place. The technology was sorted, tested and ready to go, orbiting the Earth on one of the space stations left from a former era. Local, unmanned trials of QT powered craft had proved successful. Now, for the first time since the Voyagers had left the Solar System back in the Twentieth Century, "Cutie 1", as she was called, was set to plumb the depths of interstellar space. The journey to the stars was about to begin.

It took less than six months for Cutie 1 to pass beyond Neptune's orbit. Things were looking good. The new power source was doing what it was supposed to do. Cheers and congratulatory hugs back in Endeavour headquarters. Then, a month later, came total computer failure - a huge embarrassment for the Fairfield Foundation who had, of course, supplied all the computer technology. But no one outside The Great Endeavour knew about it, so I suppose it wasn't really an embarrassment. Just a set-back.

All communication with Cutie 1 ceased, all control lost. Presumably it's still out there somewhere, en route for Centauri, but what it will find if it ever gets there, we'll never know.

Cue Cutie 2. The plan was to send it on a quick tour of the outer planets, then home in time for Christmas. Even I don't know what happened to that one. The in-house rumours spoke of self-destruction. Was something fundamentally wrong? No. All the science was spot-on, so we were told. Plans for Cutie 3 went ahead, the first manned flight.

Some argued that installing humans was an unjustifiable risk, an unnecessary complication, but of course the dream of mankind has always been for real men and women to cruise the stars, not soulless hunks of metal. Besides, Joseph Fairfield held the purse-strings and, although too old himself, he cherished the notion of his grandchildren hopping from planet to planet. And there was no shortage of prospective astronauts, eager to make history.

Dancing Mountain was dubious. He wanted more tests. What was the hurry?

Joseph Fairfield was well over eighty - that was the hurry. And, of course, he got his way. He got his way in most things - even the soundtrack that would accompany the mission. His favourite music dated back to his young hippy days, hanging out on the West Coast before he found his niche in Silicon Valley. Top of his play list was an anarchic epic by a group of San Francisco rockers calling themselves Jefferson Starship. He'd often pump it through the speakers in the control centre of The Great Endeavour:

"Have you seen the stars tonight?
Would you like to go up on A Deck and look at them with me?
Do you know, we can go, we are free
Any place you can think of, we can be.
Have you seen the stars tonight?
Have you looked at all the family of stars?"

And, not surprisingly, Dancing Mountain, who loved the wild empty plains of his native land, longed to be a part of mankind's great escape into limitless space. Except that he wasn't quite sure how mankind would take it. Which was largely why I was there: to keep an eye on the psychological states of Cutie's human incumbents.

One of many peculiar things about the QT drive was its slowness to reach decent speeds. Unlike the old rocket technology which started with an almighty thrust, this was a far gentler, less traumatic ride. It was reckoned that it could give a healthy fraction of the speed of light, but it would take a while to get there.

"Imagine a car accelerating from nought to sixty in ten seconds," I was told by one of the physicists. "That's about what Cutie does - to begin with. But it keeps on accelerating. In a hundred seconds, it's up to 600 mph. In a thousand seconds it's reached 6000 mph. Keep multiplying by ten. In a million seconds - that's about 12 days - it's up to 6 million mph, which is about one percent of light speed. At that speed, we could leave the Solar System in a few weeks. Unfortunately, though, the equations start to get a bit warped once we reach 0.1 percent light speed. But even that's pretty darn fast."

That was about as far as my understanding went. It seemed that our space craft, assembled up there on the space station, could take a small crew to the vicinity of Mars in a week or so, then on to Jupiter, Saturn and the rest in a matter of months. Within six months, she'd be back in Earth's orbit. This was to be our initial mission. Breaching the vastness of inter-stellar space was still considered to be a quantum leap away. Even at one percent of light speed, it would take four hundred years to get to the nearest star, Proxima Centauri. But the boffins were confident that, one day, the QT equations could be jiggled to take us to at least a tenth of light speed, maybe even a half, at which speed we could make the return trip in as little as ten years. But Fairfield was well content to see us exploring the planets in his lifetime, and Dancing Mountain - ever the pragmatist - thought the Solar System to be a big enough playground for the time being.

The general assumption, based on previous experience of astronauts in orbiting stations, was that isolation, confinement and the effects of weightlessness were the central problems. We'd coped perfectly well with these things before, and we could do so again. Part of my job was to ensure that our crew were as healthy, stable, well-adjusted and emotionally competent as possible. Prolonged isolation was considered to be the big challenge. We never imagined that homesickness - as it was later euphemistically called - would be a crucial factor. Our men and women were picked for their maturity and strength of character. Homesickness was an affliction of insecure little kids.

Milton Irving and Crystal Stellof were selected for Cutie 3 - Milton an ex-air-force pilot, Crystal an astro-physics PhD - both young and fit. They were good, creative, highly intelligent, happy specimens of humanity, I had to admit. At least, they were at the beginning.

They hopped up to the space station on the latest generation of Shuttle - still, after over fifty years and with surprisingly few modifications, the best way to leave the Earth's atmosphere. Cutie 3 awaited them: the most sophisticated, expensive vehicle that mankind had ever constructed. My medical colleagues and I were assigned a console at the far end of the mission control hall in The Great Endeavour HQ. Our tasks were to observe and measure every conceivable aspect of the bodies and behaviour of our two subjects. That was all we did. For months.

Halfway to the moon, Irving activated the Quantum Transmission Drive. Cutie 3 began its gradual acceleration. Within a couple of weeks, as predicted, they were well on the way towards nought-point-one percent of light speed, moving faster than any human beings had ever moved before. They zapped past Mars and reached Jupiter in a little under four weeks. Another four weeks, and they were cruising past Saturn. Everything was going splendidly. Cutie 3 behaved herself perfectly.

But something was happening to Milton and Crystal.

It's difficult having real-time conversations with someone a billion kilometres away.

"How you doing?" we'd ask from control.

Two hours later (an hour each way), would come the reply, "Fine, thanks. And you?"

We relied, more, on the medical monitors and the personal diaries each of them sent each day. At first they were predictably euphoric: full of excitement, efficiency, dedication to the mission, plus the occasional, almost obligatory, "Send my love to the folks back home" kind of thing. After Mars, their moods gradually became more subdued, their messages briefer. It was clear that they were making an effort to appear perky, but we began to wonder. Perhaps they were getting bored with the daily routine. Perhaps they were pissed off with each other's company. (Milton was gay - deliberately chosen as such, we suspected - so we knew there was no funny business going on with Crystal.)

As they approached Saturn, their moods had become worryingly low. Back at control, we were all ecstatic at the pictures they were sending back - those giant planets really are awesomely beautiful, close up - but Milton and Crystal seemed, well, frightened, I suppose. They were almost shaking with fear.

God, they looked bad. We were worried. In a matter of weeks, they'd changed almost beyond recognition. From a couple of high-flying, super-dynamic, know-it-all, top-scoring astronauts, they now came across as no-hope layabouts who'd hitched a ride to nowhere. Crystal - once a good looking woman - looked a complete mess, making absolutely no effort to spruce herself up for the daily camera session. She'd developed acne and, it seemed, a nervous tic in her right eye. Milton looked like the sort of chap you'd chuck a dollar at if you passed him lying in a back alley. He'd stopped shaving and seemed incapable of making eye contact with the camera. His words were becoming increasingly inarticulate.

The medics diagnosed clinical depression. They also noted falls in blood pressure and pulse, plus various anomalies in metabolic activity. The two astronauts took to sleeping maybe twenty hours each day and almost stopped eating. Fifteen weeks out - well on the way to Uranus - their daily messages amounted to no more than a few barely articulated words. Finally, they dried up altogether. Milton's last diary entry showed a bleary-eyed slob lying on his bunk mumbling, "Fuck off and leave me alone." Crystal continued for a few days more, alternating between silent, morose dejection and pitiful sobbing.

Her final message shook us all: a whispered, plaintive, childlike begging for mercy. "Please bring me home." Again and again, her face torn in a look of agony and grief, “For pity’s sake, please bring me home.”

Dancing Mountain, I noticed, had tears in his eyes, standing like a rock in front of the master-screen. He was silent for several minutes, all eyes upon him, as we all shared the eerie silence. Then he shouted the order. “Enough! Get to work on the calculations right away. Organise an immediate U-turn. Bring ‘em back!”

No more messages arrived from Cutie 3. By the time they’d returned to the vicinity of Saturn, the medical monitors indicated a complete absence of life on the ship. The more optimistic amongst us clung on to the hope that the monitors themselves had malfunctioned, but most of us came to accept the truth.

Fifteen weeks later, the on-board computer completed a successful docking with the Earth space station. The first astronaut to enter Cutie carried a video camera. Back home, we saw it all.

Milton had died in his bunk, his body so wasted and desiccated that he looked like an old man. Crystal was floating gently around the zero-gravity living quarters in her underwear, a syringe protruding from a vein in her arm. A massive morphine overdose.

It was all kept secret, of course. The official story that circulated around The Great Endeavour HQ blamed the tragedy on a minor technical fault in the life support systems.

Two days later, a sombre inquest took place in Dancing Mountain’s conference room. Just a few of us medics and psychologists were present, together with the leading technical staff. Joseph Fairfield was apparently too distressed to make it.

All the evidence was presented, but no conclusion was reached to explain the deaths of Milton and Crystal. The verdict of severe clinical depression seemed woefully inadequate to all of us. After all, these astronauts had been selected for their mental stability. Their psychological profiles had been as near to perfect as was possible.

Dancing Mountain - who, like Fairfield, was fond of peppering his talk with quotes from rock songs of a bygone era - summed up with a line from Bob Dylan. “So, something is happening here but we don’t know what it is, do we, Mr Jones?”

We all glanced around awkwardly, wondering who Mr Jones might be.

"Possibilities!" roared Dancing Mountain, slapping the table. "Let's have your theories."

"An effect of prolonged isolation and incarceration, Boss?" suggested one of the medics, rather apologetically.

"Nonsense. We've had personnel on the space station for five times as long."

"Perhaps the unprecedented acceleration of the QT Drive has some physiological effect we had not anticipated," ventured another. "After all, no human being has ever before travelled at such a high velocity."

"The acceleration is prolonged but gradual," one of the physicists replied. "Much greater acceleration is experienced on the Shuttle at take-off."

"But perhaps human physiology cannot adapt to point one percent of light speed."

"Any evidence? Any theory supporting your idea?" demanded Dancing Mountain.

"Not as yet, Boss" admitted the medic.

"Life conditions were stable," said Dancing Mountain. "Zero gravity, prolonged isolation, acceleration: these are all matters we've encountered before. High speed is the only new possibility, but, as the physicists keep telling us, speed is all relative."

"Some form of radiation from the QT Drive?" suggested one of my colleagues.

"God knows. Who understands such things?"

"That's not a possibility, Boss," replied a physicist. "No more radiation than from a mobile phone. I guarantee that the Quantum Transmission Drive is one hundred percent safe."

We all stared at him. We'd heard that one before - many times and about many things.

"So what else?" Dancing Mountain was a man who expected answers.

This was where I stepped into the discussion.

"There are two factors we haven't considered, sir," I said, rather tentatively, my voice rarely heard at these high-level meetings.

"Which are, Dr Er...?" (No one ever remembered my name.)

"Distance from the Earth and distance from the Sun."

"So what bearing might these factors have?"

"I don't know, Boss" I confessed. "But one certainty is that no human has ever travelled so far from home, and no one has ever been so far removed from the Sun."

"So?"

"So perhaps the bodies or the psyches of human beings cannot tolerate being so many miles from their home planet."

A slightly contemptuous murmur arose amongst the physicists, but, as a psychologist, I'm used to such things. Dancing Mountain, to his credit, kept his gaze unflinchingly on me.

"Homesickness, eh?" he said. "You reckon it's as simple as that?"

"No one seems to have any better explanation," I said, rather boldly.

He stared at me for a while before turning the corners of his mouth into the barest hint of a smile. "Work on it," he decreed. "We need a theory and we need a remedy. And we need them fast!"

Again he slammed the palm of his hand forcefully on the table, indicating that our meeting was over.

And that was how "homesickness" became the central project of my very small team of fellow psychologists. The literature and research were virtually non-existent. Most people know what it is to feel homesick, but to regard it as a real and potentially fatal affliction seemed a bit over the top. And to suggest that its intensity might be directly proportional to distance from home was absurd in the extreme. And yet... to me it all seemed somehow obvious.

At times we had to laugh. Imagine the headlines if our research was published. "Interstellar spaceflight limited not by the speed of light, not by inadequate propulsion, but by the fact that humans get homesick." Our dreams shattered because mankind can't cope with the trauma of being more than a few million miles from home.

Gradually I modified my opinion. Perhaps it wasn't the Earth that we couldn't do without, but the Sun. I recalled that day in the Welsh mountains. "This is where we are meant to be," I had thought, in the creative rush of my ecstasy. "Ninety-three million miles from the heart of the Sun, where its rays warm our bodies without burning, where its light colours our world without blinding, where its golden disc subtends an angle in the sky of just over half a degree." This is where we're meant to be, not in the blackness of absolute-zero space where the Sun is but a faint and distant speck of light. Even from the moons of Jupiter, the Sun appears no greater than a largish star - hardly the life-giving, comforting, beautiful sustainer of the Solar System.

And perhaps the "homesickness" effect was as much physical as psychological. The Sun pours out vast quantities of radiation. We respond primarily to its heat and light, but what of the countless other forms of solar radiation in which our bodies are bathed? And, of course, the intensity of that radiation is inversely proportional to distance. (In fact it's inversely proportional to the square of distance - my physics has always been a little shaky.) At 93 million miles, the distance of Earth's orbit, our bodies are perfectly suited to that radiation. At ten times that distance - the orbit of Saturn - the radiation is diminished by a hundred fold. Who knows what effects this might have? Who knows how the human being might react when the levels of radiation he receives from the Sun are reduced to a mere one percent of normal? We're talking, here, of radiation that can pass through solid planets and the protective outer casings of space craft like a hot knife through butter. I don't mean just the nasty stuff that the Earth's atmosphere and magnetic field - like the shielded walls of space craft - protect us from. The whole Solar System is simply saturated in immense spectrums of solar radiation. Perhaps this radiation is as vital to us as oxygen. Who knows? No humans - apart from Milton and Crystal - have ever been deprived of it. We live our lives bathed in the Sun's vast ocean of electro-magnetic radiation like fish forever swimming in water. We haven't a clue how its drastically weakened intensity might affect us. We're really floundering in the dark with this one.

This was the problem: a complete absence of verifiable fact; a wild theory and absolutely no evidence to support it, beyond a couple of mysteriously dead astronauts. Controlled experiments were needed. And it seemed to me that the only place to conduct such experiments was not in a particle accelerator buried deep in the Earth's crust, but out there in the depths of space. And not using machines but living human beings.

Dancing Mountain, upon reading my progress report - such as it was - wanted to see me. ("Get the English shrink up here," was the message I received.)

"So, what d'you think, Dr Er...?" he asked, after I'd briefly summarised my ideas. "Fairfield's pressing for action. We gotta make some kinda movement."

"I'd like to see a structured programme of trials, Boss" I suggested. "We could send manned Cuties out to varying distances from the Sun and closely monitor physical and psychological effects. We need data before we can venture solutions."

"Sure, sure. Mars, perhaps? We gotta have some positive goals."

"Maybe. We didn't observe any serious effects with the crew of Cutie 3 until they approached Jupiter. Maybe Mars would be a safe bet - give us some solid info without endangering lives."

"What about Venus? Mercury?"

I was puzzled. "Surely we're talking about heading away from the Sun, not towards it?"

"Why not?" Dancing Mountain, once he'd picked up an idea, really rolled with it. "If I get you right, Doc, you're saying that people get pissed off the further from the Sun they travel, right?"

"That's the hypothesis, Boss, yes."

"So why not the reverse? Head towards the Sun and see if it bucks 'em up, makes 'em happy."

"There's no evidence to suggest that possibility," I said, but I could see where the big chap was leading.

"Only because we've never tried it."

"True. We've always had our sights set on leaving the Solar System, not reaching its heart."

"So why not, eh? Old Fairfield wants us to explore planets. He doesn't mind which ones. And maybe a trip to Mercury really would be a trip. Mind-blowing. Like a massive dose of natural acid, eh? A truly cosmic orgasm. You're the consciousness altering expert, Dr Er... What d'you reckon?"

"Perhaps," I ventured, uncertainly.

To be honest, I didn't have a clue. But a part of me loved the idea. If we're investigating the correlation between state of consciousness and distance from the Sun, then why not try decreasing as well as increasing that distance? And decreasing it by half - almost as far off as Mercury - would increase the Sun's radiation four-fold. Could we expect a corresponding four-fold increase in measurable aspects of our astronauts' states of consciousness? An intriguing idea indeed.

And, not surprisingly, Joseph Fairfield was smitten by the idea. Sometimes, he and Dancing Mountain were like a couple of schoolboys together: giggling, bantering, letting their creative imaginations run riot. And sometimes they invited me to join their jovial sessions. Dancing Mountain seemed to have taken a shine to me. Perhaps I was less rigid in my thinking than all the physicists and engineers with whom he usually hung out. I think he felt that he could drop his persona and be himself with me. As the Americans say, we connected.

Occasionally he'd call me. "Come on up, Doc. Old Joseph's here and we're cracking open the tequila. Come and join us."

So up I went and together the three of us partied - as they also say. Good times. I was happy to find some relief from the concentrated seriousness of the vast majority of my Great Endeavour colleagues. Dancing Mountain and I were becoming good mates - "The Boss and the Doc", as Joseph Fairfield liked to call us.

We presented the new plan as further trials of QT Drive within Earth's immediate neighbourhood, the inner planets. The psychological aspects of the revised program were played down, but I was pushed up to head psychologist, with a salary that was itself almost astronomical and a centrally positioned console in The Great Endeavour HQ. The place was buzzing with excitement again.

Cutie 3 - refurbished and updated - went on a three week jaunt around Mars and back. Technically perfect. All equipment functioning one hundred percent. And the psychological data seemed to support my theory. Profiles of the two astronauts, throughout the flight, showed a small but significant decrease in intellectual ability, proportional to the square of distance from the Sun, and marked changes in scores on personality tests: increased depression, introversion and neurosis, decreased creativity and general mood level. These changes were corroborated by the daily video diaries. The astronauts couldn't explain what was happening to them: they just felt low, irritable and lethargic the further they travelled, yet gradually returned to their normal lively, bubbly, happy selves on the way home.

The physicists, naturally enough, pooh-poohed all this non-mathematical data, but the figures we gathered from those tests involving numerical scales were indisputable. The graphs of test scores against distance from the Sun were crystal clear: down on the way out, up on the way back. Dancing Mountain was impressed.

"I think we're on to something, here, Doc," he told me. "Could be big. Revolutionary, you might even say."

He was an astute, quick-thinking, open-minded man - that, presumably, was why he was leading the project. As his name implied, he was rock solid but, when he decided to move, the whole world felt it. He had fully grasped the implications of this research. At once, he ordered preparations for Cutie 3's next mission: the inner planets. We both looked forward to it with the utmost eagerness and scientific curiosity.

Bill Schneider would captain: an experienced space station astronaut who spent his free time trekking through Earth's few remaining wildernesses. Bob Jennings would accompany him as engineer: a brilliant scientist who topped the list of candidates in just about all the scales we psychologists could devise. We were all convinced: these were two fit, fine and spirited human beings.

"Lucky bastards," said Dancing Mountain.

I felt the same way. These two men were about to experience something that no human beings had ever before known, perhaps the high to top all highs. I just hoped they could take it.

The QT acceleration was kept relatively low as Cutie 3 set off for Venus. We wanted ample time to monitor conditions - both external and internal. Even so, a journey that would once have taken months was accomplished in a matter of days. Venus, close up, proved to be astonishingly beautiful. Not surprisingly, our two astronauts were overwhelmed with joy and wonder. They both self-assessed at 10 out of 10 on the happiness scale. There was not a trace of the low spirits that had afflicted Milton and Crystal and the Mars mission.

The mood was high, too, back at The Great Endeavour headquarters, as we sent them cruising serenely towards Mercury.

Bill Schneider was never a great talker. He chose his words carefully. Effusiveness in speech was not his way. But his body language was as open and expressive as a pet dog's. There was no doubting that he was really enjoying himself. Prolonged exposure to Joseph Fairfield and Dancing Mountain, prior to the mission, had, it seemed, turned him on to the favourite brand of music of them both - the psychedelic, space-inspired rock of the 1960s and 70s, which, as it happened, was making something of a come-back in the late 30s. Bill played it frequently, sitting at the helm of Cutie 3 - Pink Floyd, Grateful Dead and Fairfield's favourite, Jefferson Starship.

"What you going to do when you feel your lady rolling
How you going to feel when you see your lady strolling
On the deck of a starship with her head hooked into Andromeda..."

And Bill, a wide smile on his face, his feet tapping wildly, was hardly able to restrain his body from leaping into frenzied dance. We loved it too, back at HQ. Sometimes the whole place really rocked. And we loved to watch Bill and Bob go merrily about their daily astronautic business. It was like watching a ballet of joy, grace and total absorption.

"We're witnessing humanity at its absolute pinnacle," Dancing Mountain confided in me. "Controlled rapture. Single-minded intelligence coupled with gleeful spontaneous flow. I really love those guys."

Bob was a truly dedicated scientist. His eyes were constantly flicking across the bank of monitors on his console, twiddling knobs, tapping his touch-pad. But he, too, wore a constant smile and his head rocked back and forth to the beat of Bill's bizarre musical fantasies.

Bob's musical tastes were rather different. He was into Bruckner, particularly the celestial moodiness of the Eighth and Ninth

Symphonies. Bruckner and Gregorian chants - but he only indulged when he was on his own in the control cabin.

"Let me tell you something," he said once, when Bill was engaged somewhere else in the space craft. "Let me tell you this, all you lovely folk back home. I'm truly sorry you can't all be here with us to share this majesty, this... divinity. You know, I've never been a religious man, never quite understood all that God business. I'm a scientist. But, right now, I understand it all perfectly. God is this burning ball of light right in front of us. This is God, as sure as anything: not some bearded old man in the clouds, not some nebulous, ghostly, spiritual presence, but this very real, material sphere of pure beauty just out there, just a few million miles away."

Back at HQ, the control room fell silent. We all turned to gaze at the master screen and its ever-growing image of the Sun.

"Think about it," Bob continued, his voice soft but infused with the passion of an evangelistic preacher. "How is God usually described? Omnipotent, Omnipresent, Omniscient, Eternal, All-loving, the Creator and Sustainer of all life. Now consider the Sun. Obviously it's the Sun that has created and sustains all life on Earth. Clearly it's all-powerful - just look at it! It's eternal - or as near as damn it, compared to our woefully short lives. It's everywhere - not just that burning ball out there, but its emanations, its radiation, the streaming solar particles of its being encompass the entire Solar System. All-loving? Well, that light pouring from it, saturating everything, that's the greatest love I've ever known. Sunlight is the love of God, sure as hell. All those ancient, sun-worshipping, pagan civilisations we like to call primitive had it spot on, I reckon. Sunlight is love. Let's venerate it."

He gave us a beaming smile. There was no doubt about it: here was a man deeply in love. In love with the Sun.

"And what about omniscience?" he continued. "How can a ball of burning hydrogen be all-knowing? A good question. Omniscience requires consciousness. So first, tell me what consciousness is? A pretty hard question, eh? Our best guess is that consciousness is generated through the complexity of the human brain - the most complex thing in the world, even including our biggest, fanciest computers. Well, this huge shining ball in front of us is vastly more complex still. That's what the solar astro-physicists tell us. It's not just a ball of burning hydrogen. It's a billion billion different chemical and nuclear reactions every moment, all interconnected in patterns that endure from nano-seconds to millennia. Let me tell you, seen from up close this Sun of ours buzzes with life like a gigantic brain. This is consciousness on an unimaginable scale. This is the all-knowing consciousness of God. This is our Creator, our Heavenly Father.

"We're heading straight towards the loving heart of God. I don't mean that poetically or metaphorically. I mean it literally. Absolutely literally. The Sun is God. Sunlight is the love of God."

All was quiet in the control room of The Great Endeavour HQ, all eyes staring at the image of Bob, his face shining like the icon of a saint. Dancing Mountain stood mountain still in the centre of the room. Slowly he placed his palms together and bowed his head. Softly but distinctly he pronounced, "Amen."

And many of the men and women around him, as though with a single voice, echoed, "Amen."

What we were witnessing, here, was not just scientific history in the making, but the birth of a new religious awareness. Bob Jennings and Bill Schneider were transforming, before our eyes, into the enlightened prophets of a New Age.

And we loved them. We were their first disciples.

Sometimes it was easy to forget that they were just a couple of astronauts on a mission to the inner planets.

We had to insist that they leave their stations, occasionally, to eat and sleep. Their hours of sleep dropped to two or three hours per day, yet their performances never suffered. On the contrary, Bob significantly upped his already impressive scores on some of the speed based intelligence and manual dexterity tests.

Meanwhile, we noticed that, to some extent, Bill was losing interest in the constant testing regime.

"Hey, let's just be here," he said, once. "Let's just wallow in the wonder of it all."

Response times, this close to home, were only a matter of minutes.

"Don't forget, Bill," said Dancing Mountain, "that we're looking for hard data. You're not just there to enjoy yourselves. Do the tests, man."

Eight minutes later, we saw Bill giving us the thumbs up, his eyes shining. "Sure thing. Sorry, Boss." And he launched immediately into the next test programme, humming along to his music as he went.

We observed very, very closely, but we could find nothing whatsoever to criticise in Bill's or Bob's behaviour or mood or bodily responses. We replayed the final video diaries of Milton and Crystal, alongside the current ones of Bill and Bob. You couldn't imagine a greater contrast: the suicidal and the ecstatic - two extremes of human emotion. It almost felt embarrassing and intrusive to look at Milton's and Crystal's crushing despair, while it was a positive joy to share the ebullient euphoria of our two Mercury-bound heroes.

Between missions, Cutie 3 had been specially adapted for its journey through the inner Solar System. Its outer casing, so the engineers reliably informed us, could withstand the Sun's heat and radiation up to a proximity of about twenty million kilometres, probably much closer, which sounds like a pretty long way out, but it's less than half the orbit of mercury. All the portholes in the craft had been coated with layers of screening material, still transparent but blocking the full, blinding intensity of the naked sunlight. Bill and Bob, we noticed, spent much of their time just gazing ahead at the ever-burgeoning mother star, and, it seemed to Dancing Mountain and me, the looks on their faces were of pure love.

Mercury slipped by - a glowing, multi-coloured orb. They greeted it enthusiastically, marvelled at its beauty, took all the required measurements and pictures, then returned their attention to the Sun.

They were enraptured. Their verbal reports became little more than exclamations of awe and bliss - feelings for which few words exist. "Wow" and "Oh, man" and "Mmm-aah" and other inarticulate attempts to express what, for them, was way beyond expression.

Their music grew louder. Bill now interspersed Bach and Mozart with the ever-popular Jefferson Starship and Pink Floyd. Bob favoured what he called the immaculate perfection of Beethoven's final string quartets.

Their sleep and food intake declined almost to zero, yet their alertness ratings were way off all normal, Earth-bound scales, as though they were feeding on a diet of pure adrenalin - or a diet of high intensity sunlight. Their behavioural profiles - and, we had to infer, their consciousness states - suggested a couple of super-humans. Angels, perhaps.

Dancing Mountain took me to one side. “Point proven,” he said, giving me a good slap on the back. And let me tell you, a slap on the back from this man mountain is no joke.

I wallowed in pride for a bit. My theory had been suitably vindicated. There appeared to be a very definite correlation between distance from the Sun and, to put it in its simplest terms, degree of happiness. And, yes, I felt satisfied and happy that I had nailed the problem that had bedevilled the first Cutie missions. But, to be honest, I think my personal happiness was completely overshadowed by the happiness I felt for these two men heading towards the heart of the Sun.

“Good work, Doc,” said Dancing Mountain. “But what we’re going to do with this new-found understanding of ours, I’ve no idea. Looks like it rules out further trips to the outer planets. And God knows what it does to mankind’s dreams of interstellar flight. So much for all that sci-fi stuff, eh? We won’t be boldly going anyplace. We’re going to have to totally re-think our ideas of humanity’s destiny in that vast Universe out there. Looks like we’ll never see the stars any closer than when we look up at the sky at night.”

“Apart from that one very clear, very bright star of ours,” I said, “to which our two boys are heading right now with, I’m beginning to think, Boss, rather reckless abandon.”

“Yep,” said Dancing Mountain, returning at once from reverie to management mode. “I think it’s time we brought them back.”

We exchanged a quick glance, an unspoken sharing of an uneasy apprehension, then we hurried back to the control room.

The QT Drive had been turned off after Mercury. Cutie 3 was cruising at constant speed towards the Sun. The best calculations of the boffins - for this was strictly new territory - was that they could continue on their present course for another few hours, at most, before things started getting unpleasantly hot and dangerous.

"Time to come home, lads," Dancing Mountain issued his order during the next link-up.

Bill and Bob were sitting together, staring through the front porthole. The camera pointing at the backs of their heads showed virtually the entire window frame consumed by the body of the Sun.

"We can go much further yet," said Bill. "Conditions are still far from critical."

"I think not," said Dancing Mountain. "We've got all the data we need. Better safe than sorry. Let's get you back while all is well. We've programmed in the co-ordinates. You should start manoeuvring now. Change trajectory. Get into the Sun's orbit. We'll whip you round the back of the Sun and then whisk you home, past Mercury and Venus again."

There was a long pause from the other end - much longer than the expected ten minute delay as the signal zapped from Earth to beyond Mercury and back again. We could see Bill and Bob looking at each other, then looking back through the anterior port.

At last Bill spoke. "I think not, Boss. You've no idea what it's like here. It's totally beyond your comprehension. There's absolutely no way we can let this go - absolutely no way at all. She's pulling us in, Boss. We're powerless to resist. We're going all the way."

Yes, I had sort of anticipated this scenario. How can you give a couple of blokes the biggest natural high in human history, then tell them to turn it off and come home, just as they're reaching the climax?

Dancing Mountain smiled and pressed the transmit button. "OK, guys. I think I know what you mean. But, well, I'm afraid that's enough. It's time for you to bring Cutie 3 back home." A few seconds silence in The Great Endeavour HQ, then he added, "And I mean that, Bill and Bob. Turn her 'round."

As I've suggested before, no one ever argued the toss with Dancing Mountain. He was a man of exceptional charisma and authority. But no one had ever experienced what Bill and Bob were experiencing just then. They were on the point of transcending all authority. They were about to become divine beings.

Ten minutes passed very slowly. Then another ten minutes. There was no response from Cutie 3. Our screen showed Bill and

Bob with their attention locked exclusively upon the vast globe of the Sun.

"Turn them 'round, Scotty," said Dancing Mountain to the senior engineer at the central control console. (Yes, his name really was Scot.) "If they won't do it themselves, then we'll have to do it for them."

"I've been trying, Boss," said Scotty, a look of frustration, rapidly transmuting into panic on his face. "I can't budge anything. Bob's obviously been intervening in the programming. They've usurped control, Boss. Looks like they're going it alone."

Dancing Mountain calmly pressed the communication transmit button. "Listen up, Bill and Bob," he spoke, his voice as unwavering as ever. "You're sitting in a hundred billion dollars worth of machinery. You're parts of a team of several hundred back here at The Great Endeavour. You represent and carry the dreams of nine billion people on Earth." He paused and took a very deep breath. "Now get the hell back here, pronto!"

The boom of his voice echoed around the vast chamber of the otherwise silent HQ.

Five minutes later, it burst into the tiny space of Cutie 3's cockpit.

Five minutes after that came Bill's final message. "Sorry, Boss. No can do. We have our destiny to fulfil. Here. At the heart of the Sun."

We all stood silently, staring at the screen.

Then Scotty the engineer shouted, "My God, they've activated the QT Drive! They're beginning to accelerate. Straight ahead! They're really going for it!"

Someone flicked a switch and split the central screen in two. One half showed the view from behind their heads, two black silhouettes against the protected front porthole, filled with the fiery writhings of the Mother Sun. The other showed the forward looking faces of the two astronauts, their expressions not mad but completely masterful, the pinnacle of sanity - and totally blissful. They were the images of mankind at the very consummation of its billion year evolutionary journey.

Bill slowly stretched his index finger to the button of the music machine on the front console. We all recognised the first familiar notes of the bass guitar riff that poured into the cockpit and, five minutes later, poured out of the speakers at HQ, at maximum volume. Pink Floyd. "Set the controls for the heart of the Sun."

No one moved. The shimmering mass of reds and whites and yellows and oranges - and a thousand other unnamed colours - that was the living, breathing, super-conscious body of the Sun, danced, seemingly in time to the music, on the front view screen.

"Set the controls for the heart of the Sun," came the whispering voice of Roger Waters.

Bill was on his feet, arms outstretched, cruciform. Yet this cross shape was not a man dying in agony. It was a man full of the highest rapture of the human soul, a man - just like that earlier, agonised, crucified man - about to step into the Kingdom of Heaven.

Bob was on his knees. We could just make out his bobbing head, shaking with sobs of ecstasy. The consummation of incomparable enlightenment lay directly ahead of him. How could we ever have expected them to give it all up and head for home?

The whispered voice:

"Set the controls for the heart of the Sun...
the heart of the Sun...
the heart of the Sun..."

Then Pink Floyd faded, to be replaced at once by the start of the final crescendo of the last movement of Beethoven's Fifth Symphony. Two minutes of majestic, orgasmic music filled the control room.

And then...

All the screens went blank. The music ceased. We stood. Transfixed. Silent.

"They've gone," said Scotty.

"Gone to meet their Maker," said Dancing Mountain, gently. I could see tears slowly running down his cheeks, and I knew that they were not tears of anger or tears of sorrow: they were tears of wonder.

We all stood there for what could well have been an hour: no one moving, no one uttering a sound, all staring at the blank screens.

*

It was all kept very quiet. Joseph Fairfield, after all, was the world master of information control. A terse report from The Great Endeavour spoke of fundamental problems with the QT Drive that needed further research. Bill and Bob were referred to as heroes who had made the ultimate sacrifice in mankind's continuing pursuit of scientific advancement and space exploration.

The Great Endeavour HQ was put on hold for a while, as far as I was aware. According to Dancing Mountain, a period of reflection was needed. The next step had to be considered - for us Great Endeavour workers and for mankind as a whole. Lessons needed to be learned. We scientists and engineers were all given lengthy vacations and told that we would be contacted if and when.

Six months later I received a summons from Dancing Mountain and I returned to the HQ. The place was vibrant again. Something was afoot.

I was shown to Dancing Mountain's conference room, the walls now replaced by virtual reality screens depicting the wide open plains of Montana, his homeland. Even the ceiling was a perfect blue Montana sky. In the centre of a strangely sandy floor stood a startlingly life-like campfire, a steaming coffee pot on a stone beside it. Arranged around the fire were half a dozen stools cloaked in what looked like buffalo hide - artificial, I imagined, but knowing Dancing Mountain they were probably genuine antiques.

The big man led me to a stool, sat beside me, poured me a coffee and plonked his hands on his thighs - a characteristic pose.

"Good to see you again, Doc," he said.

"You too, Boss. So what's up?"

A smile constantly hovered on his face. I could see that he was excited.

"Cutie 4 is nearly prepared," he told me. "It's been under construction for several years. Much larger than the previous Cuties. Originally, it was intended to accommodate the complete living quarters for a crew of six or more on a journey of years. Beyond the Solar System. Maybe even as far as Centauri. That, you remember, was the big dream, and Cutie 4 was set to become the new Mayflower, taking mankind to the New World of the stars. OK, so now we know that's not gonna happen. Game over."

"So why do you say it's nearly prepared?" I asked.

His smile widened. "New plan, Doc. Over the last few months we've been adapting Cutie 4 to take passengers, maybe a few dozen. Towards the Sun."

He paused to let me assimilate this news. I could have asked a hundred questions, but none were necessary.

"Passengers?" was the most I could manage.

"Yep. Passengers. And I intend to be one of them," he said, his face glowing like a child's.

"To the Sun?"

"Yep. To the Sun. And back."

"Are you serious?"

"Never been more so, Doc."

I knew we were thinking the same thing. Would this be the trip of a lifetime or the end of a lifetime, a suicide mission? How, after all we had been through, could we even consider the idea? Yet how could we not consider it? I had thought long and hard about it over the months since Bill and Bob had taken Cutie 3 to its awesome fate, as, of course, had Dancing Mountain. The ship could be pre-programmed to turn back after Mercury, in such a way as to be incapable of over-ride. HQ would retain complete control. The passengers would be simply passengers, the crew little more than servants of a fail-safe computer. There could be no possibility of an act of defiance. A few dozen passengers would take a trip to the Sun and back. Was this madness? Or supreme sanity? Was this the new ultimate dream? Was it really possible that men could kiss the Sun and return to tell the tale?

Dancing Mountain was still beaming, his eyes locked on mine. "I'm in, that's for sure. When Cutie 4 heads off for the Sun, I shall be sitting there inside her. So what about you, Doc? This whole Sun theory was your baby. You deserve to be there too. There's a seat on board for you, if you want it."

Yes, it was madness indeed - the most exquisitely tempting madness I had ever encountered. I could have spent days or weeks writing lists of pros and cons. But of course, I didn't have to think about it for more than a moment. You only get an invitation like that once in your life - if you're exceedingly lucky.

"Put my name down, Boss," I replied.

Dancing Mountain's smile stretched to a wide grin. "Good one, Doc. Er... what exactly is your name?"

2
The Last Five Minutes

"Us and them
And after all we're only ordinary men.
Me and you
God only knows it's not what we would choose to do."

Roger Waters, Pink Floyd, "Us and them", 1973

The images are displayed around the walls of the gallery, a photographic record of the Modern Age: from the first sepia daguerreotypes of arrogant Victorian imperialists to the all-action, full-colour video of a passenger jet exploding into the World Trade Centre. Words may lie, reads a caption on the wall, but the photograph exudes authenticity.

A seventeen year old boy strolls around the exhibition, hands thrust into the pockets of his baggy jeans, unimpressed. This is history, no more relevant to his present concerns than the indecipherable documents and ancient portraits of kings and queens in his school text books. He dismisses, with no more than a cursory glance, the key icons of a century that, for him, is already little more than a fading childhood memory: the mushroom cloud hanging over Hiroshima, the assassination of JFK, the naked Vietnamese girl screaming the agony of napalm, Armstrong on the moon, Hillary atop Everest, Monroe atop a ventilation grid.

Suddenly his attention is unexpectedly captured by a grainy, black and white image dating back to the early years of the Twentieth Century, to 1916 and the depths of that war that didn't end all wars. Half a dozen weary, tin-helmeted, mud-caked soldiers, rifles hopelessly poised for action, clamber out of a stinking trench near the banks of the Somme and take their first and, for most, their last steps across a field of death. They're kids, no more than teenagers like himself - he can see it in their gait, sense it in some inexplicable aura that surrounds them. He can't see their faces but he knows that, despite the passage of years, they belong to his peer group, that they could be his mates, that he could be one of them. They all have their backs to the camera, of course, indistinguishable one from another, nameless cannon fodder. Yet he feels that each of them is a unique personality, each a colourful history, each a vast consciousness, each a mother's son, a cherished lover, a faithful friend, each alive with hopes and dreams and memories. Each about to die.

*

"Five minutes to go! Hold your positions."

I remember Laura racing towards me across the meadow. That were a beautiful moment: the sky a perfect blue, the grass so green and lush, spattered with golden buttercups and bright red poppies as if a painter had flicked his brush over the scene, and the apple blossom pinky-white, covering the orchard trees like confetti. I was dressed in me best shirt which Ma had just ironed and I'd had me bath that morning, it being Saturday, so I was feeling right clean and fresh, me hair all bouncy and soft. And Laura - well, she looked wonderful, as always - that summer dress - covered in forget-me-nots, I think it were - and her chestnut hair flying out behind her like a horse's mane as she rushed towards me. And that smile on her face, like I was the most marvellous thing she'd ever seen.

God, that were a happy day. Not that we did much, mind. We lay 'neath an apple tree and hugged and kissed a bit, all innocent like. I mean, she were only fifteen and I didn't wanna push her. After all, we had a lifetime ahead of us. Plenty o' time for all that cosy stuff. So we sat up and talked a while, just gossiping 'bout the weeks we'd had, me cracking a few jokes, her laughing so free and easy. She'd brought some bread and cheese. I had a small flask of cider I'd scrounged from Father. We pretended it were a banquet and we scoffed and supped it like a king and queen. Cos that's what we were, that day in the meadow - king and queen.

She'll be sixteen now, my Laura. Her birthday woulda been a few weeks back. Jesus, I've no idea 'bout dates and things. I don't even know for sure what day of the week it be. Freddie said earlier that he reckoned it were Saturday. Maybe that's why I been thinking 'bout Laura. We always met on Saturday afternoons. Sometimes she'd come home for tea. Sometimes we'd go to the dance in the evening or else take a stroll down the lanes if it weren't too cold, just holding hands, looking at the stars. And if we passed anyone I'd say, "Evening" and Laura would give 'em a bashful smile and I always felt so proud of 'er. Felt like I were walking along on a cloud, six inches 'bove the ground. Even now I can feel the touch of her hand in mine.

She cried when I told her I were joining up. I s'pose all girls do that.

"I'm seventeen now," I told her. "I gotta go."

"Why?" she sobbed.

"Why? Well... I gotta do it. It's me dooty, like."

How could I explain it to her? I couldn't even explain it to meself. It wasn't summin' I had any choice in. It was simply summin' I had to do.

Ma cried, too. I s'pose that's what all Ma's do, too, same as sweethearts. Father just stared at me, icy cold. I knew he disapproved, reckoned my place was at 'ome, working the land, though he wouldn't say aught. 'Twas up to me. We'd discussed it afore, soon after the war started.

"Course a man's gotta fight for his home, for his family," he'd said, "but I can't see as 'ow me home and me family's in any kind of danger. All these goings on in France and Germany and where-ave-ya, they mean nought to me. Them Germans come mooching into

Somerset and I'll be the first to launch into 'em with any weapon I could lay me 'ands on but so long as they's fannying about in their own land, then it ain't got nought to do with I."

It weren't that he were unpatriotic or aught like that. And he were certainly no coward. I'd seen him win many a fight outside the pub on a Saturday night, after kicking-out time. And he'd lost a fair few, too. It were just that he knew nought of the world beyond the village.

I wanted to argue with him, to present the broader picture, so to speak, but, truth to tell, I didn't rightly understand it meself. To be honest, I didn't 'ave a clue. Never seen a German in me life. Show me a blank map of Europe and I'd be hard pushed to name you a single country 'cept England. And I certainly had no idea what kind of stunt these Germans were trying to pull. Still don't. I always thought they were meant to be our mates.

So when Father mumbled his disapproval and when Laura asked me why, I had nothing to say. Made me feel a bit of an idiot, I can tell 'ee.

And now here I am with a rifle in me 'ands in some bloody foreign country and all I can 'ear in me mind is Laura sobbing "Why?" And I wish I could answer her, but it's too late now.

"Four minutes."

I feel Freddie standing next to me, me arm and shoulder pressed against his as we stare at the wall of mud in front of us. I feel him shudder. I glance over at him and see tears running from his eyes, pathways of pure pink skin down his mud-brown cheeks. Perhaps he's thinking of his girl, Lisa. Perhaps, like me, he's remembering happier times.

"You all right, me son?" I say, although my lips are so numb that the words don't come out too clearly.

"Yeah." His voice is thick, choked up. "Never better," he adds which seems such a ridiculous thing to say that I chuckle a little and he does too. Our eyes make contact for just a second, a quick exchange of warmth, of friendship and, of course, of fear. Then we both return our attention to the top of the trench and the grey sky. Looking at each other for more than a second is simply too much to bear. But I feel his shoulder pressing more firmly against mine and I press back. Feeling his body standing next to mine is me one remaining comfort, the only thing left, apart from me memories, that still feels good.

Freddie's from London. I never met a Londoner afore. Same age as me - seventeen - but several inches shorter. He makes me laugh sometimes. I've known him no more than a coupla weeks but, I dunno, seems like we've known each other all our lives. He's told me everything 'bout himself - his life, his family, his Lisa, his job in the market. And I've told him all 'bout Laura, 'bout Ma and Father, 'bout working on the farm. We've shared everything. I've never had such a good mate.

I asked him to be best man at our wedding and he said he'd be honoured although he didn't know 'ow he'd cope with our country ways. You'll love him, Laura, I know you will (although not too much, I hope), and Ma'll be all over 'im. Can't wait to see 'im down in Somerset. We'll 'ave such a time together. He ain't never drunk cider, so he says. We'll soon put that to rights.

'S funny but I really love Freddie. As much as I love Ma and Laura. I never thought I could love another bloke. Don't seem right, somehow. But we've shared so much, these past few weeks - same stinking pit of an 'ome, same bed - if you can call a coupla boards and a sheet of tarpaulin a bed - same tin of food - if you can call that slop food - even the same hole for shitting in. You can't get much closer to someone than that, can you? I s'pose he's become like a brother to me. I never had a brother, so I wouldn't know. But I feel that I'd do anything for Freddie - you know, give 'im me last tanner if he needed it. I s'pose I'd even stand in front of 'im to save 'im from a German bullet, if it came down to it. I couldn't bear to see him die. I s'pose that's what you call love, ain't it?

And I know you'll love him, too, Laura. Yeah, we'll have such good times together. I wonder what he'll look like in his suit and tie, standing beside me at the altar of St. Ben's, watching you walk up the aisle, dressed in all your pretty finery. That'll be some great day, Laura, won't it?

Right now tis good to feel ol' Freddie's body next to mine. I wish I could think of summin' to say to cheer him up.

"Three minutes."

God, I hate this place. Where is it? France? Belgium? Germany? I 'spect, when I gets home, Ma'll ask me what I thought of Europe, like I'd just been on a grand tour or summin'.

"Well, Ma, it were muddy, flat, smelly and cold," I'll say.

Just like the farm at home, I s'pose. Maybe they've even got orchards around 'ere somewhere. Maybe meadows full of buttercups. Maybe fields of hay, ripe for the first cutting. Maybe little villages and friendly taverns where the locals sup a bevy or two at the end o' the day. What d'you reckon, Laura? Shall I keep an eye out for a little farmstead where we can settle, grow some apples, keep a few cows and pigs, maybe raise a coupla kids?

Wonder what they German trenches are like. They say that's where we'll be 'aving lunch. Maybe they've got running water, decent beds, comfy armchairs. Maybe we'll 'ave a few prisoners to serve us some 'ot grub. Don't know that I fancy them German sausages, though.

I 'spect, if we ever get there, they'll turn out to be as filthy as these bloody ditches of ours. Just look at these clothes. Absolutely caked. Ma'd have forty fits. She'd 'ave me stripped in a second, get me gear in the tub and me scrubbed down in the tin bath afore me feet even touched the ground. A bit of mud never really bothered me afore. I mean, you get used to it on a farm, don't you? Now I hate the stuff. Just imagine putting on a clean shirt. A vest that's not crawling with lice. Dry socks. God, what I wouldn't give, right now, for a pair of dry socks. And boots that don't rub the skin of me feet to buggery. They 'spect us to run across to they German trenches like a pack of wolves, but I tell 'ee, we'll be more like a load o' hobbling cripples, wincing with pain every step o' the way. Freddie's got a blister on his heel as big as an 'alf crown. He can hardly stand up on it. I'll give 'im an 'and, if I can, once we're out on the top.

"Two minutes."

Jamie's standing on me left. He's a good mate, too. From Scotland. Glasgow. First few days, I could hardly understand a word he said. Nor he me, I s'pose. 'Country boy', they call me but I don't mind. It's not an insult, just a bit o' friendly banter. Me, I'm proud to be from Somerset.

Jamie's full of bravado. Always mouthing off 'bout how he hates the Germans, can't wait to kill a few. I don't say much when he's going on like that. Makes me feel a bit uneasy, like. To be honest, I've never met a German so how'm I 'spected to hate 'em? After all, they're only people, just like us. They've probably no more idea what they're doing here than we have. And they're probably as keen as we are to be done with the whole bloody business and get back home to their girlfriends - their frauleins.

Could I kill one of 'em? Jesus, I really don't know. Never shot a man in me life. Plenty o' rabbits and pigeons and what 'ave you. Even a few pheasant. But kill a man? That's a tough one. S'posing he 'ad his gun pointing at me and I 'ad mine pointing at 'im. Could I pull the trigger? God, I really don't know. I got nothing against the bloke. I'd sooner shake his 'and, share a fag and a joke. Then we could both head off 'ome to our girls. Strikes me that's the best way to deal with all this.

I shouldn't be thinking like this, should I? Tis wrong. I'd get meself shot if I said anythin' like that to the sergeant.

But what is right and what is wrong? I just don't know anymore. What d'you think, Laura? I remember you crying, once, over a poor little rabbit that had got 'imself caught in a trap. You took 'im 'ome and bandaged up 'is leg. And I remember you were so happy when he'd recovered and you set 'im free in the meadow, watching him scamper off through the grass. You know, I could never shoot a rabbit, after that.

So how'm I gonna kill a German? Answer me that, Laura. I don't know. I really don't know. Tis not right, Laura. I'm a farmer, not a soldier. I can't be doing with this whole war business. Tis not right.

Bit late now to be chick'ning out. Another minute and we'll be up over that bank and charging towards the German line, rifles at the ready. I've got no choice anymore, Laura. I've just gotta do it. It's just the way it is, I s'pose. Don't ask why. It just is.

"One minute."

God, it feels like me stomach's gripped in a vice. I feel like throwing up. I dunno how I'm gonna move, when the time comes. Only a minute to go. Or perhaps they'll abandon it all, right at the last moment. Perhaps we'll be given the stand down, relax back into our pools of mud for another day while they continue the aerial bombardment, make sure them Germans are well and truly scuppered afore we advance. Or maybe they'll even finish the whole bloody thing. Maybe they'll make peace in the next sixty seconds. Maybe we'll all chuck our rifles down and wander out into no-mans-land, Germans an' all, and hug each other and exchange fags and gossip and all 'ave a good laugh 'bout how stupid we been.

Ma and Father are always rowing. Never comes to blows or nothing but they shout at each other, sometimes not speak a word for a day or two, gloomy atmosphere in the house, that kinda thing. But they always make it up afore long, have a kiss and a cuddle and a good laugh and then everything in the house'll be bright and cheery again. Father ain't too clever, I have to say, and Ma's as stubborn as a rusty screw, but if they can manage to sort out their differences without killing each other then surely these politician chappies should be able to figure it out. Unless they're even less clever than Father, even more stubborn than Ma.

"I ain't afeared to die," Jamie said, yesterday. "Mind ye, I may be afeared tomorra."

We all laughed a bit at that one, then everyone fell silent, embarrassed like. I s'pose we were all thinking the same thing. Am I afraid to die? I dunno what fear is, anymore. All that shelling buggers your eardrums and addles your brain. Sometimes I just want it all to end - in whatever way. Sometimes I just wanna sink into a long, deep sleep.

But no, Laura, I don't wanna die. I wanna see your pretty face again. I wanna hold you in me arms and bury me face in the sweetness of your hair. I want us to run through that meadow again, hand in hand, and lie in the buttercups and munch your bread and cheese and swig Father's cider and talk of things that don't matter a damn to anyone but us. I wanna marry you in St. Ben's with Freddie grinning at me side. I want us to live in a little cottage near the farm. I'll grow tatties and you'll grow flowers in the garden. We'll have loads of kids and I'll buy a map of Europe and we'll find this River Somme and I'll say, "That's where your Father met your Uncle Freddie, back in the old days afore people learned to live in peace with each other." And you'll squeeze me arm, Laura, and kiss me on the cheek. And Ma and Father, sitting in armchairs afore the fire, will smile proudly. And our children will 'ave children of their own and they'll 'ave children, too. And maybe someday, when we're long gone, someday in the next century, p'raps, our great great grandchildren 'll look back on this distant war and think, "Thank God mankind has finally learned that killing is wrong." And maybe they'll look at pictures of this stinking bloody hell-hole and wonder how any of us could've come out of it alive.

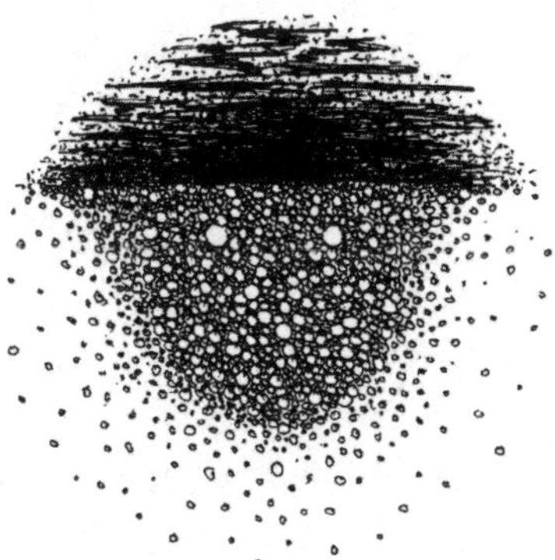

All's quiet now, Laura. Freddie's stopped shaking. I can feel his breathing, in tune with me own. In, out, in, out, in, out. Such a simple feeling, the breath of life rising and falling in our lungs. Is there anything better? Life, Laura. To be here, feeling me own breathing, feeling Freddie's beside me, to see the sticky mud of the trench, the grey sky overhead, the smell of it all, the taste, the last thoughts flowing through me mind. To be alive, Laura, you know it's so wonderful, so precious, so beautiful, like those golden buttercups reaching up to feel the Sun, like walking down the lane of an evening with you by me side. I'm no religious type, Laura. You know that. But, right now, I thank God that he's given me this life. I thank God for you, Laura. I thank God for this last peaceful moment.

A whistle blows.

We climb the ladder out of the trench. We don't look at each other. We've done all that. I follow Freddie's back up the ladder, Jamie behind me. We're standing out in the open. We begin walking forward. The guns start: a sudden, deafening explosion of ugly noise. Overhead it's like massive stars bursting through the sky, like the whole Universe collapsing in on us. Oh God, Laura, was it all a dream, that day in the meadow? I pray to God that this is the dream and that the reality. I wanted so much for us, Laura. I'm so, so sorry. LAURA!...

*

Fifty thousand soldiers died on the first day of the Battle of the Somme, one of the most ill-executed, wasteful, pointless, tragic days in the sordid history of warfare. Fifty thousand last five minutes of life, waiting for that fateful whistle to blow. Stretched end to end, those final minutes would last six months. Together, those fifty thousand streams of consciousness merge into a mighty torrent, a vast, screaming, life-affirming flood.

The seventeen year old boy bought a postcard of that picture in the exhibition and stuck it on his bedroom wall. Once or twice, alone at night, he found himself crying at the thought of it.

3
Shadow Walking

*"You were working as a waitress in a cocktail bar,
when I first met you."*

It was a seedy, back-street sort of place: peeling paintwork, dim lighting, dubious clientele. My sort of place. On a whim, I walked in and ordered a drink.

"One for the road," I said.

"Where you going?" you asked.

"West. Just walking. See where my legs take me."

"You got nowhere in mind?" you asked.

"That's right. Nowhere in mind."

We shared a smile. That was when it clicked. Not love at first sight or anything like that. Like the bar, you looked past your best, it must be admitted, but then, to be fair, so did I. No, there was just this strange, tacit understanding that flashed between us, the conviction that the pathways of our lives were somehow entwined: a certainty that defied question or doubt. In a single smile we knew that a crucial moment in both our destinies had been reached.

"Take me with you," you said.

God, did you really come out with a corny line like that?

But I took you. All the way from Lowestoft to Land's End, right across the width of England, east to west, chasing our shadows all morning and trying to walk away from them all evening. Afternoons, we usually slept, crashed out in the shade somewhere. It was a hot summer, and during six weeks on the road you develop a kind of routine.

First thing we did was hit some camping shop in Lowestoft and get ourselves equipped with rucksacks, sleeping bags, mattresses, boots and a small tent - all good quality stuff. Five hundred quid's worth. Pretty much the last of my stash, but I wasn't complaining. I was through with money. And it felt really good to be carrying my entire worldly goods, the fruits of forty years of living, in a pack on my back.

We set out that evening, following a footpath alongside the Waveney, our shadows long dark streaks dragging along behind us. When darkness fell, we pitched our tent in a tiny copse by the river. We shared a couple of cheese rolls and a bottle of water.

"Dust be diamonds, water be wine," I quoted, and you laughed. You had a laugh like the song of a skylark. I could have kissed you, then, but I didn't. We slept in our separate sleeping bags. Just to feel our bodies pressing gently together was enough.

The next morning, we ate muesli for breakfast, packed up the tent and walked on. Simple pleasures. No rush to get anywhere. Just walk on.

The stories that had brought us both to that bar in Lowestoft unfolded gradually over the coming days and weeks. Unsavoury stories, both of them. But I'm not going to tell them here. *This* is the story I'm telling. It begins at Lowestoft and it ends at Land's End. As we walked and talked, exposing ourselves bit by bit to the accepting gaze of the other, we eradicated our personal histories, watched them evaporate in the pure blazing light of the present. That, we came to realise, was what our trek was all about. Walking as catharsis. God, I wish I'd known, years ago, the natural rapture of flowing along, day after day, at a steady three miles per hour.

So I'm not writing about the sort of life I once led. Suffice to say that it was not a life of honour and pride. And it's not my place to talk of your past, although I'm sure you wouldn't mind me saying that working as a waitress in a cocktail bar was not your finest hour - nor your lowest.

I eked out the small amount of money that I had left. Bread and cheese were our staple, plus the occasional pub meal. Then I discovered that you had a soft but exquisite singing voice, and you loved to sing as much as to walk. Sometimes you sang in the market places and street corners of the towns and villages through which we passed, sometimes in pubs. We'd put down a hat and collect coins - not a lot but enough to satisfy our modest needs. Occasionally I'd accompany you on my jew's harp or some improvised bongo drum, and maybe I'd take out my harmonica and get into a bit of blues. We sounded good together: my rasping ditties and your haunting folk songs.

Sometimes we'd even carry a tune as we walked, gliding along to the rhythm of our feet, either one of my verses or your favourite mantra:

"All shall be well
All shall be well
And all manner of thing shall be well."

Repeated over and over for hours. Maybe one day we'll record it: lyrics by Juliana of Norwich - some 14th Century nun - music spontaneously created by you and me.

Each morning, as we walked, we'd take turns to tell the tale of our pasts. Nothing hidden. Why hide anything from each other? Between us, I think we must have accumulated the full pack of sins, misdemeanours and outrageous acts. Looked at objectively, we were surely a couple of distinctly unpleasant characters - not the sort you'd care to invite home to meet your folks. But looked at subjectively - which, after all, is the only way any of us can look - we were what we were: vulnerable, uncertain, weak-willed human beings, thrown into this world and struggling to cope with the challenges and mysteries of life. Who amongst us is prepared to claim that they've made a success of living? Maybe to say that we've survived - thus far - is good enough. It was certainly good enough for us.

Our pasts were our shadows - stretching way ahead of us as we walked west in the Sun all morning, but growing smaller by the hour. Come evening, they were trailing behind us, ever lengthening. Only at midday were they insignificant puddles lying at our feet.

"Darkness at the break of noon
Shadows even the silver spoon," I sang.

"Good line," you said. "Not sure what it means, but it sounds good."

You were like that: into spirit rather than substance, the ungraspable fickleness of shadows rather than the harsh light of reality. You were no great beauty - we'd both concede that - but your soul seemed to shimmer with sublime and subtle colours, the most beautiful soul I ever knew.

We never mentioned the why of our walk. We just walked. We favoured footpaths, of which there were many, defining the great line that stretches across England - the St Michael's Line or Dragon Path as it is sometimes known. First we followed the bank of the Waveney River, then the ancient Icknield Way and Ridgeway, across the chalky heartlands of the country. Pretty near the centre of the line lies the long barrow of Wayland's Smithy, a place that heaves with wonder and pastoral charm. It's one of those rare and magical healing places with the power to cleanse the human psyche of all its lingering shadows. We stayed there for two days, camping beneath the towering beeches, recounting, each, the darkest hours of our lives, shining the light of our mutual awareness into the dimmest corners.

Then on we walked, towards the stones of Avebury, down through the green fields and orchards of Somerset, over Glastonbury Tor, into the rolling hills of Devon, across the wilds of Dartmoor and Bodmin Moor, the enchanted land of Cornwall.

We were halted only by the Atlantic Ocean, the end of the line. We stood on the grassy cliff-top of Gwennap Head, England's most south-westerly point, a few miles south of Land's End, and we faced the slowly setting Sun, casting a billion quivering slivers of golden jewellery upon the ever-changing waves of the sea as they rolled gently in to crash against the rocky shore.

I held your hand - we rarely touched, at least not with our bodies. Behind us, stretched over the cropped grass of the headland, our shadows grew and grew, as the Sun sank: ten, twenty times as long as our standing forms, two vast pools of darkness, connected to our weary feet, flowing like patches of oil across the hilltop to disappear into a distant grove of hazels.

We watched as the Sun completed its farewell display, dropping behind the horizon on its way to greet the Americas. Then we feasted our eyes a while upon the pastel shades that tinged the few lazily drifting clouds. Over six weeks, we had taken daily lessons in the fine art of sunset appreciation, a pleasure that cannot be hurried.

Finally, we turned from the west to look behind us. Our shadows had vanished into the ambient twilight. We had walked free of our pasts. We live in the present.

4
The Tower

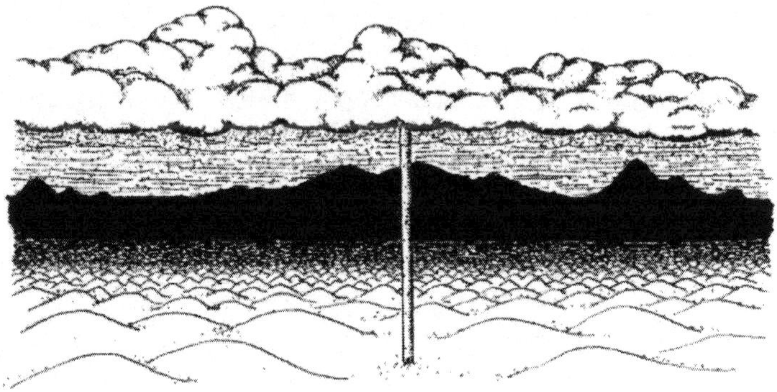

"Why does the universe go to all the bother of existing?"
Stephen Hawking, "A Brief History of Time", 1988

"It ain't why why why why why
It just is. That's all."
Van Morrison, "Common One", 1980

Between the desolate Plain of Scarn and the Unnamed Mountains, in a land that was once known as the Kingdom of Noman, rises The Tower.

Present day scholars are undecided upon the date of its construction, although all acknowledge that it precedes the days of recorded history. Two million years, some say. Others, more fancifully, attribute it to the God who created the heavens and the Earth - and perhaps The Tower to join his two domains.

The stones that comprise it are more dense and durable than any known stone, carved into cuboid shapes with roughened surfaces that appear to interlock precisely, rendering mortar unnecessary. The dimensions of the stones vary slightly - implying that they were fashioned individually rather than by some method of mass production - the average side length being exactly one foot, making the average volume one cubic foot. Estimates of the total number of stones involved in the construction of The Tower are, of course, impossible to make.

The edifice is cylindrical in shape. The circumference of its base - a perfect circle - has been precisely measured: 98.696 feet. Thus can sixteen men, with arms outstretched, completely encircle The Tower. With this circumference, the diameter is calculated to be 31.416 feet, or exactly ten times the irrational circle number, 3.1416...

As to The Tower's height: there is no way of knowing. The sulphurous clouds that continually pour forth from the Unnamed Mountains, depositing the yellow sand upon the Plain of Scarn, enshroud The Tower, allowing no more than its lower few thousand feet to be seen from the ground. The sulphurous cloud layer is estimated to be ten or twenty thousand feet thick, but whether, and to what extent, The Tower protrudes above its upper limits, there is no way of knowing.

The stonework is punctuated by regular gaps where a single stone is missing, creating a square hole - a window enabling daylight to illuminate the interior. The lowest of these is six feet above ground level and, henceforth, they appear at intervals of six feet in height, but in a spiral fashion. It is assumed - not unreasonably - that a spiral staircase climbs The Tower, flush to its interior wall. The spacing of the windows leads to the calculation that this staircase must rise up The Tower with a gradient of 1 in 1.4142..., this being the irrational square root of two.

The windows, each with an area of one square foot, clearly do not allow access to the interior of The Tower. It is generally believed that the current foot of The Tower is not indicative of its original ground level, owing to the accumulation, over countless eons, of the sulphurous sands deposited by the perpetual cloud cover. It seems reasonable to suppose that a door once existed, now submerged beneath the sand, and that once men were able to enter and climb The Tower's staircase. Suggestions have been made that excavation of the surrounding sand might reveal the hypothesised doorway and, hence, allow exploration of the interior. Regrettably, however, The Tower now lies within The Forbidden Lands to which all access is denied. Therefore we who seek further knowledge of its origin, history, nature and purpose are forced to confine our investigations to whatever documents or transmitted oral evidence we can uncover from former times.

Here, presented for the first time, is the text of a recently discovered parchment, dating back, we believe, to the early centuries of the Age of Kings. It was unearthed from the desert sands during excavations for building work on the eastern extremity of the Plain of Scarn, some two hundred miles from the location of The Tower. As to its veracity, we cannot comment. Some regard it as a purely imaginative work. Others believe it to be the true record of one Felix Sunheart, a philosopher and astronomer, some of whose earlier works are still extant. It is known that he lived at the time of the famous cryptomancer Janus Kralger, approximately fifteen thousand years ago and long before the designation of the Forbidden Lands. Some details of the life and writings of Felix Sunheart are available in the archives of the early Kings, but, curiously, no mention is made of the manner or date of his death.

We leave the reader to decide for him or herself whether what follows are the actual words of Felix Sunheart, or a much later piece of imaginative fiction, perhaps based upon an oral legend. Such remote times frustrate the historian's yearning for concrete evidence. We can do no more than present possibilities.

(Please note: we have endeavoured to translate the text into a language comprehensible to modern readers as faithfully as possible, although we have taken certain liberties with style. For instance, apart from at the opening and the ending, we have omitted the dedication to God that was customarily placed at the top of each page of writing. This practice died out many millennia ago.)

*

Be these words dedicated to the praise of The One who writes through every scribe's hand, who looks through every reader's eyes, who is the totality of all things and the beginning and end of all time.

This is the record of Felix Sunheart, who dared to enter The Tower and climb its staircase. It is usual to append a date to such accounts as this, but days, months and years have long since faded from my consciousness and, in any case, are irrelevant to the story I have to tell.

I do not propose to explain my reasons for entering The Tower. Suffice it to say that I was a healthy man in the prime of my life, a thinker, a questioner, a seeker, an adventurer. Would not any such man or woman be attracted by the greatest mystery upon this Earth? Most, it is true, remain daunted by The Tower's remote and hostile location, but I was an experienced traveller, skilled in the practices of survival in the wilds, and I was spurred by a passion that scorned the fear of death.

The trek from the civilised lands of men took three full moons: a pleasant enough journey, at first, through lush forests and across grassy savannahs where herds of wild beast roamed. Many were my adventures upon the way, but now is not the time to recount them - although I know there will be no other time.

I headed out across the Plain of Scarn, well victualled and full of resolve, my sights set on the distant sulphurous clouds that poured from the Unnamed Mountains. It was an arduous walk, for the sands were fine and unstable beneath the feet, but after many days I espied The Tower, a grey pillar thrusting upwards from the ground to pierce the cloud bank - truly the strangest spectacle I have ever witnessed. I could not believe that anything could be so high. Approaching, I discerned the small windows, spiralling skywards amid the dark stone walls, the whole structure perfectly cylindrical, it seemed to me, untapering as it rose, indeed unchanging in any way. Could this be the work of men? I wondered. And yet the masterworks of God are never seen so uniform and rectilinear. This indeed is a place of sublime strangeness. Was I scared? Who would not be? Yet I had travelled too far to let my awe and apprehensions slow my step. The Tower, I knew, was to be my destiny. I walked on, struggling to maintain a stout heart.

A single open doorway confronted me as I reached the foot of The Tower, no larger or grander than the doorway of a normal house. Perhaps I had expected some magnificent entrance like that of a palace, a huge carved oaken door, attendant guards, or, at the very least, a man to take my toll. But there was no doorman, no human soul other than me. I stepped over the threshold and entered the interior of The Tower as simply as I might step into my own home.

The circular entrance hall was empty, infused with a soft light which revealed walls of stone no different from those on the outside. Maybe twenty feet above me was a flat ceiling constructed of the same square stones, as, indeed, was the floor on which I stood. A spiral staircase wound up the interior wall, the steps made of the same cuboid stones, each rise exactly one foot, while the horizontal was somewhat more than a foot. This stairway spiralled half way around the empty room then disappeared into a gap in the ceiling. No other feature arrested my attention, save a small aperture in the centre of the ceiling, perhaps the size of a man's thumb, through which water slowly dripped, splashing on to the stone floor. I say this arrested my attention because it was a sight most welcome. My flask was empty following my trek across the Plain of Scarn and I was burning with thirst. I stood beneath the drip, mouth open, and was delighted by the taste of what appeared to be pure, life-giving water. Having quenched my thirst, I filled my flask, by which time my eyes had acclimatised to the light of the interior, and my body noted a temperature more pleasantly temperate than the baking heat of the desert. Thus was I heartened by my first experience of The Tower and, without further ado, I uttered my prayer of thanks and offering to The One that had brought me here, and began striding rapidly up the staircase, ready to encounter whatever this miraculous edifice had in store for me.

My pace soon slowed. Before long, I found a rhythm of stepping that enabled me to climb without exhaustion - up and up, round and round, on and on. For hours I climbed before I came upon anything to break the uniformity of that spiralling staircase: ever to my left, the outer wall of The Tower, its periodic square window gaps, admitting light to illuminate my way, several feet above my head height so that I could see nothing through them; ever to my right, a blank stone wall; ever above me, perhaps twenty feet, the underside of the stones of the next spiral of the staircase; ever below me, the unceasing pattern of the stone steps, ever up, up, up. This became my task: forever upwards.

I stopped, from time to time, sat upon a step and rested awhile, taking a swig of water from my flask and contemplating my state. This is madness, I thought, more than once. I am climbing into a complete unknown. Why? Because I must. This became the only answer I could find, so, rested a little, I rose to my feet and continued to climb, step by step, up and up.

Then, most unexpectedly, the right hand wall of the staircase opened up into a space, a circular room about the same size, it seemed, as the entrance hall. As before, water slowly dripped through an aperture in the stone ceiling, gathered in a tiny pool in the centre of the stone floor, then appeared to drain off through another tiny hole, presumably to emerge, I guessed, through the ceiling aperture of the entrance hall, far below. Furthermore, along part of the concave wall of this chamber grew a plant, a central woody stem with branches spreading out to left and right, clinging to the stones. Now, I am well versed in the flora of our world but I had never before seen such a plant. I may liken it to a fig, for its leaves were similarly shaped - but larger, thicker, more succulent - and its dangling fruits of a similar size, dark blue in colour. It appeared to be thriving in the soft light that bathed this room, entering through the outer wall's regular windows, and presumably it was fed by the humid atmosphere provided by the dripping water. I examined it closely but was unable to assign a family name to it. This was definitely not a plant that I had ever encountered in the natural world beyond The Tower. Rather nervously, I plucked a single fruit and bit into it. Its taste was bland, but not unpleasant, its texture seemingly nutritious. I ate and awaited a judgement from my stomach. It seemed well pleased, so I ate another, marvelling that my ascent of The Tower should be victualled with food as well as water. Then I sat a while and gazed upon the beauty of the plant, a feast for the eyes after their staple diet of stone upon stone. I think I slept a little, and when I opened my eyes I detected a lower intensity of light, as though, beyond The Tower's walls, night was approaching. Should I sleep in this well provided chamber or continue my ascent? My body chose sleep. I lay upon the stones, resting my head on one of the enormous leaves of the plant, which served as a most agreeable pillow, and sank into weary oblivion.

Once, during the night, I awoke to find the room in darkness with but a dim light penetrating the windows. Perhaps it is starlight, I thought, for I knew that the moon was new. But surely the sulphurous clouds would obscure the stars, would they not? Unless I had already climbed above them. But why had I detected no smell of sulphur drifting in through the windows? Why did the air remain as fresh and sweet as ever?

Within The Tower, I was soon to realise, all questions must remain unanswered and the asking of them becomes an intolerable burden that must finally be shed. I closed my eyes again and relished the warm silence of slumber.

The next day I launched myself up the staircase with renewed vigour and, I confess, the hope that that day would see me reach the summit of The Tower, although I steadfastly refused to speculate or fantasise upon what I might find there, or what I would do thereafter. Strangely, my vision of the future did not stretch beyond that much-imagined moment of attaining the topmost step.

For several hours, I suppose, I climbed steadily and then came upon another room in the centre of The Tower, similar in all respects to the room in which I had slept. Water still dripped through a hole in the ceiling and trickled away through another in the floor. A soft light again infused the bare stone walls of the identically sized space. A plant still reclined against the wall, its roots buried, it seemed, between cracks in the stones, its huge succulent leaves forming a mosaic of greenery covering perhaps half the wall-space of the chamber, its bluish fruits dangling invitingly. This plant, however, possessed its own shape, quite distinct from that of the lower chamber, immediately belying any notion that I had somehow returned to the same room. Hungry again, and satisfied that my meal of the previous day had done me no harm, I ate ravenously, consuming four of the fruits, each as large as, say, a grapefruit.

Thus breakfasted, I continued my climb and proceeded upwards for what I took to be the best part of the afternoon of that day before once again arriving at another chamber. Again, this was clearly different from the previous chamber, but similar in almost every respect. The crucial difference lay in the fact that, sitting cross-legged on the stone floor beside the plant, was a man.

Naturally I was startled, and he too, I think, for he leapt to his feet when he saw me arise from the staircase and, for several seconds, we did nothing but stare at one another.

I had seen no other human being for many a week and it took a while for me to don a mental persona suitable for communion. Perhaps he was similarly struggling to adapt to the demands of human society.

I was first to act. A civilised gesture was called for, I thought. I extended my right hand and approached the man. "Good day to you, sir," I said, or, at least, those were the words I intended to say. My mouth had not articulated speech for so long that its muscles were slow to respond to my intention and my message emerged rather slurred. "My name is Felix Sunheart," I added.

"And I am Zero The Number," said the man, extending his own hand.

We shook - somewhat limply, I fancied. I paid no attention to his strange name, so pleased was I to encounter another apparently friendly person. Our faces fell into unfamiliar smiles, then, overcome by emotion at this unexpected fellowship, I flung my arms around him and we embraced.

We separated and sat together on the floor, both searching our minds for the long neglected skills of conversation.

"So there are others in The Tower," I said, at last.

"Indeed," said Zero The Number. "So far I have met seven."

"And how long have you been here?" I asked.

"I do not count days," replied my companion. "I enumerate items in space, not in time."

I looked at him, perplexed. His voice was highly cultured, his clothing nought but a long smock as a farm worker might wear, his feet bare, his hair and beard exceedingly long. I estimated him to be in his thirties or forties.

"But you are climbing The Tower?" I asked, rather stupidly. What other reason might he have to be here.

"I have climbed up forty-two thousand, six hundred and eighty-one steps," he said, and then he added, "And I have descended seventy-five thousand, two hundred and four."

"Descended?" I exclaimed.

"Once, like you, I expect, I dreamed of reaching the summit. After tens of thousands of steps, I began to lose hope, but always I thought perhaps the next hundred might bring me there, and always I continued, believing that my goal must be near. Finally I lost all hope. I gave up, reasoning that to descend, a failure, must be easier than to ascend forever and never achieve my aim. So I turned around and began the long descent, back to ground level, back to the world of normal things. Forty-two thousand, six hundred and eighty-one steps I had climbed. Seventy-five thousand two hundred and four I have counted on my descent."

"But that is impossible."

"It would seem so."

"You must be mistaken."

"I am not mistaken. Counting is what I do. I count everything. I do not make mistakes."

"But how can that be?"

Zero The Number lowered his eyes from mine. "I can see that you are new to The Tower," he said. "You have much to learn."

I struggled to bring some sense to our conversation and, looking around at the chamber in which we sat, I said, "Tell me, how many of these rooms are there in The Tower?"

"How many?" he replied, rather dejectedly. "You suggest a number and I will raise it to the power of a thousand. But this I will tell you, since you ask how many. These plant rooms are not regularly spaced but are separated by different numbers of steps, as you have doubtless discovered already. Sometimes I have counted 345 steps between rooms, sometimes 1113, sometimes 5421, once as few as 55. Perhaps you recognise these numbers I quote. They are known as golden numbers and all lie upon a series that forms the basic mathematical model of the natural world. Each number of the series, added to the preceding number, forms the subsequent number. Thus, the series begins: 1, 1, 2, 3, 5, 8, 13, 21, 34, 55, 89 and so on. And every one of the numbers of steps I have counted between rooms falls upon this series, although they appear to occur in a completely random order. Now what do you make of that, my friend?"

I shook my head. This man is deranged, I thought. His head is so full of numbers that his grasp of reality has deserted him.

"And let me tell you something more about these plant rooms," he continued. "When first I counted 89 steps between two such rooms and realised that all the numbers I had counted were golden numbers, I decided to retrace my steps and count again, just to confirm my findings. So I climbed down 89 steps. No plant room. I descended a further 623, making a total of 711 - another golden number-, before I came to a plant room. Then, climbing again, I came upon another room after 327 steps."

"What of these seven people you say you have met?" I asked, growing weary of his exposition.

"You are one. I have met six others. Three were descending, two were climbing. One was nearly dead."

"Poisoned by the fruit?" I suggested.

"Of course not. The fruit sustains us. It provides all the nutrients we need. We could live indefinitely upon nothing but the fruit. No, the man who was nearly dead was starving himself. He refused to eat the fruit. There is no other way to kill yourself in The Tower. Even were we to act together, to lift one of us to a window, a hole of one foot square is far too small to allow even the smallest of men to crawl through and throw himself to his death."

My companion's tone was depressing me. I felt the hope slowly draining from my purpose. I needed positivity. Zero The Number offered nothing but numbers and despair. I leapt to my feet.

"I am convinced that the summit is attainable," I declared. "Why else would The Tower exist? I must continue my ascent. Will you climb with me?"

He sighed and slowly shook his head. "I wish you luck, although I know your task is hopeless."

"That I do not accept and I will continue to climb while the strength pulses in my limbs. And what will you do now, Zero The Number."

"I will climb or descend as the impulse takes me," he replied, a great weariness in his voice. "I have a project in mind. I am counting the leaves on the plant in each room I come upon, hoping to discover another series. This plant has six hundred and fifty-two.

Others I have counted have one hundred and fifteen, three hundred and eighty-five, ninety-two, and more besides. I discern no pattern, as yet, but my mind is working on it."

"Farewell, Zero The Number," I said, hurrying to the staircase to begin the next ascent. He made no reply, sinking into a sullen world of numerical abstractions.

And so I returned to solitary climbing, with merely a hint of regret at ending my short-lived acquaintance with the mathematician. I am accustomed to solitude and, although I enjoy the company of men well enough, I am not irked by its absence.

For many days more I continued to climb without further incident, sleeping at nights - that is, when the ambient lighting dimmed or when tiredness assailed me - in the plant rooms, of which I came upon anything between two and ten each day, although I refrained from counting the number of steps between them. In fact, after leaving Zero The Number, I found it difficult to resist the temptation to count. So monotonous was my only activity, raising one foot after the other in an unchanging environment, that counting the steps often appealed as a welcome diversion. Once, I found that I had counted one hundred and fifty-two steps without being aware of the fact that I had been counting, such was my distracted, almost mechanical state of mind. I chided myself over this and resolved to deliberately inhibit all further arising impulses to count. Instead, I tried to focus my attention solely on the one thing that was happening in my life, namely stepping, forever stepping from one step to the next. And this became my meditation, my spiritual practice, step after step, focussing upon the present.

I ate of the fruits of the plants in the rooms through which I passed, and they seemed to nourish me well. In earlier years, upon my wanderings, I had become familiar with the symptoms of malnutrition, and I must admit that I felt none of them here in The Tower. The dripping water in each room also served my needs and kept my thirst at bay. As to the excretory functions: I discovered, tucked behind the base of the main stem of each plant, a small area of waste material - rotting leaves and so forth - to which I added my own, believing that I was giving back to the plants something of what I had taken from them.

As I said, I refrained from counting the steps up which I climbed, but I did keep a tally of the passing days, and, after eight days in The Tower, I did a little reckoning. I was a fit, strong man and an experienced walker. I judged that, in a day, I could easily climb five thousand feet, maybe more, and knowing that each stone step was, on average, a foot in height (which, let me say, is considerably higher than the steps one comes upon in the normal world) I calculated that, in eight days, I had climbed at least forty thousand feet - way above the height of the highest of the Unnamed Mountains, way up into the rarefied regions of the upper atmosphere. How much further was I to ascend? How could this stone-built Tower be so high above the Earth that it pierced the realm of space? How could such a thing exist? As I have said before, these were questions that I refused to ask or even consider in my inner thoughts, although they frequently drifted, like nebulous, pulsating dragons, around the fringes of my consciousness. The mathematician had avoided their awesome unanswerability by retreating into the rational safety of numbers. I tried to avoid them by focussing steadfastly upon the present and not allowing them the chance to sap the strength of my attention. Perhaps in the outside world, beyond the walls of The Tower, there are questions that we all spend our lives evading: Why are we here? What is our Purpose? Where are we going? Here, within The Tower, with none of the fripperies of everyday life to distract me, these questions became magnified into monsters, urgently demanding resolution but achieving not a glimmer of understanding.

I think that, to keep myself sane, I had developed a certain faith: the faith that, when at last my foot stepped up the final step and I attained the top of The Tower, at that moment all my questions would be answered and perfect understanding would be mine. This faith - groundless though it might have been - is what kept me going. I suppose I could not tolerate the thought that my quest was futile, that my goal was forever unattainable and my questions would never be answered. How could any man live with such a thought?

On the ninth day of climbing, I heard soft human voices above me and, as the staircase emerged into another plant room, I encountered two more people, a man and a woman. Both were naked, and they stood staring at me as I materialised, from the top down, emerging from the staircase and stepping into the room. I stared back, joyful, once again, to have found some companionship. Within seconds, as my eyes took in the naked form of the woman, young and well-endowed with the pleasant features of femininity, my joy was compounded with a spontaneously arising feeling of lust, for, it must be remembered, I had not known the company of a woman for many a long moon.

Doubtless she noticed my lecherous look, for she stepped back behind the man and peered at me over his shoulder. He too, I saw, was a young and well-formed specimen of manhood.

After staring for far too long, I found my voice, again finding it hard to articulate words correctly after such lengthy abstinence. “Greetings. My name is Felix Sunheart.”

“Hello. Yes, welcome,” said the man. “We have not met another for some time. I am Adam, and this is my lady, Eve.” Then he smiled, adding, “That’s what we call ourselves, anyway. And why not?”

“Indeed why not?” I replied, smiling too. “And you certainly look the parts.”

The woman, I noticed, had bent to pick a few plant leaves that lay upon the floor, which she used to discreetly cover herself. She approached me and smiled. “Welcome, sir,” she said. “Welcome to our home in The Tower.”

“Your home?”

“Sparsely furnished, it may be,” said the man, “but we have come to call it home.”

“May I ask how long you have been here?” I asked.

“In this room, for several weeks,” replied Adam. “In The Tower, for many months, I suppose.”

“You came here together?”

“No. We met here. By chance, one might say.”

“And we have stayed together,” said Eve, “and bless our chance encounter, for now we are lovers and will never part.”

I could see that they were both happy with this circumstance, and I was happy for them, for, after my meeting with Zero The Number, it was reassuring to know that despair and depression were not the only moods of Tower dwellers.

"Join us," said Eve, in a tone that forbad rejection, and we sat together on a pile of leaves near the centre of the room, and she handed me a fruit and I ate, exchanging looks and smiles of friendliness and joy with both of them.

"And how long have you been in The Tower?" asked Adam.

"Nine days," I replied.

"Long enough, then, for you to realise that all our needs are met, thanks to the plants. Even our need for clothes. We discarded ours some weeks ago. The temperature of the rooms is perfectly comfortable, both day and night."

I had not previously considered this fact, but it was true. I wore nothing but a cotton vest and loin cloth, as I had worn throughout my journey to The Tower. I contemplated removing them and joining the two lovers in their nakedness, but I did not.

We talked a while longer as I ate my fruit: inconsequential talk about the room and the plants and such immediate matters. The topics of our respective pasts and, of course, our futures were avoided. Finally Eve, looking suitably coy, ventured, "We hope to have a child."

I was startled, and my two hosts laughed at my reaction.

"Yes, we, too, resisted the notion for a time," said Adam. "How could a child be reared in such a place? The very idea was madness. But then we came to see it as inevitable, as even, perhaps, the purpose of our being here. We are here to create a child of The Tower. And perhaps that child will be born knowing the secret of this place. Perhaps he will lead us to the top."

"We believe that to be true," said Eve. "We believe that to be our destiny."

And I could see, in the eyes of them both, that they were captivated and convinced by this vision. And I felt a surge of love for this latter-day Adam and Eve, and a love for the child they would hopefully produce. Yes, maybe they are right, I thought. Maybe they have found their purpose. And, although the thought of bringing a babe into the bizarre world of The Tower seemed, at times, nightmarish and reprehensible, at times it also appeared beautiful and strangely right. No, I could not and would not gainsay them. This place was too far removed from normality for conventional opinions to apply. Here, anything was permitted, for reason and the laws of nature were apparently absent.

So I clasped the hands of both of them and shared their joy and, together, we atoned a blessing and an offering appropriate to the occasion.

We sat together for several hours, conversing little but happy for our communion.

"It is good to have another soul in our home," said Adam. "Eve and I love each other, of course, but the presence of another adds a new energy to our lives. You see, we are together absolutely all the time. We cannot part. Our love and our desire to stay together, to rear a child, forever denies us the delights that solitude can sometimes bring."

"How so?" I asked, not yet catching his drift.

"I think you have been in The Tower long enough, Felix Sunheart, to realise its irrational nature. Sequentiality is unknown, here. Days follow days in a reasonable order, but rooms do not follow rooms. Were I to climb to the next room and then turn around and try to return to this room, I would not succeed. Maybe I would eventually come upon another room, but it would not be this one. Furthermore, if I were even to venture just a few dozen steps up or down the staircase, until I had lost sight of this room, I would be unable to return. I would turn around, retrace my steps, a few dozen or so, and then maybe many hundred more before I came upon another room - and it would not be this one. So, you see, Eve and I can never part, for if we did, we might never see each other again."

"It is our greatest fear," said Eve. "If we ever wander out of each other's sight, we will never return."

"We have experimented," said Adam. "Together we have climbed from our home room. Twenty steps are acceptable, keeping the room still in sight. But thirty steps, taking us beyond the domain of the room, and we cannot return. If we try, we are faced with a descent of maybe hundreds of steps before we find ourselves in a room once more - and it is not the room we left."

"So, although we call this our home," added Eve, "it is purely a temporary home. Perhaps tomorrow we will move to another home. As long as we move together, it doesn't really matter. All the rooms are very similar, and it's not as if we have any possessions. Home is where we are. We are happy with that. But it means that we can never be alone."

"And if our baby is born," said Adam, "we must be ever vigilant. If he should crawl, unseen, either up or down, he would be lost to us forever."

I contemplated this bizarre and frightening idea. Imagine it applying in the outside world, as it does here in The Tower. Imagine if you never knew where you were, nor how to get to anywhere else, perpetually adrift in the vastness. Within The Tower, place has no meaning. The question "Where?" is reduced to just two possibilities: up or down. The mathematician may have counted numbers, but here, in The Tower, numbers have no meaning. I looked around at this room of the two lovers. This is it, I thought. This, right now, is the sum total of my world. And I shuddered at the thought.

We spent many hours together in that room, Adam and Eve and I, and, although we were none of us loquacious talkers and silence would often settle upon us for long periods, we felt that silence to be like a warm blanket and our mutual looks to be perfectly satisfactory communications. I am not by nature a sociable person, but I truly enjoyed my time with these two young lovers.

"So when is your baby expected?" I asked, at one point.

"Alas, he is not yet conceived," replied Eve, looking intently at Adam. "We have been trying for many nights, now, for it is only recently that we realised that we must. But he will incarnate when the time is right, of that we are sure."

"You say he. You know it will be a boy, then?"

"So we believe."

"And what will you call him, if I may ask?"

"We will call him Son," said Adam. "Or Sun. The sound is the same and we have no means to write his name. He will be our son, our Sun."

I nodded my approval and recited a traditional blessing that, in my homeland, was often conferred upon babes-to-be: "May the long-time Sun shine upon you, all love surround you, and the pure light within you guide you all the way on."

Shortly after that, the daylight began to fade and we settled ourselves upon the floor to sleep, leaves beneath our heads, I near the staircase, Adam and Eve under the plant.

I awoke from an early snooze to the sound, across the room, of my two young friends engaged in their act of procreation. The soft noises of rhythmic thrusting, heaving and sighing had a distinctly arousing effect upon me and I felt a strange amalgam of feelings: of lust and envy combined with the love that I felt towards these two people and their optimistic quest. This feeling became unbearably intense, such that I felt I should withdraw from their presence. Very quietly, I arose and tip-toed to the staircase, climbing slowly and as silently as possible. To distract myself from the lustful feelings that I was experiencing, I counted the steps as I climbed. After thirty-four, I had left the room of the two lovers and entered another, directly above it. I lay upon the stone floor and, thankfully, soon found sleep.

The next morning, I desired to renew my delightful friendship with Adam and Eve and take breakfast with them. I quickly descended the thirty-four steps I had climbed the previous night, but, of course, I came upon no room. After a hundred or more steps, I realised the futility of my search, and the acceptance that I would never again see the two lovers brought tears to my eyes. I cursed my stupidity. I trudged wearily back up several hundred steps before I came upon another plant room - but it was not the well-loved room of my two loving friends and I was sorely saddened.

I climbed on, despondent, although it was not long before I regained that meditative state that had become an integral part of the climbing. My pace was slow - round and round, up and up - not thinking, just climbing.

After several hours, I became aware of the light changing in the enclosed spiral staircase, indicating the approach of another plant room. Then, as my head and upper body emerged into the space of the room, a missile struck my head - a fruit form the plant, as I later discovered - causing considerable pain and shock. I staggered backwards, nearly falling back down the staircase, and, at once, I became aware of a man charging towards me, long haired, long bearded, wild eyed and naked, wielding a stout stick and shouting, "Get out of here! Leave me alone! This is my room. Get out!"

I was so taken aback by this apparition that, before I could muster any kind of response, the man whacked me with his stick across my chest and arms and, as I recoiled from this, he pounced on me with every intention, it seemed, of pushing me back down the staircase. I managed to return a few punches, forcing him back and allowing me the opportunity to climb the final steps and place my feet firmly on the level ground of the room. Then again he raised his stick and, with a fierce "Be gone!" lashed out at my head, drawing blood, and lunged forward to plant a blow of his fist in my stomach.

I still hadn't uttered a word, but it was clear that words were not appropriate to this encounter. I was immediately in adrenalin mode, fighting, or so I thought, for my life. I launched myself into my assailant's chest and tried to wrestle him to the ground but he kept his balance and struck another closed-fist blow into my stomach. I doubled up, winded, and before I could return another punch, he twisted his staff between my legs, sending me toppling over backwards. Still standing by the top of the staircase, I fell headfirst down the stairs, tumbling painfully over the unforgiving stone steps. At first I tried to shield my head with my hands, but quickly had the presence of mind to throw my arms outwards to the walls on either side and thus arrest my fall.

I lay there a while, sprawled over four steps, panting wildly. The room was now out of view and it appeared that my attacker was not pursuing me down the stairs. Slowly I began to recover myself and assess what damage might have been done to my body - a gash to my forehead that throbbed and bled badly but did not appear life-threatening, painful bruises on my chest and stomach and a left leg that seemed to be unnaturally arranged upon the steps. I moved it cautiously and, judging that it was not broken, as I had at first feared, I heaved myself to my feet and, very tentatively, supporting myself against the outer wall, ventured a few steps upwards. I was still afraid that the wild room dweller might pounce again, this time to finish me off, but after a few more steps and seeing no light emerging to warn me of the approaching room, I realised that I would never see either the room or the man again.

I slowly climbed perhaps twenty or thirty more steps - reaching no room, of course - while my left leg gradually regained its mobility and my head ceased bleeding. Thence, onwards and upwards once more for I felt the urgent need to find another room in which to wash my wounds and rest upon flat ground. It was to be another hour or two before the light in the staircase signalled the approach of another room. Once my eyes reached floor level, I scanned the room cautiously for hostile bodies, but the place was thankfully empty. I limped over to the plant and found myself gratefully caressing its soft leaves and feeling soothed thereby. Then I stood under the dripping water in the centre of the room, drank my fill and soaked my battered body, then lay down and slept.

I stayed in that room for three more days, allowing my wounds to heal and replenishing my strength with the fruit from the plant. Whilst there, in relaxed and carefree mood, my mind carried me back through the events of my life. I observed the pageant of my memories, pondering their meaning and re-tasting their emotions. All the many adventures of my life, I realised, with their highs and lows, their comings and goings, their delights and sorrows, had led me here, to The Tower, which had now become the totality of my life. How many days? Already I had lost count. I recalled those people I had met within The Tower: the mad assailant, the two lovers, Zero the Number. As my mind drifted, I found myself re-telling the latter's tale of counting the steps and discovering the golden numbers between each plant room. To amuse myself, I calculated the early numbers in the list, each the sum of the two that preceded it - 1, 1, 2, 3, 5, 8, 13, 21, 34, 55, 89, 144... The list, I realised, like The Tower, goes on forever. It has no end, no upper limit. Perhaps this was the first time I had stated this to myself. The Tower was infinite. I would never reach the top, just as I could never calculate the highest golden number. I accepted this, dispassionately, as the truth. Similarly, I accepted, without fear or despondency at the hopelessness of my task, that I would continue to climb. After all, what alternative was there?

My next encounter with a Tower dweller came three days after I left my room of recuperation. As I approached yet another plant room, I sensed a presence within and, stepping silently and cautiously, I emerged into the room to find an oldish man clad only in a loin-cloth, sitting cross-legged on the floor, his eyes upon me as I climbed. At first, not surprisingly, my attitude was suspicious and defensive, but the man's benevolent smile and the aura of welcome that seemed to emanate from him put me at my ease.

"Good day to you," I said. "My name is Felix Sunheart."

He responded by broadening his smile and gesturing towards the stone floor at his side. I sat. For a long while, no words passed between us, but I would not say that communication was absent. Occasionally we looked and smiled at each other, but mainly it was a subtle quality in his presence that I sensed, almost like a warm glow that radiated from his body. And I felt, in this elderly man, a degree of placidity, of equanimity, of gentle alertness that I have rarely encountered in another man. A degree of wisdom too, perhaps, although he was yet to speak. This man, I was convinced, knew all about being in The Tower. He knew how to be here. He had mastered the art of being here.

We sat together for maybe an hour or two, then he rose, walked slowly to the plant at the wall and picked a fruit for each of us, handing me mine with a comical flourish and a wide smile. We ate and enjoyed.

"How long have you been here?" I asked.

The old man spoke no words in reply but gestured with his hand - a gesture which I took to mean that he had no idea, he had long ago forgotten and that he didn't care. The matter was irrelevant. He was here now. That was what mattered.

I realised that my question had been nothing but idle curiosity. What I really wanted to know was not how long he had been here, but whether he had found what he was looking for in climbing so far up The Tower. And I knew, with an intuitive, irrational certainty, that the answer was yes, and that words were inadequate to communicate his revelation. Stupidly, however, I kept asking him questions, even while knowing that he would not answer. His reluctance to articulate his wisdom in the words of our language began to irritate me. His smiles and looks did not satisfy my urgent desire for intellectual understanding.

Finally he responded - with just three words.

"Is The Tower an analogue of life?" I asked - a notion that had long been simmering in my mind.

"Eh?" he replied, giving me a look that combined amusement, perplexity and perhaps a slight rebuke at my obvious habit of endless questioning and analysis, perhaps even my apparent pomposity.

Some time later, I asked, "What must I do to attain your evident equanimity?"

"Be," he replied.

"But I can't just *be*," I said. "I'm an active man. I need to *do*. I can't just sit here *being*, as you seem to be doing. What can I *do*?"

"See," he said, opening his hands to indicate what he was seeing - the room, me, the plant, the total reality of that moment in The Tower.

"Eh? Be. See." Simple as that! He said no more. That was the extent of his verbal expression of his wisdom.

I stayed with this wise old man for many days, hoping that I might learn from his manner and his conduct, if not from his words. And, gradually, I learned how to marvel at the wonder of everything - to marvel but not to question, to quieten the "Eh?" that arose naturally within me. I learned how to *be*, without inner turmoil, without the constant desire to be something other than what I was, or somewhere other than where I was. And I learned to *see* - to see myself, to see the world, to see the oneness of all things.

We sat together, day after day, and I have to say that they were some of the finest, most alive days I have ever spent, just sitting in the plant room, being and seeing.

But I knew that I could not stay. The urge to continue climbing The Tower would not be subdued. I knew that, for me, being and seeing did not involve sitting but climbing.

I left him with a heavy heart, knowing, of course - although I pretended otherwise - that I would never see him again. He smiled and looked at me as I stood to leave, and his look said more than words can ever tell, and I will never forget it.

I have no idea how many days went by after I left the wise man: twenty, thirty, fifty or more. I made no attempt to count. I climbed The Tower. My life had become climbing.

And then I came upon a room which housed not another person, but the relics of a former inhabitant - a pile of white bones, clearly human and apparently of ancient origin. Beside this pile was a small book of empty pages, constructed long ago, by the looks of it, from thin sheets of what seemed to be leather. The pages had once contained words, I think, but it had been here for so long that the ink had faded completely. Nearby were a few rags that I took to be the clothing of the former incumbent of the bones, and, amongst them, a wooden stick with a pointed end that may well have been used as a quill. What ink had it contained? I wondered. The answer was clear - there were no other possibilities beyond the dark blue fruits of the plant that grew, as ever, against the wall. Piercing one with the quill, I scribbled onto a page of the book and a blue mark appeared.

What a wondrous delight this was to a one-time wordsmith such as me! Now, in addition to climbing, I could write!

I set to it at once, taking my time - for time was the one commodity I had in abundance. Using my most ornate handwriting style, I meticulously recorded the details of my days within The Tower, filling that little book with words crafted by the wooden quill in the dark blue ink of the fruit of the room plant. For two days I wrote, my goal, beyond the joy of writing, to crystallise my experiences, for the benefit... Of whom? It mattered not. Perhaps I might have left the book in the room in which it was written, to be read by another Tower climber. Perhaps the words would have faded over time, as, it appeared, had the words of my bony predecessor. But no, I felt I had to release my story from The Tower, into the wider world where providence might do with it as it wished.

The windows, of course, were the only possible means of egress - at a foot square, too small for a man but ample for a book. I constructed a kind of holder out of the bones, tied with fibrous material from the plant, giving it a winged, bird-like shape in the hope that it might glide gently to the ground and give some meagre protection to the precious pages it contained. My device, with the book strapped in place, seemed to glide quite well as I sent it flying across the room. But the lowest window was several feet above my head height. I would have to carefully cast it upwards and, to avoid the possibility of it becoming stuck on the wide sill of the window, out of my reach, I tied a length of plant fibre to its tail so that I might pull it back down if it did not fly through cleanly. My plan seemed sound, and a few practice throws convinced me that it would work. Once through the window, perhaps it would fall like a stone, or perhaps it would glide on the wind of the outside world and be carried who knew how far. Probably it would be lost. Probably it would plummet to the ground and be dashed to pieces by the impact, or become buried deep in the fine sands of the Plain of Scarn. But what else was I to do? Just as I kept the faith - beyond all reason - that I would one day climb to the top of The Tower, so I held on to the hope that my words would one day be read by another.

So now I write for the last time before launching the record of my tale into the unknown future.

Be these words dedicated to the praise of The One who writes through every scribe's hand, who looks through every reader's eyes, who is the totality of all things and the beginning and end of all time.

*

As we stated at the beginning of this work, the book - clearly of ancient provenance - was found in the sand of the Scarn Desert, some two hundred miles from the base of The Tower. We cannot comment upon its authenticity and will offer no opinion as to whether these are indeed the words of Felix Sunheart. Nor is it our place to speculate upon what might have become of him within The Tower. We let the tale stand on its own and leave the reader to interpret, embellish, criticise or dismiss as he wills.

5
Pooter II

Fig. 1 A pooter in operation

*(Matthew Pooter first appeared in the book "*Tales of Kaph*". In this story he is about thirty years older, but probably no wiser. Familiarity with the original story is not necessary. Pooter is an easy character to get to know. Or maybe not.)*

"Time flies like an arrow.
Fruit flies like an apple."

Old joke of unknown origin

My father was a lighthouse keeper. But that was long ago, when men still manned the great stone pillars and lit the lamps that proclaimed the safe watery way for passing seamen. Today the lighthouse keepers are electronic robots - efficient but soulless. They don't need feeding, or days off, or even paying: a twice yearly maintenance session is all they require. They do a good job, it must be said, despite their lack of consciousness and humanity. But no-one writes myths and romances about inanimate machines.

What became of all the erstwhile lighthouse keepers? I thought perhaps they had formed themselves into a society - the Society of Redundant Lighthouse Keepers. I thought perhaps that I might join their society, not as a bona fide member, of course, but as the son of one of their legendary number. But I could find no mention of any such society. And even if one did exist, it probably would not have admitted me. I don't belong in societies. I am an outsider. Once, I thought this a wondrous thing to be - like Camus, Dostoyevsky, Pirsig, Salinger: my literary heroes. But outsiders don't join societies. They avoid them. And even if there did exist a Society of Outsiders, I wouldn't really have fitted in. I would, at best, have been a very peripheral member. I would sooner join a Society of Peripherals. Perhaps I'll be the founder member. We'd never meet, of course. We'd keep our distance. But it would be comforting to know that we belonged to something larger than ourselves. Like computer peripherals, we'd enjoy a flimsy connection with the core of things, both independent of and dependent upon the wider world. And we'd have our uses - turned on only when needed. Like the lighthouse keeping robots.

My name: Matthew Pooter, esquire.

My age: no longer young.

My occupation: I work as a laboratory technician in a university biology department. It sounds professional, academic perhaps, high-tech even, but it's none of those things. Basically, I'm just a dogsbody, doing what the doctors and lecturers and graduate students tell me to do. Well, actually, they ask me reasonably politely and sometimes, if I don't much feel like it or if their question is plainly impractical, I say no. I have a certain authority, slowly acquired over the years. I've worked my way up through the ranks, you see: junior laboratory assistant, ordinary laboratory assistant and now senior laboratory assistant. To be fair, there are only three of us - it's a very small laboratory - so being the senior laboratory assistant is really no big deal. The junior laboratory assistant is usually some new graduate who has yet to find a proper job. They tend not to stay long. Except for me - I stayed for years - as did my successor as junior assistant when I became ordinary assistant.

His name's Barry. He progressed up the ladder to ordinary assistant when I was promoted to senior assistant and a new junior assistant joined us from the ranks of lower second class graduates. Maybe Barry has his sights set on the lofty heights of senior laboratory assistant when I leave. But I've no plans to leave, and I'm not sure that Barry really wants my job. He's not exactly the career lab assistant type. His heart lies in painting. He daubs massive areas of brightly coloured acrylic paints onto huge canvasses. An interesting style. A few of his works adorn the walls of local cafes and one particularly impressive specimen is permanently propped up against the coffee machine in our tiny staff room. The best adjective I can offer to describe them is "colourful". Beyond that, I struggle a little. But Barry loves his art. It's what truly turns him on. I try to encourage him as much as I can. It's a healthy hobby. And every laboratory assistant needs an interest outside the laboratory.

We get on well together, Barry and I. He's a couple of decades younger than me and we don't talk much at work, but there's always a genial atmosphere between us. Like a long-time married couple, we rub along well enough without scratching each other. Barry concentrates on the botanical side of things within the lab. I've never known anyone enthuse so much about the colour of flowers. He tries to create them with his acrylic paints and then describes the colours using the names of the paints he has blended. Thus an orchid may have a colour he would call "purple madder with a hint of alizarin crimson and cobalt violet". Having devised the correct colour, he then blends vast quantities of it and splodges it liberally on to a canvas - never in the form of a flower, as such.

"I'm not into form," he tells me. "I'm more into colour and emptiness."

"Emptiness is form," I reply, "and form is emptiness." But he doesn't appreciate that I'm trying to be facetious or ironic or whatever it is I'm trying to be. I don't know. I really don't know what to say about Barry's paintings apart from "colourful".

Our latest junior laboratory assistant is a pleasant and rather endearingly naive young man called John Crumb. "Call me Crumb. Everyone does." So we do.

On his first day, we take him to the staff room for our morning break and, naturally enough, his attention is ensnared by Barry's huge painting leaning against the coffee machine.

"What d'you think, Crumb?" asks Barry.

Crumb studies the large, formless blue blob for several minutes before asking, "What is it?"

"Basically it's a blend of cobalt, Prussian and French ultramarine," says Barry. "The background is a very thin wash of cerulean."

"But what is it?" asks Crumb.

"That's what it is," says Barry.

"But what's it meant to be?"

"Exactly what it is: a blend of three blues on a light cerulean background."

Crumb nods his head slowly and strokes his chin. "Ah. Right. Yes. I like it. A lovely blob of blue."

Barry and Crumb become good chums after that. Crumb even reveals a certain talent for watercolour painting, spending his lunch breaks capturing the likenesses of Barry's favourite flowers.

"A reasonable feel for form," Barry confides in me, "but he's got little sense of the nuances of colour. I shall instruct him in a deeper appreciation of chromatic sensitivity"

I sometimes wonder why I always seem to find myself surrounded by such odd people. Is this my fate? Or is it just that all people, when you get to know them, are fundamentally odd? And what is the norm by which we judge the oddness of our fellows? Perhaps we are each our own norm. Objectivity, I believe, is the unacknowledged myth of scientific endeavour. It doesn't exist. We can none of us escape our subjective personal viewpoint.

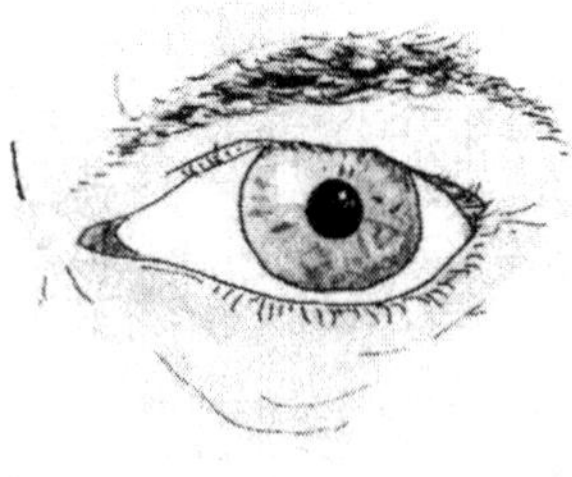

My area of expertise, as senior laboratory assistant, is entomology - specifically fruit flies. *Drosophila melanogaster.* They are absurdly tiny insects - no more than a millimetre or two from head to tail - but they're incredibly interesting to geneticists because they breed so quickly and the passage of their genes through vast numbers of generations can be very closely observed. To be honest,

I'm rather fond of the little buggers. They're not much to look at with the naked eye - little more than a speck of black that you would probably flick from your hand, if you noticed it, without a second thought. You can only take a good look at a fruit fly when you've captured it in a pooter and stuck it under a microscope lens, and such treatment doesn't do the poor blighter much good - it is rare that one is returned intact to its vivarium after a microscopic examination.

A pooter, in case you've never come across one, is a tiny transparent plastic bottle with two tubes attached, one of which is sucked while the other is pointed in the direction of the fruit fly in question. A quick suck - or poot, as I like to call the procedure - and it's whisked up the tube into the bottle, ready for the microscope.

All the academics in the department are used to me by now and don't think anything of the peculiar coincidence of my name and occupation, but new undergraduate students are always amused. Matthew Pooter the pooter. Sometimes I pretend that I invented the first fruit fly trap and named it after myself. Some gullible young people even believe me. Visiting North American students tend to snigger: a pooter to them is a farter. I take their sniggers in good humour and sometimes I like to entertain them, if I'm feeling inclined, by letting rip a small fart while enacting a poot. Always goes down well.

Fortunately, we lab assistants, particularly senior lab assistants, have little contact with undergraduate students. The graduates and doctors take over when the students invade the lab for their three hour practical session. We just prepare what they need, hover in the background, then clear up the mess after them.

The senior scientist in charge of the laboratory is Dr Charlotte Darwin. She's fed up with the inevitable first question and always appends "no relation" when stating her name. Everyone calls her simply CD. She's been working on fruit fly genetics for five years. I like to think of myself as her right hand man. Sometimes I like to think of myself as something more than that. She's a good looking woman. The cut of her white lab coat nicely accentuates the curves of her body. She keeps her long, dark hair tied back when engaged in microscope work, and I often have the pleasure of working alongside her at the microscope bench. Our delicate manipulations necessitate very close proximity. Our hands are apt to touch. Her hair sometimes brushes against mine as she invites me to examine a specimen through her microscope. Occasionally we even share the same double-eyepiece microscope and our cheeks are virtually touching. I can feel the warmth of her breathe, smell the subtle odour of her femininity.

"Got the hots for CD, eh?" Crumb taunts me. I silence him with a glare. The boy should have more respect for his elders.

And that's really the trouble with me and Dr Charlotte Darwin. She regards me as a generation above her. She's in her late twenties and I'm... considerably older. I may lust after her but I know that I haven't got a chance. She regards me more as a genial father figure than a potential lover - I can see it, unmistakeably, in her body language towards me.

Middle age! God, where did that come from? When did I cease to be young? Tis a strange time, indeed, middle age. It's not even clearly defined when it begins, nor when it transforms into old age. Teenagers would say it begins at twenty. Those in their twenties would say thirty, and those in their thirties forty. By fifty, I think it's undeniable that one's youth is gone. That's me: crashing through middle age like a bull in a china shop: one year speeding away into the next: spring, summer, autumn, winter - God, it's so relentless. I've given up on Christmases and Easters. Once every three or five years would be good enough for me. Summers come and summers go. I have to be reminded to take a holiday each year. Usually I decide at the last minute and take off walking somewhere - the South Downs or Dartmoor. I'm not really into travelling abroad. I claim that it's the carbon footprint of flying that puts me off, but probably it's more the language and the culture differences. I much prefer English and England. I like to lose myself in nature, in the depths of a deciduous forest or the open expanses of the wild moors. It might just as well be in Somerset as Siberia. The advantage of Somerset is that, wherever you might be lost, if you walk in one direction for long enough, you'll come across a welcoming pub, a pint of cider and a hot meal. You don't get those sorts of things in Siberia. That's why I steer clear of the place.

"What about spirit?" says Barry. "You don't want to neglect the spiritual side of things, old bean."

He goes off on a Buddhist retreat in Wales every year. Seeking enlightenment, he tells me. "So what's enlightenment?" I ask. He comes out with all the usual stuff - awakening, seeing into your true nature, self-realisation, the mystical union and other such nebulous synonyms. I've heard it all before.

To be honest, I don't get on with religions, with isms and ologies, with rituals and ceremonies, with priests and proselytizers. They're all right for some, perhaps - each to his or her own - but not for me. And I've no time for the so-called word of God, spoken only in Eastern tongues to rare individuals who lived a few millennia ago in remote, hot and sandy Oriental countries. If God's got something to say, why can't he say it directly to me - now - here in England?

Nature, the Earth, the Sun - these are my gods. And I prefer to worship them, to commune with them, to unite with them while walking in the woods or high on the rocky moors or sitting under a tree or listening to the sound of waves breaking on a seashore or gazing at the clouds. This is where I find spirit: in abundance and free from the trappings of religion, intellect and ego.

But maybe I'm missing something. I often feel that there's a terrific party going on somewhere, and I'm not there: that the entire world is privy to some great secret, but no one has let me in on it.

That's okay. I'm happy as I am. And when my life is over, that's okay too. All things must pass; nothing lasts forever. When I die - Amen: so be it. I'm not going to lose any sleep over it.

What do we expect? Some great reward for having lived? Fanfares heralding our soul into the Kingdom of Heaven? St Peter at the gates? "Well done, there, Matthew Pooter. Well done indeed. You've lived your life and now you're dead. Congratulations."

"Thanks a lot, Peter. Glad to be here. Oh, and by the way, what was all that denying Jesus three times before the cock crows business all about? Bit wimpish of you, wasn't it, giving up on a friend like that?"

"For Christ's sake," yells Peter, "that was all over and done with two thousand years ago. Can't you people just forget all that ancient history and start living in the present?"

"I'm dead, don't forget. My moment living is over. Just eternity to look forward to now."

Honestly, I mean no disrespect to anyone. I'd be a good Christian if I could. Or a good Buddhist. Or A Hindu. Or even an atheist. I just don't get it, that's all. Why do we always imagine that there's more to life than simply living it?

I spend a lot of time looking at fruit flies - good old *Drosophila melanogaster*. Close up, they are beautiful creatures. Magnified a hundred times, they are as wondrous, as vital, as perfect as ourselves. Are we any better, any closer to Heaven than them? Are we any more special in the eyes of God or the Universe or whatever than a humble fruit fly? We like to think we are. Fruit flies don't think they are the chosen ones, the crown of creation. That's not because they aren't, but because they just don't think. Thinking is what humans do, not fruit flies. That's our trouble. We think that thinking makes us somehow superior.

Yes, we're bigger than your average *Drosophila*, and we live longer, but that's about it when it comes to superiority. As far as survival goes, they totally outdo us. They've been around for millions of years - masters of adaptation and evolution. We, by comparison, are upstart newcomers, a freak experiment on the tree of life. Who knows, they might well have the last laugh when humanity pollutes itself into extinction and the fruit fly flies on into the future. Who knows that God is not more keenly following the spiritual development of *Drosophila melanogaster* than the noisy thrashings of *Homo sapiens*.

A typical fruit fly weighs in at about a milligram. Let's say a sizeable human specimen may be one hundred kilograms. That's a hundred million times heavier. A typical fruit fly lives for about a couple of weeks. We humans can hope for a lifespan of two thousand times as long. Okay, we're bigger and live longer, but does that make us any better? The Sun is many trillions of times bigger than us humans and its lifespan is hundreds of millions of times as long. Size and age are relative quantities. We need to transcend our narrow, blinkered perspectives.

But of course, we can't. We look at the world from our own viewpoint, just as the fruit fly looks at the world from his or her own viewpoint, and the Sun, no doubt, from its own very lofty viewpoint.

Humans, it is true, can think and write lengthy, rambling discourses, as I'm doing. Fruit flies can't. But fruit flies can beat their wings at two hundred times per second, and their love making antics put our clumsy gropings to shame. When it comes to reproduction, *Drosophila* is the master lover. Male courtship behaviour is prolonged and intricate, including the licking of the beloved's genitalia and making music for her with vibrating wings. Copulation itself lasts for twenty minutes. Considering that the fruit fly only lives for a matter of days, that's a massive chunk of its lifespan. And they do it many times each day, with different partners: polygamy is not an issue amongst *Drosophilae*.

"Well, they all look the same, anyway, so how do they know?" says Crumb.

CD's passion is the reproductive behaviour of *Drosophila*. She is probably one of the world's leading experts on the subject. Sometimes this passion pours out in lengthy, colourful monologues on fruit fly courtship and copulation. It's actually quite arousing to listen to her. Sometimes Barry, Crumb and I are her rapt audience in the laboratory staff room. We all fancy her. Common gossip in the department once had it that she was a lesbian - she was never seen with a bloke - but I reckoned that she loved fruit flies more than humans, of whatever sex. Is there a technical term for the love of fruit flies? *Drosophila*-philia, perhaps?

"Look at this, Matthew," she says and leans aside to allow me to peer down the second eyepiece of her binocular microscope. "Look at that wonderful eye. Over seven hundred separate units, seven hundred separate lenses and retinas, and yet we must assume that he perceives a unified image of his world."

It is indeed a wonderful sight. Magnified a hundred times, the fruit fly eye resembles nothing so much as some geodesic structure of man's devising, a piece of precision optical engineering a fraction of a millimetre across.

"Imagine the consciousness of *Drosophila*," says CD pensively. "Imagine seeing the world through those eyes. Imagine being such a tiny living thing yet with all the urges and appetites that we experience. This little fellow lives a life no less vivid and vital than our own, of that I am sure."

My face is no more than a few inches from CD's. I can smell marmite upon her breathe. I can see the shimmering of her eye lashes as she looks through her eyepiece. I can feel her white coated shoulder pressing against mine.

"Beautiful," I murmur - not an adjective usually used to describe fruit flies.

We raise our heads and share a glance for a moment: nothing personal, but a brief, wordless communion of our mutual sense of wonder. Then we return to our eyepieces. We share an empathetic feeling of love towards the miniscule beasts. It's not a feeling that many people know.

"We can never know what this fruit fly sees of the world through this remarkable eye," CD muses. "We each of us - you, me, this *Drosophila* - have a unique viewpoint into which the world is made manifest. And our personal, subjective viewpoint, right here at the centre of our Universe, is all we can ever know. For us, it is what is."

I consider her remark. This is a moment of momentous seriousness. I sense that we are juggling with concepts and intuitions so subtle and immense - so sacred, one might even say - that words can do them no justice.

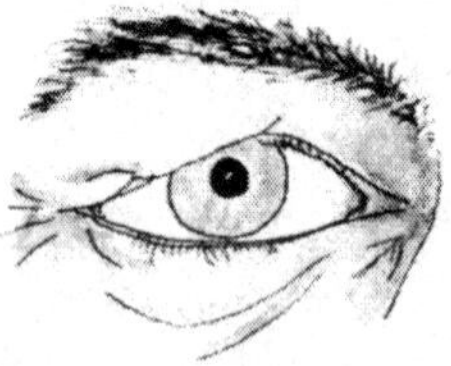

"What of the scientific ideal of objectivity?" I venture.

"But where does the objective world exist," says CD, "save in the imagination of the scientist? We tacitly assume that there is a real, objective world out there, independent of consciousness, a world in which we are merely peripheral. It's an assumption that is rarely challenged. Our humble *Drosophila* suffers no such delusion."

We are silent a while, gazing at this *Drosophilian* compound eye. Then CD looks up. "Pooters away: it's time for tea," she says. Our Dr Darwin is not your typical scientist, it has to be said.

CD may or may not be a *Drosophila*-phile - there's no law against it - but she is most assuredly an agoraphobe. She hates the outside: the space, the chaos of "things", the endlessness of the sky, the sheer uncontainedness of it all. She keeps all the blinds down on the lab windows, always shuts doors, runs from the lab building a few short steps to her car and, once at home, runs quickly indoors and draws the curtains. She exercises on bicycle and walking machines in a windowless gym. Although fascinated by the intricate details of tiny invertebrates, she can't stand to be confronted by the immensity of Nature.

I'm completely different. I love the sky. I love to be beneath it, free, unrestrained by walls and ceilings and doors. I love to look through windows. (From the inside out, I should add: I'm no peeping Tom.) I spend much of my time looking through windows.

"Hey, man, take a look out the window, see what's happening." - Jimi Hendrix: one of the great lines of modern popular music.

One sunny day, after a claustrophobic morning in the lab, I suggest to CD that she might like to accompany me on a lunchtime stroll in the park, to eat our sandwiches on the grass. It's a bold suggestion: the nearest I've ever come to an invitation to do anything outside work. But I can see her recoil at each outside word I utter - "stroll", "park", "grass". Or maybe it's me rather than the outdoors that repels her.

I mention it to Barry and Crumb during our afternoon break in the staff room that day.

"Some say that phobics can be cured by total immersion in the object of their fear," says Barry. "Perhaps you should have dragged her out and forcibly marched her over the grass, beneath the sky."

"I think what she'd really like is to live in a giant vivarium, getting intimate with her beloved fruit flies," offers Crumb. He's probably right.

For reasons unknown, CD rather likes Barry's paintings. This surprises me. I would have thought that their formlessness might have disturbed her need for rectangular walls and ceilings, for limits to her view of things. But no: she gushes over his colours. She often stands in admiration before "Blob of blue" in the staff room.

Barry asks her if she'd like to model for him. Also to my surprise, she agrees. The next day, I detect a certain sparkle in Barry's eyes. CD is not around, that day, but Barry has brought along the painting he made of her and he displays it proudly in the staff room. It feels rather strange to look upon the naked image of our boss - but, of course, there is very little form to her nakedness. The three feet square canvas contains a vaguely humanoid flesh-coloured shape, the outline fuzzy, the interior lacking any kind of detail at all apart from a brown smear to represent her pubic hair.

Crumb giggles and points at the brown patch, saying, "What's that, then?"

"Burnt umber," replies Barry, "mixed with a hint of Indian red."

The modelling/painting episode triggers the start of a romantic relationship between CD and Barry. I don't ask Barry for details and he doesn't give me any. It seems that the intimacy of his studio and the nakedness of his model had aroused the passion in both of them.

I confess to feeling somewhat jealous. Of course, I have no real hope with CD, but I fancy that our mutual interest in fruit flies might go some way towards bridging the generation gap. Barry and CD are of a similar age and Barry, I have to admit, is not a bad looking bloke in an eccentric artist/lab assistant sort of way. I swallow my disappointment and help it down with a few stiff drinks that evening. Barry and CD, after all, are a couple of my best friends and I should feel happy for them. I am, eventually. But first I allow myself a short wallow in self-pity.

Their relationship progresses, as I observe it, from frequent glances and smiles across the lab, through brief affectionate comments as they pass each other, to blatant touching and kissing at every opportunity. After only a week or two, I walk into the laboratory store room and find them hard at it on the floor. Bit of a shock, I can tell you. My sudden appearance must have shocked them, too, for they roll over right onto a large plastic bag containing our entire reserve supply of pooters, crushing most of them between their combined weight.

Crumb thinks this is highly amusing - making love on a bed of crushed pooters. Barry is embarrassed. CD apologises profusely and even insists on paying for a consignment of replacement pooters out of her own pocket - an offer I decline, saying a few breakages are acceptable in the pooting business. What price a few dozen pooters compared to the love of an agoraphobic doctor and her artistic laboratory assistant?

I don't expect their relationship to last. Crumb thinks CD should spread her favours more liberally amongst the laboratory assistants. Others in the department affirm that relationships between academic staff and either students or lab assistants are inevitably doomed to failure. But we are all wrong. Barry and CD become engaged. Soon after, they are married.

I am invited to the wedding, of course, but purely in a peripheral role. Crumb is best man. This, I must admit, rather hurts me. I've known Barry for quite a few years and Crumb is a relative newcomer to the laboratory. Shortly before the wedding, I approach the staff room and overhear CD and Barry discussing their big day. I keep my distance but listen carefully.

"Why didn't you ask Matthew to be your best man?" I hear CD say.

"Oh, I never thought of him," replies Barry. "A bit old for best man, don't you think?"

"I suppose so," CD agrees.

"Besides, Crumb's a good mate. And a good laugh."

I slink away, unobserved. I take the rest of the day off. In fact, I take a long walk in the woods and along the river and across the fields. That's something Barry will never do with CD, I think.

But I soon get over my feelings of rejection. I'm a resilient type. And the wedding is a joyful affair.

They honeymoon in Paris but apparently rarely leave their hotel room, which doesn't surprise me. Even The Louvre or the Cathedral of Notre Dame are much too massive open spaces for CD's liking.

One Saturday, while they are away, the university lab is raided by a group of animal liberation activists, under the impression that we are breeding and conducting cruel experiments on rats, mice and other poor furry creatures. But our only live animal specimens are fruit flies, plus a few tadpoles, goldfish and assorted microscopic coelenterates and protozoa. No doubt the activists, after scaling a wall, smashing a small window in the staff room toilet and entering the building with some considerable difficulty, are disappointed by the lack of mammals to liberate. Not wishing to waste their illegal visit, they decide to liberate our extensive *Drosophila* population. They open the doors of all the vivaria, then the windows of the lab. Several thousand fruit flies find freedom for the first time in their short lives. Most, like CD, can't handle the emptiness of the open skies after a lifetime of captivity. Many politely decline the offer of freedom that the liberationists present to them and stay put in the comfort of their vivaria where fruit, water, warmth and mates are supplied in copious quantities and they never have to worry about a thing. The majority of the more curious flies who decide to take a peek beyond their vivaria merely flutter around the lab for a while before settling dejectedly on every available surface, no doubt wondering where all the free fruit juice have gone. The really adventurous ones find the open windows. Some think it too cold in the outside world and fly right back inside. Presumably many others perish. But a sizeable number of the hardiest *Drosophilae* make it to the orchard that sits, fortuitously, right next door to the laboratory, and there they make their home amongst the apple trees, breed at their usual phenomenal rate and, later that summer, devastate an entire crop of cider apples. (There is a pleasing irony in this, for the animal liberation activists who raided the lab are, it transpires, from a well-known local lodge whose favourite alcoholic beverage is cider.)

I expect CD to be horrified, when she returns from her honeymoon, but she, like most people, sees the funny side. Besides, her work on the genetic make-up of *Drosophila melanogaster* is virtually complete. Her paper on the subject has just been published in a scientific journal. Normally, it would sink into academic obscurity, but it is given a massive boost of publicity by the press coverage of the animal liberation raid. The papers have a field day. "No cider for fruit fly liberators." "Animal rights activists fly in the face of reason." "Fruity feast for freed flies." Such are the headlines. CD is consulted as a *Drosophila* expert and a picture of her looking particularly sexy in her white coat standing beside a vivarium circulates amongst the tabloids. David Attenborough is asked to comment on Radio 4's Today programme ("You know, I've always had a soft spot for the *Drosophila* genus") and the story even stirs a laugh on *"Have I got news for you"*.

As for me, I get on with my daily tasks - there are still plenty of fruit flies remaining and plenty of pooting to be done - and, as senior laboratory assistant, I relish the fifteen minutes of fame that our laboratory has achieved.

Strangely, the whole episode seems to bring us all together. Shortly after the media furore has subsided, CD and Barry take Crumb and me out to a nearby pub, after work one day, and buy us a slap-up meal. We all get inebriated, to varying degrees, and all have a really good laugh about the whole business - a free-flowing, uninhibited, utterly joyful laugh that spreads, as laughs do, throughout the entire pub. I feel a peripheral no more, but an integral, even central part of this peculiar group of friends and colleagues.

Even Crumb has his endearing side. At the height of the evening, as we all sup cider in honour of our liberated flies, he comes out with this old limerick:

"A *Drosophila* doctor from Hyde
Ate so many apples she died.
The apples fermented
Inside the lamented
Making cider inside her inside."

And we all crack up. It's so good to laugh.

Unaccountably, at that moment I think again of my father, the lighthouse keeper, standing on the balcony of his lonely seashore home, gazing out across the troubled waters. Did he ever laugh, I wonder? I have never before imagined him laughing, but of course he did. And now I picture him throwing back his head, opening his mostly silent mouth, and releasing a huge bellow of a laugh that radiates, like his light, across the ocean: the laugh of the lighthouse keeper, the laugh of the laboratory assistant. Perhaps even fruit flies can laugh, in their own *Drosophilian* way. That's one thing that robots can't do. Whoever heard a machine laughing? Laughing is the exclusive, luxurious speciality of conscious beings. Laughing and loving and gazing out from the unique viewpoint that is, for each of us, the very centre of the world - whether that world is a desolate seashore, a scientific laboratory or the inside of a fruit fly vivarium.

And that's where I'll end this tale: The Laughing Pooter: Son of a lighthouse keeper: Senior laboratory assistant: Conscious being: Centre of the Universe.

(Author's addendum: Matthew Pooter re-appears in at least two more tales further on in this volume.)

6
The Colour of Trees

A whimsical little tale

Paul was quite a catch, she had to admit - good looking in a Hugh Grant sort of way, with a certain naive charm and floppy hair that cried out for you to run your fingers through it. And he was the first half decent bachelor she'd met in years. There was just one thing wrong with him. Well, two actually. Well, three, to be precise.

For a start, there was his name. Green. Terri was not at all happy about the prospect of becoming Mrs Green.

"What's wrong with that?" her friend Jo asked when they met for their usual Saturday lunchtime gossip in the local pub.

Terri knew that she was being silly, that it was a trivial matter. "Teresa Green," she said. "How can anyone take me seriously with a name like Teresa Green?"

It took Jo a few seconds and a few thoughtful sips of lager to catch on. Her face erupted into a wide smile.

"See what I mean?" said Terri.

"You think that's a problem?" scoffed Jo. "I married Mike King, remember. God, I've lost count of the number of clever dicks who've greeted me with 'You must be Jo King!'"

Terri had to laugh. But it never seemed to worry Paul that he was called P. Green. Nor his mother, Olive.

Of more serious concern - this was the second problem - was her fiancé's atrocious sense of time-keeping. Terri prized punctuality as one of her finest assets. She was never late for anything. It was a matter of basic consideration for others. Keeping people waiting was simply discourteous.

But Paul was always late.

"Oh, well, better late than never," he'd joke as he arrived at the cinema, half an hour after a film had started, to find Terri standing forlorn in the empty foyer.

"Sorry I'm a bit late," he'd excuse himself to her mother with a winning smile as he rolled up at three o' clock to the charred remains of Sunday lunch.

"Late again," he'd laugh as he burst, red-faced, into the pub, ten minutes before closing time, where Terri had been sitting, gooseberry-like, with Jo and Mike for the entire evening.

She tolerated his habitual tardiness because... well, because she loved him, presumably. And because, when he did finally show up, he always showered her with affection and conviviality. Never with reasons for his lateness. That was always taken for granted. And that was the third problem.

Paul was an amateur ornithologist. A bird watcher. He wasn't just interested. He was fanatical. He was the sort of bloke who'd go charging all over the country with his binoculars and zoom lens because some fellow twitcher had reported on the Internet that he'd spotted a lesser spotted something-or-other.

That was what had happened during the only holiday they'd ever taken together. He'd been late booking anything up, of course, so Terri had organised a last minute cancellation, a flight to the Canaries. She was packing for a week's lazing on a sunny beach when the ornithological grapevine whirred into action. Paul, beside himself with excitement at the prospect of glimpsing some obscure feathered creature she'd never even heard of, pleaded with her and she, as always, succumbed to his boyish enthusiasm. So they ended up spending a week in a damp guest house on the Norfolk Broads, peering at mist-choked reed beds all day.

She tried to share his interest. She tried desperately hard.

"Look! Over there!" he'd yell, pointing at some distant speck of black, hovering above the horizon. "It's the first merlin I've seen for weeks."

By the time she'd got her binoculars focused and found the right patch of sky, the damn thing had disappeared.

She preferred swans. They were big, white, easy to identify and they stayed in one place for more than a few seconds. Swans, sparrows, robins, ducks and seagulls - that was pretty well the extent of her ornithological knowledge. It wasn't that she had anything against birds. They had their place in the scheme of things. (In the sky, and preferably not directly above her car or washing line.) They were nice enough to look at or listen to but she felt no desire to get to know them more intimately, to distinguish one from another.

"What is this thing that blokes have about naming things?" Jo asked one Saturday as they sat in the pub, sipping their lagers.

"God knows," Terri replied. "I suppose they get it from Adam, rushing around the Garden of Eden, frantically giving everything a name. I think it's some basic need to be masterful. Give it a name and you feel you've got control over it."

"Is that why Paul wants to give you his name, d'you think?" said Jo, grinning. "Teresa Green. It grows on you, I suppose. It's just that it's going to sound a bit silly in winter."

"Very funny," said Terri, sardonically.

He proposed to her one afternoon as they were driving across the marshes. He slammed on the brakes and they sat in some desolate lay-by for half an hour while he followed the slow progress of a distant heron strutting through the reeds. He had an uncanny ability to detect an avian presence in the most uninspiring of landscapes.

When finally the heron had disappeared from view, he replaced his binoculars on the dashboard and turned to her.

"I love watching birds with you, Terri. Somehow it adds a whole new dimension."

He wasn't one for romantic speeches or verbal expressions of affection. This was probably as good as it would get. She leaned over and kissed him on the cheek.

"Why don't we get married?" he asked.

She was taken aback by the suddenness of his proposal. She must have flushed, lowered her eyes.

"How about it, Terri?" he persisted. "We'd make a good breeding pair, don't you think? How about getting into a spot of nest building?"

Did he really say that? Surely not!

But before she could even begin to think about a yes or a no, something black and tiny and probably winged and feathered flashed across the windscreen.

"Hey, what was that?" Paul yelled, grabbing at his binoculars.

She never actually gave him an answer. Their engagement was tacitly assumed. They started making plans. Neither of them wanted a big do. A register office would suffice. Just a few friends and then a decent honeymoon. The Canary Isles, this time, maybe. Apparently, at this time of year, they were a haven for migrating birds.

Jo seemed to be more ecstatic than Terri, when she broke the news. They hugged and kissed.

"I'm so pleased for you, Terri," Jo gushed. "The two of you are obviously so much in love."

What made her assume that? Terri wondered. And were they? Certainly she was excited. After all, she'd never been proposed to before. Paul was, as she kept telling herself, quite a catch and she was well over thirty and beginning to feel nailed to the shelf. All her friends had long since married and settled down. Some were even on their second or third go.

But was it love? She couldn't decide. Could she really accept the prospect of a lifetime of embarrassing unpunctuality, of sitting beside primeval swamps scouring grey skies for signs of bird life? Could she really give herself to a man who would give her such an absurd name?

They waited in the reception area of the register office - just Terri with Jo and Mike as witnesses. The minutes ticked by. Jo kept looking at her watch and huffing. Terri just sat there, fiddling with the engagement ring on her finger and trying to imagine herself saying 'I do'. Twenty minutes after the appointed time, the door flew open and Paul burst in, his hair tousled, his tie awry.

"God, I'm so sorry, Terri," he jabbered, hastily adjusting his clothing. "I was in plenty of time. No problem. Then, crossing the marshes, I swear I glimpsed a bittern. Can you believe it? Of course, I had to stop and take a closer look. I mean, a bittern, Terri! You understand, don't you?"

Terri just stared at him. Yes, she understood. She understood perfectly.

Paul glanced at his watch. "Still, better late than..."

"Don't say it," Terri interrupted him.

"Don't say what?"

She pulled the ring from her finger and plonked it into his unsuspecting hand.

"This time I think it's better never than too late. Goodbye, Paul."

Terri stepped outside into the spring sunshine and breathed a long sigh of relief. No, it wasn't too late in life to start being decisive. And, as Jo would doubtless say, there were plenty more fish in the sea. Or birds in the sky.

She looked up. The trees were green (but not her!) and a bird was singing somewhere, hidden in the leaves. She didn't know what sort of bird it was. And she didn't care.

7
Tales of Kaph II

"That which is before you now is **IT**, in all its fullness,
utterly complete and perfect...
Immediately refrain from conceptual thought.
Let a tacit understanding be all!"

The Zen Teaching of Huang Po

During the early years of the second decade of the Twenty-first Century, The Society of Kaph underwent a dramatic expansion in numbers as its aims and practices became increasingly well known. One might say that it was truly flourishing, were it not for the peculiar paradox that the Society steadfastly denied its own existence and eschewed the very notion of membership.

A crucial reason for the burgeoning interest in the concept of Kaph was the unexpected success of my first book, '*Tales of Kaph*'. No one was more surprised than I. The collection of stories evolved into a bone fide book quite suddenly, thanks to various fortuitous arrangements of circumstances (or synchronicities, as one might say). That it should sell in such numbers astonished all concerned. Within a matter of months of its humble launch in a Somerset library, copies of '*Tales of Kaph*' had found their ways to six continents: and I live in hope that some Antarctica-bound explorer or scientist may stow one in his pack, to complete the worldwide count of continents. Within six months, reports of distinctly Kaph-like incidents were appearing in the media, and within a year some wag had coined the term 'kaphinated' to describe acts or events that manifested or epitomised the ideals of the Society, and 'de-kaphinated' for those that were clearly opposed to its lofty aims. I like the words, I must confess, and would be happy to see them appearing, as someone has suggested, in a future edition of the Oxford English Dictionary.

A brief explanation is needed, I feel, to update those who have not come across the original *'Tales of Kaph'*, in which the Society was first introduced. The word itself is an acronym derived from the four qualities of Kindness, Awareness, Patience and Humility. The Society of Kaph, as I portrayed it in that book, is a loose collective of men and women who have resolved to put these qualities into practice in their daily lives as often as possible - which means, in effect, as often as they remember, for we all tend to forget or get distracted by other things. The perfection of the human spirit - as personified by individuals such as Jesus or Buddha or St Francis or Ramana or whoever may be your favourite spiritual role model - may be considered as the ideal and complete expression of kindness, awareness, patience and humility. Thus, any act or thought or feeling that is inspired by or infused with any of these four qualities makes the world a better place and, one might say, makes oneself a better person.

Awareness, of course, is the fundamental nature of our being. But kindness is placed first in the acronym because kindness (or love or compassion, if you like) is the greatest thing in the world. There is nothing one can do that is better than an act of kindness, and no greater feeling than the giving or receiving of kindness. We of the Society take this to be an unarguable fact of life.

Patience and humility refer to attitudes of mind. Both involve letting go. Patience is the letting go of all grasping, all attachment. It is the complete acceptance of and surrender to That Which Is. Humility is about letting go of the ego, and all its absurd, chaotic thoughts. It is the realisation that, in our essence, beyond the noisy prattling of ego, we are all the same, no better and no worse than one another, each one of us an immaculate fount and receptacle of Being, each one of us the Holy Grail.

A friend of mine, after reading '*Tales of Kaph*', was uncertain about the inclusion of humility in the acronym, regarding it as something of a negative character trait. It is true that our modern, acquisitive culture emphasises self-assertion, confidence, pushing oneself forward, and so on. But arrogance is the antithesis of humility and has no place in a healthy mind or a civilised society. Humility is about letting go of the self-aggrandising tendencies of the ego. It is no accident, I think, that in the medieval tales of the Quest of the Holy Grail, the most successful knights were said to embody the noble qualities of patience and humility, rather than those dubious ego-based characteristics more normally associated with the great heroes of more recent times. And didn't Jesus himself affirm that, "The meek shall inherit the Earth"?

The first 'kaphinated' character I met, as I recounted in the original '*Tales of Kaph*', was Kaph the Philosopher - a wise and genial grey-haired man with an infectious chuckle and the remarkable talent of putting anyone at ease in his company with the merest word or gesture. He earned his living as a ferryman and spent his free time freely scattering the fruits of his philosophising amongst those who sought his wisdom. Kaph the Philosopher became my friend and mentor, and he it was who encouraged me to commit to paper many of the stories I had heard from various 'members of the Society'. We met only occasionally, usually in the cafe in his home town where he was apt to sit at his customary corner table behind his card advertising:

"Philosopher offers free consultations"

Through contact with Kaph the Philosopher and other Kaphs of the Society, I developed my own kaphinated routine, enacted largely in a small back-street cafe in my own home town, where I would sit behind my own card proclaiming:

"Writer, walker and listener offers services, free of charge."

Following the publication of '*Tales of Kaph*', I had become something of a local celebrity and my 'clientele' in the cafe was sizeable. I spent increasing amounts of time seated at my table performing kindly acts of writing or listening - and I can confirm that I had never before in my life found such a satisfying occupation.

It was on a morning in early May that I entered the cafe with the intention of giving my services for a couple of hours to all who requested them. I was surprised and delighted to find, sitting at my usual table, a trio of fellow Kaphs: my old friends Kaph the Philosopher and Cath the Storyteller, plus a newer acquaintance, Kaph the Herbalist, who collected wild plants from woods and meadows, concocted tisanes and tablets and prescribed herbal remedies to those who consulted him with physical or psychological problems.

These three Kaphs greeted me effusively, and I them, for the company of fellow Society 'members' always gladdened my heart, but I could feel a certain reserve and apprehension in their communal manner and, after a brief exchange of jovial banter, Kaph the Philosopher got straight to the point.

"We are concerned," he began, "that, in your obvious zeal to promote our ideals, you are yourself, perhaps, straying from those ideals."

His tone, as always, was kindly and I felt, within myself, no more than the hint of a defensive reaction. "Please explain," I said.

"Your book," said Kaph, "contained many finely written tales and we all enjoyed reading them."

"Thank you," I responded. *'Tales of Kaph'*, as I have previously stated, was entirely my own project, produced independently of the 'Society', and I had rarely discussed it with other Kaphs.

"Our concerns, however, are two-fold," continued the Philosopher. "First, we feel that you portrayed the 'Society of Kaph', as you called it, as something too substantial, too real. Even using the term 'society' evokes ideas of constitution, membership, aims and procedures, and you imply that it is somehow an elite group. I have, indeed, heard many refer to it as a secret society."

"I endeavoured to depict it as I saw it," I responded. "Perhaps others have misinterpreted my observations. The idea of a secret society has always appealed to the popular imagination."

"And therein lies the problem," said the Philosopher. "Many people are searching for something different, something that takes them beyond the mundane and conventional. And many seek to belong - be it to a church, a religious group, a football club or even simply a crowd of mates down the pub. Hearing tell of a society that appears strange and secretive, benign but passionate in its aspirations, many are curious. Many are allured by the prospect of membership of such a society. They desire a subtle badge of belonging, a special handshake, perhaps. They desire fellowship and a shared secret. Fair enough: these seem to be natural longings. But we are not secret and we are not a society. All we offer is openness and freedom."

Cath the Storyteller spoke up - a pleasant-featured woman whose soft, lilting and exquisitely articulate voice had an immediate magnetic effect. "Too many tales are told of secret societies. The theme is perennial, down through the history of storytelling. Perhaps the secret society is an archetypal symbol, fulfilling some primal need of the human psyche. The thinking mind is forever curious, forever seeking some esoteric meaning behind that which is given. There is an excitement, a mystique, a glamour about the idea of a secret society that open societies clearly lack."

"But we are neither secretive nor, in any formal sense, a society," said Kaph the Philosopher, addressing me. "We are a group of people who share certain ideals and practices. We are nothing beyond that. We have no organisation, no leadership, no constitution, no funds, no specific objectives. We don't even have a name, although you delighted in calling us the Society of Kaph."

"Isn't it rather difficult to talk about a group of people without applying some generic label?" I defended myself.

"Labelling immediately introduces boundaries, definitions, restrictions," said the Philosopher. "And labelling groups of people immediately sets them apart from the rest of humanity. And that's where the problems begin, as the entire history of the human race has demonstrated, again and again."

"But aren't we all happy that ever increasing numbers of people are coming to embrace our philosophy?" I said. "Is this not a desirable state of affairs?"

"Of course," replied the Philosopher. "And we are happy, too, that your book has helped to spread this philosophy. But now we must beware lest crystallisation sets in. Once words appear on paper, they solidify. Speech and dialogue have a vitality and openness that printed words lack. Plato attempted to calcify on paper the ever-dancing dialogues of his teacher Socrates. By so doing, he created a dogma that has persisted for millennia. Similarly, the sayings and teachings of the prophets and spiritual masters - spontaneously given to a particular group of people at a particular time and place - became immortalised and set in stone as scriptures. Once written, they were regarded as sacred and could not be challenged. Thus was fundamentalism born."

"And once a group of creative individuals come together and call themselves a society," said Kaph the Herbalist, making his first contribution to our conversation, "then creativity and individual freedom tend to get squeezed out and the collective viewpoint becomes ever narrower."

"The fact that we do not exist as a tangible body, the very nebulosity of our 'Society of Kaph' as you call it - this is our strength," said the Philosopher. "As our numbers grow and our ideas spread, so others seek to attack us, for we are egalitarian and egalitarians always evoke mistrust in those dominated by the cravings of ego. But how can we be attacked if we do not exist?

"It is common to think in terms of 'them' and 'us'. That's the way the human mind works. But who are 'they'? '*They*'re out to get us', people affirm. '*They* ought to do something about it!' '*They*'re watching us.' But there are no 'they'. There is no conspiracy, no plot to suppress the rights of the little people, no Orwellian-like establishment. All '*they'* are is a collection of individual men and women - just like 'us'. Once you begin to label 'them' and 'us'; once you use concepts like 'secret society' and 'establishment conspiracy'; once you start taking sides; once you start thinking, 'you're either with us or against us', then you're lost in the ugly aggression and competition that has choked and warped all human history."

"We are nothing special," said Cath the Storyteller. "We are just individual people attempting to do what we think is right. If we change anything, it's by telling stories, not by winning arguments."

"It's by being as we are," added the Philosopher, "not being something that we are not."

We sat in silence for several moments, contemplating the flow of our respective thoughts.

"So what is to become of us?" I asked.

"We shall see," said the Philosopher. "There is no master plan. The world is changing, that much is certain. But the world has always been changing. So let's sit back and enjoy whatever happens next. Who knows? It might surprise us all. The unknowable future is only just beginning."

And, with that, he began to chuckle, and, of course, we all fell under the infectious spell of his chuckling and chuckled along with him. And our chuckles spread throughout the cafe, as chuckles do, until the whole room was gently shaking with quiet chuckles.

"Now that," said the Philosopher, regaining his composure, "is how the world is changed: not by fighting or arguing, but by chuckling."

With that, Kaph the Herbalist slapped his thighs with a force that must have been painful. "Herbal teas all round," he proclaimed cheerfully, rising to his feet. "I know you lot are all coffee addicts, but on this occasion something more transformative is called for. Agrimony, I think, should hit the spot."

He made his way to the counter. Kaph the Philosopher sat back in his characteristic pose, hands clasped across his rather profuse stomach. Cath the Storyteller, upon the return of the Herbalist with a tray full of beverages, regaled us with a story fitting to the occasion which, adapted in my own writing style, I have included in this volume - I will refrain from stating which story.

Then we chatted freely and amicably, enjoying each other's company, relishing the society of fellow Kaphs.

After the Storyteller and the Herbalist had left us, I sat on with the Philosopher who, as I well knew, liked nothing more than to sit at a cafe table, to watch the world flow by and to engage in philosophical dialogue with anyone who felt similarly inclined.

"You mentioned earlier that your concerns about my '*Tales of Kaph*' book were two-fold," I said. "So far we have just discussed my depiction of our Society as too substantial."

"Ah, yes," said the Philosopher. "The other matter concerns yourself. I wonder if the success of your little book and your perceived position of, as you said, 'unofficial spokesman for the Society' have perhaps had a rather ego-enhancing effect which, you must admit, runs contrary to our ideal of humility."

"To be sure," I responded, immediately adopting a defensive mode, "I take a certain pride in my book. I am a creative artist. Is it so bad that I should be pleased with and proud of my creations?"

"Of course not. We all enjoy performing whatever services we each offer. If we didn't enjoy them, then their value would be less. But we prefer to act anonymously. Celebrity may have its pleasurable aspect, but it hinders the cultivation of patience and humility. We must guard against thinking of ourselves as any better - or, indeed, any worse - than any other man or woman. Pride is a very tricky little feeling to deal with. At first it feels good and positive and worth indulging in for a while, but it carries the danger of irreversible ego inflation."

I took this slight rebuke rather personally - and justifiably so, I believe, for, ever since my first encounter with Kaph the Philosopher and the ideals of the Society, I have deliberately tried to cultivate humility and subdue the vanity of the ego. And yet, I have indeed taken pride in my book and in the 'Society of Kaph'.

"Pride and prejudice," continued the Philosopher, with a chuckle. "A good book about a couple of tricky little blighters - the concepts, I mean, not the characters Elizabeth Bennet and Mr Darcy. Once they get rooted in our minds, they run amok. We must be ever vigilant."

I nodded, considering his words.

"Thank you. Your advice is timely," I replied in a sincere and friendly tone, for there was a quality about the Philosopher's manner of discourse that forbad the taking of offence. He spoke, I could tell, from genuine concern.

"Think on it," he said.

And I did.

A few weeks later I paid a visit to the cafe frequented by the Philosopher in his home town. I was happy to find him 'at home', seated at his favourite table, the chair opposite him vacant, awaiting his next philosophical consultation.

He greeted me affectionately, as always, and signalled to the waitress to bring me a 'kaphinated' coffee.

"My problem," I said, getting right to the crux of things, "is that I think too much and write too much and imagine that, by extolling the qualities of Kaph both to others and to myself, I am actually manifesting those qualities in my life."

"Quite so," responded the Philosopher. "You share this problem with many of history's great thinkers. Even Socrates, who first formalised the ideals of right living in a right society, was, by all accounts, a miserable bastard. Thinkers and writers are not, on the whole, known to be a happy bunch. And we've all come across preachers who deliver fine, inspirational sermons but whose lives are chaotic and unfulfilled. Thinking about how to lead a good life is one thing: actually doing it is entirely another matter."

"So what am I to do?" I asked, my tone plaintive, for I had indeed given this much thought yet had reached no resolution.

"We both follow the same way," said the Philosopher. "We practise kindness, awareness, patience and humility as often as possible, which means as often as we remember. This is our method and its fruits are abundant."

"Then perhaps I forget too easily."

"As do most people. We forget to remember the simplicity of it all. There is no arduous path of training required, no gruelling uphill trudge to salvation. Happiness, equanimity and the awareness of the wonder of Being are right here, right now. Bliss is, as it were, the default mode of consciousness. Switch off or see through the noisy babblings of the thinking mind, and there you are."

He was silent for a few moments, holding my gaze, the light from his eyes seeming to emphasise the beautiful simplicity of his words. But my mind was noisily babbling. I could not grasp what he was trying to show me.

"Every moment is an opportunity to practise Kaph," he continued. "Every apparent setback or problem or worry is a chance to surrender, to let go and patiently accept the reality of That Which Is. All the events of your life have led you to this moment, right here, where it all begins. The entire future story of your life - in fact the entire future story of the Universe - starts right here and now. And whatever went before doesn't matter. Of course, the present moment is created out of the entire previous history of the world, but that's all gone and all we're left with is the reality of now. Regret, blame, guilt, remorse - all these are so much useless baggage, weighing us down as we try to step gracefully from moment to moment. Let them go. Surrender, with a great sigh of relief, into the bliss of present moment awareness. Simple as that."

And his face erupted into a wide grin and his head shook with a quiet chuckle. And I tried to share his chuckle but a massive "Yes, but..." had become fixated in the forefront of my mind.

He picked up a discarded napkin, extracted a pen from his shirt pocket and began to rapidly scrawl a few lines. I looked on, my "Yes, but..." dangling forlornly in the space between us. It wasn't that I felt the need to argue with him - there was no one in the world whose words I respected more than his - but my mind, I suppose, was predetermined to find difficulties and reluctant to accept such a simple philosophy.

With a flourish, the Philosopher handed me the napkin. I read:

CONCISE INSTRUCTIONS FOR THE RE-DISCOVERY OF THE BLINDINGLY OBVIOUS:

LET GO
SURRENDER
BE AS YOU ARE
DO AS YOU WILL
BE KIND
LOVE
ALL IS WELL

"Yes, but..." I finally managed.

The Philosopher chuckled some more. "You're not convinced?"

"Yes, but..." I was struggling to express my dissatisfaction. "Yes, they're fine aphorisms, to be sure. I've heard them before, and of course I can't argue against such wisdom, but... I am unsatisfied."

The Philosopher nodded. "The bread of humanity is thickly spread with yes butters."

I smiled. "Yes, but..."

"The path to happy living really is so incredibly straight-forward," he said, "but you, I gather, would rather hear the annotated version than the concise."

"Maybe," I replied with a shrug. "You know I'm fond of words."

"Okay," said the Philosopher. "Just for you, I present the annotated instructions for the re-discovery of the blindingly obvious. Where would you like me to start?"

"The blindingly obvious, perhaps? I'm not sure that I share your confidence."

"This is what we've just been talking about. The Kingdom of Heaven, Enlightenment, Awakening, Self-realisation, Happiness – call it what you will – is right here, right now. It is blindingly obvious but usually we do not see it because we imagine that it lies at the goal, the fulfilment of a lifetime or more of practice and effort. This is the so-called spiritual path, which we tend to see as a very long, uphill climb, do we not?"

"I suppose we do."

"Well, we are deluded. This present moment – right here, right now – is **IT**. This is as good as it gets. There is nothing more, no spiritual way along which we slowly trudge, no mountain to climb, no quest to pursue. The light shines through us and from us and within us and all around us **RIGHT NOW.** We have nothing to achieve. We are already the perfect children of God."

"Philosophically, perhaps I can accept that," I responded, "but I don't necessarily feel it. I am not directly aware of it. I feel that I still have much to achieve."

"Consider other animals," said the Philosopher. "The birds of the air, the beasts of the field, the fish of the sea, the myriad living things. They are conscious beings. They are aware of the urge to feed, to reproduce, to be secure, to **BE**. Is it not so with us? Why do we feel the need to infer something more, some great destiny that awaits us? Why can we not simply be as we are and rejoice in our Being?"

"Because we are thinking beings," I suggested. "Our inner lives are dominated by words and thoughts."

"Words delude us. They weave themselves into fantasies which, like cobwebs, soil the spacious purity of our minds. Let them go. Let them drift off into the sky like children's balloons."

I looked down to the napkin. 'Let Go' was the first of his aphorisms. "Easier said than done," I said.

"Yes, I agree. It is one of the many ironies of human life that it is easier to grasp than to let go. Grasping involves maintaining tension. Letting go is the release of tension. Why should this be so difficult? We are grasping, acquisitive beings. Grasping is highly valued in our materialistic society: acquiring possessions, acquiring property, acquiring a comfortable lifestyle, acquiring knowledge, acquiring spiritual progress, then grasping them tightly for fear of losing them. Letting go is seen as weakness. Yes, we all need to relax from time to time, but the dominant ethos of our culture values effort above relaxation."

"This is true," I reflected. "I can rarely relax for long without feeling a little guilty that I should be doing something."

The Philosopher chuckled. "The malaise of modern man, succinctly put. The reluctance to let go. But it really is a very simple process. Just experience this moment, then let it go, ready for the next."

"And surrender?" I said, moving on to his next maxim.

"Surrender is acceptance. Surrender is saying 'Yes!' with that huge sigh of relief we spoke of earlier. 'Yes' to these life conditions in which we find ourselves. 'Yes' to our idiosyncratic talents, our tendencies and our failings. 'Yes' to whatever circumstances come our way. **YES!** (And notice the absence of a 'but' following the 'yes'!)"

"Be as you are. Do as you will," I said, reading further down his list. "Rather platitudinous, wouldn't you say? They smack of outdated hippy ideology."

"Don't knock the hippies," replied the Philosopher with a smile. "Some of my best years were spent wearing beads and kaftans. And is there any alternative but to be as you are and do as you will? Life flows through you from the Source within. You are the manifestation of Being. Let it be. You are the dance of life. Let it flow."

"Okay. Next we have, 'Be kind'. No, I can't argue with that."

"I should hope not. We take this simple advice to be, unquestionably, *the* fundamental spiritual truth. Kindness is giving to another – whether the gift is a moment's attention, a look of sympathy or empathy, a smile – yes indeed, a smile! – a cheery word, a comforting embrace, a helping hand, a piece of heartfelt counsel, a listening ear, a ten pence coin, a million pounds - whatever. Kindness is perfect beauty.

"And love, of course. Yes, it's been said many times before: Love is all you need. Love is the Sun, ceaselessly showering the entire Solar System with its light, its love.

"So we reach the end of the list. All is well. How can reality be anything other than perfect? It is perfect by virtue of its Being – every tiny particle and vast galaxy, every moment.

"No, don't argue," he said, holding up a hand to inhibit my interjection. "You're about to hit me with another 'Yes, but...' You're going to tell me that the world is far from perfect, that all is anything but well, that suffering and ugliness and oppression and defilement and pollution are all around us, wherever we look. Look within, that's what I say. First see who you are, then you will see the blindingly obvious truth that all is well, that perfection is actuality.

"And now I see, as if on cue, another customer hovering nearby, awaiting a philosophical consultation, I suspect. So, my friend, Kaph the Tale Writer, the time has come for us to part."

He rose from his chair and clutched my right hand firmly between both his hands. "God's speed, God's Grace" he whispered, and the look he gave me was so intense, so infused with love, that tears sprang involuntarily to my own eyes and I tried to say something in return but failed. So I stood and left the cafe and stepped out into the first moments of the start of the rest of my life.

Remember that sign I sat behind in the cafe of my home town:

"Writer, walker and listener offers services..."

Well, I had done a lot of writing and a lot of listening. Now was the time to do some walking. I walked out of the cafe in the Philosopher's town and just carried on walking, one step after another, just walking, walking, walking. My first destination was my own town, a journey of three days, spending nights in wayside bed-and-breakfasts and eating in pubs. I walked slowly, contemplating the Philosopher's words until the resolve had formed within me to, as he had said so often, **'let go'**, to abandon myself to the pursuit of the ideals of Kaph, to hit the road, like the questing knights had done in days of old, and see what might befall.

Once back home, I considered the practicalities of my quest and realised that there was really nothing to stop me from walking on. Within a few days I had closed up my flat, quit my job, sold my car and other possessions of value, amassed a modest but satisfactory stash of money in the bank to support my wanderings, obtained a light-weight pack, sleeping bag, mat, a tent into which I could just crawl, a remarkably sparse list of sundry baggage, donned my walking boots and set off into the world.

Simply walking.

And being.

And seeking the mystic Grail and the realisation of which the Philosopher had spoken so passionately.

Now, I am a walker. Call me Kaph the Walker. I flow from place to place, chasing no goal beyond the joy of placing one foot after the other. As was said of the questing knights in the Grail romances, I follow the signs of adventure, never knowing, each morning, where evening might find me. And those signs rarely let me down. I feel guided by a divinely drawn map, revealed to me through my intuition, devoid of reason and yet infallibly precise. At each junction in the path, I make a choice - left or right - in the ever-growing certainty that I can do no wrong, for my destination does not lie on man-made maps. It is right here, right now. Like a toposcopic map on a hilltop, I am always at the exact centre of the world, looking outwards and marvelling at the view.

I rest when weary, eat when hungry, sleep when night descends, arise when dawn has broken, pack my bag and step out upon my way. I pass through countryside that stuns me with its beauty and shames the chattering of my thoughts into silence. I fall in love with my native land: its rolling hills and valleys, its woods and pastures, its trees and flowers, its rocks and streams, its birds and beasts and insects, its radiant skies, its fertile earth. I dive into the depths of Nature and am refreshed, invigorated, enriched.

I give and receive kindness to and from those I meet along the way, and, when I travel alone, I give myself up to the tacit awareness of motion and landscape and atmosphere and the spirit of place. Sometimes I follow thoughts through strange verbal labyrinths and sometimes I let them roam as they will, paying them scant attention. Sometimes I compose tales and songs as I walk and send them off into the world - fleeting creations that no one but myself shall hear: but I hear them and am pleased. And sometimes I tell my tales of Kaph to those I meet , and maybe they, in return, tell me tales of their own, or share their food with me, or buy me a drink in a wayside tavern, or I them. For now I am a traveller. Now I am of the road, the footpath, the woodland, the wilderness.

From my Somerset home, my two trusty feet carry me first to the coasts of Devon and Cornwall and Dorset, then lead me through the chalky hills of Wiltshire and across the Severn Estuary into Wales where the Wye Valley finds me and magically transports me through its wondrous wooded hills into the Cambrian mountains. Where next? This is a question I never ask. Forever a path opens up before me and I walk it. Forever a tree or a rock beckons and I sit beside it a while. Forever a cheery face draws me into conversation and I enjoy the company of men. Forever the sound of a flowing stream entices me to its banks and I meander along with it. Forever the signs of adventure direct me on my way. I leave no trace of my passing save occasional footprints, and invisible thoughts that drop from my mind, discarded mental litter that vanishes into nothingness in the spaciousness of the physical world. I let go of my thoughts, my long-held opinions and beliefs, my past regrets and future aspirations, my hopes and fears. I let them all fall away, like the dry brown leaves of autumn scattered on the path, the dead debris of my living mind. My internal monologue - now often an ecstatic eclogue - slows with my pace. Words fade into a rich, comforting, quiet emptiness, a "Rediscovery of the Blindingly Obvious", as the Philosopher had put it.

I recall his final words to me, that day when my walk began. "God's speed. God's Grace." God's speed, I see, is slow and sedate - a steady two or three miles per hour. And God's Grace falls constantly upon me, like gentle rain from the sky, cleansing and life-giving. The Grace of God is the present moment - enfolding me, caressing me, nourishing me, filling me with light and love, with kindness, with awareness, with patience, with humility.

A journey into vastness. I fade into the firmament at night; vanish amongst the trees and fields and clouds by day. I merge into the world...

Atop these shoulders sits the Holy Grail -
an immaculate vessel overflowing with the Universe,
an ever-creative fount from which all things pour forth.
It is, at one and the same time, nothing special and something wonderful,
the birthright of everyman and the crown of kings.
All intellection misses the point.
The point is right here and now.
The point is to see, to enjoy, to be.
This is the nature of Being.
We are all like this.

8
The Value of Money

"Money, it's a gas
Grab that cash with both hands
And make a stash."

Roger Waters, Pink Floyd, "Money", 1973

What do you do when you find a twenty pound note lying in the street? Hand it in to the police is what you're meant to do, I suppose. Or maybe, as in this case, give it back to the person who probably lost it in the first place. Or keep it, perhaps?

Jesus, it's not often I even see a twenty pound note. Fivers and tenners are the most I usually get my hands on. But here, tucked under a bush beside the path, was a little see-through bag containing, unmistakably, a twenty pounder. Just the one - that was the first thing I checked as I eagerly picked it up. But a whole twenty quid. Jesus! More than I earned in a fortnight.

The Old Man had stopped giving me pocket money on my fourteenth birthday.

"Old enough to earn your own, from now on," he informed me.

"Thanks very much," I said.

Pretty soon I found a job delivering Sunday morning papers. Sunday paper rounds are the great prize amongst us young earners. Only one early rise each week and, even then, you can lie in till seven thirty. We have these nifty little fluorescent trolleys to push around, the Sunday papers are so ridiculously bulky. And I pick up over a fiver for a couple of hours' work.

I'd only been at it for a few weeks when I first encountered Old Git Gittings. He lives on his own at Number 31. The Mirror is his Sunday read, which is at least a reasonable size, although the spring on his letterbox is rusted up to buggery and has a bite like a crocodile. Number 33 is next on the round. Damn Sunday Times - as big as a telephone directory. I usually take a short cut across the lawn in front of old Mr. Gittings' window.

"Oi! Get off there!" he shouted at me, first time I did it, waving his arms wildly and giving me a menacing glare through his window.

The next Sunday, I did the same again and he came charging through his front door, ranting and raving, still dressed in his pyjamas. I gave him a cheeky smile and carried on across the lawn to Number 33. Stupid old git!

The Old Man knew him from way back. "Tight-fisted old bloke," he told me. "The state of his paintwork's a disgrace to the estate and he never does a damn thing to his garden. Neighbours cut the lawn for him."

"Be reasonable," Mum defended him. "He's only got a pension to live on and he can't get about too well. Arthritis, I think. His wife died years ago and he's all on his own, poor chap."

"So he should sell up and move to a nursing home or something," was the Old Man's verdict.

God, I hope I never get as old and grumpy as Mr. Gittings. Nor as mean and selfish as the Old Man, come to that.

So anyway, what was I going to do with this twenty quid? First thing I did was stuff it quickly into my pocket and get on with the round. I'd walked to Number 57 before it began to sink in. Twenty quid. Enough for a couple of CDs or the occasional burger or bag of chips of an evening. Maybe I could even invite Alice out to the cinema or something (nice fantasy), or get some decent clothes instead of the cheap crap Mum's always buying me. Honestly, my needs are quite modest, really. And, after all, twenty quid is twenty quid.

I knew it belonged to Mr. Gittings, of course. Must have fallen out of his pocket as he fumbled for his key. Apart from having found it just up the end of his path, the plastic bag was a give-away. He always kept his cash in a plastic bag. I'd seen him, a few times, paying his bill in the paper shop. First, it took him about ten minutes to withdraw the tiny bag from his trouser pocket, then another ten while he counted out the few paltry pounds to pay his week's bill.

You'd think he was handing over his life savings to a robber at gunpoint. Old Dixon, the newsagent, would almost look guilty taking it from him. And never a thank you would emerge from old Gittings' puckered mouth, never a smile or even the barest hint of a smile. Nothing but the scowl that had lived on his face for so long it had taken root, grown, died and become fossilised.

Once I stood behind him while Mr. Dixon handed back some change - about 3p. Old Gittings counted it at least ten times before placing it, coin by coin, into his little plastic bag, huffing and puffing to himself and refusing to budge an inch from the counter so that I could get there to buy my Mars Bar. And the smell that came from him! Jesus! Why is it that old people always stink of putrid cabbage?

"See you next week, Mr. Gittings," Dixon shouted with remarkable cheerfulness as the old bloke left the shop.

"Hrumph," he replied and hobbled off, muttering to himself under his breath.

The old git didn't deserve to have his twenty quid back.

And yet, I thought as I crossed the road to Number 74, it's only money, after all. Probably means more to him than it does to me. To be honest, I hate the stuff. It causes nothing but trouble.

Nothing divides people as much as money - those who have it and those who don't. I mean, we go on about discrimination based on sex or age or race. What about money? No one seems too bothered about that, do they? Money is the biggest divider there is. You've either got it or you ain't. And if you ain't - well, tough luck, mate. Why can't I walk into a posh restaurant and order a fancy meal? Because I'm poor, that's why. No headwaiter's going to come up to me and say, "I'm sorry, Sir, we can't serve you here because you're black: or you're female: or you're too old: or you're too ugly." So how come he can say, "Sorry, chum, you ain't got no money. Out!"?

It's a fair point, don't you think? How is it that some rich bloke can blow ten million quid on a Van Gogh while some Indian kid has to work for six months to buy a pair of sandals? Why is it that some fat arse company director earns a million a year while his cleaner is on just seven quid an hour? Why is it that Jason Double-Barrelled What's-his-name, at school, gets thirty quid a week pocket money while I get bugger all? Valid questions, don't you think? Or am I turning into a communist? Or a cynic, as the Old Man often calls me. (Not quite sure what it means, to be honest, but I sort of like the sound of it.)

The thing about money is that it's rather good for getting you pretty well anything you want. "Money talks," Mum's always saying, to which the Old Man replies, "Money doesn't talk, it swears." I used to think that was quite clever till he told me it was a quote from some Bob Dylan song, back in the Sixties when twenty quid could buy you a car and still leave you with enough change for a slap-up meal on the way home. I wonder what twenty quid will be worth forty years from now. Maybe enough for a packet of mints.

By the end of the round, I'd sort of decided. I marched back up the road, deliberately went down the path of Number 33, then across the lawn to Number 31.

Old Gittings opened the front door before I'd even knocked.

"Now what?" He glared at me as though I'd rudely interrupted his extremely busy Sunday morning.

"Found this at the end of your path," I said, holding up the plastic bag. "Thought maybe you'd dropped it."

The scowl dropped from his face like a discarded crisp packet, his eyes lit up and, for the first time in seventy-five years of miserable existence, he smiled - a huge, toothless, face-cracking smile. For a moment he looked like a newborn baby, cooing with ecstasy at the first sight of his mother.

"Thanks, lad," he said, taking the twenty quid from my hand.

I stood there, awaiting a slightly more profuse expression of gratitude or even, perhaps, a small reward –ten percent would have done fine - but he just slammed the door and was gone.

So much for the new CDs, I thought. So much for inviting Alice to the pictures.

Twenty quid just to see old Mr Gittings smile.

Yep, I decided as I trotted home, it was worth it. Good value for money.

9
The Dancing of the Lord of Weir

(This is a retelling of a tale from Robin Williamson's 1971 album "Myrrh". The opening and closing lines are direct quotations from his song.)

"In the third part of the year
when men begin to gather fuel against the coming cold
hear hooves ring hard on frosty ground
begins our song..."

In those times, we lived well apart from the tribes who professed to rule our lands, the miners of copper and tin, the makers of metal tools and weapons. We favoured the old ways: wood and stone our materials, horn and bone and leather. We lived on the moorlands, herding deer and goats, collecting fruits and herbs from the wilds, growing barley and oats on rough patches of ploughed ground. Enmeshed in the seasons, at one with the world, we basked in the beauties of the rolling hills, of the skies, of the Mother Sun. We carried the ways and legends of the Ancients into the future.

Our homes were deep caves in the rocky cliffs, and huts of earth and willow, flush with the grassy hillsides. Our meeting hall was a low dome, built long ago from ash and beech boughs dragged up from the valleys, covered in turf and planted over with heather, merging into the surrounding mounds and wild contours. We cared not to mingle with the men of metal, nor they with us. Our paths would cross from time to time, but always we, small and fleet-footed as we were, would scamper quickly away, secreting ourselves in the undergrowth or the canopies of trees. They dismissed us as urchins, uncouth beings of the wilds, outlaws, even insubstantial sprites and, for the most part, they let us be, many even believing that we possessed a breed of magic stronger than their own. As for us, we avoided those tall men of the lowlands, their smell seemingly putrid to our noses, cleansed daily, as they were, by the fresh winds of the moorlands. We offered them no welcome to our upland homes, although welcoming strangers of our own kind was both our custom and our delight.

My father, Kaph, was Bard of our tribe, a singer and story teller who wove his wondrous tales around our evening's fire in the domed hall, ensnaring the rapt attention of every one of us and holding us captive till his tale was told or his song cycle sung. He taught me the words, the tunes and the moods of his songs and stories, whose histories, he said, were buried deep amongst the ancestral roots of our people. He taught me, too, to play upon the pipes, creating rhythms and melodies and tonal colours to punctuate and illustrate the telling of sagas.

I tried to learn his words and tunes as thoroughly as possible, to recite them as he did, but for this he chastised me.

"Create, don't copy," he said. "When your time comes and you inherit the bardic mantle from me, you must find your own voice. Tell the tales in words that are your own, allow your own melodies to arise, for the tales of our tribe are like trees, rather than stones: they grow, they change, they take on the colours of the seasons, they are living beings with their own courses to pursue.

"Never," he told me, "tell twice a tale in the same words."

And these words I have remembered unto this very day.

"The shining time of the bard is at day's end," spoke my father, "when the people gather around the evening fire, their bellies full. And, just as the splendour of the sunset is anew each day, so must your stories live in the moment, even whilst retaining their ancient essence."

Once, just before my initiation as a man, my father took me out onto the moorland, far away from all listening ears but ours, and there he taught me to play the magic tune of the eternal dance, the strangest sound I ever heard.

"Within these notes lies a strength beyond reason," he told me, "an enchantment too potent to be heard save in the most dire of circumstances. Learn it well, in solitude, and keep it hidden till it be needed."

This I did, little thinking that the day of that necessity was but a few weeks away.

It happened that we, the men-folk of the tribe, were out hunting salmon in the river valleys on the edge of our moorland, when a party of the Lord of Weir rode up to our home amongst the high tors and, finding the grassy door of our hall open to the sun and air, and the women-folk at work within, they leapt from their horses and entered. They were soldiers, armed and clothed in stout leather jerkins, yet their eyes and postures, so the women told us later, betrayed their apprehension, their fear, even, for they all knew the stories that were told of us and they were not comfortable in our presence. So, although they had swords and clubs raised to attack, they hurt no one, hoping, rather, to intimidate and scare us into submission.

Our women kept their composure as our tribal Mother, small but carrying the wisdom of eighty summers atop her shoulders, stepped forward.

"What brings you here?" she said, her voice, although soft, combining authority, a tentative tinge of welcome and an unmistakeable undercurrent of displeasure.

The captain of the soldiers stepped forward and lowered his sword.

"We mean you no harm," he said. "My master, the Lord of Weir, has commanded that we seek you out, for he desires to bring magic into his domain by taking as bride one of you hill-folk."

"Why does he want magic?" asked the Matriarch.

"Who knows?" replied the captain. "To steal a march on his foes and rivals, I presume. The power of magic would be a fine weapon to add to his arsenal."

"Our magic may be used only for good," said the Matriarch.

"The Lord of Weir will use it only for his own good, of that I can assure you," replied the captain, with a smile.

The Matriarch snorted. "He'll have none of our magic for his evil ways. Be gone!"

Her tone belied her frail appearance. Her words were the final authority of our tribe. But the captain stood his ground and, hesitantly, he raised his sword above the Matriarch's head. "The Lord of Weir will not be gainsaid," he spoke. "We will take what we came for, and if you try to resist us, you will all suffer."

"This one!" shouted one of his men, dragging by the hair a young maiden from the ranks of women cowering against the walls of the hall.

"Well chosen," said the captain, lifting the maiden's chin and brushing back her tangled locks to look upon her face. "This is a wild beauty of a beast."

She glared at him, her feral stare reminding the captain of the eyes of a wild lynx he had once encountered.

"Yes, here is fitting magic and passion for our Lord of Weir. Take her!" he commanded his men.

The soldiers of his company dragged away the woman, who made not a sound, for she was as dumb as a rabbit and had been since birth. But, as the captain rightly observed, her spirit was as wild and free as a cat's.

Her name was Gelda, my sister, the only daughter of Kaph the Bard, the beloved totem of our tribe, for never did a hostile or unkind word fall from her lips. Furthermore, though her mouth made no sounds, her hands could beat a rhythm upon a deer-skin drum that was as bewitching as the tumbling of water down a mountain stream.

But our lovely sister was bound, hands and legs, and carried off, hanging from a pole like a carcass of meat. The captain bowed before the Matriarch and, his sword still raised, turned abruptly and led his men and their burden from the hall. And though the soldiers of the company might well have had a mind to further looting and raping, every one of them thought better of it, scared by the tales of our magic powers, eager only to be gone from that enchanted place, back to the fields they knew.

At sunset, our fishing party returned, lugging bags and baskets replete with fat salmon, and apples, plums and damsons gathered from the trees that grew upon the banks of the lowland rivers. Our fare was the makings of a lavish feast and our conversation merry, anticipating a day or two of jollity and repose in the warmth of our hall. But our mood soon turned sour as we learned of the loss of our wild sister, Gelda.

Instead of the expected feast, we ate sparsely and drank little of our mead, for our thoughts and discussions were focussed on the making of plans to rescue our loved one.

The next day, a band of twenty of us - men and women alike - set off at dawn towards the lands of Weir. We carried no weapons - for it is not our way to fight - but rather we had dressed ourselves in the manner of minstrels and travelling troubadours, gaily coloured and festooned with dangling bells and garlands of flowering heather. Where others might have taken clubs or staves or slings and other instruments of aggression, we held only pipes and horns, drums and diverse stringed instruments.

The castle of the Lord of Weir stood high upon a rocky crag, a league away, where the moorlands fell away to gentler hills, wooded valleys and green meadows. We arrived at the castle gates and announced ourselves as merry-makers, come to entertain the lord and his company in exchange for food and a night's quarters. The home of the Lord of Weir had the reputation of being a dour, austere place where music and laughter were rarely heard, so the guards at the gate, not recognising us as the magical moorland folk, ushered us in gleefully, hoping for some more uplifting evening than they usually endured. We were shown into an ante-room where we rested and prepared ourselves. Then, as the Sun set and the castle's company gathered in the great hall around their fire and their lord, so were we introduced and we skipped cheerily into the room, playing our instruments.

Our lost one, Gelda - as we observed at once - was tied to a stake in a corner of the great hall, for the Lord of Weir had yet to tame her. Rather, he delighted in taunting her and feeding her not, presuming that hunger and thirst would soon make her relent and soften to his advances.

"Who leads this motley band?" cried the Lord of Weir, when we had completed our jig around the hall and gathered in the centre.

"Tis I," said Kaph, stepping forward, removing his hat and presenting the lord with an extravagant bow and a bright trill on his pipes.

The Lord of Weir was not a man prone to smiling. The features of his face had frozen, long ago, into a perpetual scowl. "And what have you to offer us this night?" he spoke, his voice as cold as his face.

"We bring the gifts of song and dance," replied my father, Kaph the Bard.

"Then play a tune, while we eat," proclaimed the Lord, "but keep your songs subdued lest they cause us indigestion." Thus saying he picked up a leg of chicken from the table and bit into it with relish, a sign that the rest of the company should commence the feast.

The Bard began his tune, soft and relaxed, at first, as requested, creating a mellow mood conducive to banqueting.

The Lord of Weir nodded his approval.

But gradually, as the diners concentrated on their food and forgot the background music of the minstrels, Kaph quickened the tempo of his piping and the accompanying drummers and string strummers, initially restrained, matched his speed and slowly raised their volume. I noticed feet tapping amongst the feasters at the Lord of Weir's table, and the table at which sat his courtiers. The commoners and servants of the castle sat at benches around the perimeter wall of the great hall, and here, too, feet were a-tapping and bodies swaying as the assembled company tucked in to their meal. The atmosphere in the hall was changing, and I believe it was not due to the intoxicating ale that the diners were swigging between mouthfuls of food. No, it was as if someone had thrown a huge bunch of ash logs on the fire and the blaze was radiating throughout the room, reddening the faces of all. It was as if a window had been thrown open, flooding the dim hall in golden light; as if a mood of restless jollity was flitting from one to another like an irresistible aroma.

Then, while the drummers and strummers maintained their rhythm, I became aware that my father had slipped into a new tune, the secret series of piped notes that he had taught me: the melody of the eternal dance.

The foot-tapping of the banqueters became more insistent. Some began banging their pewter tankards upon the table, some swinging their elbows and arms along with the beat. The meal became forgotten. First one, then two, then more and more leapt to the floor in the centre of the hall and there let their bodies move in an unrestrained dance of spontaneous vivacity: feet stomping, hips swaying, arms tracing curves upon the air, heads bobbing in glorious abandon. This was the dance of the world in motion; the dance of the wind in the trees; the dance of the planets around the Sun, of the stars across the sky; the dance of blood flowing around the body, of images swimming through the mind; the dance of yesterday, today and tomorrow; the dance of all time; the eternal dance.

Within minutes, all in the hall were upon their feet, their bodies gyrating, their arms and legs flying in all directions, their faces aghast with joy or wonderment.

Last to succumb was the Lord of Weir himself, but even he, despite the joyless grumpiness that habitually cloaked him, could not resist the magic dance. He threw back his chair and leapt onto his table, kicking bowls and tankards aside, his legs splayed and shaking, his hands describing all manner of spirals, his torso writhing in ways he would never have thought possible, his long locks of greying hair a constantly churning curtain before his eyes. With lordly abandon, he let go. And the whole of that great hall surged like a raging cataract to the dancing of the Lord of Weir.

My father had told me that the secret tune of the eternal dance was irresistible. Dance one must, and dance forever, until, as it is said in the legend, the dancer thinks one kind thought. And thereby he would escape the spell of the dance. Thus the men and women of our company, we minstrels and players, were not endangered, for kind thoughts come as second nature to us. So we played and played, loving this spectacle, while the Lord of Weir and his retinue danced themselves into a frenzy.

Kaph, still piping the magic tune, opened the doors of the great hall and the dancers followed him out of the castle and across the drawbridge, on to the stony road that led into the valley.

"Over to you, now, my son," he shouted to me, growing exhausted from his piping.

And I raised my own pipe to my lips, and the tune emerged, just as I had learnt it, flowing from me as smoothly as it had from my father, note after note, conjuring the spell of sound that conquered the will of even the strongest and most stubborn of men. There I was, enchanting even the mighty Lord of Weir with a simple tune played upon a pipe.

Oh, that moment I will remember all my life, a moment for which I was born!

I piped on, and on danced the dancers, down the rocky path from the castle and into the valley. But now the expressions on their faces were changing, from glee and wonderment, at first, to alarm and fear, for each of them was coming to realise that, despite their exhaustion, they were unable to stop. The Lord of Weir himself wore the grimmest grimace: the man of control was out of control. He had sought to use our magic for his own ends, but now our magic was using him. And he was sorely a-feared for he was defenceless, gripped by a power of which he knew nothing. I saw him struggling to halt the lashings of his arms, the leapings of his legs, but, try as he might, he could not break free from the spell of the eternal dance.

Is it true, I wondered, that they needs must dance until they think one kind thought?

My question was answered forthwith. An oldish woman in the dance - one of the castle cooks, I think - tripped on the rough ground and tumbled into a ditch beside the path, her ankle clearly twisted. Her body still writhed to the rhythm of the dance, but she could not raise herself to her feet. Many passed her by, captured by the dance and careless of their fellow in distress. But then a young man - a servant boy, I suspect - took pity on her, stopped, helped her to her feet, wrapped his arms about her and supported her tenderly, leading her back onto the path. With this one kind thought, he escaped the magic of the dance and, standing still at last, he panted in exhaustion. The old woman, too, acknowledging the kindness of the young man with a smile of heartfelt gratitude, shared his kindly thought and her own moving limbs were stilled. Arm in arm, serene at last, they turned and sauntered wearily back towards the castle, while the rest danced madly on down the pathway.

Far from the castle, upon the banks of a wide river that meandered into the meadowlands, I ceased my piping. But the dancers danced on, the music of the eternal dance now firmly fixed in their minds, its insistent rhythm residing in the muscles of their limbs. The procession wove on, following the riverbank, but through weariness the dance had transformed into a crazed parody of its first joyful, abandoned steps in the great hall of the castle. Now the dancers seemed possessed by madness and despair, rather than the euphoria with which they had first leapt to their feet. I watched as, one by one, they dropped to the ground, exhausted - or dead, perhaps - or perhaps that kindly thought had finally found them. But of this I am sure: many of the company of the castle of the Lord of Weir danced on into the distance, till they vanished from my sight. And the Lord of Weir himself was certainly amongst them. And it was later recounted by the future bards of our people that, being ever incapable of a kind thought - a notion totally alien to his personality - he may, for all we know, be dancing still.

I climbed happily back to the castle where Kaph, my father, had cut the ropes that bound his daughter, Gelda, and she was in his arms while the rest of our minstrel band gathered around with merry faces.

"Today has been a day of great wonder," proclaimed my father when he saw me approaching, "a day to sing about down through the future generations of our kind, a day upon which a new tale has been born."

Cheers and whoops arose from the assembly. The bard let them continue for a few moments, then silenced them with a raised arm.

"Furthermore," his voice was softer now, more intimate, "this day has seen the passing of two remarkable milestones for my family. First, my son has become a true bard, of proven worth and power. And second, most joyously, my daughter, through the shock of her captivity and release, has broken the spell that kept her silent and she has found her voice."

"Is this so?" I asked, incredulous.

"It is, my brother," replied Gelda, my sister, a voice soft and hesitant but full of love and magic.

And I wept for joy, not only for the delight of hearing her voice at last, but also for the sweet felicity of being addressed, for the first time in my life, as "my brother".

We slept, that night, in the empty castle of the Lord of Weir, having first eaten and drunk our fill from what remained on his banqueting table. The next day, our beloved Gelda in our midst, our band of happy minstrels walked home to our hill upon the moors...

"...and entering in
made fast the grassy door."

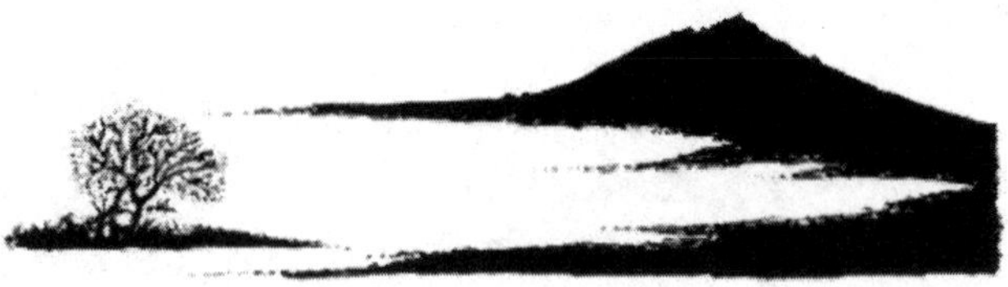

10
Pooh Sticks at the TIE Club AGM

"What is this life if, full of care,
We have no time to stand and stare,
No time to stand beneath the boughs
And stare as long as sheep or cows."

William Henry Davies, "Leisure", 1911

Some consternation followed the announcement that the Annual General Meeting of the Take It Easy Club would feature, as the main event, a "Pooh sticks" tournament.

"The man's gone batty!" spluttered Maximilian Gavel as he read the letter of invitation over a late breakfast.

"Take it easy, dear," said his wife who, in accordance with the ideals of the Club to which they both belonged, was doing just that: gazing contemplatively through the window while sipping at a cup of chamomile tea.

"But Pooh sticks?" persisted Maximilian. "Who in their right mind plays Pooh sticks?"

"Exactly," said his wife. "That's why I think it's quite a fitting activity for the TIE Club AGM. Toby has chosen well again."

"Depends which bridge over which river he has in mind," responded Maximilian who, after many years, was beginning to attain occasional vague glimpses into the peculiar mindset of his old friend Toby, founder and chairman of the Take It Easy Club.

"Probably a rather sluggish river," his wife conjectured before returning her gaze to the window.

Presumably he had some reasonably common surname, but Toby always signed his letters, "Toby Ornotobee", and when giving his name to a stranger he contrived to make the "Ornotobee" sound quite natural, so that he was rarely challenged.

"When a chap gets to my age he can call himself what he damn well likes," he once said to some officious young clerk who had raised an eyebrow at his name. "That's Ornotobee - spelled O-R-N-O-T-O-B- double E."

In fact, he was only fifty-two, although he could easily have passed for any age from thirty to seventy. Despite his many behavioural eccentricities, his face was remarkably unremarkable: a bland visage of expressionless indifference. "Anonymity is an asset worth cultivating," he often opined. "To drift through life observing closely but rarely closely observed is my preferred modus operandi. Others may flaunt dynamism and panache, if they care to. As for me, I just like to take it easy."

The Take It Easy Club was born during a particularly lazy summer's afternoon upon the grassy bank of a slow flowing Somerset river. Toby, Maximilian and Fiona Gavel, John and Joan Smith and Seamus O'Verdun, the unknown Irish poet, were loafing in the sun while passing a bottle of German wine amongst themselves, each filling his or her glass and transferring the bottle to the next picnicker at such a leisurely pace that it took at least fifteen minutes to complete the circuit, by which time each participant was ready for a top-up. A freezer box containing several more such bottles was readily to hand.

"Job lot," said Maximilian, whose job it had been to supply the wine. "A neighbour of mine found a case of the stuff on a roadside verge. Apparently it had fallen off the back of a lorry. Mine for a couple of tenners."

The Smiths had brought a tin of home-baked scones and strawberry jam, which pleased Toby immensely and he became somewhat annoying to the rest of the party by the frequency with which he passed the tin to the two Smiths, saying, with great glee, "Another scone, John? Another scone, Joan?", shifting between the two variant pronunciations of "scone" accordingly.

Toby himself, as usual, had provided the sandwiches for the riverside repast: as usual they were filled exclusively with blue cheese and marmite.

Seamus, misunderstanding his allotted task to bring some poetry, offered an earthenware goblet and a Wedgewood vase.

"Pottery, poetry," he defended himself, "Are we to quibble over a couple of re-arranged letters?"

The question remained unanswered for Toby, as was his wont, was holding forth. "You know, taking it easy is a very under-valued skill," he proclaimed, shortly after pouring himself his third glass of wine. "By eschewing arduous activity, we serve humanity, relaxing the collective consciousness of mankind. Our afternoons of easy-going lethargy are the perfect counterpoise to the frenetic hurly-burly and brouhaha of the modern world. The value of doing very little is not to be underestimated."

None of the company ventured to gainsay their host. Toby, as always, had organised the al fresco party, or, at least, he had stated time, place and personal contributions. All present, it must be admitted, shared his oft-voiced views on idleness and the delights of leading a simple, undemanding life of ease and indulgence. Others may have dismissed them all as useless loafers, over-privileged and under-employed, but they tended to rationalise their chosen lifestyle as a challenge to the prevalent pace and ethos of modernity, and themselves as champions of the art of relaxing into the present moment, with a smile on one's lips, a song in one's heart, a light fancy tripping through one's mind and, ideally, a glass of wine in one's hand.

"We should form a society to celebrate ourselves, and recruit like-minded fellows," Toby announced. "The Take It Easy Club. And, as all good societies need an acronym, we'll call ourselves the TIE Club."

"Absurd idea," muttered Maximilian.

"I like it," said his wife, Fiona.

"Ludicrous," said John Smith.

"Delightful," said his wife, Joan.

"A splendid touch of English eccentricity," said Seamus.

"So that's it," said Toby. "Unanimously carried."

"What do you propose we do in this club?" asked Maximilian.

"Why, take it easy, of course."

Subsequent discussion - such as it was, for Toby remained the principal speaker - led to the resolution that the TIE Club should have no written constitution, no officers, no agenda beyond taking it easy, and that members should wear no badge, indulge in no fancy handshake or other gesture of recognition, follow no prescribed rituals and adopt no obligations or responsibilities.

"But perhaps we could proclaim ourselves," suggested Toby, "by, appropriately, the ties that we wear. Let them be outrageous in the extreme. I, for one, am sick of the ties of dreary conformity that I am apt to wear."

Thus saying, he ripped off his tie - a particularly nondescript grey specimen with absolutely nothing to commend it beyond its greyness - and, snatching up the bread-knife with which the scones had been cut, he sliced the offending tie into several pieces and flung them into the air. They all watched silently as the fragments of tie slowly fluttered to the ground amidst the remains of the picnic.

The next time they met, Toby set the trend by wearing a wide blue tie decorated with huge white daisies - a tie guaranteed to elicit a smile from even the most stony-faced, hard-hearted observer.

"A grey day is brightened by a spry tie," he offered, by way of explanation.

Seamus took up the challenge by wearing a silk tie painted to resemble a full-sized salmon, hanging by its tail from his collar, its wide-eyed head staring out just above his belt. He had even embellished the image by smearing it with fish oil, giving it an unmistakable but unwelcome air of authenticity.

The Gavels and the Smiths hadn't bothered to dress up at all, in accordance, as Maximilian asserted, with the principle of taking it easy. The Smiths had gone one step further by not even bothering to turn up.

"Of course, attendance at TIE Club get-togethers is entirely voluntary," said Toby, "although the absence of John and Joan's scones and scones is to be regretted."

A mild groan drifted lazily around the group, like the aroma of Seamus's tie, as Maximilian drew the cork on the first bottle of wine.

"So, here's to the inaugural meeting of the TIE Club," said Toby, raising his glass.

"May it live long and prosper," said Fiona Gavel, causing a simultaneous and tacit realisation to pass amongst the other three members of the Club: that her face and ears bore a distinct resemblance to those of Mr Spock of Star Trek fame.

Numbers grew slowly, as befitted the nature of the Club: from six in the core group to, over the years, seven, nine, ten and peaking at eleven after five years.

"Pity we couldn't have made twelve - you know, like the apostles," said Fiona Gavel, as, once again, the momentary image of Mr Spock flashed around the group.

"It's thirteen," said Maximilian, "if you count the Jesus character."

"I think it propitious for us to avoid all religious allusions or connotations," said Toby. "Besides, eleven is a good number - a prime, no less."

"Perhaps I'll compose a poem to the number eleven," said Seamus, "something that's probably never been done before."

But he never did. Seamus was a man of ideas rather than actions. He liked nothing so much as to take it easy, to sit and watch his mind create forms and patterns in words and images, and to send them drifting off - always unrecorded, often unuttered - into the oblivion of the past.

Toby was more a man of action - albeit deliberately slow action. He had no car and never went anywhere that he couldn't reach by walking or slow cycling. He wrote his letters meticulously using a plume pen and a bottle of ink. His most favoured method of cooking - for he fancied himself as something of a culinary aesthete - involved a slow pot in a low oven. His gardening efforts were confined to bonsai trees. And his pursuance of the arts of courtship had been so protracted that he had never maintained a woman's interest for sufficient time for adequate wooing and thus remained a reluctant bachelor. But once he had had an idea, and once he had resolved, after considerable thought, that it was a worthy idea, he tended to see it slowly through to its actualisation.

Thus it was with Pooh sticks.

"Why not Pooh sticks?" thought Toby Ornotobee, idly pondering, one afternoon, the forthcoming AGM of the TIE Club.

The tradition had evolved that those members who turned up should engage in some kind of activity other than sitting, eating and drinking. Nothing too strenuous, of course, neither physically nor intellectually. Ideally something relaxed, amusing, slow-paced, undemanding, occupying perhaps an hour, maybe more, depending on how the mood of the meeting developed.

"Why not Pooh sticks?" thought Toby. What could be more conducive to the spirit and aspirations of the TIE Club? Equally as appropriate, he thought, as the activity of the previous year's AGM: cloud watching. That idea, as outlined by Toby, was that members should assume recumbent, upward-gazing postures upon a grassy surface and observe the passage and gradual transformations of passing clouds, perhaps offering remarks upon shapes resembling recognisable forms, perhaps simply marvelling at the ongoing pageant. Unfortunately, as with many outdoor English endeavours, the proposed activity was scuppered by the vagaries of the weather: a perfect day, the sky a uniform blue from horizon to horizon, not a cloud in sight.

"Rather defeats the object of the exercise," Maximilian had murmured.

Toby had been a little disappointed. Even a sky of dull grey stratus would have been more interesting. "Perhaps we should wait till sunset," he suggested, "then at least we could get into some star gazing."

But the encroaching cold as the Sun set sent the company indoors. Besides, prolonged recumbency was taking its toll. Half the Club had dropped off, Seamus snoring like an elephant, Fiona Gavel loudly articulating her dreams, which seemed to involve Maximilian and assorted objects of torture.

"Time to retreat indoors," Maximilian had said, nudging his wife firmly in the ribs.

Seamus had snorted. "Sky blue apples upon a sky blue platter. Being and Emptiness, spirit and matter." It is well known that Irish poets dream in rhyming couplets.

"Yes, Pooh sticks, this year," Toby resolved, wondering why such a fitting idea had never before occurred to him.

No doubt the game originated in the depths of prehistory, when mankind first laid bridges across flowing rivers, but it took a small bear and a young boy to earn it a specific name and elevate it to the status of a popular pastime. It all started when the bear, Winnie-the-Pooh, absent-mindedly kicked at a pine cone while crossing a bridge. The pine cone plopped into the waters of the river. Pooh, being an absent-minded sort of bear, strolled across the bridge and, peering over its downstream railing, observed his pine cone passing by beneath. Hm, he thought and repeated the experiment, finally graduating from pine cones to sticks.

Thus was the game of Pooh sticks born, in 1928, in A. A. Milne's "The House at Pooh Corner", and from such humble beginnings in children's literature it grew, if not exactly into an Olympic sport, then at least into a common, easy-going recreation amongst Pooh-reading children - and adults sufficiently liberated to indulge in the fancies of childhood.

Toby was convinced. Pooh sticks was the ideal, idle afternoon's entertainment for ladies and gentlemen of leisure.

The rules are simple and seldom made explicit in written words. The sticks should be similar but identifiable, preferably but not necessarily composed of willow. Two or more participants should hold their sticks, at equal heights, over the upstream parapet of a suitable bridge. At the pronouncement "Ready, steady, drop" - whether from the participants themselves, in unison, or an independent referee - the competitors should drop their sticks into the river below. (Throwing is prohibited and punishable by disqualification. A simple "drop" is all that is allowed.)

Participants and spectators then run or amble - depending on the speed of the river's flow - across the bridge to the downstream parapet where, peering over, they await the emergence of the dropped sticks. Whoever's stick is first to appear is proclaimed the winner. Competitions may constitute a single "drop", the best of three or five "drops", or any other predetermined odd number. Alternatively, the duration of the competition may be defined by time - an hour or two, for instance - or the availability of sticks. Disputes are settled by a "re-drop". The spirit of sportsmanship is regarded as paramount. Winning or losing are equally irrelevant: it is the taking part that is important.

Is success at Pooh sticks attributable to luck or skill? Several academic treatises have been written, advocating either position. Toby decided to exclude this question from possible discussion. Inevitably, the winner of a tournament will claim his or her victory is achieved by skilful "dropping". Inevitably the loser will dismiss it as blind chance. But to Pooh stick purists, enjoyment is the name of the game. All else is vanity: dust upon the water, chaff in the wind.

"Poppycock!" said Maximilian, when Toby had completed his summary of the above dissertation on Pooh sticks at the TIE Club AGM.

"Thanks a million, Maximilian," said Toby. "A useful contribution which perhaps puts our forthcoming endeavour into perspective. I'm sure poppycock is a word of which Pooh would approve."

"You realise that Pooh is a fictional character, I presume? As such, his approval or disapproval of a particular word is irrelevant."

"Don't deride fictional characters, Maximilian," said Toby. "It's conceivable that you might be one yourself."

Maximilian snorted. "Shall we just get on with it," he said, hopping restlessly from foot to foot in a manner rarely seen amongst members of the Take It Easy Club. Despite his innate tendency towards derision and cynicism, Maximilian usually turned out to be the most enthusiastic participant in Toby's activities.

"Right. Round One," announced Toby, who, as usual, had appointed himself Master of Ceremonies. "Gather your sticks."

Eight Club members had responded to Toby's invitation to the Annual General Meeting: the two Gavels, the two Smiths, Seamus the poet, Wittgenstein the bricklayer (a recent addition to the Club), Matthew Pooter (a rather reticent biology lab technician recruited by Seamus who had met him in a pub) and Toby himself.

"We shall call it a quorum," said Toby, ticking off the names on his Club register.

"Quorum my arse!" said Maximilian, unaware of both the exact definition of the word 'quorum' and of how his speech had become infected by the catchphrases of popular TV sitcoms.

The location, chosen by Toby, was a small, picturesque stone bridge that carried a seldom used lane over a very slow running stream - or ‘rhyne’, as they called it in those parts (“Rhyne my arse,” Maximilian remarked. “Anyone can see it’s a bloody stream.”) on the lowlands of Avalon, beneath the towering pyramid of Glastonbury Tor.

Toby had chosen to adorn himself with a tie festooned with Poohs, Piglets, Roos and Eeyores. Seamus sported a Velcro tie to which adhered a random spattering of what appeared to be plastic imitation dog turds of the sort supplied by joke shops (at least, the other members of the Club assumed they were plastic: no one looked too closely). “My interpretation of Pooh sticks,” he announced. Wittgenstein the bricklayer’s tie bore a design of terracotta bricks resembling a brick wall. The other gentlemen exercised their right to abstain from the wearing of ties.

“First round, ladies only,” Toby decreed. “Mrs Smith and Mrs Spock - er, I mean Gavel.”

Fiona Gavel and Joan Smith stepped forward, sticks at the ready.

The rest of the party fell silent, expectant, a frisson of excitement stirring amongst them.

“Ready, steady, drop,” said Toby, slowly and precisely.

The two ladies released their willow sticks.

The company peered over the stone wall to observe the two Pooh sticks drift very slowly under the bridge, carried by the brown water of the distinctly sluggish rhyne. Once they had disappeared from view, the watchers turned as one and made to rush to the downstream parapet, eager to see what might befall.

“Take it easy,” said Toby.

They all checked themselves and began sauntering slowly across the bridge, some gazing about, others exchanging snatches of conversation or humming whimsical tunes. Finally they found themselves at the opposite wall where, leaning lazily over, they observed the gentle drift of the brown fluid. First to emerge, after a minute or two, was Fiona’s stick, followed, a few seconds later, by Joan’s.

“First point to Fiona,” said Toby.

“Beautifully done,” said Maximilian, throwing an arm around his wife’s shoulder.

“Bad luck,” John Smith consoled his wife. “But it was a near thing. No cause to be downhearted.”

“Round Two,” announced Toby. “The poet versus the bricklayer. Take up your sticks, gentlemen.”

Seamus and Wittgenstein stepped forward, brandishing their willow sticks.

“Ready, steady, drop,” proclaimed Toby, affecting an air of solemnity.

Seamus had dressed for the occasion, wearing not only his Velcro “Pooh sticks” tie but also a frilly white shirt with long, loose, embroidered lace cuffs, emulating, he fancied, his compatriot writer and role model, Oscar Wilde. As chance would have it, at the moment of ‘dropping’, a sharp node in his stick became snagged in the lacework of his cuff and by the time he had shaken it free, Seamus’s stick fell to the water several seconds behind Wittgenstein’s.

“Shame, Seamus,” said Toby.

They ambled across to the downstream parapet where, a few minutes later, they were astonished to see Seamus’s stick drifting slowly into view on the moribund current. Of Wittgenstein’s stick there was not a sign.

They waited several minutes more. Matthew Pooter examined a tiny insect that had landed on his sleeve. Joan Smith cleaned her glasses. Fiona Gavel started whistling. Maximilian twiddled his thumbs. Still Wittgenstein’s stick failed to emerge.

“Whereof one cannot speak, thereof one must be silent,” quoted Toby.

“Ah, well, not to worry, eh?” said Wittgenstein. “It’s only a game, after all.”

“A profound thought, indeed,” said Seamus. “Worthy of your exalted namesake.”

“This is becoming increasingly preposterous,” muttered Maximilian who, despite his firm allegiance to the underlying principles of the TIE Club, often felt less comfortable with the seemingly surreal antics of his fellow members.

"Your turn now, Maximilian," said Toby, "in competition with, I think, our newcomer, Pooter the lab technician."

The two men stepped up to the wall of the bridge, Maximilian holding his stick with an expression of intense concentration on his face, while Pooter's pose was positively nonchalant.

"Ready, steady, drop."

Perhaps the flow of the rhyne was dwindling to a snail's pace in the sultry heat of the afternoon sun. This time ten minutes elapsed before the sticks emerged. Their tips were almost touching each other.

"A tricky call," said Toby.

"Nonsense," said Maximilian. "Mine's clearly a few millimetres ahead."

Pooter conceded defeat without argument.

"Who's keeping a tally?" asked Maximilian.

"We've no need to keep score," said Toby. "We play for the fun, not the result."

Seamus stepped forward in a posture indicative of a forthcoming poetic gem:

"It matters not, to he who plays, who wins and who shall fail.
What matters most, in future days, is the telling of the tale."

"Quite so," said Toby.

"Fair play," said Maximilian.

And so the afternoon continued with paired bouts interspersed by ever-increasing intervals of idleness: John Smith versus Toby (a dead heat, and they agreed to forgo the re-drop), Wittgenstein versus Fiona Gavel (another victory for Mrs Gavel while Wittgenstein's stick, once again, mysteriously failed to re-materialise on the downstream side of the bridge) and, finally, Pooter versus Seamus. (Match abandoned. It was decided that the flow of the rhyne had at last given up the ghost. Stasis ruled the waters. The Pooh sticks sat motionless on the mirror-flat surface.)

"And so to tea," said Toby, leading the way to a grassy bank beside the rhyne and spreading, with a flourish, a large, red-and-white squared tablecloth. Maximilian carried the wicker picnic hamper from which he extracted a bottle of wine, eight glasses and a cake-tin full of scones. The company reclined upon the grass, relaxed, light-hearted, gently imbibing the afternoon sunlight and the peace of the English countryside. Smiles and sighs of contentment spread from soul to soul. The day's activity over - such as it was - the time had come to get down to the serious business of the Take It Easy Club: taking it easy.

"You can't beat it, eh?" mused Toby. "Who needs adventure? Who needs the world of endless possibilities, of places to go and things to do? No one has the time to see and do everything that may be seen or done, so why the frantic desire to cram as much as possible into one's brief life? Better to slow down, look around and contact the place in which we live, to enjoy the intimacy of the little picture rather than worry about the wider view of things. Better to keep a space for stillness and silence."

"Well said," said Maximilian.

The assembled TIE Club members nodded their assent.

Toby, a soft smile dancing lightly across his face, reached for the scone tin.

"Scone Joan? Scone John?"

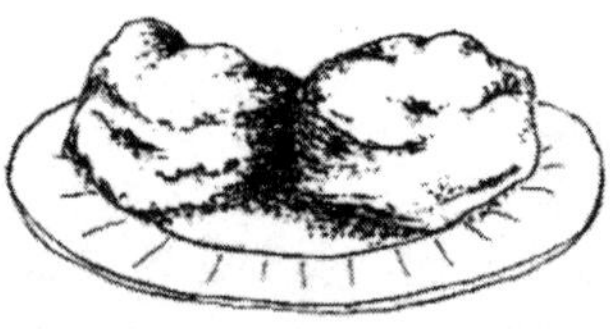

11
The Executioner's Paradox

(This is a retelling of an old tale, the origin of which I do not know.)

No one doubted that the verdict would be guilty, and it was generally accepted amongst those who had witnessed the trial that the death sentence would be passed. But the judge, thoroughly outraged by the details of the crime and by the arrogance and lack of remorse shown by the defendant, decided that a straightforward death sentence was too lenient a punishment. (He was a judge with a reputation for merciless severity to maintain.)

"So utterly despicable was your crime," he pronounced, almost spitting his venom across the courtroom, "that I feel compelled to make you suffer the most awful of sentences. Death it must be, of course. Beheading at dawn, as is the custom. And within seven days, as the law decrees. But the exact day of your execution must come as a complete surprise to you. You will suffer the agony of not knowing when your end will come, of not knowing which night's sleep will be your last, which meal will be your final one upon this Earth. You will spend what little remains of your wretched life in uncertainty and constant worry."

The condemned man bowed his head - through shame and horror, it was generally supposed, but in truth it was to conceal a self-satisfied smirk. For this was an exceedingly clever condemned man - a logician, no less - and, knowing that the judge was a stickler for ensuring that his sentences were carried out to the letter, he knew that this particular sentence could never be enacted. He would live! And the jailors, as they marched him off to the dungeons, noticed that he walked with a more sprightly step than did most of those they led off to their doom.

The executioner studied the docket that was tied around the neck of the condemned man when he arrived, hands strapped behind his back, at the dismal, subterranean corridor of cells known as death row.

"Sentence: beheading," he read. "Time: dawn. Date: within seven days, on a day unbeknown to the prisoner, such that it will be a complete surprise to him."

Strange, thought the executioner, but it was not his place to question the wisdom of the judge whose sentences kept him in business.

The prisoner sat on the stool on the straw-strewn floor of his condemned cell, looking remarkably cheerful, while the executioner perused the docket.

He was a friendly sort of executioner who liked to get to know his prisoners a little before separating them from their heads. He took a pride in his ability to ease them swiftly but gently from this world to the next. And he regarded it to be a vital part of his job to assess the mental state of each beheadee, to judge the likelihood of resistance, of whether it would be necessary to tie his hands, whether he would kneel at the block with dignity, whether a blindfold was desired. The executioner considered himself to be a caring man who valued the personal needs and temperaments of his charges. Besides, he needed an opportunity to examine the man's - or woman's - neck, to gauge which weight of axe to use and with how much force he should swing it. Beheading, he firmly believed, was an act that could all too easily be executed sloppily.

"Do you enjoy your work?" asked the condemned man, seeking to make conversation.

"Of course I do," replied the executioner. "Mine is an ancient and noble profession."

"And you've no shortage of work, what with the brutal laws and sanctimonious judges of our country."

"I'm kept fairly busy, yes," said the executioner. "But it is not my place to comment upon our legal system. All countries must have laws. I am a law-abider and a law-enforcer. That's good enough for me. Others may regard the job of executioner as a miserable and bloody line of business, but I must admit that I derive a measure of satisfaction from it."

"And they pay you well, I presume?"

"Well enough that I am not susceptible to bribes, if that's what you're thinking."

"Of course not," said the condemned man, feigning offence that such dishonesty might be on his mind. "I have the utmost respect for your professionalism. And already I feel sorry that my peculiar case will inevitably place an intolerable strain on your integrity."

"How mean you, sir?" asked the executioner.

"I can see that you are not one to shirk your duty. And your duty compels you to decide upon a day for my execution, in the next seven days, that will come as a complete surprise to me."

"Indeed. An odd command, to be sure, but I shall fulfil it."

"I fear that will be impossible," replied the prisoner at once, now warming to his topic and regarding the executioner with a look of glee that the latter was not accustomed to seeing in the eyes of his prisoners.

"How so?" he demanded.

"Well, let us consider on what day you might surprise me," said the condemned man. "Clearly not on Saturday, which will be my seventh day on death row. If I survive until dawn on Saturday, then I will know that I must die that day, therefore it will come as absolutely no surprise when you awake me with your axe in your hands."

"Indeed so," said the executioner, "for the task must be completed within seven days."

"So, that rules out Saturday as a day on which to surprise me, which means that Friday is the final day for you to spring my surprise execution upon me, is it not?"

"It would seem so."

"So, if I survive till Thursday night, I will be assured that I will die on Friday morning, so where's the surprise in that? Thus, having ruled out Saturday and Friday, Thursday will be your final chance to surprise me. Therefore, I will not be the least surprised to see you at my door, axe in hand, at Thursday dawn. Which brings us to Wednesday morning, your last opportunity to surprise me, therefore it will be no surprise at all."

"I see your point," said the executioner. "As each day becomes the final day to surprise you, then surprise is not a possibility."

"Exactly," said the prisoner, a beaming smile on his face. "Similarly, Tuesday and Monday are ruled out. All that remains is tomorrow, Sunday, on which, logically, I must expect my execution, so I shall not be in the least surprised to see you. I am afraid, Mr Executioner, that you will be unable to carry out my sentence as prescribed so precisely by His Honour, the judge."

The executioner pondered this a while. The argument appeared sound.

"Logic defeats you, I'm afraid," said the condemned man, leaning contentedly back against the wall of his cell.

That night, at home in his bed, the executioner found no solace for his troubled mind and lay awake mulling over his strange paradox. Again and again he ran through the confidently uttered syllogisms of the logician's argument, but he could not refute the rationality of a single statement. It appeared true, as the man so arrogantly asserted, that there existed no day of the coming week on which the executioner could spring a surprise execution. With the final day obviously precluded, each preceding day thus became the final day which, in its turn, was similarly precluded. The days fell away like a line of tumbling dominos. The executioner was flummoxed. The surprise demise of the logician appeared logically impossible. Logic, he decided, was a real bastard of an adversary.

Meanwhile, the condemned man - the logician - slept easily, for, having convinced himself of the irrefutability of his argument and the impossibility of his surprise execution, he relaxed into the prospect of a prolonged confinement in his cell, wherein he might indulge at leisure in all manner of philosophical investigations. Yes, he would enjoy the duration of his death sentence. It pleased him greatly that he had been able to preserve his life purely through the exercise of logic and its eloquent exposition. Well endowed with intellectual satisfaction, he found the strength to stoically endure his time in his tiny cell on death row: the meagre rations of bread and water, the cold dampness, the fleas and lice, the hard palette on which he slept, the pervading stench of excrement from the bucket in the corner - emptied only when a sentence was complete - and the pitiful wails of nameless souls in neighbouring cells. For them, each day brought their pre-specified death-day a day nearer. But for him, each passing day strengthened the conviction that he was immune to surprise, and therefore freed from his sentence.

The executioner puzzled on. He could see no escape from the paradox that paralysed him. In his spare time, he consulted a professor from the city's university, who puzzled with him but could not refute the logician's logic.

"Your hands are tied," proclaimed the professor. "Either you fail to surprise your prisoner, or you fail to execute him. Either way, you are failing to carry out the judge's sentence."

The executioner was not happy. It was not his place to judge, but to execute the judgements of others. He made a point of never learning of the crimes committed by those who knelt beneath his axe, and he always refused to listen if, within the unusual intimacy of the condemned cell, a prisoner started blabbing about the deeds that had led him there. Murder, treason, theft, insurrection, even adultery: all these acts, in various countries of the world, were punishable by death. But the executioner never enquired. His job was to execute. His conscience was never troubled.

Except that now he was sorely troubled. He had never disobeyed a judge's ruling.

As he lay awake on Monday night, tossing and turning in his bed in agitation, his wife solicitously offered to share the burden of his thoughts. Normally, they spoke nothing of his profession.

"Good day at work, dear?" she would ask each evening.

"Yes, thank you, my dear," he would reply, and that would be that. The executioner was not a man to bring his work home with him.

But, on this occasion, he told his wife of his disturbing paradox.

She listened and summed up the situation succinctly. "So, how can you surprise someone who has persuaded himself that he cannot be surprised?" she said.

"Exactly," said the executioner.

"Well, if he's convinced that he can't be surprised, then you can surprise him on any day and it will come as a complete surprise to him," said his wife, turning over to resume her sleep.

And that was when the resolution of his paradox suddenly dawned on him. He had simply to ignore the entire logical argument of the logician.

At dawn on Tuesday morning, the executioner flung open the door of the logician's cell, pulled the man from his palette and bustled him along the corridor to the execution chamber.

"But... This cannot be!" stammered the condemned man.

The look of total surprise on his face cheered the executioner's heart and convinced him that he was about to execute his duty with customary scrupulousness in accordance with the judge's decree.

And finally, kneeling before the block, the logician turned his head slightly to look up at the executioner and, with the barest hint of a smile, he whispered, "Well done, sir."

"Thank you, sir," replied the executioner, as the swing of his axe reached its zenith and began its rapid fall towards the back of the logician's neck.

12
Diverse Antecedents

"There's nowhere you can be that isn't where you're meant to be."

The Beatles, "All you need is love", 1967

My maternal grandfather fell asleep whilst on guard duty at his company's camp and, falling from a standing position, he accidentally discharged the rifle he was holding. The bullet, as chance would have it, struck the wheel of the bicycle of the husband of the daughter of the village elder who was cycling past, holding a pumpkin pie in a glass dish in one hand, en route to his weekly visit to the camp commandant to offer bribes. The shock of the gunshot and the jarring of the bullet against the bicycle wheel conspired to topple the poor man sideways and, not wishing to relinquish his hold on the pie dish, he fell unprotected to the road. The dish smashed and a four inch shard of glass penetrated the chest of the husband of the daughter of the village elder. He died instantly in a pool of blood upon the dusty road outside the camp.

The elder, not prepared to accept that his son-in-law's death was accidental, and following local tradition, demanded either that my grandfather be buried up to his neck in the parched ground beneath the tropical sun for three days, or that he should marry his newly-widowed daughter. Not surprisingly, my grandfather chose the latter option, especially as the lady in question was young, pretty and was offered along with a sizeable dowry. The union was a happy one. Within a year a baby was born who, twenty-two years later, was to become my mother.

Thus one quarter of my genetic make-up is derived from a British colonialist guardsman, formerly of Gloucestershire, and one quarter from the Tamil speaking tribal aristocracy of southern India.

My father's genes enjoy a less curious history.

My paternal grandfather - a man known to all, for reasons that have long since faded from family memory, as Glob - was a labourer on a cider farm in Charlton Mackrell, in mid-Somerset. My grandmother, Elsie, worked for Clarks in nearby Street, stitching leather to make shoes.

They met at a barn dance in Charlton Mackrell, to which the girls of Street were transported by bus on alternate Saturdays.

"I likes 'ee," said my grandfather, being untutored in the ways of courtship.

"I likes 'ee, too," replied Elsie, coyly, for the girls of Street were brought up to respond politely but cautiously when approached by eligible gentlemen.

They danced together all evening: reels and jigs and squares, following the directions of the step-caller. Cider was flowing freely from the barrels in the barn, and the mood was merry. At nine o' clock, the bus arrived to take the girls back to Street, and Glob ventured a quick parting peck on the cheek of my grandmother, who blushed and made to squeeze his hand in return, but being somewhat inebriated, her aim was unsteady and instead of his hand she grasped and squeezed his crotch, which he took to be a good sign.

Two weeks later, for the next barn dance, they both dolled themselves up in their smartest togs and danced and drank and chatted exclusively with each other.

"Can I call on 'ee tomorra?" he asked.

"P'raps," she replied.

The routine of alternate Saturday dances followed by Sunday teas with Elsie's family continued for a few months, their conversations low on content but high in affection. Those were slow-moving times, back in the late nineteen-thirties in rural England.

Relationships, like good cider, required time to mature. Finally, they became engaged.

"Will 'ee marry I?" he asked her. (Correct usage of personal pronouns was not an art much practised in Somerset.)

"Aw right," she replied, as though he had offered her a second cup of tea.

"Right then. That be that, then," he said, and they had a second cup of tea.

They married in Street parish church, one Saturday, the reception a modest affair in the church hall. For their honeymoon, they took the bus to Weston-super-Mare, twenty-five miles away, where they had booked into a small guest-house. Their first sexual encounter was an unsatisfactory experience. Glob came prematurely, all over the freshly starched sheets, and Elsie insisted upon immediately washing the offending patch in the tiny sink in their room, lest the landlady should discover it and think them unclean and careless guests. Glob was acutely embarrassed and further sexual activity was postponed until the following night and preceded by the judicious placement of a towel upon the bed, but the iron bedstead rattled at the slightest movement and Elsie was concerned lest the other guests should hear and insisted that Glob should perform his actions very slowly.

Of course, this story was not in general circulation in my family circle. When I first heard it, told with a snigger by my grandmother when she was in her eighties, I could not help recalling the accidental discharge of my other grandfather's rifle that had played such a crucial part in the genesis of the maternal side of my genetic make-up, but I refrained from dwelling too closely upon either unplanned discharge.

Clearly my paternal grandfather soon got to grips with the business of copulation, and my father was the result of a more controlled discharge in the marital bed of the farm labourer's cottage where Glob and Elsie lived for many years, my grandfather growing cider apples and my grandmother, while bringing up a family of three, still stitching shoes for Clarks, delivered to her each month by the outworkers' van of the good Quakers.

Meanwhile, my maternal grandfather and his Indian wife returned to England and took up residence in an army camp on Salisbury Plain where, without much delay, my mother entered the story. To the tacit but nonetheless evident delight of all but my grandmother, my mother appeared to be of undiluted white English stock: brown haired and blue eyed like her father, with the characteristic family dimple firmly embedded in her chin. My grandmother, naturally enough, had felt disorientated and lonely in her army quarters on the desolate plains of chalky Wiltshire, having never before in her life ventured more than a few miles from the village of her birth, nor known any other weather conditions than the relentless heat of the tropics, but she was comforted by the birth of her daughter - my mother - and the beautiful new babe gave her some standing in the community of army wives. She discarded her sari in favour of smocks and skirts and replaced her cumin, cardamom and coriander with salt and pepper, determined to cultivate a fondness for what she regarded as the boiled blandness of English cuisine. She was a good wife and mother, of that I have no doubt, and my grandfather came to bless the day that he had fallen asleep on guard duty in the tropical sun.

Then the Second World War happened, wiping clean the slate of everyday life and thrusting a harsh new reality into the faces of Europe's millions. My grandfather, being a regular soldier, was immediately posted abroad to the front line of some French battle zone, but before ever he had a chance to fire a shot in anger, he was captured by the Germans in peculiarly unremarkable circumstances and incarcerated in a prisoner-of-war camp, where he remained for the next six years, far removed from all areas of conflict.

"Why didn't you escape?" I once asked him, under the impression, gleaned from films, that this was the first duty of all captured British soldiers.

"I tried, once or twice," he replied, "but escaping into an occupied war zone wasn't a comfortable prospect and most of those I knew who attempted it were either killed or speedily recaptured and thrown into solitary confinement cells."

To be frank, he was something of a wimp, my grandfather.

"So what did you do for six years?" I asked.

"I stayed put and kept my head down. And I recommenced my education, which had been abruptly curtailed at the age of fourteen when I joined the army. The prison camp might have been short of books, but it was full of scholars and teachers who loved to impart their knowledge. A highly organised school existed for those, like me, who had little interest in table tennis or digging escape tunnels. I learned mathematics and history, even a good smattering of Latin. And German, of course, so that we could converse with our captors, most of whom were happy to join our classes, either as pupils or teachers. Astronomy, philosophy, physics - I learned them all, often, if the teachers were good, to an astonishingly high level. There wasn't much else to do, after all.

"Some of the best years of my life, they were, in POW camp. A shortage of freedom and feminine company, it was true, but the compensations were many. We even grew our own grapes and brewed our own wine. Good camaraderie. Good days of sparse but wholesome living. Of course, we heard very little of how the war was progressing for our compatriots and that worried us a bit, but the Germans we encountered seemed a decent bunch so we assumed we'd all come to some amicable agreement. I must confess to even feeling a little sad rather than jubilant when our camp was finally liberated by the Americans. Our captors surrendered without a fight - it was clear that their war was a lost cause. We shook hands with them like old friends as we locked them in the sheds that had once confined us. Good chaps. I still correspond with a couple."

Back in Britain, my grandfather was treated as a hero and cosseted as an invalid. And my mother, a seven year old girl, could always recall crying when first embraced by the unfamiliar figure of her father.

Glob, my paternal grandfather, had greater claims to being a war hero. Conscripted in the first year, he fought in North Africa, Turkey and Italy and survived the D-Day landings, but a leg full of shrapnel resulted in a speedy shipping home and a lifelong limp.

My grandmother, Elsie, still stitching shoes in Somerset, was always proud of the wartime efforts of her husband, who, though not the brightest of men, was, for her, one of the bravest. And their son, my father, spent his boyhood playing fantasy games of fighting, emulating the glorious deeds of his father, the wounded soldier.

So here, the war over, my grandparents step aside and leave the stage for my parents to continue the tale.

My father, Glob junior - or Richard, as he was christened, or Richie as he came to be called - passed his childhood quite contentedly as a country boy in Charlton Mackrell. His father taught him orchard maintenance, apple pressing and cider making. His mother taught him leatherwork. But Richie dreamed of greater things.

As a teenager in the 1950s, he left the confines of his tiny village for the slightly larger village of Street, five miles away, where he worked on the Clarks shoe production line - a dull job, to be sure, but it earned him his first money. And it was there, in the factory social club, that he discovered music - not the jigs and reels beloved by his parents, but blues of the American South and the nascent stirrings of rock 'n' roll.

Richie was hooked. He bought a second-hand guitar and spent every free minute learning to play the tunes he heard on the wireless: Muddy Waters, Bo Diddley, Chuck Berry, then the Everly Brothers and Buddy Holly. By the early sixties, he had formed a rock 'n' roll band with a couple of mates, calling themselves The Cobblers.

The Beatles were on the point of blossoming in Liverpool, The Rolling Stones in London, but the quiet shoe-making community of Street had little time for the noisy love songs of hormonal youths. My father always maintained that it was merely lack of opportunity rather than lack of talent that held back his career as a pop star. I don't wish to be disloyal, but I've heard some of his early recordings and I'm inclined to think it was simply lack of talent that kept him out of the Premier League. The Cobblers were strictly Third Division players in the pop business. Richie didn't give up his day job in the shoe factory, but every Friday and Saturday the Cobblers piled their gear into the back of the bass guitarist's van and headed off to a gig in some local club or town hall.

And that was how - and I know you've been waiting for and wondering about this bit of the story - my father eventually met my mother.

She was called Sally - a distinctly un-Indian but most assuredly a rock 'n' roll name, although it was the music of Bach and Mozart that moved her rather than the frenetic chords of the electric guitar. Her wireless stayed tuned to the Third Programme rather than Radio Luxembourg.

Enthused by her father's POW-induced love of learning, Sally became an avid student, sailing through her school exams and earning a place at university, which for a girl in the early sixties was a notable achievement. She chose to study psychology, craving knowledge not just about the world, but about the mind that knows the world. And there, at Bristol University, she discovered both sex and C. G. Jung.

The reader will forgive me, I hope, if I gloss over the sexual business - she was my mother, after all - and concentrate on Carl Gustav Jung who undoubtedly had a bigger influence upon her life.

Jung was never mainstream psychology, and certainly not in 1960s universities where the subject was struggling for scientific respectability, but Sally, encountering his works by chance, was fascinated by him. His autobiography, *"Memories, Dreams, Reflections"* ranked, thereafter, as the crucial book that changed her life, and it was his little book *"Synchronicity"* that shook her mind awake. The term was not widely known, in those days, although the power of remarkable coincidences has always been a fruitful topic for writers and raconteurs. But Jung explored and extrapolated the "how weird!" factor of coincidences and hinted at an overarching unity of all things. Thus he coined the word "synchronicity": the meaningful coincidence connecting an inner and outer event in a way that defies rationality yet evokes an immense emotional response.

Synchronicity is a subject which, if pursued eagerly, leads into all manner of strangenesses. Once you begin to accept that two apparently independent events are somehow connected by an experienced meaning, then the soul-less world of objective science begins to crack and the light of a greater reality shines through.

Stranger still, as Sally found, is the common report that, once you become aware of and start thinking about synchronicities, then they start happening all over the place. You find yourself bombarded by synchronistic events wherever you turn until it seems that you are living in a different world, a world in which subtle threads of meaning connect all things and you feel yourself to be a part of some beautiful cosmic web.

Most of the synchronicities Sally experienced were seemingly trivial - she is thinking a particular word at the same moment that the word is spoken on the radio: a man coughs on a bus and the rhythm of the cough exactly aligns with the Mozart sonata currently playing in her mind. Trivialities such as these are easily dismissed with a smile. Equally easily, as they pile in, one upon another, they can herald a spiritual awakening.

Immersed in such Jungian thoughts, Sally was walking the streets of Bristol, heading home after a day in the university library, when she passed alongside a van, stopped at a traffic light. Looking out through the passenger window was the face of a young man. It was a face she had met in her dreams the previous night - and since finding Jung, her dreams had exploded into technicolour epics of vast import. Her dream self had endowed that face with sublime beauty and vital meaning. Somehow - she knew not how - it mattered immensely. The man behind that face had a part to play in her life. (This is what absorption in ideas of synchronicity does for you: everything, even a passing stranger, becomes infused with significance.)

They exchanged an expressionless few seconds of eye contact through the window, then the van drove on and Sally realised both the futility of trying to pursue it, and the certainty that they would meet again.

She walked a few steps further and, in her distracted state, tripped on a raised paving stone, twisted her ankle and cracked the rather high heel of her shoe. She cursed silently and examined her foot. The heel of the shoe was broken. A shoe repairer - a cobbler, no less - was urgently required. She looked up and at once her eyes fell on a poster on a billboard: an advert for a gig, that evening, at a local club. Top of the bill was a group she had never heard of. The support act, in smaller letters - and this was where her gaze spontaneously landed - was “The Cobblers”.

Of course she had to be there, such was her obsession with "the numinous", as Jung called it. Following synchronicities had rapidly become the major motivating force of her life.

There were about fifty people in the small hall behind a pub, mostly students, mostly girls, mostly twisting on the dance floor. Sally had never danced in her life. It fact, she had never been to a pop gig in her life. It was loud. She arrived late. The support act had already started. She stood at the back. And there he was, her man in the van, the vision from her dream, standing on the stage in a trendy suit and bootlace tie, strumming away at his electric guitar. She recognised him at once, both from her dream and the face at the van window. His image touched her. His music didn't. She would rather have been at a chamber concert.

The Cobblers played a dozen short, indistinguishable songs then left the stage to a subdued round of applause. Sally tried to find her way to the stage door, with several other girls. One of the roadies told them that The Cobblers would be in the bar presently to sign autographs. Most of the other girls were more interested in the main group, who had apparently once appeared on "Saturday Club" on the Light Programme. Sally found her way to the bar and bought a lemonade. The Cobblers drifted in. She approached Richie as he stood at the bar.

"We meet again," she said, stupidly assuming that he would remember the five seconds of eye contact they had shared through the van window, a few hours earlier.

Richie couldn't recall the face but guessed that she was one of the girls from Street who sometimes followed the band. Still high on adrenalin from the performance, he replied, "Yo there. 'Ow be on, me lover?"

"I'm sorry?" said Sally, unfamiliar with Somerset dialect.

"Hey, that's cool, babe," replied Richie, remembering himself and his rock 'n' roll star persona.

"I'm sorry?" said Sally, unfamiliar with the youthful language of hip.

Richie looked her over. Not much of a groupie, he thought. She was still dressed in her student gear; her mousy brown hair tied back, black rimmed glasses, a shapeless woollen skirt below her knees, black stockings, a broken shoe. But her eyes are beautiful, thought Richie, and she seems to be taking an interest in me. He had his charms, my father, but they were not immediately obvious, and his trendy pop suit and electric guitar persistently failed to attract the flocks of girls he had imagined they might.

"Getcha drink?" he said.

"I'm sorry?" said Sally, and this time it occurred to her that perhaps she was apologising for not being the woman he'd hoped she might be.

"I'm Richie," said Richie, finally finding a comment she understood.

"Sally," said Sally. "I saw you in a dream."

"Well, I'll let you be in my dream if I can be in yours," said Richie, proud to be able to quote a line from one of the popular albums of the moment. (And a hint, here, to those in the know, of the year of this episode.)

"I'm sorry," said Sally, who had no more heard of Bob Dylan than The Cobblers.

Their conversation continued thus: assorted staccato exchanges mostly failing to elicit meaning in the mind of the other. Their communication was predominantly non-verbal: looks, smiles, shrugs, nods - a display of largely unconscious gestures.

Then the band members mustered, ready to load the van and head back to Street.

"May I write to you?" said Sally.

"Sure," said Richie, and he scribbled his name and address on the back of a beer-mat.

And that is the rather unromantic story of how my mother and father met.

Sally spent the next week composing an epic ten page letter, summarising her life history, her studies, her ideas on the nature of the unconscious mind, the archetypes that currently had meaning in her life, her relationships with Jung, Freud, Maslow and Rogers and her tastes in music, which, she regretted, did not yet embrace the modern idiom. She barely mentioned Richie in her letter, although she held his face constantly before her as she wrote. After three years at university, she was accustomed to writing only academic essays. The notion that this should be a love letter never occurred to her.

Richie skimmed through it, then tossed it aside. He had never read an academic essay. Come to that, he had never received a love letter, either. But he sent her back a postcard: “Playing at Bath, next weekend. Come if you can.” Followed by a time and place and an illegible signature. Sally studied the handwriting. It was clear that Richie was not an intellectual type.

She went to the Bath gig. Afterwards, they talked a little, rather awkwardly, then he pulled her into a smoochy dance on the dance floor and, in the dimness, deposited a slobbery kiss on her lips. Caught in the excitement of the occasion, she let him lead her to the group’s van, in the back of which lay a little used but ever-hopeful mattress. With minimal preamble, they made love. Neither of them were virgins, though nor were they experts. I imagine Richie to have been an ungainly sort of lover, Sally overly passive. In truth, I try not to imagine the sexual relations of my parents. Rather, my thoughts dwell on their motives. Richie, of course, was just happy to have a bit of nookie with anyone who seemed to fancy him. His motives were purely carnal. But Sally? She was a sensitive, refined, deep-thinking woman. The one thing that attracted her to Richie was the compulsion of her dream. I believe she loved him for who he represented - a powerful dream archetype - rather than for who he actually was. But maybe she, too, was just after a bit of undemanding nookie.

Their relationship progressed spasmodically. Every few weeks, Sally would take the bus from Bristol to Street and they would spend a day together, their time divided between his tiny flat and the local pub where The Cobblers hung out. And every few weeks, Richie would come to Bristol and they’d frolic on the bed in Sally’s student bedsit in the attic of one of Clifton’s Georgian townhouses. One day at a time in each other’s company proved quite enough. Their union was devoid of intensity, commitment and, for the most part, conversation. Yes, there was affection, but not real love. For Sally, the synchronistic excitement had rapidly drained away. What remained was comfortable habit.

And then, for reasons I have never investigated, an embryonic I popped into life to complicate the situation. Certainly I was never planned. I was, as they say, an accident. And, thankfully, in those days abortion was rarely considered to be an option. Marriage was out of the question. Clearly it would have been a disaster. Sally, by that time, had graduated and was training as a Jungian psychotherapist in Bristol. Richie was working on the shoe assembly line in Street and, at weekends, playing rhythm guitar with a third rate pop group. The only thing they appeared to have in common was me, and Richie could find no place to fit a baby into his busy life. Sally decided she would bring me up alone. Richie made no objection.

Sally's predicament was not as dire as might appear. She inhabited a wide and caring community of intellectuals, cultural aesthetes and assorted bohemians who praised her liberal views and admired her courage and energy to juggle a career and a child single-handedly. Before long, she found a soul-mate: a university psychology lecturer, twenty years her senior, who shared her academic background and gladly opened his fine house to Sally and child, the darlings of the Clifton Jungian fraternity. They never married, and I never called him "Dad". He was always Julian. But he was truly good to me and I loved him from the first.

Sally maintained a tentative contact with Richie, and I saw him occasionally. We never bonded. You see, I think I was both a disappointment and an embarrassment to him. He would have liked a tough, white skinned, brown haired boy with whom he could play football and guitar. Sally gave birth to me: a girl - black hair, brown eyes and the dark brown face of a southern Indian.

Richie had never met my maternal grandmother, so the shock was natural enough.

"You sure she's mine?" was amongst his first comments to Sally, upon seeing me.

She responded with a curt "Yes", and thrust a photo of her mother under his nose.

So Richie never really took to me, just as I didn't to him. The liberal bohemians of Clifton, however, were delighted to have a mixed-race baby of a single mother in their midst. They lavished love, attention and gifts upon me. My childhood was unusual, it must be admitted, but it was not unpleasant. My mother became a well-respected and well-paid psychotherapist; my step-father, Julian, a distinguished academic. At the school I attended, I was considered to come from a privileged background.

Richie, as the sixties blossomed into the strange days of modern legend, gave up his job at Clarks, gave up with The Cobblers, and gave up on his parents. He took his guitar to London to confront his destiny. I know little of how things went for him in the metropolis. It seems he earned some money as a session musician, then, as was expected of a young man in the sixties who played rock 'n' roll guitar, he got into drugs, rapidly progressing from cannabis to the heavy stuff. He died from a heroin overdose at the age of twenty-seven. It might have sealed his rock star reputation - but it didn't. He remained a minor player in the sixties milieu.

"'Ee were a good lad," said Elsie, my grandmother, at his funeral.

"Aye, that 'ee were," said Glob.

The three remaining Cobblers played one of his songs. It was not appreciated by the small family gathering.

I was seven at the time. I cried. Poor Richie, my father! I feel for him, even now. His life never amounted to much.

"It amounted to you," my mother reminds me. Fair enough. If it wasn't for Richie and his youthful dreams of playing in a rock 'n' roll band, if not for Sally and her youthful dreams of the archetypal animus, then I wouldn't exist. It's a strange way to consider our parents, but perhaps we should all do it from time to time. And consider our grandparents and the unlikely stories that brought them together. And their parents and grandparents. And the first ape that swung down from the trees and tried keeping his balance on two legs. And the first fish that flapped his fins and found himself on dry land. So many contingencies, leading to me, standing here now. Who'd have thought it, back at the beginning of time!

I visit all my grandparents regularly. They all survive: Glob and Elsie, still living on the cider farm in Charlton Mackrell: my mother's parents, now in a bungalow in Cheltenham. I've even returned with my mother and grandmother to the place where my grandparents met - a village in southern India. Too hot by far! Despite my skin colour, I feel little affinity for the land of my forebears.

My mother, Sally, had two more children with her gentleman friend, Julian: both boys, both with browny-white skin hues

As for me, in order to add a dash more colour to the genetic cocktail of our family, I married an Inuit from Greenland, known by everyone as Nanook - his real name being unpronounceable by us English. We live in Swindon, where Nanook runs a company that produces small, plastic igloos for children. We're probably the only English/Indian/Inuit couple in town.

And now I'm pregnant. In frivolous mood, we take bets on the skin colour and racial characteristics exhibited by our child. We don't care. Fortunately, none of us is privy to the selection of genes and life stories that Nature spins for us. We are each dealt our hand and we must play with it: aces and kings, a royal flush or a random mix of spades and clubs from the lower echelons of the pack. We have no choice in the antecedents and circumstances that are thrust upon us from the moment of conception. In the end, the best we can do is be as we are.

13
A Curious Elliptical Interlude

...being an essay from the periodical "Ellipse", *the journal of the Society of Ellipticologists*

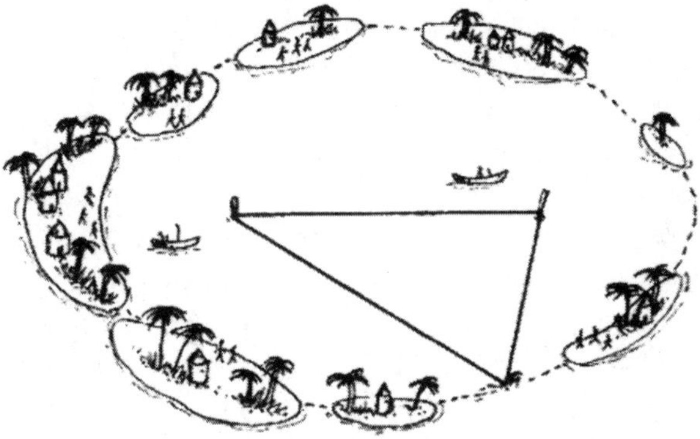

There is an archipelago of islands in Eastern Polynesia - the name of which we withhold to preserve its privacy - which possesses an almost perfectly elliptical shape. Geologists argue over the formation of this archipelago; mathematicians marvel at its geometric precision; and anthropologists are astounded by the customs, pertaining to its elliptical nature, that have arisen amongst its natives, a highly cultured race.

Unaware, it is presumed, of the uniqueness of the shape of their group of islands, the archipelagonians conduct a ceremony, once every seven years, that demonstrates remarkable geometrical knowledge and must be regarded as one of the anthropological curiosities of the Pacific Ocean.

The equipment for this ceremony is stored in a hut belonging to the tribal chief, and is held to be of inestimable value, representing the pinnacle of this people's cultural heritage. It consists of two wooden poles, some twenty feet long, and a loop of thin rope, made from palm fibres, of circumference approximately half a mile.

Two small fishing boats carry the two poles into the lagoon in the middle of the archipelago where the poles are thrust into the sand beneath the relatively shallow water, at the exact positions of the two hypothetical foci of the ellipse. These poles protrude vertically several feet above the water surface. The loop of rope is then placed around the poles and rowed to the shore of the main island where a young man of the tribe - the “island runner” as he is called - steps within the loop and, keeping it as taut as possible, alternately runs and swims around the archipelago, from island to island, thus tracing out the circumference of the ellipse in a manner known to every western schoolchild.

As the island runner emerges from the intervening sea onto each of the archipelago’s islands, all the inhabitants of that island, gathered on the shore line, reach out and either quickly grasp his hand, in the case of males, or deposit a small kiss on his passing cheek, in the case of females. The entire elliptical run and swim takes about two hours, during which time all members of the population stand silently upon the beaches of their respective islands, apparently in a state of meditation, all eyes following the progress of the island runner. Once the ellipse is completed, great jubilation ensues, with feasting, music and dancing continuing for three days. The poles and rope are then stowed away in their special hut to await the next ceremony in seven years.

It is commonly thought that the purposes of this ceremony are to reinforce and cement the identity of the archipelagonian community, to re-affirm the status of their tribal leader and, some anthropologists claim, to pay homage to the deity whom they believe created and sustains their ellipse of islands.

Several peculiar features of the ceremony have been reported by various independent observers. (The archipelagonians, themselves, discourage all talk concerning either the ceremony or the elliptical nature of their homeland, regarding such talk as bordering on the sacrilegious, and although they do not object to the presence of outsiders, their culture forbids all manner of measurements, so that even the precision of the ellipse of the archipelago has never been verified by observers.)

Curiously, the men who place the poles in the lagoon - the “pole-placers”, as they are called - are blind - or, at least, very short-sighted - and, it is believed, thrust their poles into the sandy seabed when they intuitively feel that the rowers of their boats have transported them to the correct focal points. On one observed occasion, the rower of one of the boats rowed his craft in random directions around the middle of the lagoon for nearly an hour before his pole-placer felt that the moment was right. Nevertheless, the two poles appear always to be placed precisely at the two foci of the ellipse, as is attested by the fact that the runner, taking the loop of rope around the circumference, invariably traces out the required figure, setting foot upon the beaches of each of the eight islands whilst keeping the loop of rope taut all the while.

Equally strange is the timing of this seven-yearly ceremony. The archipelagonians possess no calendar and their island world, situated between the tropic of Capricorn and the Equator experiences little seasonal variation. Each day of the year is pretty similar to every other day. Yet the ceremony always takes place upon either the 3rd or 4th days of January, according to our calendar. These dates should be familiar to students and followers of ellipticology - the study of ellipses. The perihelion of the Earth's elliptical orbit about the Sun - that is, the point at which it is nearest to the Sun - occurs on the 3rd or 4th of January. The aphelion, when the Earth is furthest from the Sun, occurs around 4th July. This fact often puzzles those unfamiliar with the arcanities of ellipticology. How can it be that the Earth is furthest from the Sun at about the time when we experience the height of our northern hemisphere summer? The answer is that there is only a 3.3% difference in the perihelial and aphelial distances of the Earth from the Sun (147 million kilometres at the perihelion and 152 million kilometres at the aphelion). This tiny difference in the amount of heat energy reaching the Earth from the Sun in January and July is overwhelmed and rendered imperceptible by the effect of seasonal variation, caused by the 23 degree tilt of the Earth upon its axis, although, as previously mentioned, seasonal variation is not a significant factor in the day-to-day experience of the Polynesian archipelagonians.

The elliptical nature of the Earth's orbit is usually diagrammatically represented in a considerably exaggerated form, the better to demonstrate its non-circularity. In fact, the orbit, if viewed from an external vantage point, would appear to be an almost perfect circle. Indeed, it is only very slightly *not* a perfectly circular orbit. Ellipticologists like to talk about the eccentricity of ellipses. Eccentricity can be calculated from a simple mathematical equation relating the distance between the two foci to the overall length of the major axis of the ellipse. It is measured on a scale between zero and one. A perfect circle is said to be an ellipse with zero eccentricity. Ellipses become increasingly more ovoid as their eccentricity increases from zero to one. An ellipse of eccentricity 0.9, for instance, would appear to be an extremely flattened oval shape. At 0.99 it would be approaching a straight line.

Elliptical eccentricity may be most readily appreciated by a quick experiment performed in front of a mirror: first, the subject makes an "o" shape with his or her lips, then slowly relaxes into a closed-mouth semi-smile. The shape of the lips has thereby passed from a circle (eccentricity zero) to a highly flattened ellipse (eccentricity approaching one.) (This experiment may also be performed by two or more subjects in the same room, each observing the lips of the other participants, thereby adding a degree of merriment and bonhomie to this instructive lesson in ellipticology.)

The elliptical eccentricity of the Earth's orbit around the Sun is usually drawn in a very unrealistic form, suggesting a value of maybe 0.3 or more. In fact, the eccentricity of our planetary home is a mere 0.0167, an eccentricity which, if represented graphically, would be scarcely distinguishable from a circle. It is not surprising that, before the advent of the great astronomers and mathematicians, Kepler and Newton, it was commonly thought that our orbit was indeed perfectly circular.

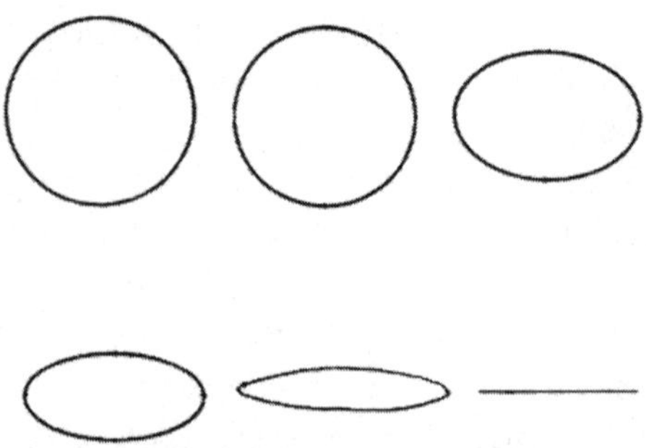

Fig. 2 Ellipses of varying eccentricity (upper row: 0, 0.2, 0.5 lower row: 0.75, 0.9, 1)

The eccentricity of ellipses is aptly matched by the eccentricity of many ellipticologists who, when expounding upon their favourite subject, invariably digress into unnecessarily elaborate descriptions of the finer geometrical features of their beloved ellipses, thereby not only endangering a loss of interest or concentration on the part of the reader or listener, but also engendering a selective amnesia whereby they completely forget about the topic that led their discursive train of thought along its elliptical sideline. In extreme cases, this ellipsicoidal amnesia can result in the permanent neglect of the original subject matter, no matter how interesting it might once have been. Thus it is that ellipticologists are frequently described as having an eccentricity of between 0.5 and 1, while circulologists -those who favour the study of circles - often exhibit near zero eccentricity. (Although, it must be said, judging the psychological eccentricity of a collective group of scholars on a scale of zero to one is a far from exact science, and many ellipticologists often go to very great lengths to refute the suggestion that they are eccentric or amnesic or that they are prone to excessively long-winded digressions.)

The eccentricity of the orbit of Pluto, it is worth mentioning, is 0.248, making its orbit of the Sun by far the most elliptical of all the planets, nearly 15 times more elliptical than that of the Earth.

And it is interesting to note that the eccentricity of the elliptical Eastern Polynesian archipelago - about which we had almost but not completely forgotten - as estimated from photos taken of the two poles thrust at the two foci in the middle of the lagoon during the seven-yearly ceremony, is approximately 0.25. The elliptical eccentricity of the archipelago is therefore a very close match to that of the orbit of Pluto - a distinctly peculiar coincidence that has led diverse Forteans, conspiracy theorists and anomalous phenomena seekers to posit all manner of Plutonian/Polynesian connections.

There is some debate, amongst the more unorthodox fringes of anthropologically and astronomically inclined ellipticologists, about the significance of this fact. Theories have been rated, following the eccentricity scale, from zero - of absolutely no significance - to one - of the utmost significance.

The archipelagonians themselves - who have no word for "ellipse" in their vocabulary and who confess a total ignorance of the movements of the planet Pluto - possess a curious counting system that begins at two and contains neither zero nor one. Consequently they have never grasped the scale of elliptical eccentricity and their views on the matter of the correspondence between their archipelago and the orbit of Pluto have never been sought.

Clearly there is scope for further research in this field, should any student of ellipticology wish to take a study trip to a group of idyllic South Sea Islands. Funding is available from the Bursar of the Society of Elliptiocologists. Candidates should be able to demonstrate an eccentricity of at least 0.5.

14
Whim's Tale

"All animals, except man, know that the principal business of life is to enjoy it."

Samuel Butler, "The Way of All Flesh", 1903

Whim liked to think of himself as a gentleman of the streets. Others called him a tramp - or perhaps, less derogatively, a disadvantaged homeless traveller. But Whim didn't care much for labels. It was true that he gave his address, when asked, as "no fixed abode": it was true that his entire worldly possessions amounted to the clothes he wore, the contents of the pockets thereof and a plastic bag he carried containing a waterproof blanket and diverse "collectables", as he called them - objects picked up from the street and kept for no other reason than that he liked the look of them: and it was true that he rummaged and scavenged and gathered and very occasionally stole to supply his daily needs. Such a précis of his life, thought Whim, could be applied to the vast majority of the world's living beings. He considered himself to be in good company, the latest in a long history of hunters, gatherers and scavengers. He was neither proud nor ashamed of himself.

He never spoke of his past. If ever asked how he came to be a gentleman of the streets - which wasn't often - his reply was a curt, "Fallen on hard times." This was usually accepted. No-one ever asked if the hard times had been of his own making or were attributable to the sad economic conditions of the day.

"Hard times happen," he frequently opined. "They happened in the Victorian England of the great Charles Dickens, and they continue to happen in Twenty-first Century England. Hard times are always happening to someone."

But people rarely questioned the provenance of a tramp. They were more likely to be curious about the origin of his name.

Whim had answered that question so many times that the patter rolled effortlessly off his tongue, giving the erroneous impression that he was an articulate talker, perhaps even a cultured man.

"I was christened William. My father was a great shouter. 'William!' he shouted, then gradually shortened it to 'Willum!', then 'Wilm!' and finally 'Wim!' He was also a great believer in saving time, my father."

'Wim' had stuck, changed to 'Whim' by a pedantic school master who disliked both nicknames and badly spelled words. But Whim rarely had occasion to actually spell out his own name.

His life had its share of ups and downs, before the hard times hit. More downs than ups, to be honest. The capacity for earnest endeavour, he would happily admit, was not one of his prime characteristics. And good fortune was a very rare companion. Until, that is, a certain day upon which this tale begins...

The day had followed its usual course: much sitting around punctuated by occasional circuits of the waste bins behind restaurants and supermarkets, feasting lavishly on rich pickings that more choosy people had discarded. Then, as evening drew on, he turned down a side-street in search of some secluded spot in which to spend the night, and there he came upon a doorway in which was placed, neatly folded, a pile of clothes: a man's grey suit, complete with white shirt and a colourful but tasteful tie. Naturally, Whim tried it on - a perfect fit. He swaggered off, back to the main streets of town, feeling uncustomarily jaunty in his newly acquired apparel, having first folded up his old clothes, rather tatty and soiled as they were, and left them in a neat pile on the doorstep. Exchange is no robbery, he thought to himself, not that he considered it to be robbery to pick up anything left out in the streets. Rather he saw it as a service to the community, keeping the neighbourhood free of unwanted debris.

The new suit of clothes seemed to transform his mood. Striding down the main street, he observed his reflection in shop windows, confidently swinging his arms, shoulders back, looking every bit the dapper man-about-town. (The trousers, it must be said, were a few inches too long, but they effectively concealed his soiled and weather-beaten boots, preventing any too noticeable flaw in the picture he presented.) By chance, he reached into the inner pocket of his new jacket and felt a leather wallet. Hm, my luck's certainly in today, he thought, for the wallet felt full. He opened it and nearly released some choice expletive that would have damaged the impression of the cool, collected city gent that he was delighting in projecting. The wallet was stuffed with fifty-pound notes - a casual flick suggested a hundred or more, which, Whim calculated, amounted to a very considerable amount of money. He'd never before set eyes upon a fifty-pound note, let alone a hundred of the things. Feeling somewhat overcome, he flopped down on the pavement and sat a while, leaning against a shop window: not the sort of pose commonly adopted by a man in a smart suit. Certainly not a fitting pose for a rich man, thought Whim, heaving himself back onto his feet. He replaced the bulging wallet in his inside pocket, patting it several times to assure himself that it was real. He allowed the thought to briefly flit across his mind - "This is the most money I have ever possessed in my entire life" - before seizing upon the subsequent, much more familiar thought - "I deserve a drink."

A rather smart hotel stood just a few yards down the street. Whim had walked past it many times, and often rummaged in the waste bins at its rear. Now he entered through the front door - a revolving contraption that seemed to epitomise opulence - and approached the reception desk.

"A room for the night, if you please," he said, quietly congratulating himself upon his acting skills.

"Certainly, sir," replied the receptionist, a most pleasant looking young lady. "What sort of room."

"Large. Posh. With a bath. Expensive," said Whim, realising, as the words emerged, that they were not quite right. Nor was the gesture that accompanied them, a quick but telling flash of the wad of fifties in his wallet.

"Room 250 should suit," said the receptionist, reaching behind and plucking a key from the board.

"I'm sure it will, "said Whim, "but first I fancy a meal and a drink or two."

"Certainly, sir," said the receptionist, gesturing across the foyer towards the restaurant, and Whim had his first inkling of the economic truth that, if you have money in your wallet, you can say and do anything you like.

He ate and drank well, that night. His choice of courses was based not on what he fancied - for the menu was written largely in French - but on their prices. He chose the most expensive. And, when shown the wine list, he scanned it very quickly then plonked his finger on the highest priced bottle, which turned out to be red and a little too tart for his taste. In truth, he would rather have had a pint of cider, but that didn't seem to be an option in this restaurant.

His plates cleared, his bottle emptied, he staggered up to room 250 and, contrary to his usual habits, found the presence of mind to remove his boots and his suit before collapsing onto the bed. His head was spinning - past straitened circumstances had forced him to be a far from regular drinker - but he was aware of a recurrent thought that dominated his inner world as he slipped into slumber: "This is remarkably good fortune. Looks like my hard times are over at last."

Whim awoke the next day with a headache and a feeling that the day would be a memorable one. He took a shower, donned his suit and boots and descended to the restaurant for breakfast, which he didn't really feel like eating but, as on the previous evening, he stuffed himself so full that the trousers of his new suit began to feel a little tight and he surreptitiously loosened his belt.

The hotel bill, including meal and wine, came to nearly two hundred pounds. Whim handed over the cash from his wallet with overdone flippancy, as though paying a few coins for a loaf at the bakery. "This is all right," he thought. "Very pleasant indeed."

He spent the day eating, drinking and walking the streets - for these were the three activities that usually occupied his days and had done for many years. When he had money, he ate and drank. When he had none, he walked the streets until such time as he had acquired enough money to do either or both of the other alternatives - and we will not dwell on the means whereby that money came into his possession. The streets provided his sustenance in ways unrealised by those of us to whom streets are merely the intervening spaces between buildings.

By mid-afternoon, thoroughly replete with food and well inebriated, he found himself sitting in a bar and, for the first time that day, he contemplated his situation. Despite a pocket full of more cash than he had ever imagined, he began to feel the niggling suspicion that something was missing from his life. What he missed, of course, was hunger. Having satiated his desires, he missed desire itself. "You can't properly enjoy eating unless you're good and hungry beforehand," he said to himself. In fact, he spoke this thought aloud, not realising that he wasn't saying it to himself.

"Too true," responded a man sitting a little further along the bar, dressed, like Whim, in a nice smart suit, a white shirt, a colourful tie and, unlike Whim, a pair of highly-polished black brogues. "Unless you know what it is to be without, then how can you enjoy what it is to be with?"

Whim nodded pensively.

"Will you have a whisky with me?" added the stranger.

Naturally Whim accepted, and naturally, for now he was in a position to do so, he reciprocated the offer.

Before long, the two men were sat at a table in the corner of the bar, two glasses and a bottle of whisky between them.

"Name's Merryweather. Tobias Merryweather," said the stranger, proffering a hand to shake and a cheery smile.

"Whim," said Whim.

"A curious name, Mr Whim," said Tobias Merryweather. "A pseudonym, I suspect, and no doubt a curious history lies behind it."

"Quite possibly," replied Whim.

His companion smiled. "Yes, we all have curious histories, sir. But, right now, all we have is today and, let's hope, tomorrow. Let's drink to that fine thought."

They clinked their glasses.

Thence their conversation rambled amiably - as befitted their rising intoxication - until Whim, seeking to learn more of his new-found friend, asked, "You seem to be a rich man, Tobias. So tell me, how did you come by your money?"

Such a question was common and expected amongst gentlemen of the street, always eager to learn how one of their number had come by a tenner or a bottle of wine or a lukewarm take-away, and Whim had forgotten that talk of personal finances was taboo amongst gentlemen of the city who wore smart suits and frequented bars in the afternoon.

But Tobias laughed again. "I admire your forthright attitude, Mr Whim. A frank and pertinent question. And I'll answer you frankly. Basically, I'm a gambling man."

"Horses or dogs?" asked Whim who had dabbled fecklessly in both.

"Good Lord, no. Mug's game, gambling on animals. Stocks and shares - that's where the money's to be made. Buy low, sell high - that's the secret."

"I know nothing of such matters," said Whim. "How do I buy stocks and shares?"

"You don't. You get someone like me to do it for you. Someone who's in the know. And let me tell you this..." He leant forward and lowered his voice conspiratorially. "...I know of a beauty, right now. A sure-fire winner. Shares set to rocket over the next few days. I'm putting a packet on it. That's why I'm here - a little early celebration. You interested in joining me?"

"By doing what, exactly?" asked Whim, a little slow on the up-take as ever.

"By investing some money in my winner, of course. Don't worry; I'll sort it all out. You just relax and, in a day or two, pick up the profits - less my usual twenty percent commission, of course."

Now any normal person would have run a mile from a proposal like this, conducted in a sleazy bar on a dull afternoon with a complete stranger. But Whim was not a normal person. And, furthermore, he was drunk, carefree and he had a wallet-full of fortuitously acquired cash.

"How much do you need?" he asked.

"Whatever you care to invest," said Tobias. "I'm in for fifty."

"Fifty pounds?" No big deal, thought Whim. He could spare a single note from his wad. The spell was beginning to weave itself around his will.

"Do me a favour!" retorted Tobias, laughing: "Fifty grand. We're talking top league stuff, here."

"Beyond me," said Whim.

"So how much can you spare?"

"Five hundred pounds, maybe." Okay, why not? he thought. Easy come, easy go. And he'd still have more money left than he'd seen in years.

"Fair enough. Start small. That's not a bad policy," said Tobias, topping up both their glasses.

Whim reached into his jacket for his wallet and counted out five hundred pounds in fifty-pound notes. He handed it across the table.

"Jesus, man, are you crazy? Are you prepared to trust me, just like that?"

"Yeah, I trust you. You seem like a decent chap. And we're friends now, aren't we? Friends trust each other. That's what makes them friends."

There were tears hovering around the rims of Tobias's eyes as he reached out both his hands to Whim, one taking the wad of money, the other clasping his hand and shaking it firmly.

"You won't regret this, Whim, old man. There are no cast iron guarantees in this business, so I'll make you no promises, but I reckon that, in maybe two days time, I'll be handing you back twice this amount (less my usual twenty percent commission, of course.)"

They emptied the whisky bottle, their talk flowing freely, then Tobias rose unsteadily to his feet and shook Whim's hand once again. "Must get this in motion before the market closes," he said, patting the pocket that held his wallet. "Let's give it two days and see what happens. Same time, same place?"

"I'll be here," said Whim, adding, "Happy trails, Tobias, my friend."

Did he have second thoughts? Did he feel any emptiness, sitting alone in the now empty bar at a table with two empty glasses and an empty whisky bottle? No. He basked in the warmth of his new friendship, in the warmth of uncustomary afternoon inebriation, in the comfort of a wallet still bulging with notes, in the thrill of the commencement of a new adventure. For he was a simple man who liked to bask in simple pleasures. Perhaps he had known too many troubles and hardships in his life to waste time and energy anticipating the possibility of more. 'Sufficient unto the day is the evil thereof': thus runs the philosophy of gentlemen of the streets.

So Whim wallowed a while in pleasant feelings, then fell asleep, awaking only when the bar began to fill with early evening drinkers. He returned to the hotel in which he had spent the previous night and booked in for two nights more.

"Anything you require?" asked the receptionist who had taken his two hundred pounds that morning.

Whim considered the question for many moments before replying, "How about some polish to clean my boots? They're looking a little the worse for wear."

"Certainly, sir," said the receptionist. "If you'd like to leave them outside your door, they will be cleaned for you by morning."

"No need for that. You can have them now," said Whim, removing his mud-caked boots and depositing them on the reception counter, then walking off in his bare feet.

For the next two days, Whim luxuriated in the luxury of his hotel, eating and drinking like a king, lounging on his huge soft bed, idly flicking through the dozens of channels on the vast television screen that faced him across the room. Occasionally he'd spend a while staring from his window, down into the street, wondering what was happening out there in the street-level world he knew so well. And occasionally he'd have the feeling that something was amiss, that this hotel room was not where he was meant to be. But he dismissed the feeling. Just dig it while it's happening, he said to himself, a mantra from the distant days of his youth.

After two days, he donned his suit and newly shined boots and returned to the bar where he had arranged to meet Tobias Merryweather.

No doubt the cynical or worldly-wise reader is anticipating, at this point, a disappointing outcome for Whim: the loss of his five hundred pounds and the loss of a new-found friend. He would have coped, of course, with the aid of a few stiff drinks, for he was well accustomed to disappointments and, anyway, his wallet remained healthily full. But our story treads a different path. Tobias awaited him in the bar, a bottle of champagne and two glasses at the ready, a beaming smile upon his face and a handshake and shoulder slap that almost caused Whim to wince with pain.

"Great news, my friend," said Tobias, pouring the champagne. "Our investment behaved as I had expected. The market is volatile, these days, but I know it well and played it judiciously."

"So your gamble was a winner?" asked Whim.

"A highly propitious winner, indeed. Allow me to present you with double your initial investment (less my twenty percent commission, of course.)"

He handed Whim a cheque for nine hundred pounds, payable to Mr Whim. Whim studied it a while. "I'd rather have cash," he said.

"Then cash it shall be," said Tobias, laughing and, extracting his wallet from his jacket, he counted out eighteen fifty pound notes.

"Thank you," said Whim.

"And I'll tell you what," continued Tobias. "I greatly admire your trust in me. Most people, witnessing our last meeting, would have immediately labelled me a conman - and you a naive fool for handing me so much money without even a signed contract. But now you know. I'm no conman and you're no naive fool. Integrity: that's what it's all about, Whim. Integrity. Were it a marketable commodity, it would be worth millions."

Whim nodded and smiled. Integrity was not a word he ever used, nor really understood. Whatever it was, he tacitly assumed that he didn't really have much of it. To be sure, he tried his best to do what he supposed was right, but he tended to be a feckless man who had achieved little in his life. But he accepted that that was the way he was and, hey, that was okay. That, for Whim, was integrity of a sort: being as he was. So he smiled and raised his glass and clinked it against Tobias's.

"The market's hot, right now," Tobias said. "Big things are looming. What say you? Are you up for another little investment?"

Of course Whim was not going to refuse. He had just made five hundred pounds in two days (less twenty percent commission). So they talked a little about it - Tobias talked and Whim listened and sipped his champagne, thinking it an over-bubbly and over-rated drink - then the deal was struck and Whim handed back the nine hundred pounds he had just been given.

"We'd best give it a week, this time," said Tobias. "Allow the prices to rise to a maximum before cashing in. That all right with you?"

"Sure. You do what must be done."

Whim's trust in his new benefactor did not waver. A week went by...

And what, now, does the reader think will happen? Have we seen the last of Tobias? Will Whim exhaust his funds on a lifestyle of which he has had no previous experience and which, to be frank, he is pursuing ineptly and with scant satisfaction? Will he end up back on the streets from whence he came?

Fear not, dear reader, for although Whim might appear more suited to a tale of intolerably hard times and unremitting misfortune and woe, this story is one of morality and good-humour.

A week went by and again Tobias was waiting in the bar of their rendezvous, again with a grin enlivening his pleasant features, and a large bottle of cider at the ready - for Whim had confessed his tastes. More cash changed hands - less twenty percent commission - more talk of new opportunities and more investments made.

Tobias, this time, urged prudence. "My policy is to invest no more than half of what I can afford to lose if things go badly. If you do the same, Whim old chap, you'll watch your wealth increase without fear of failure."

Whim had no fear. He was not a worrier. If the bubble of his recent prosperity were to burst, he would accept his return to the streets without complaint. But he heeded Tobias's advice. The original find, that fateful day, of suit and wallet was a fortuitous circumstance indeed, like an apple falling from a tree into his open hand. Why shouldn't he enjoy it? He had considered, once or twice, the possibility of trying to find the proper owner, but neither suit nor wallet offered any clues to his identity. Informing the police was, of course, an option, but Whim had never felt pleasantly disposed to any forms of authority. So why shouldn't he enjoy it? And why shouldn't he try to amass a little more of the stuff, if only to continue to pay his extravagant hotel bill.

"I don't believe in working for money," Tobias imparted his wisdom, "I believe in making money work for me."

Thus Whim's life continued for several months. Tobias proved to be a shrewd and successful broker, and, furthermore, an honourable man who never missed an appointment and was always open with Whim about the handling of his money (less twenty percent, of course). They became firm friends, and watched their fortunes grow together, sealed with champagne and cider and pleasant afternoons in bars and restaurants. Whim never sought to probe into Tobias's past, nor to wonder how he passed his time between their weekly meetings. And Tobias, while accepting that Whim was most assuredly not like his other investment clients, never enquired into his former life, nor asked him how he had come by his stash of fifty pound notes. Instead, they chatted of the present and the future, their relationship one of banter and inebriation and comfortable, undemanding companionship. Tobias was used to dealing with the rich, the greedy and the anxious. He came to greatly value his friendship with the strange and equanimous Whim, who always wore the same suit and tie, the same boots. Their meetings were oases of jovial conviviality in the midst of a life of dry figures on paper and screens, of transactions devoid of substance and humanity. Tobias looked forward to them as much as Whim, the bond of friendship forged spontaneously and unconditionally, both relishing the flow of feeling that united their two disparate lives.

Their meetings became weekly, always in the same bar, the same afternoon drinking session. Occasionally Tobias had bad news to convey concerning the progress of their mutual investments, but far more often there was profit due - which Tobias soon learned was always to be paid in cash - and much talk of the fickle ways of finance.

"Why do you do it?" asked Whim, one day, his mind well lubricated with alcohol.

"Why do I do what?" responded Tobias.

"Make money. Make so much money, seemingly so effortlessly. Why?"

Tobias pondered the question. Perhaps it had never before been put to him. Perhaps he had never even considered it himself. "Why? Because I can. It seems I have a talent for making money. I am simply using that talent."

Whim nodded. An acceptable answer.

"I have a friend," continued Tobias, "who has a remarkable talent for piano playing. He's a concert pianist, and when he's not playing Mozart or Chopin, he's banging away at the keys in a rock 'n' roll band. He's rich and famous, but he doesn't do it for the money or the fame. He does it because he can - and because he loves it. Same with me. No one ever asks this mate of mine why he plays the piano. It's what he does."

"So you're not in it for the money?" asked Whim.

"Money is what I make, just as an artist makes paintings and a pianist makes music."

Whim nodded again and raised his glass, saluting his money-making friend. The thought occurred to him - although he didn't voice it - that paintings and music were beautiful things, but money was essentially rather ugly. True, it could make life comfortable, but what can you do with a comfortable life? Even comfort palls after a while. What's so great about being comfortable?

He stayed in his hotel because it was the easiest thing to do. Perhaps he could have sought a cheaper place to rent, but why bother? He paid his exorbitant hotel bills once a week - always in cash - and no one ever questioned him. No one ever questions a man with money. What more did he need beyond a comfortable room and good meals served whenever he fancied? He had a decent suit, which he wore constantly, so he had no reason to buy clothes. He had a big TV in his room that had 30 channels to choose from, and he had diverse entertainment to amuse him in the bar and other ground floor rooms of the hotel. He had a restaurant and bar at his constant disposal, and a staff who, happy to receive his extravagant tips, treated him like a king. What more did he need? What does a man with money actually do with his life? Other than, like Tobias, make more of the stuff.

Gradually - for Whim was not the quickest of fellows - he began to realise that his indolent lifestyle was basically unsatisfying. In the past, when he had no money, he had spent a large proportion of his days either trying to get money or food, or just being with others of his kind, light-heartedly bemoaning their pecuniary predicament. Now that he had money in abundance, he didn't know what to do. He spent most of his mornings dozing in his huge bed, for he could see no particular reason to get up. After a few days, he had discovered that it wasn't even necessary to rise for breakfast. A simple phone call was sufficient to have it delivered to his room, prepared to his personal specifications. By lunchtime, he rose reluctantly, showered and donned his suit and boots, then ventured out into the streets. But the streets seemed to lack the vibrancy that had once coloured them. They lacked the challenge and excitement that he had once felt when walking them. The streets merely carried him from one smart bar or restaurant to another. They had become like hotel corridors, bland spaces through which to pass as quickly as possible.

Yes, without hunger, without thirst, without needs and desires, without companionship, Whim was depressed. Without money, he had at least known a kind of transient happiness, or so his memory convinced him. Without money, he had truly valued every penny. Now he fingered the thick wad of notes that filled his wallet and he felt indifference.

The solution was clear: rather than try to make money, which he seemed to be doing with no trouble, he would give it away. He tried it in the streets, proffering fifty-pound notes to passers-by. Most steered well clear of him, as they had when he was dressed in shabbier clothes and held out an empty hand, asking rather than giving. A few took his offering, but suspiciously, scrutinising the note to see if it was fake. Even fewer thanked him. The looks he received were of doubt and fear, even pity. He was seen as a madman. Only madmen gave away money in the street. Either madmen or little-known television personalities out to make some novelty programme. Many people glanced around in search of a hidden camera.

Whim changed his tactics. He switched from fifty-pound notes to fivers and pound coins, which people seemed more willing to accept. He took to sitting in those street pitches at which he had previously plied his beggary, handing coins to passing pedestrians. He even placed his hat on the pavement, filled it with pound coins and wrote a note on a scrap of cardboard reading, "Help yourself". At first, few did. But Whim persisted and gradually he became known to the people who used the street and many would pick up a coin, sometimes a handful, smile, perhaps, or mutter a few curt words of thanks before walking on.

Giving money, thought Whim, felt better than making it. But still he met Tobias each week, and still his wealth continued to increase - faster, it seemed, than he could give it away.

Tobias sensed his unease. "What's up, Whim? Does wealth not agree with you?"

"There's something not quite right about it," pondered Whim. "How can we justify having so much money when so many others have so little? Can it be right that we indulge in any luxury we fancy while the world is full of people struggling to find their next meal?"

"Don't get all egalitarian on me, Whim," said Tobias. "The world is not a fair place. Some have and others don't. Let's just be grateful that we belong to the former category."

"It doesn't bother you?"

"No, it doesn't. Wealth cannot be evenly distributed. It's just not the way the world works. Look, I'm a fairly short chap. You're fairly tall. Should height be evenly distributed? Should we all be the same? Should we all live in colourless, uniform equality, sharing everything like a bunch of kids sharing out a bag of sweets? Get real, Whim."

Whim thought back to his days with the gentlemen of the streets. When one of them somehow acquired a bottle of booze, they all shared it till it was gone. If one of them was given a couple of fivers by some madman giving away cash in the street, they'd all go down to the takeaway and have a good feed. No one ever accumulated money. It was like accumulating sunshine - impossible. It's there for everyone to enjoy. You can't rush around stuffing sunshine into bags, saving it for a cloudy day.

So Whim continued to give money away - which wasn't easy. More often his random recipients regarded him with suspicion rather than gratitude. Large tips to those who served him seemed to be more graciously received. He would buy a cup of coffee in a cafe and leave a twenty pound tip, or give a fifty pound note to the doorman who held open the door for him at his hotel. And, best of all, he'd come upon a beggar or a busker and nonchalantly drop a handful of notes into his hat on the pavement. Once, he had dallied with picking pockets in busy streets. Now, he used those skills in reverse, delighting in slipping bundles of notes into the pockets of unsuspecting passers-by then walking on, unnoticed, imagining their surprise and bewilderment when his gift was discovered. He even exchanged some of his notes for bags of pound coins which he'd scatter at random while walking the streets, knowing that, while few but the poorest would stoop to pick up a penny, few but the richest could resist a pound coin lying in their path.

Strangely, Whim enjoyed the giving of money more than the making of it. Like Tobias, who made money because he could, so Whim gave away money because he could. He had few talents, he readily admitted, but giving was certainly one thing he could do better than most.

And finally it dawned on him that the neatly folded suit of clothes containing the healthily replete wallet that he had found upon that doorstep, many months before, had not been left by accident - as he had often supposed - but as an act of kindness, a gift to whoever might find it from someone who had stepped beyond wealth. Could this be so? He had no way of knowing, but it was a notion he cherished.

Tobias, despite his rant against egalitarian ethics, applauded Whim's money giving behaviour.

"I make, you give. That's OK," he said. "Let's each do what we're good at."

So Whim gave him five hundred pounds.

"I can double this for you in a fortnight," said Tobias.

"Double it for yourself. Keep it," said Whim. "I believe you've taught me the value of money. That's your twenty percent commission for the lesson."

They parted amicably, toasting each other with a final glass of whisky in the bar where they had met.

"Maybe next time we meet, I'll be begging on the streets again," said Whim. "I hope you'll drop a couple of coins in my hat as you walk past."

"I never give to beggars," said Tobias. "That's my policy."

Whim spent a last night in his hotel, ensuring that his boots were well polished for the coming day. He looked at himself in the full-length mirror in his room. His suit had become rather shabby. He needed a new one.

The next day he visited a tailor and bought the finest suit he could find. He folded it neatly and carefully inserted his wallet into the inside pocket. After this final spending spree, it contained approximately a thousand pounds. He walked the streets until late afternoon, then found a little-used alleyway along which he spied a suitable doorstep. He lay down his burden, gave it a fond farewell pat and walked away in his shabby old suit and his weather-worn but newly polished boots.

Let's see what else the world has in store for me now, he thought. Dusk was falling. He walked out of town for an hour or more, far enough to be free of the din of civilisation, the glare of street lights. The full moon shone upon a grassy bank beside the road. Behind it stood a willow tree, bejewelled with leaves, white in the moonlight. Whim sat himself down, a gentle smile on his lips. He thought, "What treasure is moonlight! You can't eat it or drink it, you can't own it or save it or spend it. But it is more beautiful than a million shining coins, more valuable than a bank full of paper notes. And that's good enough for me."

He lay back on the grass and closed his eyes.

15
Mr Perkins gets it right

(Ralph Perkins and Irene Firth first appeared in the story "Mr Perkins gets it wrong" in ***Tales of Kaph.*** *This time, perhaps, Mr Perkins gets it right.)*

The County Council's proposal to close the library (or "withdraw funding" as they euphemistically expressed it) caused quite a stir in the town. It was not entirely unexpected. Local government cuts were the hot topic of the day. Libraries were seen by many councillors as easy targets.

"The town library was established in 1837," Mr Perkins wrote in a letter to the local Gazette. "Since then it has steadily grown and moved twice, bedding down in its present, purpose-built home only ten years ago. It is a well used and friendly place. Its proposed closure is an abominable outrage."

He went on to harangue the Council, both collectively and individually, directing his most caustic remarks at the Council leader, Len Craddock, and reiterating his oft-expressed opinions of local government politicians. He was a well-known letter writer.

"Bad business, Mrs Firth," he said, on his next visit to the library. "All these proposed cuts and whatnot. Don't know what the Council's playing at."

"I tend to share your sentiments, Mr Perkins," replied Irene Firth, "but as a Council employee I really can't comment on Council policies."

"Nonsense, woman. Say it as it is. Bad business."

Realising that he had perhaps overstepped the mark, he flushed - he was a ready flusher - and flustered over the library book he was returning. Irene took the book without looking at him, desperately but unsuccessfully trying to control her own flush - she too was a ready flusher, especially in Mr Perkins' company.

"I saw your letter in the paper," she murmured.

"Ah, yes. Venting my spleen, I call it, Mrs Firth. A cathartic exercise. Don't keep your feelings bottled up, eh. Better out than in, that's what I say."

Realising that the allusion was perhaps a little inappropriate, he cleared his throat, flushed a little more and turned away, picking up the nearest book from the returns trolley and feigning inordinate interest in a randomly chosen page.

Irene resumed her behind-the-counter duties. For the past year, she had barely spoken to Mr Perkins, beyond the usual civilities of "Good morning", "Thank you" and "Goodbye." In fact, Mr Perkins' once weekly visits had dwindled to monthly or less, their former fleeting friendship reverting to a cold, customer/librarian exchange of platitudes. Once, he had asked her to call him Ralph and she, in a rare relaxation of her public role and persona, had invited him to call her Irene rather than Mrs Firth. Once, she had even dared imagine that there might have been something more between them, a glint that might have grown into a wholesome fire. But Mr Perkins - a not unattractive, widowed, retired, well-off gentleman of leisure - had set his sights elsewhere. What was her name? thought Irene. Ursula, wasn't it? Some totally unsuitable money-seeking floozie. Dreadful woman.

She had heard the story second-hand. Mr Perkins had been jilted at the altar. Ursula - give her her due, thought Irene - had thought better of her mercenary motives. Some said she had taken what she could and ran before she became too entrenched. It was generally agreed that Mr Perkins would not have been the easiest of husbands to live with. He was left standing at the altar in his best suit, his son from his first marriage beside him, waiting, waiting. After half an hour, the vicar had closed his service book, stepped forward and whispered, "I'm sorry. I have another wedding due soon." "Bad business," Mr Perkins might well have said. Or thought, at least. But who knew what he thought and felt, that day? His face had been inscrutable as he politely apologised to the small congregation and hurriedly left the church.

He had kept a low profile, after that. It was a few months before he ventured into the library.

"Morning, Mrs Firth."

"Morning, Mr Perkins."

They didn't even exchange a glance, let alone a smile. Of course, Irene wasn't going to say anything. What could she have said? "I was sorry to hear about..." That would have been a lie, for a start. And Mr Perkins, how was he feeling? Heartbroken? Humiliated? News travelled fast in a small town. He must have known that everyone he met would have been imagining him, standing there in the church, shuffling from foot to foot, huffing and puffing and looking at his watch, finally accepting that his newly blossomed dream of happiness was over. No, it was certainly not Irene's place to comment upon the personal traumas of her customers.

At least the Council's proposed cuts had broken the ice that had formed between them. At least now they had a reason to converse again.

"Something must be done," said Mr Perkins on his next visit, the following week. "We're not just going to sit back and let those Council jackals rip the guts from our beloved library. We must fight them, Mrs Firth. We must show them how highly the people of this town regard their library."

"The Council are meeting in a month to vote on the proposals," said Irene. "I gather an internet group has been formed and there's talk of a petition and maybe even a legal challenge. Perhaps you could join the group, Mr Perkins."

"Internet group? I can't be doing with all that computer stuff. I'm a book man, as you know, Mrs Firth, a man of words. Time for another letter to the paper."

The following week's Gazette devoted two pages to letters on the library question. Most were well-argued essays listing the many services provided by the local library, reminding non-users that libraries were not just about books. There was much talk of DVD and CD hire, free internet access, a space for public meetings and exhibitions, and many autodidacts extolling the library as an almost sacred seat of learning at the heart of the community. A few Councillors responded with statistics about debts and the need to save so many millions over the coming years, positioning libraries in direct competition for money with social services, facilities for the elderly and disadvantaged, and so forth. “Where do our priorities lie?” asked one, “Books or abused children?”

Mr Perkins’ offering was severely edited and appended at the foot of the page, a vitriolic attack on Len Craddock, the Council Leader. “Is the man a complete moron? He’s more interested in power than the needs of his electorate. He should be ashamed of himself.” Mr Perkins vented his spleen.

The Council refused to waver. At meetings and consultations, the people of the town expressed their views vociferously and passionately. The internet group flooded cyberspace, mobilising public opinion across the county and then the country, drafting in library and legal experts. The Council listened - or so they said - but claimed their hands were tied by national government and budget deficits accrued by the poor management of previous administrations.

Irene Firth, following the instructions of her superiors, tried to remain aloof from it all, to give information only and not appear to take sides. Of course she was concerned. Her job was at stake, after all. But she was not a woman to dwell on future possibilities. She’d had enough of that. Once she had dreamed the dream of matrimonial and maternal bliss, but no children came and her husband of ten years exchanged her, like his car, for a younger, sleeker model. Once she had dreamed the dream of literary fame, of being the next Iris Murdoch or Joanna Trollope or even J K Rowling. But her angst-ridden manuscripts of former days remained unpublished and unread, rotting in a cardboard box in the back of her wardrobe. Once she had fancied travelling the world, but her concern for the world forbad flying in jet planes and, besides, in her globe-trotting dream she was never alone. Once, she dreamed that the companion at her side might be Mr Perkins - Ralph - but that dream had faded, along with the rest. Now she cared not to look beyond the affairs of the day. She was not bitter - not very - but resigned to a life of comfortable mediocrity and content with what gentle pleasures came her way. Her attitude tended to be that of acquiescence, and she had yet to decide whether that was a positive or a negative attitude.

Besides, she had little time to ponder her future. The coverage in the Gazette had awoken the curiosity of those townsfolk who were more or less unaware of the library in their midst. Every day new faces appeared, wondering what all the fuss was about. Many joined. Business was booming. Irene was exhausted, returning to her solitary, book-reading, evening existence at the end of each day. No time for dreaming.

The Council meeting to decide the fate of the library was scheduled for 16th February. On 14th February, just after opening time, Mr Perkins appeared bearing a single red rose.

"For you, Mrs Firth," he said, proffering it bashfully.

Irene didn't know where to look or what to say. She took the rose clumsily and muttered, "Thank you, Mr Perkins."

"No, no. Please call me Ralph. And the rose is a Valentine's gift to express my love of this library of yours. Long may it prosper."

"Thank you, Mr... er, Ralph," said Irene, bending to find a small vase from beneath the counter. Her emotions were suddenly in turmoil. It was many seconds before a coherent thought entered her mind. Two thoughts, in fact, both accompanied by exclamation marks: "Oh, Ralph!" and "Bloody cheek!" She held them both at bay and attended to her next customer.

Two minutes later, Mr Perkins re-appeared, a book in his hand. She took it from him and scanned it, giving him no more than a quick but, she supposed, affectionate glance. The book was Thoreau's "Civil Disobedience".

"Enough words," said Mr Perkins. "Time for some action." But Irene had no idea what he meant by this.

The single red rose sat in a vase on the corner of the counter. Throughout the day, its petals slowly unfurled, releasing a fragrance that seemed to weave a soothing web over the counter area. Many customers noticed it. A few commented.

"You have an admirer?" asked one, her tone almost incredulous.

"An admirer of the library," said Irene, distancing herself from the rose's overt expression of love.

During her afternoon break, she took the rose into the staff room and gazed at it as she sipped her tea. She had forgotten it was Valentine's Day, and now that she was reminded of the fact, she thought back and counted off the years. My God! The thought nearly made her spill her tea. Valentine's Day, February 14th 1971, exactly forty years ago to the day. The day she had lost her virginity. My God! Was it really forty years? She'd been a university student. The height of the hippy era. Free love and all that, but love never seemed to freely flow her way. Until that night. He'd been a local boy, an office worker, not a student. Oh yes, it had been good. She still tingled at the memory of it: not love exactly, but passion and thrill and the wonder of physical contact. They repeated the pleasure a few times, over the coming weeks, then drifted apart. It was to be several years before she met the dashing Mr Firth. And since the disastrous end of that debacle, no one had really stirred her apart from Mr Perkins - Ralph. And of course he was completely unsuitable. He was ten years older than her. Ex-military. Ex-civil service. Set in his ways. A charming but rather curmudgeonly old man. But his Valentine rose seemed to shine in the dusky afternoon light. She thought she had closed the book of their imaginary flirtation - closed it and stashed it on a remote upper shelf of the bookcase of her memories. But perhaps it deserved dusting down and re-opening. Perhaps it might yet have a happy ending.

Shortly before closing time, Irene became aware of activity outside the front of the library. She left her post at the counter to investigate. There, immediately beyond the library door, was Mr Perkins, a pack on his back, a picnic hamper on the ground at his side, in the process of erecting an old army-style camp-bed.

"What on Earth are you up to, Mr Perkins?" she asked.

"Direct action, Irene. It's the only way. Purely non-violent, of course. We'll stop our library closing by simply stopping it from closing."

With that, he produced from his pack a long, heavy-duty chain, of the sort used to tow lorries, which he entwined through the handle of the library door, the steel n-shaped bicycle stand cemented into the ground immediately outside the library, and once around his own ankle, securing it with an equally heavy-duty padlock. Next, he removed a large banner from his pack which he unfurled and attached with big blobs of blutack to the door, proclaiming the message: “OUR LIBRARY WILL NOT CLOSE!”

“So what do you think of that, Irene,” he said, sitting down on his camp-bed with a self-satisfied grin. “Bit of civil disobedience, eh?”

“And how long do you propose to sit there?” asked Irene who, though she tried to hide it, found her own face folding into a reciprocal grin.

“Long as it takes. I’m well prepared.” He opened his picnic hamper and withdrew a large plastic sandwich box, a bottle of port and two glasses. “Will you join me in a drink, Irene? A little act of defiance against the County Council?”

“I’ve got a library to close, Mr P... er, Ralph. You can’t sit there. How am I going to lock up?”

“Both you and I know, Irene, that there is an inner door to the library that can be locked from within. This outer door only gives access to the lobby. Our precious books are quite safe, I assure you.”

“Do you propose to stay here all night, then?” asked Irene, as his intent slowly dawned on her.

“Looks like it. I’ve called the local press who should be here soon to record the event for posterity. Hopefully, too, some TV cameras will show up. Perhaps we’ll even go national. And I’m hoping that we can persuade Councillor Len Craddock to come along. This is his local library, after all.”

Irene felt, in equal measure, both annoyance and pride: annoyance that her end-of-day routine would be disrupted, and pride that Mr Perkins - a man in his sixties - was prepared to take a stand for the sake of her library. Pride and affection won the day. This is real human life, she thought. This is something more than books and internet groups and petitions and public meetings in the town hall, something altogether more positive, more noble. She felt like hugging Mr Perkins. She didn’t, of course.

But she was also worried. She had no idea how things might develop, and she was none too keen on uncertainty. She vaguely supposed that, once the press had been to take a few photos, once darkness had fallen and, with it, a probable cold night, then Mr

Perkins would pack up and go home, job done. She suspected, however, that this would not be the case.

Once she had switched off all the computers and lights and closed up the library for the night, she put on her coat and went out to sit with Ralph on his camp-bed. She was off duty. She could do as she pleased.

He poured them both a glass of port.

"Happy Valentine's Day, Irene," he said, and a momentary image of that Valentine's Day forty years ago flashed through her mind. She dismissed it without pursuing any thoughts or feelings, past or present, that might have accompanied it.

The photographer from the Gazette appeared and took a few pictures. (Irene withdrew into the shadows, allowing the hero of the day to bask in the flashlight.)

"I'll phone a few contacts," the photographer said. "Tomorrow, hopefully, we'll get the regional TV news here. Maybe even some national newspaper articles. Old man defies council cuts - that sort of thing."

"I'm not so old," replied Mr Perkins indignantly. "Sixty-four, if you must know, and as fit as a fiddle. Same age, I believe, as our great Council leader, Len Craddock, and if he's still young enough to wield his axe against our library, then I'm certainly young enough to stop him."

A few cheers and claps arose from the small group who had gathered around the library door to witness Mr Perkins' solitary act of civil disobedience. After a while, Irene succumbed to the cold and withdrew, but she was determined not to desert her library saviour. A couple of blankets were kept in one of the cupboards. She pushed some easy chairs together in the staff room and laid herself down, enwrapped in the blankets, for a fitful night's sleep.

The next morning, she paid an early visit to a nearby cafe and brought back a tray containing a full English breakfast for Mr Perkins, who was out of his sleeping bag and sitting on his camp-bed. By mid-morning, word had spread around the town and many people turned out to greet their local hero and join him, for a while, in his vigil. Irene, content that he was well catered for, set about the business of running the library.

A crew from the regional BBC news appeared. Mr Perkins reclined on his camp-bed, the chain that tied him to the library door in full view, and adopted a defiant pose.

"How long do you propose to keep this up?" was the most obvious question.

"As long as it takes. At least until tomorrow when the Council makes its decision. And if they decide - against all reason and sanity and public opinion - to close this library, then I shall stay on. I shall physically prevent them from closing this library."

"For how long?"

"Well, I'm not a young man, of course, but I've got a good few years ahead of me yet."

"And what do the library staff think of your stand?"

"Irene Firth's the one to ask. Admirable woman: diligent worker, stern in appearance but a soft and kindly heart. Great expertise in bookish matters."

Irene herself declined when asked for an interview.

A report went out on the regional TV news at six o'clock. The national media picked up the story and it earned a slot on the BBC ten o' clock news.

Meanwhile, the library attracted twice its usual number of visitors. Irene was rushed off her feet, but there were plenty of other willing supporters to take care of Mr Perkins, sitting like a king upon his throne in the doorway. Irene selected a few books that might help him pass the time: Mahatma Ghandi's autobiography, Ray Mears "Survival Handbook" and Eckhart Tolle's "The Power of Now."

"A fitting selection," Mr Perkins thanked her.

She popped home during her lunch break to pick up her own sleeping bag and a small camp-bed and, that night, she slept again in the staff room - unobserved, of course, for she thought it prudent not to be seen publicly condoning Mr Perkins' behaviour, although she took personal responsibility for quietly administering to his needs and comforts throughout the day, even to the extent of bringing out the library display screen so that Mr Perkins could have some privacy in which to attend to his ablutions, for he adamantly refused to unlock his chain.

Following the TV appearance on the second night and front page coverage in several national dailies, the leader of the Council, Len Craddock, turned up at eight in the morning, along with a police car and two policemen.

Irene observed his arrival through the staff room window and went outside, first making a quick phone call to the Gazette photographer who lived down the road and who, in his turn, scrambled the regional BBC crew who were staying in a hotel in the town.

"A noble effort," said Len Craddock, cheerily. "You've made your point and made it well. I think now you should call it a day, don't you?"

"And if I don't?" (Mr Perkins had rehearsed this moment many times, and was resolved to maintain both his ground and his civility.)

"I'm afraid," said Councillor Craddock, "that this is County Council property. I've instructed these police officers to remove you, if you will not go willingly."

One of the policemen brandished a long-handled pair of wire cutters.

"You'll have to do better than that," said Mr Perkins, holding up a length of the chain which was clearly too stout to be more than scratched by the wire cutters.

"The point is, Mr Perkins," said Len Craddock - and by this time, Irene, the Gazette photographer and the BBC camera crew were on the scene, together with a rapidly growing crowd of onlookers - "The point is, the Council is obliged to make cuts. Our budget has been slashed. Money must be saved. This is one of a whole raft of ways that we propose to do it. These are hard times, Mr Perkins. We all have to make sacrifices. We have to prioritise. What are we to do; withdraw money from libraries or deprive abused and disadvantaged children of the care they need and deserve? Believe me, no one regrets the closure of this library more than I do. I've been coming here all my life." (Never seen him before, thought Irene.) "But money must be saved. That, unfortunately, is the bottom line."

"How much would it cost to keep this library open for another year?" asked Mr Perkins, leaning towards the microphone that the BBC sound man was holding.

"The figures are all in the public domain, Mr Perkins. We have staff salaries to pay, building costs, ground rent, electricity and gas bills, all the support facilities that keep the library running."

"How much?" Mr Perkins persisted.

"Well, taking off revenue from DVD and CD hire, overdue fees and so on and so forth, we're talking about saving fifty-three thousand pounds a year."

"You're closing our library to save such a piddling sum?"

"Hardly piddling, Mr Perkins."

Mr Perkins pulled a cheque book and pen from the inner pocket of his jacket. "Fifty-three thousand, you say? OK. Who shall I make it out to? The County Council?"

"I'm afraid it's not that simple, Mr Perkins. You can't just write a cheque, a generous gesture though it may be."

"Why not? Strikes me it's pretty straightforward. It will cost fifty-three thousand pounds to keep this library open for another year. So here it is. No cuts necessary. You save your money and we keep our library."

"And next year?"

"Next year, if necessary, I'll do the same again. But remember, Councillor Craddock, that we live in a democracy and we're not far off elections for the likes of you. Are you so confident that you'll still be here next year? You're not exactly the most popular man of the moment."

Thus saying, he ripped the cheque from his cheque book and stretched out his arm towards the Council leader. "Might take a day or two to clear, but it will be honoured, I assure you."

Len Craddock attempted his favourite camera smile. "I can't take that, Mr Perkins. This is about council policy, not just the money to keep a single library open for a year."

"Take it." Mr Perkins' tone was soft but resolute. "You need money. I'm giving it to you. What's the problem? Take it. I'm offering this library a lifeline. Are you going to reject it in front of the good people of this town, in front of the nation's television cameras?"

Mr Perkins stretched his hand to within inches of Mr Craddock's. Mr Craddock hesitated for a moment more then tentatively closed his thumb and index finger around the cheque. At that moment, cameras and mobile phones clicked all around, and the TV camera zoomed in on the councillor's face as it struggled to maintain its genial public persona.

Mr Perkins nodded his head in gentle satisfaction. "So, I think that concludes our business." He extended his hand to the Council leader who shook it curtly and turned away, disappearing from the scene as the ever-gathering crowd cheered.

"All right, move along now, move along," said the policemen, half-heartedly, for they too were enjoying the occasion.

Mr Perkins reached into his trouser pocket, extracted a key, unlocked the padlock and removed the chain. Amid the general clamour he quietly packed up his bed and belongings and, accepting Irene's offer to come into the library for a wash and brush-up, he withdrew from the scene as discreetly as Mr Craddock had done.

"A celebratory drink?" he said, a while later, sitting with Irene in the staff room. He produced his bottle of port.

"Certainly not at this time of day," said Irene. "I've got a library to run."

"So you have, Mrs Firth. So you have."

He leant back in his chair and poured himself a large glass of port, a smile of glee on his face. "Ah, I do so enjoy a story with a happy ending, don't you, Irene?"

"On this occasion, Ralph, I'll make an exception and agree with you," said Irene, hoping that perhaps this would not be the end of the story.

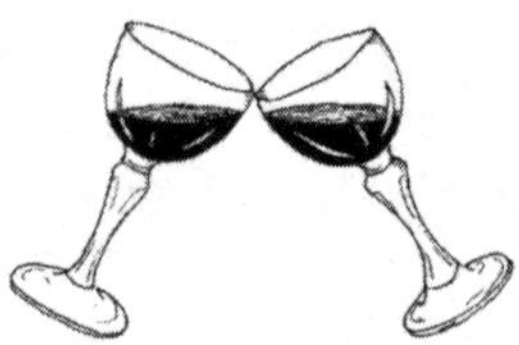

16
A Tale of Misfortune

"Man is born, lives, dies, builds houses, writes books,
not as he wants to but as it happens.
Man does nothing. Everything happens."

G.I.Gurdjieff, from **P.D.Ouspensky's** "In Search of the Miraculous", 1949

Fred Shearman changed his name by deed poll to Freddie Fortune in an attempt to break into the big time in the burgeoning pop music business of the late 1950s. National fame eluded him, but he achieved a modicum of local renown with his smoochy, blues-like ballads.

His wife, Felicity, the daughter of the town fish'n'chip shop owner, also adopted the surname Fortune, as did their daughter, Melody, the heroine of this tale.

Freddie Fortune's pop star ambition slowly evaporated as he took over the chip shop from his father-in-law, but he still sang on Sunday evenings in the town's sports and social club where the ladies admired his wistful crooning and the men smirked, part mocking, part jealous, part pleased that their local lad could enliven their dull lives. Fortune's Fish'n'chip Cafe flourished - Freddie, it seemed, had found his true niche in life. Felicity Fortune grew fat and happy and Melody Fortune became the darling of the street.

The Bishop of Bath and Wells once entered the shop, in need of sustenance after a particularly gruelling synod in Winchester. Felicity - a church-goer - recognised him at once and gave a curtsy, which wasn't easy with her voluminous body cloaked in a tight white apron. But the Bishop was touched by the gesture and, when he noticed Melody lurking behind her mother's legs, he reached forward and patted the top of her head.

"And what's your name?" he asked, in Father Christmassy tones.

"Melody Fortune," replied the little girl, shyly peeping around her mother.

"A name like that is surely a blessing," proclaimed the Bishop, then grabbed his bag of fish and chips and swept out of the shop without further conversation.

Felicity's eyes glazed over. "A blessing indeed," she intoned, dreamily. Her husband humphed and attended to the next customer in the queue. And Melody wondered what a blessing might be.

Everyone called her Melody. She was, after all, the only Melody in town, and she loved her name as much as her parents did. A rather taciturn but ever-smiling girl, it seemed that she had inherited the felicitous demeanour of her mother and, aptly, the melodious tones of her father.

At school, she neither excelled nor disappointed - good at singing and sports, like her father; good at sewing and social skills, like her mother; poor at arithmetic and spelling, like both her parents. In those days, children were tested, graded and ranked within their class each term. Willie Atkinson, the doctor's boy, always came top, while Joe Slade, who lived with his grandmother in a flat above the butcher's, was always bottom of the class, although it never seemed to bother him because football was his only love and he was captain of the class team. (He went on to play the game professionally for Bristol Rovers, becoming the only child from that class who attained any degree of fame and fortune.) As for Melody Fortune, she was regularly placed in the middle of the class of 30, swapping 15th and 16th position each term with Gordon Seward, whose father mended broken wirelesses, televisions and diverse electrical appliances in the shop next door to Fortune's Fish'n'chip Cafe. Gordon was the only boy in the class who wore spectacles - round, wire-framed, thick-glassed contraptions that would later look fashionable on John Lennon: but on chubby-faced, lank-haired Gordon, they just looked ugly and gave rise to his nickname, "Goggles", later shortened to "Gogs".

Gordon accepted his nickname and his lack of good looks with a stoicism rarely seen in children. His school report, one year, summarised his character in the single word "meek", a word probably not properly understood by the teacher who used it, the parents who read it, nor, most certainly, by Gordon himself. "Is meek good or bad?" he asked, not unreasonably, but the Seward's could not answer him and the house, though full of all manner of electrical appliance manuals, did not possess a dictionary. Gordon wondered if meekness might be a quality admired by ladies, particularly by the lovely exemplar of the female sex who lived on the other side of his garden fence in the form of Melody Fortune. He never asked her, of course. He kept his infatuation with Melody a complete secret, satisfied only by stolen glances over the fence as they both played out their separate fantasy games in their respective gardens, or across the classroom as they struggled over arithmetic exercises, or during the weekly country dance lesson, in which he would often contrive to be Melody's partner so that she might hold his sweaty hand.

Melody - albeit the paragon of feminine beauty in Gordon's eyes - was, regrettably, not quite as pretty as her name might suggest. Her slightly skewed nose gave her face an asymmetric appearance and her teeth protruded when she smiled, revealing an abundance of gaps. But her long blonde hair, flowing in waves across her shoulders, was considered by her parents and others - and especially Gordon - to be her greatest asset. Her mother brushed it lovingly each morning: fifty full brushes while Melody closed her eyes, relished the sensation and felt like purring the pleasure of a stroked cat.

Thus far, our heroine appears a charming young girl, her life gently charmed: blessed by a bishop, loved by her parents, adored by the mild-mannered boy next door. It seems that fortune favours Melody Fortune. But a crushing blow awaited her on the first day of her third year in junior school, at the age of nine.

Her new class teacher was a man, Mr Jekyll - the first male teacher she had ever encountered. In the judgement of the female members of staff at the school, he was young and dashing and full of bright, modern ideas. In the eyes of the children he was just another adult, a teacher to be respected and obeyed. During the first registration of the term, he tried to win over his pupils with a bit of jovial banter to which they, wondering about this new man in their lives, responded very tentatively and without the laughter he had hoped to induce. Going down through the register, he came upon Melody's name.

"Ah," he said, "so it is my misfortune to have a Miss Fortune in the class."

He paused for the anticipated titter at his little joke, but the titter didn't come. No one thought there was anything particularly funny about Melody's name. They had lived with it all their lives. Besides, the word "misfortune" was not exactly common in the vocabulary of a group of nine-year-olds, as Mr Jekyll should have known.

Melody, as it happened, was an avid Enid Blyton reader and had already had dealings with the word "misfortune" but, strangely, she had never connected it to her own title and surname. Now, apprehending for the first time that her once delightful name was capable of a less delightful interpretation, she was shocked and a dark cloud began to grow over her happy life.

The cloud deepened and darkened as the weeks of that term passed, fuelled by My Jekyll's insistence upon always addressing Melody as "Miss Fortune", imagining it to be a witty and playful joke and rather disliking what he took to be the unwarranted quirkiness of her fore-name, Melody. And, though she tried not to show it, she was hurt indeed, shuddering within every time he used the expression. An ugly resentment began to grow in her soul. She hated her new teacher, even as he played for and won the affection of most of the rest of the class, as the days went by. Most, that is, except Gordon, who was also an Enid Blyton fan and sympathised with his young love's plight. Besides, it was not long before Mr Jekyll caught on to the fact that Gordon's chums always addressed him as "Goggles", so, in an attempt to win his friendship, he decided to do likewise. But Gordon was not impressed. His nickname was fine amongst his friends but did not sound friendly when coming from an adult. Mr Jekyll, in his first weeks at the school, had forged two enemies.

Probably Freddie and Felicity Fortune had never even considered the potential embarrassment that could result from their daughter's name, and they might well have remained ignorant of her distress - for, unable to articulate it, she hid it from them - had it not been for a visit to their shop by Mr Jekyll, one evening, in search of a fishy takeaway.

"So, how's our little Miss Fortune?" he said to Freddie the fish fryer, cheerfully.

"What misfortune is that?" replied Freddie.

"Your daughter, Melody."

Both Freddie and Felicity, behind the deep fat fryers, stared at him, expressions of grave concern on their faces.

"Misfortune?" said Felicity. "What misfortune is that? What's happened to her?"

"No, no, nothing," responded Mr Jekyll, beginning to wish he had not brought up the matter. "It's just my little joke. Miss Fortune. Her name."

"But Melody's a lovely name," replied Freddie. "Everyone thinks so."

Mr Jekyll sighed. "Indeed so. I was merely... Not to worry. Fish and chips once, if you please, Mr Fortune."

Freddie attended to his business, firing occasional furtive glances at Mr Jekyll, which, the latter fancied, were far from friendly. Felicity handed him his paper-wrapped package and took his money without looking at him. The coldness of the Fortunes dulled the poor man's appetite. He hurried home wondering what he had said to offend.

Miss Fortune's misfortunes began, it may be said, that day in the classroom with the flippant and rather insensitive jest of her new teacher. The remark, lightly spoken, penetrated the as-yet unhardened periphery of her being and burrowed inwards, like a parasite, feeding upon her former confidence and joie-de-vivre. Perhaps those few words of intended levity had awoken her self-consciousness, her vulnerability, bursting the fragile bubble of childhood innocence.

Her first physical rather than psychological misfortune occurred a few weeks later when, walking home from school absorbed in an unfamiliar childish sulk, she stepped into the road in front of a passing cyclist. She sustained a broken arm; the cyclist, falling from his bike, a fractured skull.

"What a misfortune," the nurse said as she plastered Melody's arm in the local casualty unit.

The next day, struggling to cope with her plastered arm, she dropped her school satchel into a roadside puddle, ruining the three Enid Blyton books she had borrowed from the school library.

"Well, I'm afraid your parents will have to pay for that misfortune, Miss Fortune," said the school librarian, who had taken a shine to Mr Jekyll and liked to imitate his jokes and witticisms which, it appeared, tended to spread rapidly around the staffroom.

Misfortunes, it is said, invariably come in threes. The third occurred a few weeks later when her father, Freddie the fish fryer, slipped on the greasy floor behind the counter and, arms flaying to control his fall, he thrust his right hand wrist deep into the boiling fat of the chip fryer.

His scream could be heard throughout the town. Some recalled that he had once had a more melodious voice.

The shock, confusion and horror of this incident sent Felicity Fortune's blood pressure soaring. Already eight months pregnant with her second child, a brother for Melody, her waters spontaneously broke and she went into a very premature labour. Two ambulances arrived at the fish'n'chip shop in rapid succession, one taking the agonised Freddie to Accident and Emergency, the other the frantic Felicity to the maternity unit. Freddie's hand was badly damaged. Felicity gave birth to a still-born boy.

Thereafter, and not surprisingly, the ambience of the once merry cafe became unpleasantly sombre. Freddie struggled to fry as best he could with one hand, his left hand wrapped in bandages. At random intervals, and for no apparent reason, Felicity would burst into tears and run off sobbing. Business fell. Regular fish'n'chip suppers dropped off the menus of many families. The situation wasn't helped by the opening, during that period, of an Indian and a Chinese takeaway in the vicinity. The fortunes of the Fortune Fish'n'chip Cafe took a serious dip.

Melody ended her academic year under the tutelage of Mr Jekyll with a drop in the class rankings from midway to 21st. (Gordon

Seward finished in 22nd position, perhaps in sympathy for his secret sweetheart, perhaps in deliberate and futile protest against the teacher who persisted in calling him "Goggles", even when his few friends in the class had shortened his nickname to "Gogs". Gordon retaliated by trying to get all his classmates to refer to their teacher as Dr Hyde, but no one else had even heard of Stevenson's story, so the joke fell flat and the appellation did not catch on.)

The following year proved no better. Melody's unfortunate epithet - Miss Fortune - had stuck in the staffroom and her fourth year teacher, Miss Lomax, who, like the school librarian, had fallen under the spell of the handsome Mr Jekyll, invariably referred to her as Miss Fortune. Miss Lomax blatantly favoured the high-flying academics of the class and tended to be dismissive of the also-rans such as Melody and Gordon. Melody, disillusioned by her education at such a young age, withdrew from active participation in the class, secreting the current novel she was reading under whatever work she was supposed to be doing and sneaking a glance at it at every opportunity, to the neglect of all else. Concluding the entire works of Enid Blyton, she moved first to The Silver Sword and The Secret Garden, and then, taking a giant leap, on to Wuthering Heights which occupied her for the best part of that year. (She was a slow reader who needed to silently articulate each word with her tongue and lips.) The dark moodiness of Emily Bronte both infected and inspired her. Heathcliff became the first fantasy lover of her life, to be replaced, the following year, by Charlotte Bronte's Mr Rochester and then Jane Austen's Mr Darcy. Melody's contact with the real world dwindled as she roamed the Yorkshire moors and Georgian houses of her imagination.

Further misfortunes followed. The Fish'n'chip Cafe burnt down one night after closing time. Apparently one of the fat fryers had not been turned off. Some suspected a deliberate insurance scam - the business was in deep trouble - but those who knew Freddie knew that he would never put his family at risk. The Fortune family, in the flat upstairs, survived unscathed but were forced to relocate. Freddie found a job as a cook in a truckers roadside cafe on the other side of the county. Felicity sank deeper into depression and Melody withdrew further from her formal education into the works of Dickens and Hardy.

Gordon, meanwhile, was devastated after the fire when the Fortune family left town. Melody's departure tore a hole in his world which he felt would never heal. His journey into adolescence was a rough one. At the age of fourteen - lanky, spotty, severely low in both confidence and friends - he considered his future. Four possibilities presented themselves. One involved joining his father in his electrical appliance repair business. The second consisted of working hard at school, getting some A Levels, going to university and getting a decent job. Third was dropping out and becoming a hippy. (This was the late 1960s, the height of hippydom, and "dropping out" had the same allure as "joining up" might have had for previous generations.) The fourth option - a seriously considered possibility - was suicide. Life, for Gordon, was not what he had once hoped it might be. Despair greeted his first moments of wakefulness each morning and hopelessness lulled him to sleep at night. Meekness, he decided, had little to commend it as a personal quality.

At sixteen, still completely uncertain as to the direction in which his life was taking him, he abandoned his glasses in favour of contact lenses, drifted through various unsatisfactory jobs, examined most of the world's major and minor religions and enrolled as a novice Zen Buddhist monk at a small, family-run monastery in the hills of Devonshire. There, immersing himself in inner and outer emptiness, he discovered the equanimity and happiness that had slumbered away, unnoticed, at the centre of his being throughout his teenage years. He began to glow again with the same light that had illuminated his childhood days, playing in his back garden while Melody played in her garden over the fence.

Meanwhile, Melody's life seemed to be a perpetual stumble through a succession of misfortunes which sculpted her body and soul in ways that were not altogether pleasing to the eye.

Her father, Freddie Fortune, one-time singer, former fish'n'chip shop proprietor, died in a tragic accident: drowned in a slurry pit on the farm that bordered his roadside cafe. He had been out walking the fields, between shifts, when he noticed a stranger's dog running with careless abandon and hurling himself, unknowingly, into the unwholesome brown quagmire of the unfenced slurry pit. Without thinking, Freddie charged to the rescue, not realising, as he waded in, that the pit was a good ten feet deep.

"It doesn't take long to drown in a slurry pit," Melody and her mother were informed by the doctor who attended the scene, himself something of an expert in the field of agricultural deaths. "Probably a matter of seconds. The airways are instantly choked by the filthy stuff. Unpleasant but quick."

If this was meant to console, it didn't. Felicity grieved for many months - she was a great advocate of protracted periods of grieving - then, in need of a sturdy masculine shoulder to cry on, she took up with one of the lorry drivers who frequented the cafe. He was not a good man. He beat Felicity Fortune and tried to force himself upon the unfortunate Melody, bursting into her bedroom one morning while Felicity was out. At the time, Melody was reading Dostoevsky's Crime and Punishment - a large, hard-backed copy she had borrowed from the local library. When her would-be molester made his move, she somehow managed to slam the book shut, entrapping his ready penis and causing him such pain that he was temporarily incapacitated and she was able to push him away and run screaming from the house. She never returned. The farmer's wife at the farm of the fateful slurry pit took her in. The library refused to accept her story of what had happened to Crime and Punishment and she had to pay five pounds for a replacement. She never did find out what happened to Roskolnikov.

Leaving school at sixteen without turning up for her GCE examinations, she returned to her home town and moved into a flat with an old friend from her junior school. She began to feel a resurgence of her former happy, childish self, the Melody whose head the Bishop of Bath and Wells had patted. She was young and free and the world lay before her, offering itself. She resolved to accept the first offer of a job that she received. As fortune would have it, that offer involved working behind the counter in the fish'n'chip shop that had replaced her father's - not quite the glamorous position she had had in mind, but at least it provided a steady income and regular meals.

It was not long before Mr Jekyll appeared in the shop, still at the same junior school, now risen to the heights of deputy head. He didn't recognise Melody after so many years, but she certainly did him, despite his balding head and bulging stomach. She glared at him, overcome by a flood of memories and strange emotions, for it was only dimly that she connected him with the commencement of her misfortunes. Yet his presence repulsed her. The long submerged feelings from that awful year in his class exploded into a sudden surge of hatred. She summoned up a mouthful of saliva and, while Mr Jekyll chatted jovially with the fish fryer, she spat abundantly upon his portion of chips.

An unfortunately placed mirror on the wall opposite the counter revealed this furtive act to the fish fryer, Melody's boss. He said nothing - Mr Jekyll was a regular and valued customer - but shovelled another ladle-full of chips onto the platter, hoping to conceal the glutinous glob of gob. As soon as Mr Jekyll had left the shop, he turned to Melody.

"Take off your apron, get out and don't come back," he said, firmly but quietly, not wishing to upset his queue of customers.

"Bloody stinks in 'ere, anyway," said Melody, ripping off her apron and storming out.

She left town that night, carrying her meagre possessions in a backpack, walking through the dark lanes of her childhood. It was not a walk of shame but of hope. She was leaving her past behind her, heading into a future that, after all, could only be better. Her fortune beckoned and she welcomed it.

Until the rain started.

She found a leaky, disused barn and spent a cold, wet and miserable night in the company of bats and noisy, unseen rodents.

Walking on, the next day, she came upon an encampment of hippies who took her in and fed her - first brown rice, then hash, then cocaine and speed. She gladly embraced this chemical escape from herself and stayed with that group of drug-fuelled drop-outs for weeks that turned into months that turned into years. They moved from benders and barns in the country to squats in the city. Melody moved from man to man, just like the joints that were passed around the circle, giving her love and her body in exchange for food and drugs and a spurious sense of security.

They called her Blondie, after her most obvious physical feature, her hair hanging in long drapes that, thanks to her habitually downcast gaze, obscured most of her face. She never told them her real name, a name that she had come to feel as a curse rather than a blessing.

Drugs dominated the group's lifestyle. She smoked or snorted or popped whatever she was given - although she drew the line at injecting, having always been squeamish about needles. None of them was addicted to any particular substance, just to mind altering drugs in general, to altered states of consciousness. Normal consciousness was simply too normal. They'd lived with it all their lives and they'd had enough. They called themselves psychic explorers, always searching for some other mental place, anything other than the tedium of the quotidian. The aim of each day was to end it in a state that they called "wasted". To get wasted was not a waste of a day but a day well spent.

Melody never questioned this philosophy, this lifestyle. She was beyond questioning the things that happened to her. At least here, amongst these hippies, she was a part of something. At least here she could be herself - if only she knew what that might be.

The years past in a psycho-chemical blur: sometimes good, sometimes bad, sometimes happy, sometimes sad. That phrase seemed to encompass the prevailing world view of her new peer group, and she was happy enough - or sad enough - to accept it.

Thus the flow of fortune carried her from her teens to her twenties, from the sixties into the middle years of the seventies where, one evening in some strange city, she found herself sitting on a pavement in the aftermath of an acid trip, her head drooped, her matted blonde hair dangling in the gutter - alone and nameless.

"Melody Fortune?" she heard.

Some still shining part of herself responded instinctively to the sound of her own name. She looked up.

His expression was concerned, compassionate, questioning, a little hesitant. She didn't recognise him. His glasses were gone and his head was shaved.

"You don't recognise me?" he said.

His voice had deepened, of course. They hadn't seen each other since they were eleven. She tried to place him, but her memory span had dwindled to days. The last month had all but vanished: the distant days of childhood nought but a rarely probed blur.

"What d'you want?" was the question she asked, not "Who are you?"

"To help," he replied.

"I don't need no fucking help."

"We all need to be helped and we all need to help. That's why we're here."

Suddenly something clicked. Perhaps it was some subtle intonation in his voice, the minutest of gestures. She remembered.

"Gogs?"

He smiled.

"Goggles?"

He grinned.

"Gordon Seward?"

His eyes filled with tears.

"Bloody hell! You're Gordon Seward!"

He reached down and placed his hand on her shoulder. It was the first time he had ever touched her - apart from holding her hand in country dance lessons.

"Bloody Goggles!"

"These days I'm called Ananda."

"What kinda name's that?"

"Preferable to Goggles, that's for sure." He laughed. And she fell into the infectious pool of his laughter.

He led her to his dormobile, parked in a nearby car-park, and there he set about making her a cup of tea.

"Got anything stronger?" she asked.

"Chamomile or Jasmine?"

She looked him over. He'd improved a bit since those old days in junior school, but he still wasn't much to look at. But his company felt warm and, recalling flashes of those childhood days when they had played in their adjacent back gardens, she felt a connection with her happy, carefree past that she had not known for years. She smiled at him as he busied himself at the sink of the cramped vehicle, and he smiled back.

"D'you remember that bloody teacher we had? Mr Jekyll?" she said.

"Not my favourite," said Ananda. "He wasn't the greatest teacher in the world, but he was only trying to do his best. Just like all of us. We've all made mistakes. We've all suffered misfortunes."

And it was with these words, spoken in the warm emptiness of Ananda Seward's dormobile, that the wall of self-defence that Melody had been painstakingly building in her mind throughout her years of misfortune, the wall that separated what she was from what she thought she was, the wall that kept the world at bay, that wall began to crumble. She watched it fall, like one of those films of a collapsing factory chimney. And when it was gone, she stood naked amidst the rubble; and the freedom, the space, the glorious open space filled her heart.

And the tears of relief flowed and flowed, like a dam burst, until it seemed that the dormobile was bobbing on a sea of tears. And those two young people clung to each other as their bodies shook, sobbing for the sadness that had touched both their lives, sobbing for the vulnerability and the fragile sensitivity of all humanity, sobbing for the misfortunes of the whole world.

On the 28th June 1979, Miss Melody Fortune abandoned her unfortunate name forever, becoming Mrs Melody Seward.

17
The Walker

"Afoot and light-hearted I take to the open road,
Healthy, free, the world before me,
The long brown path before me leading wherever I choose."
Walt Whitman, "Song of the Open Road", 1856

Tommy travelled with his guitar slung across his back. Sometimes he'd play it in a pub, in exchange for a meal and a few drinks. Sometimes he'd gently serenade the setting Sun, alone on a hilltop. When walking, he'd keep it safe in its weathered leather case upon his back. He carried his other possessions in a hold-all, swinging along beside him as he walked: some spare clothes, a sleeping bag, ground-sheet and a few blackened cooking implements.

They came upon him as he tramped down a long, straight lane in the pouring rain, splashing through puddles in sodden sandals. Every few steps, he'd use his free hand to sweep his lank, dripping hair from either side of his face. At first sight he looked like a teenager. On closer inspection, he could have passed for anything between fifteen and fifty.

Jenny was driving. Ben had had a couple of early evening pints and she never let him drive home from the pub.

"We must give him a lift, poor chap," she said, slowing down as they approached the bedraggled figure.

"Don't be silly. He's absolutely soaking."

"Exactly."

There was no time to argue about it. They never argued, anyway. They merely agreed to differ in protracted silences. Jenny drew up alongside the walker and reached across Ben - who persisted in staring straight ahead - to wind down the window.

"Where you going?" she shouted.

"Where you going?" he replied, flicking his hair back over his shoulders. His smile was the first thing she noticed, completely immune to the unpleasantness of the rain.

"Only a couple of miles, I'm afraid."

"That'll do."

Without another word he was in the back seat.

"Nasty weather," Jenny commented as she pulled off. "Been out in it long?"

"I love the weather. Rain or shine, it doesn't bother me."

Jenny glanced at Ben, hoping he'd say something. She wasn't good at conversing with strangers. But Ben continued to stare through the windscreen, ignoring their passenger. They sat in silence until they reached the driveway of the cottage.

"I'm afraid this is it." Jenny glanced over her shoulder as she slowed. It was still several miles to the nearest town and the lane was deserted.

"Thanks very much," said Tommy, opening the door. "Very kind of you."

As he smiled at her again, Jenny knew that she had no alternative.

"Listen, we can't leave you here in the pouring rain. Why don't you come in and wait for it to ease up?" She glanced at Ben who inhaled deeply but said nothing.

"Very civil of you." Tommy's smile opened up into a wide grin. "How can I refuse such an offer?"

The rain didn't stop. Darkness was falling and Jenny insisted that their guest should stay the night. Ben followed her into the hallway and caught her arm as she started to climb the stairs to prepare the bed in the spare room.

"This is absurd," he spluttered, trying to keep his voice to a whisper. "The chap's a complete stranger. We can't just put him up for the night."

"Why not?" Jenny surprised herself with the rapidity of her response. At the back of her mind, she felt that perhaps she should be sharing Ben's concern, but, overpowering this niggling doubt, was the conviction that she was doing exactly the right thing: showing a little compassion for a fellow being in distress. She sighed. "Well, what do you suggest we do?"

"Send him back to the bloody road, that's what I suggest."

"But it's pouring. He'll have to walk for miles to get anywhere."

"That's his problem, not ours." But, even as he spoke, he knew that his argument was lost. Perhaps he wasn't a particularly compassionate person but he prided himself on his tolerance of others and liked to think that he was capable of seeing through the superficialities of appearances. And Jenny's contemptuous look burned into him until he had to look away.

"Okay." He raised the palms of his hands. "Okay, if that's what you want."

"Remember Germany," she said, softly.

He remembered. They'd been hitch-hiking across Europe, many years before, a couple of penniless students in love with each other and with the adventure of the open road. They, too, had been soaking and beginning to despair of surviving the coming night. A German farmer had picked them up, taken them back to his house, fed them and let them stay for two days until the skies cleared.

Together, without another word spoken, they relived the entire memory.

"Right." Jenny turned back to the stairs. "I'll get the spare bed ready."

Ben returned to the living room. Tommy was standing by the unlit fire in the vain hope of drying off. Ben managed to twist his face into the nearest he could approach to a smile. "Put a match to it, if you like. It's all ready."

"Thanks, mate." Tommy grabbed the matchbox from the mantelpiece and set about lighting the fire. Minutes later, following a few judicious prods and blows, it was blazing away merrily. Ben, watching from a distance, was impressed. The fire could be a stubborn beast to coax into life, but Tommy clearly knew what he was doing.

Somewhat grudgingly, for he felt wary of leaving a stranger alone in his living room, Ben wandered into the kitchen. It was the custom for him to prepare the evening meal. Rice and stir-fry could easily be made to stretch to three, he thought, and set about the task. The sound of Tommy's guitar drifted through the doorway, a few twangs as he quickly tuned it then a soft strumming and picking. The style was free and tuneless, the mood soothing. He's good, thought Ben who had once dallied with the instrument himself.

Tommy had dried out by the time they sat to eat. Ben and Jenny felt awkward with their unexpected guest. They usually ate in silence, but now that silence seemed strained, hanging over the dinner table like a mist over the moors.

"Good grub," said Tommy, clearly more interested in eating than conversing.

"Thanks," said Ben.

A minute went by. The mist thickened. Ben and Jenny glanced uncertainly at each other, but it was Tommy who dispelled the spell.

"So what d'you do with yourself, man? Apart from cooking." he addressed Ben, between hearty forkfuls of rice.

"I'm a salesman. Stationery, office supplies, that sort of thing. Mainly mail order. Stuck in an office, most days."

Tommy nodded. "You don't sound too keen."

Ben shrugged. "It's a job."

"So what would you really like to be doing?"

The question did not seem strange. Ben had asked it himself, many times, and he knew the answer well, although it felt odd to admit it in public, to voice it, even, in front of Jenny. "I'd like to make it as a writer. You know, the old best-selling novel thing."

Perhaps he expected a laugh or a grimace. It embarrassed him to confess to such a hackneyed fantasy. It made him sound like a dreamy kid.

But Tommy responded seriously. "So you seek fame and fortune?"

"I suppose so."

"Along with five or six billion other people. Unfortunately they can't all be rich and famous. Not even for fifteen minutes."

"But you've got to strive after something," Ben defended himself. "You've got to have a goal, a dream." His dream was more than an idle fantasy. It was a desperate imperative, a life force. Yet, as the years slipped by, he realised that he was no nearer achieving it than he had been half a lifetime ago. The fear of failure polluted his everyday thoughts, the sickening fear of spending the next twenty years selling stationery, of sinking into old-age obscurity.

"You've got a nice place here," said Tommy, looking around at the homely comforts of the cottage. "Decent pad to live in. Good food. A good wife. Strikes me you've got it made, man."

Ben contrived a smile. There was no way that he could express the frustration that dominated his life. Certainly not to a homeless hippy. Perhaps even less to his wife. He pretended to be, if not ecstatically happy, then at least reasonably content. The facade seemed to remain intact fairly well with friends and acquaintances, but he had worn it for so long that he had forgotten how to let it down in front of Jenny. And now, when he sat at his computer at the weekend, awaiting inspiration, he despised himself. His shelves were full of books by people who had achieved success. He longed to be amongst them. Jenny imagined that it was nothing more than a casual hobby, like his abandoned guitar playing. He joked about it and never let on how inadequate he felt.

"And what about you?" Tommy turned to Jenny. "What d'you do with yourself?"

Jenny hesitated. It was not that she was reticent to give an account of herself in front of a stranger. It was more Ben's presence that inhibited her. They were accustomed to speaking of trivial daily incidents, of practical matters and local gossip. They talked of brief moments in time and avoided the larger patterns of their lives.

"I work part-time in a shop in town," she said in a dismissive tone. "Other than that, looking after the cottage and the garden keeps me pretty busy."

"I'm sure it does. But I can see there's more to you than that. What drives you? What's that flame burning inside you?" Tommy's gaze was unnerving although its intensity was always modified by the hint of a smile. "Your husband seeks fame and fortune. What about you?"

Ben, too, was staring across the table at her, as curious to hear her response, it seemed, as Tommy. She felt herself flushing, not because of Tommy's presence but Ben's. Why was it, she thought, that they never discussed the deeper feelings of their lives? It wasn't that they lied to each other. It was just that they each tried to present themselves as the sort of person they believed the other wanted them to be. The truth can hurt, they both knew that, and in a comfortable marriage you try to avoid hurting and being hurt. You avoid touching old sores.

She dropped her eyes to her food. "I don't know," she muttered. "Adventure, maybe. Excitement."

She glanced quickly at Ben and noticed his raised eyebrows. Well, what did he expect her to say? Certainly not that.

"Aha." Tommy grinned. "It appears that I've stumbled upon your little secrets. Two dreamers securely ensconced in the heart of Middle England."

Jenny's flush deepened. Ben laughed awkwardly. A change of topic was clearly called for. "What about you, then? I detect a bit of a northern accent. Where d'you come from?"

"Just come up from Cornwall," he replied. "Been walking the coast path for a few months."

"And before that?"

"Oh, I've been on the road for years. Just me and the old guitar. Don't get me wrong. I'm no scrounger. I work when I can get it and when I can't, I just walk."

"Freedom, eh?" said Ben. "Sounds rather good."

"As the song says, freedom's just another word for nothing left to lose. Yeah, I suppose I'm free. Never know where I'll be tomorrow."

Jenny gazed at him. At first she'd felt pity but now it was changing to envy. She knew perfectly well where she'd be tomorrow - and a thousand tomorrows after that. The security of such a thought was supposed to be comforting but she'd had her fill of comfort. Yes, it was excitement that she sought, that vital feeling, each night, that the next day, if not better than today, would at least be different. It was a feeling she'd last known during that hitch-hiking trip across Europe, and she'd secretly longed for it ever since. She'd lingered for ten years in the shadow of Ben's un-talked-of dreams of fame and fortune. She'd woven herself into a cocoon of genteel country pleasures. And the taste of adventure she'd relished during the months of their European trek seemed, now, no more real than the distant days of childhood. Even the adventures of childbirth and parenthood had been denied her. They'd told themselves that they'd wait until Ben's big breakthrough into the world of the published writer. Or, rather, they had implied this to each other. Or, at least, Ben had implied it. They told each other little, these days. Beneath their conventional outward lives, their fantasies seethed, fit and strong, but years of frustration had taught them the great lesson of adulthood: how to keep fantasy and reality well insulated from each other. Tomorrow, Jenny knew, she would stay at home in her cottage. Yet her dreams, she knew, would be flying through a completely different world.

And Ben knew that he'd be in the office again tomorrow, still treading water while his ambition bubbled away below the surface, still pretending that his job was merely a temporary stopgap while he awaited the mythical coming of success. During that trip to Europe, he'd given himself ten years to make a name for himself. At the time, it had seemed more than reasonable. Then he'd embraced the notion that life begins at forty. And now, in those bleaker moments as he sat in front of his blank computer screen, he counted the years towards the possibility of early retirement.

The next day, it was still raining. Their breakfast conversation was easier - trivial but jovial. Tommy felt almost like an old friend.

"You're welcome to stay till it eases off," said Jenny.

"Appreciate that," he replied.

Ben was busying himself with preparations to leave for work. His lack of comment, or even a glance in the direction of either Jenny or Tommy, was evidence of his uncertainty about leaving their unexpected guest alone in the cottage with his wife.

Tommy sensed his unease. "Hey, trust, man," he said. "Trust."

Ben looked at him. Their gazes locked for a few moments. Trust is a strange and nebulous thing, thought Ben. Perhaps it's more visceral than rational. He waited for a confirmatory feeling to arise. It did not, but neither did its opposite: mistrust. He picked up his car keys from the dresser, kissed Jenny goodbye in his usual manner and made to leave.

Tommy followed him to the front door and touched his shoulder as Ben reached for the latch.

"Hey, man," he said, "I dig your dream. It used to be the same with me. Guitar playing, singing-songwriter. The old pop star thing. That was my dream. But then I realised that what I really loved doing was just playing me ol' guitar."

"Good music," said Ben. "I enjoyed it."

"And what about you, man? Do you enjoy your writing? Do you love watching the flow of words onto paper?"

Ben knew the answer, of course. He smiled. "Apart from Jenny, there's nothing I love more than surfing on the creative flow."

"Then just do it, man. Just ride it. Enjoy it. See where it takes you."

"True words, Tommy," said Ben, "but I also feel that I want to communicate. I feel that I have something to say, to write, that I want others to listen to, to read."

"Sure you do. Me too. I like to play my guitar to myself, but I like it even more to play it to a couple of people like you and Jenny. I don't wanna big stadium or a recording studio. Just a couple of mates - listening, maybe singing along. Can't beat it, eh? So write for Jenny, man. Write for me. Write for your mates. You don't have to write for the whole bloody world."

With that, he slapped Ben's shoulder and turned back to the living room.

When the Sun broke through, in the early afternoon, Tommy went into the back garden and set about chopping wood for the fire. Jenny watched through the kitchen window as he removed his shirt, the muscles of his tanned back bulging as he swung the axe. She felt desire arise within herself. But it was not a desire for his body. Rather, she lusted after the freedom of his lifestyle.

Later, she listened while he strummed his guitar. He wasn't trying to impress her. The music flowed from him like the easy manner of his conversation, like the smiles into which his face naturally fell whenever he looked at her.

They walked together through the fields. His pace was quick but unhurried. Ben regarded walking merely as a means of getting somewhere, tolerated only when a faster form of locomotion was unavailable. Even when they took a turn over the hills on a Sunday afternoon, he was always counting the miles they had covered and the miles left to reach their predetermined destination. Tommy's, though, was the walk of life. It was self-fulfilling movement. The past was gone, the future yet to come. Here, in the present, it was simply good to walk. Or to play guitar. Or to talk.

Ben returned from work and the three of them sat at the kitchen table, drinking tea. They talked of mundane matters, joked and laughed. Then Tommy stood, packed his guitar away in its case and made to leave.

"Reckon I'll be on my way," was all he said. "Thanks for the hospitality."

He kissed Jenny on the cheek and gave Ben a hug. They watched him walk off down the lane, his guitar slung across his back.

They stood in the living room, before the unlit fire. Suddenly the cottage seemed cold and lonely. But the space left by Tommy's departure was not a vacancy: it was filled with a seemingly tangible potential energy.

Ben was first to speak. "How about another trip across Europe this year?"

Jenny squeezed his arm. "Let's get the fire blazing again and talk about it."

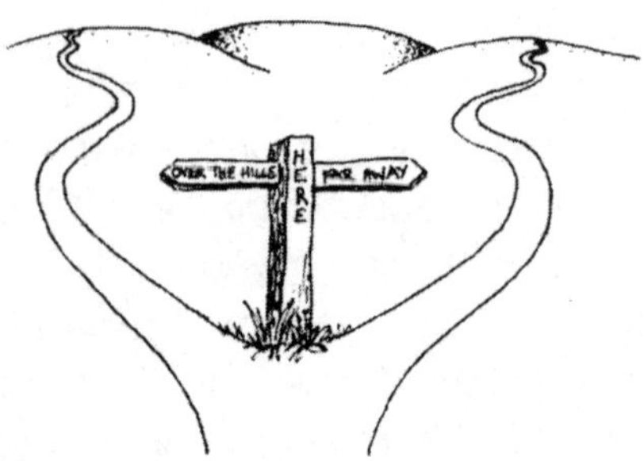

18
The Departure of the Cryptomancer

Readers of "The Tower", *earlier in this volume, may recall that the narrator of that work, one Felix Sunheart, was known to be a contemporary of the great cryptomancer Janus Kralger. The following work, one of very few surviving writings of Felix Sunheart, explores a peculiar episode involving both Kralger and Sunheart. We believe - but have no way of verifying - that this work pre-dates* "The Tower".

When the world was younger, I, Felix Sunheart, seeker of strangeness, walked the streets of diverse cities and enjoyed the company of many misfits and mystics, like myself. Most of us were loners, solitary adventurers through life, but the turn of circumstances had a tendency to draw us together, and our occasional colloquies fed energy and inspiration to our individual paths.

Thus it was that I came to make the acquaintance of the renowned cryptomancer Janus Kralger. And thus it was that, after several years of sporadic friendship, I found myself incarcerated, for a while, in a prison cell that he had recently vacated.

I knew at once that it had been his cell. Every single brick of all four walls had a letter impeccably scratched upon it. Janus always surrounded himself with random patterns of letters. Where others may have daubed paintings upon the walls, he preferred to contemplate the anagrammatic possibilities of twenty-six letters.

As a young man, he had accidentally amputated his left index finger with a meat cleaver. He claimed to have been pre-occupied by some cryptogrammatic conundrum while preparing a meal and felt no pain at the first swing of the cleaver. Looking down, he was puzzled, for an instant, to see the finger-shaped lump of meat lying next to the joint he was chopping. Perhaps the second swing would have severed another digit, so obsessed was he with his mental machinations, but he remembered himself just in time and froze his motion before any more damage was done.

He constructed a replacement finger for himself, its steel tip shaped to a stylus-like point. With this he was able to scratch a letter onto each brick of his cell. Who else would have gone to so much trouble to adorn those bleak walls in such a fashion? A poet may have scrawled lines of verse, but only a cryptomancer would chose a completely random array of letters.

The details of his crime and sentence were well-known. Janus had broken one of the fundamental Laws of Cognition. He had dared to think the unthinkable, and then compounded the offence by speaking the unspeakable. The unthinkable and the unspeakable were, of course, never prescribed within the written documents of the Laws of Cognition, making it difficult for the profound thinker and eloquent speaker to avoid thinking or speaking them. Janus's principal defence was that no evidence of his having thought the unthinkable or spoken the unspeakable could be presented at his trial without a further breach of the law. Without speaking of the unspeakable of which he had spoken, how could any witness claim that he had actually heard him speak it?

The judge dismissed this defence as ludicrous, a mere sophism. The guilty verdict was delivered without anything approaching a fair trial. The judge, it was generally thought, acted through spite rather than jurisprudence. He had taken a personal dislike to Janus Kralger who, practising his cryptomantic arts upon the name of the judge, had prophesised his imminent death from a blow on the head. The judge had been so outraged by this prophecy that he resolved that Janus should never again ply his cryptomantic profession and should be duly incarcerated for the rest of his life.

That day, the trial and sentencing over, the judge was leaving the courthouse when a stone gargoyle resembling a grimacing gorilla, perched high on the edge of the roof, was suddenly dislodged by a gust of wind and collapsed, showering stones upon the street below. The judge was struck upon the head and fell in a pool of blood.

"Damn that cursed cryptomancer!" were apparently his final words.

Meanwhile, in his prison cell - a cell with which I was later to become intimately familiar - Janus continued all the activities of his former lifestyle: philosophising, meditating, delving deeper into the mysteries of letters and conducting cryptomantic readings. At first he performed this latter procedure in response to questions asked by his guards, who sought expert divinatory knowledge of their future lives. Then he was visited by the prison governor, similarly curious and impressed by the prophecy he received. As word spread of his captivity, Janus would give audience to nobles of the court and even the king himself, who would occasionally appear at Janus's stark steel door seeking counsel and the casting of cryptomantic oracles pertaining to the tasks of kingship. Janus was happy to oblige, especially as the king brought pleasant luxuries from the kitchens of his palace to supplement the prisoner's meagre diet. The one thing he could not offer was a royal pardon, for the Laws of Cognition were deemed immutable, beyond even the power of the king.

I had observed Janus at his cryptomancing on many occasions. He usually employed wooden or clay cubes, each face bearing a letter of the alphabet. Different numbers of cubes would be thrown, with due ceremony, depending on the question asked, and the resulting letters would be studied intently by Janus who would arrange the displayed letters into words - whether real or imaginary - and offer interpretations on their meaning in the light of the petitioner's question. This was the art of cryptomancy, and I had no doubt that it was an art at which Janus Kralger was a Grand Master.

"Letters and words have powers beyond their symbolic meaning," he once told me. "In certain arrangements, their sound or their written form can pierce the subtle film that separates our world from a much greater reality that encompasses all time from distant past to distant future. Words can heal and transform, they can change the nature of things, and they can transcend the limits that we normally imagine are imposed on our experiences.

"And there are certain words," he continued, raising his metallic finger in an idiosyncratic gesture, "words known only to the greatest of cryptomancers and magicians, which, when spoken or written, possess an energy that can rip the very fabric of reality. The writer or speaker can then step through that rip into nowhere. And from nowhere, he can reappear anywhere he likes."

"How can this be?" I had asked.

"How? I cannot say. I know only that it is so. This much was understood by the cryptomancers of old who, for obvious reasons, kept their knowledge hidden, to be used only in exceptional circumstances. A single rip in the fabric of reality can quickly heal itself. But a multitude of willy-nilly rips is likely to tear that fabric apart completely. That is why the Word of Departure, as it is known, is the most closely guarded secret of our fraternity of cryptomancers."

"And do you know this word?" I asked. As a seeker of strangeness, this was, to me, something strange indeed.

"The configuration of letters was given to me, in coded form, by my former cryptomantic master," said Janus, "who had himself received it through spontaneous intuitive transmission from his own master. The Word of Departure may be used only once and then transmitted to another. I, in my turn, shall use that word when the time is right. I shall depart through a rip in the fabric of reality. But, having departed, I shall linger a while near that rip until such time as I may be called upon to transmit my knowledge to another who ardently seeks it."

And so it was that, after a year in his cell, Janus Kralger spoke or wrote the Word of Departure and departed.

The next day, when the guards looked in, the cell was empty. No trace remained. There was no way that any man could have escaped from that cell. The steel door was firmly locked from the outside, the brick walls intact, the single window too high and small and protected by bars, the stone slabs of the floor sitting upon bare rock.

The night guard was accused of treachery. It was the only reasonable explanation, for the possibility of the prisoner creating and disappearing through a rip in the fabric of reality was clearly absurd. Even to think such a thought would have contravened the Laws of Cognition. So no one even thought it, let alone spoke it. (No one, that is, but I.)

Janus Kralger was never seen again. The official version recorded death by natural causes, that night in his cell. Deaths in cells were not uncommon and rarely questioned.

His cell remained empty for no more than a week before I became its next incumbent. My crime was heresy, which, like Janus's, fell under the strict Laws of Cognition, the bane of all free-thinking men and women in our country - and the end of many.

My heresy was to suggest, in a written essay, that the Sun, far from being a ball of chaotically burning gas, as was generally supposed, was in fact a supremely conscious living being, the creator, the sustainer and the ruler of our Solar System: God, no less, by any other name.

I had long been a student of astronomy, and this seemed to me to be a perfectly reasonable view based on the evidence of direct experience and intuitive revelation. But it was not a view that conformed to the dogmas of the judges who upheld the Laws of Cognition. They deemed it a heresy to suggest that God was anything other than that strangely insubstantial divine Being depicted in the ancient scriptures, written long ago in a far off culture. To question the word of the scriptures was heresy.

A friend of mine had fallen foul of the heresy law, many years before. Seeking a true and rational understanding of the nature of God, he had reached the conclusion that the word "God" was merely the mythological or religious name for the Universe, the totality of Being, and the word "Universe" was the secular or scientific name for God. My friend was sufficiently satisfied with this conclusion to utter it in public, incurring the wrath of listening bigots.

Similarly, I had simply stated that those characteristics normally applied to God - omnipotence, omnipresence, omniscience, eternal, creative, life sustaining and so on - could equally well be applied to our loving Sun.

I was given no opportunity to defend my case. Indeed, it was considered that my case was indefensible. I had thought and disseminated what was considered to be a blatantly false and inflammatory idea. Indefinite incarceration was my sentence. With Janus Kralger departed, I had no friends willing to risk pleading my cause.

I accepted my fate stoically. The Laws of Cognition were an abomination devised by a sick society. Men like Janus and I regarded it as our duty to the freedom of the spirit to speak our minds and write those things that we believed were true, fearless of the repercussions. I had no regrets. But I was sorely depressed by the prospect of prolonged captivity, for I have always been a man who loves to feel the open skies above his head and the endless road stretching before his feet.

My spirits revived, however, when I discovered that the cell I would inhabit was to be the one recently vacated by Janus. Suspecting that he had utilised the Word of Departure to procure his departure, I was immensely cheered and I determined to find the same means of egress from my own imprisonment.

We had spoken of it in past, happier days. I knew that the Word of Departure was twelve letters long. Surely I could discover it. After all, in how many possible ways can twenty-six letters be arranged in twelve letter words?

This was the first question that taxed me. I quickly realised that the number of possible twelve letter words was rather large: to be precise, 26 to the power of 12. This I worked out, performing calculations in the dust of the cell floor, to be a little under one billion billion.

How long would it take me to write one billion billion words? I tried scratching a single 12 letter word in the dust. Possibly 6 seconds, if I was extremely quick. Ten words per minute. 600 words per hour. Working 20 hours per day, that's 12,000 words. Multiplying by 365, that's over 4 million in a year. Despondently, I realised that my task would take me many billions of years. Such a prospect may well have deflated a lesser man's resolve, but I was passionate in my desire to be free and could see no alternative but to find and employ that liberating Word of Departure.

A different approach was required. Clearly it was highly unlikely that, before I died, I would ever write the Word in the dust of the cell floor using either a random or a systematic method. But my life has always been strewn with highly unlikely events. I live at the very limits of probability. Therefore, why should I not find the Word of Departure, not after a billion billion attempts but after only one?

The probability against it was a billion billion to one. But, thought I, I shall be that One! I shall find it at my first attempt!

I considered the matter thoroughly, refining my plan of action, before I made any attempt to write a 12 letter word. First, I spent a day in meditation to quieten my mind as completely as I could. To be sure, this is a difficult task in the noise and bustle of the outside world, but in the confines of a silent cell, featureless save for a pallet on the dusty floor, four walls strewn with scratched letters and a tiny window through which nought but sky could be seen, it was relatively easy to still my mind.

On the second day, experiencing a great inner emptiness, I very quietly asked the question: "What is the Word of Departure?"

I asked it over and over, very slowly and with full concentration, not seeking to conjure up the Word, but just waiting, waiting, waiting...

"What is the Word of Departure?"

This was my question for two whole days and nights - for I was too focussed on my task to sleep.

"What is the Word of Departure?"

Then, after two days, I heard a voice in my head, quiet but sure. It was Janus Kralger speaking to me. Of that I was convinced.

I listened very, very intently.

"K," said the voice.

I opened my eyes and, as though to confirm Janus's pronouncement, my gaze fell instantly upon the letter K carved into one of the bricks of the cell wall.

I wrote the letter carefully with my finger in the dust upon the floor. Then I waited.

It seemed that an hour past before I heard Janus's voice again.

"U," it said.

My eyes snapped open, and there was the letter U before them on the cell wall.

I wrote it in the dust and waited another hour.

"G," came the voice. Again my gaze alighted at once on a G scratched onto the wall. I transcribed.

Another hour - clearly time flows differently on the other side of the fabric of reality.

"V," said Janus's voice, soft but clear.

I must, of course, in accordance with the hidden ways of the cryptomancers, refrain from imparting the following letters, from five to eleven. Suffice it to say that the twelfth letter was finally revealed to me.

"O," spoke Janus in my mind. O was the letter that jumped out of the cell wall to meet my gaze.

"O," I transposed to the dust.

"Erase the Word," said Janus, a command I could not defy.

With a sweep of my hand, the twelve letters of the Word of Departure in the dust of the cell floor were gone.

And so, too, were the walls of my cell. So, too, were the floor and the ceiling.

For a while, I was nowhere. My visual world appeared grey, but I knew that this greyness was most assuredly not my cell. I could feel a breeze upon my face. I could feel the warmth of the Sun on the top of my head. I could feel nothing beneath my feet.

Then I began to discern far vistas, faint, at first, but gradually gaining definition, perspective, colour and structure: distant mountains, green plains through which wide blue rivers meandered, forested hills, meadows grazed by sheep and cows, pleasant cottages and gardens, white cumulus clouds. I knew that I was floating high above this new world. I could feel my body - I was not discorporate - but neither was I falling. Rather, I was floating, gliding like a bird or an angel - a feeling which, before, I had known only in dreams. Slowly I descended to a more terrestrial level, but I remained in flight, learning, it seemed, how to propel and direct myself with subtle movements of my limbs. I hovered and soared and swooped, exploring, from above, this beautiful land.

But the strangeness, the wonder of this experience was as nothing compared to the joy I felt at the release from my cell.

I was free.

Like Janus the cryptomancer, I had departed.

19
Pooter again

"Lighter than air, clearer than glass, altogether released from myself, I was nowhere around."

Douglas Harding, "On Having No Head", 1961

"My father was a lighthouse keeper," I sometimes say during lulls in the conversation at social gatherings, if I'm trying to impress. Not that that happens very often - that I'm at a social gathering, or there's a lull in the conversation, or I'm trying to impress. I tend to be a listener, a nodder, an "Oh, really?" sort of converser. Well, most people like to talk so much and there are so few taciturn types like me that it seems to be a kindness to let the talkers talk while I listen, sipping from a glass of wine, furtively glancing at my watch, from time to time, to decide when would be a suitable time to politely withdraw. No, I'm not a party person, it must be said. One-to-ones are fine, but when three or four or more are gathered together, I tend to slip into the background.

"So what do you do, Mr Potter?"

"Er, it's Pooter, actually."

"I'm sorry. So what do you do, Mr Pewter?"

"My father was a lighthouse keeper."

Yes, I know it doesn't answer the question, but it's more interesting than saying I'm a laboratory assistant (a senior laboratory assistant, to be precise, with special responsibilities for fruit flies, or

Drosophila melanogaster as we like to call the little creatures), which generally elicits a contrived "Oh, really?" and a glazing over of the eyes.

"You're a lighthouse keeper? Really?"

"No, not me. My father was a lighthouse keeper."

No glazed eyes now, but wide-eyed expressions of wonderment. Everyone is intrigued by the image of a lighthouse keeper. Most imagine a fat, old, bearded man with a ruddy face and weather-worn features, dressed in a chunky polo-neck sweater, wearing a peaked nautical cap and staring out to sea, possibly with an outstretched arm and a pointing finger indicating the far horizon. And lighthouse keepers, in the popular imagination, are always seen as verging on the edge of insanity, if not barking mad - a consequence of all that solitary staring out to sea and the constant noise of crashing waves.

"Which lighthouse did he keep?" I'm sometimes asked.

I have to confess that I'm not sure - in fact I haven't a clue - but that doesn't matter because, by now, my conversational partner is off into his or her own memories and fantasies: of lighthouses visited or seen, of holidays on the coast, of scrambling over rocks and delving into rock-pools, of raging seas and wrecked ships. The image of the lighthouse is an infallible prompt to the imagination, an archetypal image that dredges up dreams and reminiscences from the depths of the unconscious.

Sometimes, some know-it-all wag professes to be an expert on lighthouses and starts bombarding me with names and places. I take a furtive glance at my watch.

But my father really was a lighthouse keeper. I am the latest in a long lineage of lighthouse keepers. Yes, I know that the job of lighthouse keeper is now obsolete and that I occupy the much less romantic position of senior laboratory assistant, but still I feel a vital connection with the grand tradition. And are we not all lighthouse keepers, shining our own light of awareness out across the turbulent ocean of life? This world that I see before me now is my world, illuminated by the light of my consciousness, my special, personal viewpoint, the viewpoint of Matthew Pooter. And so it is for each one of us. The lamps are many, but the light is One.

We can't all be life savers, like my father. We can't all have epic adventures, do great deeds and be significant figures upon the stage of time. But we are all, each one of us, the hero, the master, the central character of our own short story, the raison d'être of our own world, the world that we view through the window of our individual awareness. Even the most lowly of us has a vital part to play in the ongoing story of the Universe, for we are each the centre point of everything, the king pin of all creation, the glorious jewel in the heart of the lotus.

That's how I like to look at it, anyway. That's my point of view. And I know that it's all just words, thoughts, ripples on the surface of Being. That's okay. I like creating beautiful patterns of ripples.

I once had it in mind to visit all the lighthouses in Britain. Like most of my dreams and schemes, this one fizzled out fairly rapidly in the practical light of day, but I still like to gaze upon a distant lighthouse, whenever the occasion arises.

Many years ago, I resolved that, at least once every year, I would both take a swim in the sea and look upon a lighthouse from as close a vantage point as possible. It's one of the few resolutions that I've dutifully maintained.

I'm a bit timid when it comes to immersing myself in very cold water, but I love the experiences of floating, swimming and cavorting in sea water, of lying upon my back and staring up into a blue sky, the noises of the world muffled by the ocean, of flowing with the incoming waves, of diving down and exploring the magic land below the surface, of using my limbs in an unfamiliar way to propel myself through this glorious medium. I don't much care for swimming pools, but an annual dip in the sea on a warm summer's day I count amongst my favourite luxuries.

And a trip to the seaside is incomplete without the sight of some lighthouse perched upon a rocky headland.

Sometimes, on a sunny summer's day, the fancy takes me to see the sea and, after work in the lab, I drive to Brean, the closest coast to my Somerset home, and walk the beach in the evening quiet, or climb the high promontory of Brean Down to view the setting Sun.

Brean Beach is not a place for swimming, regrettably, but it has its own delights. The water of the Bristol Channel becomes increasingly muddy as one travels east into the Severn estuary, and the slope of the beaches at Brean, Burnham and Weston-super-Mare is so incredibly slight that, when the tide is out, the walk to the water's edge can be a kilometre or more. Even at high tide, one can wade out to sea for half an hour and the water level is merely up to one's knees. And one's feet sink into a squidgy bed of wet mud making every step a trial. Good fun for playful children, no doubt, but it's not the place to enjoy the full pleasures of sea swimming.

The beach is remarkable for its lengthy simplicity: three or four miles of featureless flat sand, shielded from caravan and amusements parks to the east by a ridge of dunes. To the south, it merges into the beach of Burnham-on-Sea: to the north it is abruptly curtailed by the cliffs of Brean Down, projecting like a recumbent dragon into the Bristol Channel, the last vestige of the Mendip Hills.

It is the emptiness of the beach that draws me. I walk slowly out onto the low-tide sands, my body gliding easily across the soft, flat surface. It seems that I am just a globe of visual awareness floating over the sand, a huge, transparent bubble silently sliding towards the sea. I am alone. A few people linger near the dunes, a few stride along the beach much closer to the shore. But here, half a mile out into the Bristol Channel, I am alone. I could scribe a circle around myself of several hundred yards radius and it would include not a single soul, and not a single object beyond amorphous, damp sand. And me: this globe of awareness, drifting silently along...

I find myself thinking of this Earth, and of humanity's rather unpleasant presence upon it. My thoughts emerge as negative, almost hopeless. I have little hope for humanity. A few hundred years at most remain before we burn ourselves out. Probably much less. We're well on the road to extinction, poisoned by our own avarice. Maybe a few communities of intrepid individuals in remote locations will survive the coming environmental crises to carry the ways of humanity into the future, and perhaps they will develop some new form of civilisation in which men may live in harmony with their planetary home. I have some slight hope of that - but very little, it must be said.

Yet I am full of hope for the Earth. The Earth will, of course, survive this passing plague of humanity. Life will continue. Change. Evolve. The flow of the natural world will follow its natural course. Trees will remain. Perhaps new lines of animals will evolve, new intelligences. Perhaps they will avoid the many mistakes we made. Perhaps the spirit of life and consciousness that we carry within ourselves will be carried by other forms, their own purposes to pursue. That's okay. The Earth will no more lament the passing of humans than it laments the passing of each day. Does God look down on us humans with any more feeling and love than upon all the other beings in its creation? We humans have always liked to think so. That's because it's us who are doing the thinking. It's possible that dolphins can think, in which case they would probably think of themselves as the chosen species, the top of the evolutionary tree. So would fruit flies, if they could think.

Crumb, our junior lab assistant, doesn't think much of fruit flies.

"I mean, they're pretty stupid little buggers, fruit flies, don't you think?" he says.

"What do you mean stupid?" I ask. I'm loyal to my *Drosophilae* and don't like them to be insulted.

"Well, all they do all day is sit around, drinking fruit juice and shagging."

"What's so stupid about that?"

Crumb considers the matter, then smiles. "Okay, you've got a point."

"Besides," I continue, "it seems that it's not just ordinary fruit juice that they drink, but cider. CD tells me that their saliva contains an enzyme that nourishes yeast and hastens the fermentation of the juice. Perhaps they sit around all day, drinking and shagging, because they're completely pissed most of the time."

"Not a bad life, I suppose," says Crumb.

"So maybe they're not so stupid. Maybe they've got a far firmer grip on the business of living than we humans have. After all, they've been around for millions of years."

"Maybe you're right," says Crumb.

The trouble with us humans is that we think we're the bee's knees, the be-all and end-all of life on Earth.

I think we are deluded. Arrogant and deluded.

And yet... Am I not here? Am I not now? Am I not Matthew Pooter, the centre of the Universe, the crown of creation? Am I not, this very moment, a globe of awareness rolling across the sands of Brean Beach?

A question arises, unbidden but insistent. "Where do I end and where does this empty beach begin? Where do I end and where does this world begin?"

I let the question linger, making no attempt to think up an answer. Perhaps it's just a rhetorical question, a childlike wonderment. I let it quietly sit there in my mind, weaving its spell.

And then, as spontaneously as the question arose, the answer comes - a sudden shock, an intuitive revelation, an Oh My God! moment.

There is no separation.

I am both the outside and the inside: the very far and the very near.

I am the infinite sky and the intimate I.

I am the circumference and the centre-point of awareness.

There is no boundary between I, the experiencer, and the world that I am experiencing.

I am totally absent: This world is totally present.

We are One.

I carry this truth with me as I walk on over the wet sands. No more questions follow, demanding further explanation. Enough has been said. Bliss and equanimity are now my companions as I meander across the sandy emptiness. Nothing is lacking. Enough said, indeed.

The fact is, I'm not certain that my father really was a lighthouse keeper, or whether this was just a myth created by my mother to explain the perpetual absence of my father. It was a subject we never discussed. On the rare occasions that I might ask her about her past life or my provenance, she would reply, very curtly, "Your father was a lighthouse keeper," and stare off into the unfocussed distance, a sad, wistful expression on her face. Over long years of practice, she had mastered the art of staring off wistfully into the distance and saying nothing. I learned not to bring up the subject of my father. And now my mother, too, is gone, and it's too late.

I believe I inherited my mother's taciturn nature and her wistful, far-away look. And from my father, I inherited... What? A love of lighthouses, I suppose. Nothing else springs to mind. A love of the sea, perhaps. But certainly no love of travelling. Like my father in his lighthouse, I prefer a sturdy home base upon the shores of my homeland. Like my father, I suspect, I am no adventurer. I prefer to view the vast panorama of the sea from the security of solid ground, rather than sail over its savage depths.

And, like my father in his solitary lighthouse, I have come to accept the absence of feminine company. My lovers have been few and mostly short-lived affairs. I'm inclined to think that this was also the case for my father. Perhaps my mother was his one brief liaison. I do not know. But I like to think his love-life was, like mine, sparse but sporadically intense.

As for me: I don't complain. Although it must be said that one consequence of a dearth of female company is a constant alertness to the possibility that, with each new encounter, that dearth may be nearing its end.

And so it is that I feel the first stirrings of romantic possibility when - to return to the present and my evening stroll at Brean - I come upon a woman called Cathy Hardy.

Still basking in the glow of my beach experience, feeling cleansed, vacant and receptive to whatever might befall, I wander back to the shoreline, back onto firm, dry sand, and decide, on a whim, to climb the steep path that zigzags up to the top of the three hundred feet high Brean Down. This rugged peninsula reaches a mile out to sea, a single ridge, no more than a few hundred yards in width, covered in scrub and grassland on which cows and goats are grazing. Its westernmost end slopes down to a rocky point where the gentle waves of the Bristol Channel converge from three directions. Across the Channel, the hills of South Wales are visible, while, sitting placidly in mid-channel, are the twin islands of Steep Holm and Flat Holm, their shapes aptly described by their names. The latter, perilously perched within a busy shipping lane, sports a white lighthouse.

She is sitting on a bench beside the track, quite near the end of the Down, her mind elsewhere, I fancy, her gaze seemingly fixed upon the island of Flat Holm and its lighthouse.

I stop, feeling pleasantly amicable and desirous of a few moments communion with another soul.

“Evening,” I say, giving a quick bow of my head and adopting a genial smile.

She turns slowly towards me, as though awakening from a reverie, but her eyes, at length alighting on me, suggest no surprise at seeing me there upon this lonely path, intruding into her solitude.

Her first words, softly spoken, startle me - and rightly so, I think.

“My father was a lighthouse keeper,” she says.

The look I give her must display the astonishment I feel at hearing this remark from the lips of another, but she takes the look for incomprehension and, raising her arm to point at the distant white lighthouse, she says again, “My father was a lighthouse keeper.”

“Really?” I reply. “That’s strange...”

But before I can explain what is so strange about it, she continues. “But that was long ago. They’re all automated now, you know. Lighthouses.”

“Yes, I know,” I say.

“My father was one of the last,” she says.

“Right,” I say, coherent speech beginning to fail me.

“One of the last flesh and blood lighthouse keepers. Before the machines took over.”

“Right,” I say. “Was that on Flat Holm?”

“No, no. Elsewhere.” But she declines to reveal where. “But all lighthouses fascinate me.”

“Right,” I say. “Me too.”

A curious but unstrained silence descends upon us, she on her bench, I standing beside it, both of us staring over the muddy water towards Flat Holm. Then I turn me attention to my unexpected companion and run my eyes over her. She is a little younger than me - in her forties, I guess - a swarthy, red-faced, outdoor type with stout arms and legs, her body concealed by a blue anorak which, I notice, is precisely the same brand, style and colour as my own. Her long dark hair is tousled by the gentle breeze on the Down, necessitating occasional sweeps of her hand to keep it from her eyes.

Yes, I like the look of her. No classic beauty, but a pleasant aspect and her smile wins me over. To be honest, I have never needed much winning over where women are concerned.

"I have a mind to walk the coast of England and Wales to see all the lighthouses," she says.

"Right," I say. "Me too."

She flashes me a quick glance, as though questioning my sincerity - or even, perhaps, my suitability as a conversational partner.

"How many are there, d'you know?" I ask. Strangely, it's a question I have never before asked.

"About seventy in England and Wales," she says, returning her gaze to Flat Holm. "Over two hundred on the Scottish coast. All automated now, of course. The profession of lighthouse keeper became extinct in the 1990s."

"Right," I say, adding stupidly, "Shame."

Was her father really a lighthouse keeper? I wonder. Presumably there were several hundred lighthouse keepers who were made redundant when all the lighthouses were finally automated, and presumably there could well be several hundred children of lighthouse keepers, some of whom might well be wistfully walking the lighthouses of England. It is quite likely that this meeting of ours is nothing but a rather strange coincidence: two children of former lighthouse keepers, meeting by chance on a site that overlooks a lighthouse. Thus runs a thought through my rational mind, while a hundred less rational thoughts surge away beneath it, seeking expression, and a cloak of wonder descends to smother all my thoughts.

"My name's Pooter," I say. "Matthew Pooter."

A mischievous residual thought that will not be silenced imagines that she might reply, "Good Lord, Pooter's my name too," and thence we might discover that we are siblings, or, at least, half-siblings boasting the same mysterious, unknown, lighthouse keeping father. But she expresses no surprise at my name.

She smiles. "Cathy Hardy," she says.

I am gratified that she feels sufficiently comfortable with me to reveal her name, but that name, I think, does not bode well. Cathy immediately evokes an image of my favourite tragic heroine, Cathy Earnshaw of Wuthering Heights, and Hardy makes me think of Thomas Hardy and his notorious unhappy endings. Tess! Oh, how I longed for a happy ending, but Hardy would not permit it.

No, Cathy Hardy is not an auspicious name upon which to hope for a happy ending to this particular tale that we are currently living. But who can say?

She stands. "Shall we get a bit closer?" she says.

The look of astonishment I give her causes her to lower her eyes and maybe even flush a little.

"I mean to Flat Holm," she adds, swiftly. "To the lighthouse. Shall we walk to the end of the Down?"

"Right," I say, and fall in step beside her.

"Flat Holm is still about eight kilometres beyond the end of the Down," she says. "Steep Holm is only about five, but it has no lighthouse."

And suddenly I am immersed in a new adventure, walking along Brean Down with an unknown woman who is called Cathy Hardy, the daughter of a lighthouse keeper. We are silent, keeping pace, step for step, our eyes upon the white pinnacle of the distant lighthouse. Internally, too, I am wordless, thoughtless. Once again, as it was upon the empty beach, I feel myself to be nothing but a globe of awareness, effortlessly floating along. And I feel myself, my ego, all that which I might once have clung onto and labelled as mine - my thoughts, my personal history, my opinions, my petty problems - drop away, falling behind me as I walk, like a trail of discarded litter. I am disappearing, gently fading. And in my place, this whole world is taking on a lucid, vibrant reality. In full, delicious colour. In 3D panoramic vision. With accompanying sounds, smells, tastes, sensations of touch, of the cool breeze, of moving limbs, of occasional thoughts and feelings popping into existence and then popping out again, like bursting soap bubbles.

We walk on, side by side. Moment walking. The long life histories that have brought us both to this point have no more meaning than finished stories. Whatever future lies before us is utterly unknown. We are here. We are now.

She turns to me and says, "I get the feeling that we've got something in common, you and me."

And she smiles. And it is a smile that expands from her lips to the outer reaches of her face and continues to expand until it encompasses the outer reaches of this beautiful world through which we walk together.

And I smile back, a smile that breaks spontaneously forth out of the joyous emptiness that is what I am - for it feels that I left my ego, with all its cumbersome baggage, back there on the beach of Brean, to be washed away by the incoming tide.

Yes, looking out from my emptiness and into hers, it seems that we have much in common. A common humanity. A common divinity.

We walk on.

A thought occurs: Perhaps this story will have a happy ending after all. And a new beginning.

She says, "Yes, my father was a lighthouse keeper."

I say: "Yes, my father was a lighthouse keeper, too....."

20
Epilogue I: Return from the Heart of the Sun

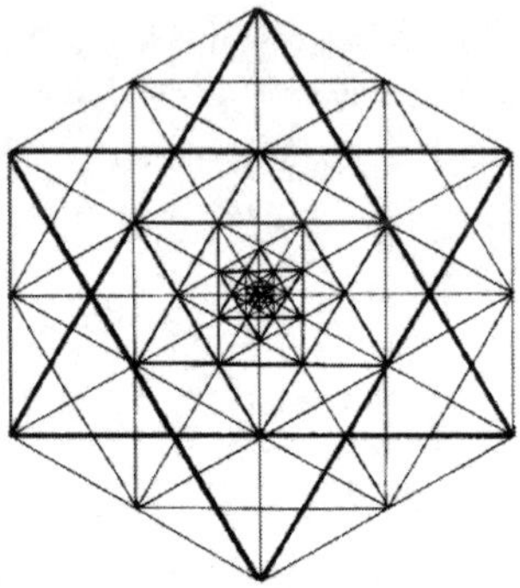

"Stranger than that, we're alive.
Whatever you think, it's more than that
More than that."

Robin Williamson, "Job's Tears", 1968

We spoke very little on our journey back from the Sun. Somehow it seemed disrespectful, almost sacrilegious, to clothe our feelings in words. We had transcended words, transcended the desire or need to speak. We communicated, rather, with shared looks, with smiles, hugs and, yes, even with tears of overwhelming joy. Compassion lay at the heart of our experience of touching the Sun, a compassion for everything: for our fellow passengers and crew upon Cutie 4, for the strong but vulnerable world to which we were returning, for our own selves and all our many foibles and failings, for every last object in this vast Universe, from the smallest speck of dust to the most distant galaxy. Compassion was our lifeblood.

I found myself spontaneously adopting the gassho gesture that I had learned and practised during my younger days of attending Zen retreats, where silence had been obligatory: palms together in front of the heart, accompanied by a bow of the head. The gassho - from the Japanese meaning "united palms" - serves a multitude of functions, from greeting to thanks to wonder to the simple acknowledgement of the shared Being of the other. So much can be communicated through such an easy gesture, palms together, head slowly bowed. Dancing Mountain caught on at once, and very quickly gasshos spread throughout the ship, replacing all manner of more normal conversations. Our journey home seemed like one long gassho of love and respect and thanks to our wondrous Sun.

Back at The Great Endeavour Headquarters, there were none of the usual de-briefing and conferencing sessions that we might have expected.

"A period of peace and contemplation is required," announced Dancing Mountain. "We must all assimilate what we have experienced in our own personal ways before we can consider what will come next."

His PA had arranged for a series of cars to whisk us off at once to wherever we wanted to be. Dancing Mountain himself was, I knew, headed for the wide open spaces of his Montana homeland. As for me, I was jetted discreetly back to Britain and driven to my old cottage in Somerset. And there I stayed for several weeks - just Being: sitting, walking, pottering, simply relishing every moment of the mundane. I didn't talk much, didn't write, didn't even give much thought to what had happened. Just to Be was enough. Call it what you will - bliss, satori, awakening, divine union, the Kingdom of Heaven - words are so much less than the glorious reality of that experience we shared as we approached the heart of the Sun. I prefer to call it simply Being. We were truly Being.

And then, that day on Cutie 4 as the great globe of the Sun virtually filled the front-facing screen, the fail-safe computer kicked in, whipping us around the back of the Sun and home again to our green and pleasant land.

After a couple of weeks I had a call from Dancing Mountain, inviting me to meet him in his virtual-reality room. Alas, my little cottage lacked this great luxury of modern life. Technologically, I have always lagged a few decades behind the latest trends. I drove up to Bristol and hired a virtual-reality booth for a few hours. First, I entered a black room the size of an antique telephone box where I was scanned from all directions to create a holographic image of myself with which my virtual-reality companion could communicate. Then I donned a sensi-suit and allowed my attendant to connect me up to assorted wires, goggles, ear-phones and God knows what else. Finally, suitably attired, I stepped into the empty V-R booth, a featureless four metre cube.

"Connecting you," I heard the attendant say, and the next words were Dancing Mountain's.

"Welcome, Doc."

The big man's image gradually took shape out of the ambient greyness. He was dressed in a brightly embroidered, knee-length Native American poncho, his long grey hair tied back in a pony tail, his face beaming. His hands were already in gassho gesture to greet me.

The room seemed to materialise around him, the same image I had seen in his conference room at the Great Endeavour HQ - the wide open plains, distant purpling mountains, the sky tinged with the colours of sunset. A small camp-fire burnt in the centre of this virtual environment, a couple of stools covered in buffalo hide sitting on the sandy floor. A coffee pot bubbled on a stone beside the fire. The aroma of coffee was just about discernible - the olfactory mode of virtual-reality had yet to be developed to the high standards of visual, auditory and tactile perception.

I returned Dancing Mountain's gassho, as my holographic image appeared before him. Then he reached out his arms and we met in a quick embrace, and together we broke into hearty laughter at the strangeness of embracing a hologram. We sat upon the stools and laughed some more, about nothing in particular. We were both ready laughers and this was the laughter of friends enjoying each other's company. For friends we were - no longer awesome boss and timid employee. Our communion had been forged in the loving heart of the Sun and was as strong a bond as I have ever known with another person.

Dancing Mountain was first to articulate any words. "Well, Doc, how's it been for you?"

What could I say? Finally I managed, "It's been good, Boss."

Dancing Mountain threw back his head and again roared with laughter. "Your adorable English reserve! All you can say is 'good'."

"So how's it been for you?" I asked.

"Absolutely bloody amazing," he replied. "And a hundred other superlatives that I won't bore you with cos I know you've felt them too."

We laughed again, as Dancing Mountain poured the coffee. I felt the sensation of lifting the mug, taking a sip, registering the warmth, but it didn't really taste much like coffee. Like the dream of interstellar space flight, virtual-reality has failed to live up to its glorious promise.

Perhaps Dancing Mountain's coffee tasted better than mine. He took a big gulp. "So, what's to become of us, Doc?"

"When you say 'us', do you mean you and me or the whole of humanity?"

"The latter, of course," replied Dancing Mountain. "You and me - we've got nothing to worry about. It's the other nine billion of us that concern me. Now even the dream of zapping off to another planet, of cruising through the galaxy has been crushed in its prime."

"The other day I read an article about Stephen Hawking," I said. "It included a quote of his from way back in the early years of the century. He said, 'I don't think we'll survive another thousand years without escaping beyond our fragile planet'."

"Well, he got it wrong on that one," said Dancing Mountain. "Even Stephen Hawking was not infallible. We're here to stay, for better or worse. So let's stop dreaming about what's out there and turn our attention to cleaning up the mess we've made of this place."

"As we've been saying for the past fifty, maybe even a hundred years," I said. "We've got all the science and technology. All that's lacking is the will to use it."

"These days," said Dancing Mountain, "I'm a firm believer in an old adage that's been around for quite a while: it's not science and technology that'll save the world. It's love. Love is all you need, as those old Beatles sang."

"There's nowhere you can be that isn't where you're meant to be," I added.

We sat sipping our coffees, our gazes locked. Yes, this is where we're meant to be. Here on Planet Earth, third rock from the Sun.

"You've spent your whole working life in the space business," I said. "Aren't you a bit disappointed that that dream's over?"

"Hell, no," replied Dancing Mountain. "This place is paradise, this world of ours. Why should we wish to be anywhere else."

He opened his arms to indicate the wide open plains of Montana and the sky, coloured by an ever-changing but never-finishing sunset. The irony that we were, in fact, both sitting in empty, windowless rooms on either side of the Atlantic Ocean, did not pass without a shared smile.

"But we've both been radically transformed by that experience we had, journeying to the heart of the Sun," continued Dancing Mountain. "We've seen the light, one might say. What of those nine billion who haven't? Simply recounting our experience is not good enough. I've tried it many times. So have you, I expect. No one truly understands. How can they? It's like trying to describe a taste to another person, or to describe an uplifting piece of music you've heard. No one's gonna understand. Everyone's gonna want to experience it for themselves. Talking about it just ain't good enough."

"So what's to be done? Send the entire population off on a trip to the heart of the Sun?"

"I wish we could. Perhaps we could build bigger ships, maybe carrying hundreds at a time, maybe even thousands. It only takes a matter of days to get there, after all. We could have them going back and forth like a regular train shuttle."

I nodded. "But even so," I said, "it's an option open only to very lucky insiders, like ourselves, or to the extremely rich. That's what bothers me."

"Of course," said Dancing Mountain. "We're talking very big money here. Spaceships like the Cuties don't come cheap. And tickets to the Sun and back, if the whole thing is to be viable, are going to be selling for mega-bucks. We're talking about several million dollars a piece, probably much more. It'll be a trip exclusively for the very rich, the famous and the powerful. But, you know, that doesn't necessarily bother me."

I expressed my surprise. "What, it doesn't bother you that it'll be like offering enlightenment to only the obscenely wealthy?"

"Maybe not."

"Come on, Boss, I know you well enough to know that you're no elitist capitalist. That's Fairfield's field, not yours."

"Consider this idea," said Dancing Mountain. "We use Cutie 4 to take twenty or thirty of the world's leading statesmen and billionaires on a trip that we know will change their lives. They're gonna come back transformed. So what are they gonna do when they get back home? Continue in their same old ways? Or, like us, perhaps they'll find love infusing everything they do. Total attitude change. Consider what that could mean, Doc."

"Interesting," I said. I could see where he was heading with this.

"Interesting indeed," he continued. "Why don't we spread this thing from the top down, rather than from the bottom up? Imagine all the world's leaders putting kindness, awareness, patience and humility at the top of their political agenda. Imagine the masters of industry doing what's best for their workers rather than their shareholders. Imagine the bankers acting through compassion rather than greed. Let's take the tyrants, too, the gang leaders, the slave traders, the arms dealers, the war mongers. Let's fill the ship with the world's worst and bring 'em all back as better people. Imagine the political and economic structures of the world run by men and women whose hearts are filled with boundless compassion. Imagine what kind of world that would be to live in."

For a few minutes we sat in silence, contemplating the prospect. Then, together, we threw back our heads and roared with laughter. (Dancing Mountain roared: I tend to be a gentler laugher.)

"Well you gotta laugh at such a ludicrous idea," said Dancing Mountain, recovering his composure. "And the really ludicrous thing is that it's an idea that just might save the world."

He poured more coffee - real for him, virtual for me.

"You know, Doc, all of us on board Cutie 4 were radically transformed, there's no denying it. As yet, we've kept things pretty low key. Just imagine the reaction when we go public. We're no bunch of religious fanatics. We're scientists, astronauts, technologists, managers, establishment figures with sound reputations. People are going to listen to us and think, hey man, I want some o' that. And who's going to be at the front of the queue? I reckon it'll be the rich and the powerful."

I nodded. He certainly had a point. And a plan. And I knew from experience that when Dancing Mountain had a plan, then there was no stopping him seeing it through to its conclusion.

"So what about you, Doc?" he said, conscious, perhaps, that he had been hogging our virtual-reality air-time. "What've you been thinking?"

"Well," I began hesitantly, "I've been thinking along somewhat different lines, I must say. You know, many of us psychologists, these days, are very much into the idea of morphic resonance. It's never been a particularly popular idea - certainly not mainstream science - but increasing numbers of us are thinking there's something to it. Ideas, feelings, modes of behaviour seem to spread so rapidly amongst our species. Our minds resonate with other minds in ways that go way beyond rational, materialistic explanation. Ideas spread like wildfire.

"We call it the hundredth monkey phenomenon. There's an old story of a group of ethologists - animal behaviourists - observing macaques monkeys on some remote Japanese island, back in the 1950s. They introduced the monkeys to sweet potatoes, left on the sandy beach. The monkeys loved them, but weren't too happy that they were covered with sand. Then along came a clever monkey who had the idea of washing them in the sea before eating them. Other monkeys copied him. Before long, a hundred monkeys had learned this new behaviour. And at that point it was discovered that monkeys on a nearby island also learned the behaviour, even though there was no actual communication between the populations of the two islands. The new idea, it was said, had spread throughout the species by morphic resonance. Once a critical number had learned it - a hundred, let's say - then the idea just zapped through the entire species.

"More than likely, the monkey story's a fabrication, but the idea behind it seems to be real enough. Change in human behaviour spreads at a phenomenal rate. Once the critical mass has been reached, then the new idea or behaviour pattern seems to spread throughout our collective consciousness. This is what happened at the beginning of the internet age. Things went 'viral', as they used to say.

"So I'm thinking, maybe when a few more of us have taken that trip to the heart of the Sun, maybe when, as you say, we go public about what we experienced, then maybe we'll see something happening. Maybe we'll see a new light spreading across humanity, the dawn of a new age."

Dancing Mountain had followed my drift. "You could be right, Doc. I certainly get the feeling that we're standing on the edge of a new era for mankind, and hopefully a reprieve for this wounded world of ours, before it's too late."

"We could be talking massive paradigm shift, here, Boss."

"We're talking revolution, Doc. And this ain't just a scientific revolution. It's a goddam religious revolution. D'you remember Bob giving us that sermon, that impassioned discourse on the Sun as God, while Cutie 3 was hurtling way beyond Mercury?"

I nodded. It was something I would never forget.

"Well, his words have been dancing through my head ever since. And I believe he was dead right. You scientists think you know quite a lot about the Sun, but everything you think you know begins from the assumption that the Sun is just a vast ball of burning gas. Of course scientists don't think of the Sun as a conscious, living being. Why should they? But why shouldn't they? You wouldn't approach the study of, let's say, an oak tree or a beetle except with the assumption that it is a living being. And yet people approach the study of the Sun with the assumption that it is certainly not living. They say, how can something that is so absolutely vast, composed of 85% hydrogen and helium, how can that be a living thing? The trouble is, we can't define life except in terms of our own kind. We can't define consciousness except as something that living things somehow possess - particularly carbon-based, organic living things like us. How can the Sun be alive, we say? How can it be conscious? The idea is absurd."

He paused and took a sip of his coffee, his eyes locked on mine all the while - oh, such playful and wise eyes.

"It's absurd," he continued, "until we abandon the idea and just look for ourselves, just let the truth into our hearts. And then it's obvious. Not only is the Sun a conscious, living being, it is also God - our creator, our sustainer, our Heavenly Father. We are all creatures of the Sun. Knowing this, then everything falls into place, simply and naturally. The extraordinarily complex patterns of electromagnetic changes that solar physicists observe in the Sun are no more mysterious than the changes of energy and matter that we see in a single living cell, or, let's say, the human brain. Looked at in this way, the Sun is like an enormous brain, its consciousness, we must assume, unimaginably vast and complex. Once every 365 days, we orbit the body and soul of God. Every moment of every day, we are bathed in the glorious love of God - otherwise known as sunlight or solar electro-magnetic radiation. Our entire bodies, thanks to the miracle of photosynthesis, are composed of that love of God. Can ya dig it, Doc? Can ya dig this idea?"

I nodded enthusiastically, grinning widely. "Yes, I can dig it, Boss."

"Scientists scoff. Call us a bunch of pagan pantheists. But we have come close to God, Doc. We've been there. We've communed with his presence. We know. The old religions demanded an irrational belief in the deity called God. We need no such belief in our deity, the Sun. We've felt its divine kiss. We know it beyond all doubt. It's God, it's love, it's the light of the Sun. People ask for proof. Well, let them step outside in the hours of daylight, let them look up. There's God: sitting there in the sky, looking at us, loving us, knowing us, flooding us in his divine grace. What more proof do you need?"

*

Just then I heard a voice in my ear that was not Dancing Mountain's.

"Your virtual-reality session will terminate in ten minutes."

"Gotta go soon, Boss," I said. I think he had also heard the message.

"We'll meet again, Doc," he said. "Our Great Endeavour is really just beginning. We're bonded, you and I, forever companions in the heart of the Sun."

He stood and presented me with a gassho, bowing lower and more slowly than is customary. I reciprocated the gesture, feeling a great love for this great man, and, through that love, a love for all men.

"Hey, Doc, one more thing before you return to your part of the world."

I awaited his final words.

"Will you dance with me?" he said.

"Dance?"

"Sure. That's what I enjoy doing more than anything. I'm a Dancing Mountain, ain't I?"

Music began to emanate from somewhere, rising, in a few seconds, from silence to pretty damned loud. I recognised it at once. I'd spent enough time in Dancing Mountain's company. It was from the early nineteen-seventies era of American West Coast rock: Jefferson Starship, who had provided the signature tunes of the first Cutie missions at the Great Endeavour HQ. The album was '*Sunfighter*', and the song now rising in volume was the finale, '*Holding Together*', a slow rock-n-roll masterpiece: snippets of inspirational Paul Kantner verse upon a piano-led tapestry of drums and exquisite Jerry Garcia guitar playing.

Dancing Mountain was moving his mountainous body, feet pounding slowly in the Native American way, body swaying, arms tracing patterns in the air.

I joined him in the dance: a free-flowing, spontaneous expression of the joy of movement. For the most part, our eyes maintained contact, relishing the sight of the other's gyrating body - mine tall and slender, his massive in all directions.

We danced, bathed in bliss.

The song finished with Paul Kantner's electric, anarchic voice:

"We leave the Earth to the wind,
To the cool, clean air that should have been here,
As we go...
As we go...
Into Nova."

The music faded, as did the dancing hologram of Dancing Mountain and the image of the Montana desert at sunset.

I was back in a featureless virtual-reality booth in England.

I was soaring through space, ninety-three million miles from the Heart of the Sun.

Surging ever onwards.

Flowing into Nova.

Into Newness

Into Nowness.

21
Epilogue II: The Sun of Kaph

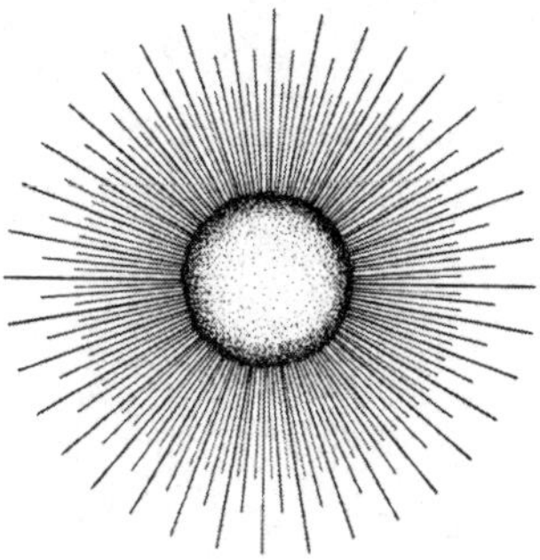

"At first, I was iridescent
Then, I became transparent
Finally, I was absent."

Paul Kantner, final words of "*Starship*", 1970

Kaph the Tale Writer disappeared without trace. Believe me: I tried very hard to find him. I followed leads that led all over the country, reported sightings from as far afield as Loch Ness, Lowestoft and Land's End. They all proved fruitless. Rumours of people called Kaph were rife. Everyone, it seemed, had met a Kaph somewhere, usually sitting in a cafe, freely dispensing help or advice or even just a listening ear to all who asked. The 'Society of Kaph', as it was called by some, had spread its branches and twigs across our land.

My search was personal. Kaph the Tale Writer was my father.

I was still a teenager when he set out on his never-ending walk. He and my mother had split up a few years before. The circumstances of their divorce are irrelevant and I will allow them to remain a part of our private family history. Suffice it to say that my parents retained sporadic but reasonably amicable contact and I saw my father quite frequently. Our father-son bond was undemonstrative but sound. I confess to feeling a certain pride in the success of his book, "*Tales of Kaph*". He gave me a number of signed copies, several of which I distributed amongst the friends I made in later life. That was how Dancing Mountain came to hear of the concept of Kaph.

We became close friends, Dancing Mountain and I, during the period preceding our trip to the Sun in Cutie 4. I was ensconced in a small cabin on the campus of the Great Endeavour while preparations for the trip were made. The big man would often visit of an evening, and we'd drink port or tequila and chat freely together into the early hours. Good times. He became one of the best friends I ever had.

My possessions in the cabin were of course sparse - I was only there for a matter of months - but a copy of "*Tales of Kaph*" was prominent amongst a small shelf of books.

"Who's Kaph, Doc?" asked Dancing Mountain.

"It's a book. By my father. Take it away and read it."

The time was not ripe for me to get into a discourse on the matter of Kaph. I'd let him discover it for himself. Not surprisingly, he loved the book - its style, its stories and the underlying themes of Kindness, Awareness, Patience and Humility.

"Good man, your father," he said, the next time we met. "Where is he now?"

"I wish I knew. It's been well over thirty years since I last saw him."

"Still alive, then?"

"No idea. He'd be in his eighties, now, I suppose."

Dancing Mountain nodded thoughtfully. He had no personal experience of father-son relationships. He was an orphan, brought up by a string of foster parents, and he'd never married and started a family himself. "Married to the job," was his response, whenever the question was asked. "Space was my bride; the Sun my lover."

If the Society of Kaph still existed in those strange years of the 2040s following our shared journey to the heart of the Sun - indeed, if the Society had ever existed - then Dancing Mountain surely deserved to become its honorary president. He was a natural advocate of all the Society stood for. And his fame rapidly became worldwide.

He was always Joseph Fairfield's golden boy and, when the nonagenarian trillionaire died, he inherited a good part of his fortune.

Fairfield wanted a part of the bliss that Dancing Mountain, myself and a few others had experienced on that first Cutie 4 trip to the Sun. He insisted on booking a seat for Cutie 4's second Sun-bound mission. We all knew that his health was rapidly deteriorating and that the adrenalin surge of it all may well prove too much for his frail body to take. He knew it too, but this was his life's dream and nothing could deter him. He was over ninety, a life replete with adventure and achievement. All that was left for him was the one ultimate experience of a space flight to the Sun. Of course Dancing Mountain granted this final wish and gave him a seat on Cutie 4, and another for his personal physician. A dozen of the world's top politicians and businessmen had also signed up, each contributing the required millions. Dancing Mountain's master-plan was ploughing full steam ahead.

Shortly after Cutie 4 had whipped around the back of the Sun and was on its computer-led journey back to Mercury, Venus and its Earthly home, Joseph Fairfield retired to his cabin, complaining of severe heart pains. His physician, realising that the end was near, recorded his final words:

"I've lived a good life and now it's time to die a good death. Thanks, Boss. It's been great."

It was commonly thought that he was directing these words to God, the great "Boss" in the sky - a deathbed conversion, perhaps. Fairfield hadn't had a boss for half a century or more. He was always the top man. But to Fairfield, as to all of us who had worked on the Great Endeavour, there was only one Boss and that was Dancing Mountain. Fairfield, in his final words, was using the common epithet of the man mountain who had made space flights to the Sun a reality.

Dancing Mountain didn't grieve over the demise of his friend and patron. He video-phoned me to tell me the news. I saw only awe in his face, the hint of a smile playing across his lips - a permanent feature since that enlightening experience on Cutie 4. Yes, they had been close, but Dancing Mountain knew that Fairfield had died with a smile on his own face. "A good man," he told me. "One of the best. He made a fortune for himself, not by trampling over others but by having bloody good ideas and by working bloody hard to make them happen."

Fair enough. Joseph Fairfield was the only trillionaire businessman I'd ever met. A strange taste in music, but basically a kind and decent man.

He left a substantial amount to Dancing Mountain in his will: several billion dollars, it was said. That still left billions more for his family and friends, plus a sizeable percentage to the US taxman, easing, to some extent, a struggling economy. His death was kept low-key in the mass media that he had always manipulated to his own ends. On the same day as the funeral, a government spokesperson announced that certain proposed cuts to services would not, now, be necessary: Joseph Fairfield's silent legacy to the people of America.

At first, Dancing Mountain was rather perturbed by the billions he received. He had no need of money. He had quite enough of his own, earned through years of work as head of the Great Endeavour. He retired from all active involvement with the Endeavour and settled, for a while, back in his Montana homeland. Then he began giving away Fairfield's billions.

For a year or two, that became his chief occupation: giving away huge sums of money. He chose his recipients carefully, ensuring that his gifts were used efficiently and ethically and spreading them liberally throughout the world. Wherever there was genuine need, he did what he could to assuage that need. Once he had been the "Boss" of the space business. Now he became the Boss of philanthropy.

He set up a company called simply "Kindness", the stated aim of which was not to make money but to give it away. His office in Helena, the capital of Montana, was visited by leaders of the world's nations, businesses and charities, pleading their various causes. He listened to all but gave his money only to those he deemed presented the most needy, ethically sound and environmentally beneficial cases. Photos started appearing in the media of various famous statesmen or charity celebrities, standing beside him, dwarfed by the huge man with his beaming smile, his massive white T-shirt emblazoned with the word "Kindness" - or, on occasion,

"Awareness", "Patience" or "Humility", for he had taken my father's book to heart and tried to live by and promote its principles whenever he could.

When all his fortune had been suitably distributed, he set out, like my father, to walk the world and see what might befall, to take the ideals of Kaph on the road and cultivate them, both in the world and in his own soul. Unlike my father, though, who carried a small backpack of very basic camping provisions when he set off on his great walk into oblivion, Dancing Mountain, as one would expect of the man, went to great lengths to prepare himself.

Remaining in contact with many of the top scientists, technologists and innovative designers of the day, he secured what was probably the most sophisticated, hi-tech backpack ever assembled. His sleeping bag weighed in at 300 grams - a super-lightweight material with adjustable thermal properties that had been developed for the latest generation of external use space-suits for space station astronauts. His tent, of a similar material and weight, was, when packed, the size of a tin of beans, but it unfolded to amply accommodate the big man plus, if needed, a companion. Likewise, every item of his personal backpack was as light, as durable and as efficient as modern science could devise.

Food was another matter. You only had to look at the man to realise that Dancing Mountain was a prolific eater, but few people were aware that he was a vegetarian. He loved all living things with such a passion that he could not accept that something should die in order that he might continue to live.

"I'm not prepared to kill another animal," he once told me. "I've done so in the past, but no more. And while I will happily employ other people to do various tasks for me, I believe it is wrong to ask anyone to do something that I am not prepared to do myself. So that excludes slaughtered meat from my diet. A pity," he added with a smile. "I used to love a good, juicy beef steak. These days, I content myself with extraordinarily realistic imitation beef steaks made from plant material. Fairfield used to jibe me about this, but I've cooked him many a beef-substitute soya steak and he's scoffed it with relish without suspecting anything vegetarian."

"And vegetables? You're not averse to killing plants, then?" I asked.

"I try my best not to. Most fruits and seeds and flowers and leaves and so forth can be picked without destroying the donor plant. Most plants positively thrive on donating their produce to animals' diets. And with those that don't, like root vegetables, for example, to which I am particularly partial, I take care to sow more seeds than I harvest."

Dancing Mountain decided that, despite his enormous appetite, throughout his walk he would live as much as possible as the plants live: making his own food from sunlight, carbon dioxide and water.

I knew, from Great Endeavour days, that one of his pet projects had been the development of artificial photosynthesis. During the early decades of the Twenty-first century, much progress had been made in the production of fuels, particularly hydrogen, by using sunlight to break down water molecules. But the great goal of artificial photosynthesis research was to create food, to replicate the manufacturing processes of a simple green leaf. Not too challenging a project, one would have thought. Raw materials: water, carbon dioxide and sunlight. End products: glucose and oxygen. Sextillions of plants did it every single day, with no apparent effort. Even the tiny leaves of a weed growing in the pot of a house-plant in a scientific laboratory could do it, easy as pie, but the scientists in the laboratory lagged miserably behind. They could build staggeringly complex computers, design and construct all manner of synthetic plastics, make artificial human hearts, even send space ships to the Sun - but they couldn't join six molecules of water to six molecules of carbon dioxide to make a molecule of glucose and six of oxygen. Every green plant in the world knows the secret, without even thinking about it. But our top scientists at the pinnacle of our civilisation were flummoxed.

The scientists at the Great Endeavour eventually cracked it, as they cracked most problems if enough cash was poured into the pot. It took a bit of doing, though. They estimated that the first artificial photosynthesis run produced a test tube of glucose costing several million dollars a kilo. Things were going better in the latter days of the Great Endeavour, which had always championed artificial photosynthesis (or "artfo", as it came to be called in typically American fashion) as the solution to the food problem on manned space flights beyond the solar system. Of course, that dream of cruising the galaxy had died along with the two astronauts who flew Cutie 3 into the heart of the Sun, but the research into artfo had continued, largely thanks to Dancing Mountain's passion for the project.

The problems were many and seemingly insurmountable. The equation for photosynthesis, learned by every schoolchild, simplifies the process to its basic starting and finishing points:

Water + carbon dioxide + sunlight → glucose + oxygen

In chemical symbols it looks even more elegant:

$6H_2O + 6CO_2 + \text{sunlight} \rightarrow C_6H_{12}O_6 + 6O_2$

But the arrow in the centre of the equation belies its immense complexity. This is not one chemical equation but a chain of dozens, perhaps hundreds, each of which is dependent upon specific enzymes produced in the plant cell, which is akin to a vast factory making, say, cars on an assembly line. And all of this happens every day in the humblest blade of grass. I'm no biologist and don't pretend to understand the chemistry of photosynthesis, but I am staggered by this monumental miracle of life.

The research and development finally bore fruit with the creation of the prototype "artfo jacket", which Dancing Mountain wore upon his epic walk. Shaped like a reasonably normal jacket, it was covered with small photocells capable of soaking up any degree of sunlight. Carbon dioxide was absorbed from the air (a tricky matter which plants cope with admirably, for CO_2 exists in the atmosphere as less than 500 parts per million, so it's not exactly in plentiful supply.) Water was added to the system via an aperture in the collar.

The artfo jacket performed its plant imitating work in tubules that made up its inner lining. A pouch in one pocket slowly filled with glucose in gel form. In the other pocket, various other organic substances were manufactured in small quantities.

Three times a day during his walk, Dancing Mountain would sit down to his artificially prepared meal, extracting a pouch of glucose from one pocket and a pouch of assorted nutrients from the other.

Even for a man of his bulk, the artfo jacket provided an adequate daily food intake. He was completely self-sufficient, reliant upon no one and nothing for his daily needs except the Sun and the atmosphere.

"How's it taste?" I asked.

"As you would expect: sweet, synthetic and basically pretty repulsive. But good enough to keep me alive and walking. And of course, if I'm offered a decent normal meal, I never refuse. Plus, I gather natural plant food whenever I can."

"And coffee?" I asked, knowing his favourite addiction.

"Unfortunately the jacket doesn't make coffee - although I'm told the boffins are working on that one."

Dancing Mountain's entire backpack and jacket weighed only 10 kilos. He'd given away all his possessions and this, he claimed, was all he needed to live indefinitely. He had no need of money, and he carried none. He was happy to live the rest of his life without ever touching a coin, a note or a card. He even had his embedded dermal ID chip removed.

"One day, we will all live like this," he told me. "Dependent on nothing but the Sun. Living on light, they call it. I prefer to call it living on the Love of God."

(I didn't like to remind him that his prototype artfo jacket was approaching the production stage: estimated retail value, fifty million dollars apiece. It would be quite a while before we could all live like that.)

I followed his progress from afar as he walked all over America. We spoke almost daily by mobile (he still carried a good selection of his favourite gadgets) and I'd often catch videos and audios of him on assorted programmes. Typically, he'd be pictured just standing there, legs apart, arms folded, that characteristic half-smile upon his face, gazing benevolently into the camera, his grey hair in a pony-tail way down his back, maybe posing in front of some iconic location - the Grand Canyon, the White House, the remains of the Golden Gate Bridge, the Last Californian Redwood, the Texas Apocalypse Memorial. His was an imposing figure, head and shoulders above any intrepid reporter who dared to interview him. And his bizarre jacket added to his already enormous girth, reflecting light in all directions as he moved.

"And what exactly is it you're doing, Mr... er... Mountain?" some interviewer would ask.

"I'm being," he would reply, widening his smile into a grin.

"Being what?"

"Being what I am."

"For what purpose?"

"Being doesn't need a purpose. Its purpose is simply to be."

He could have said much more. He was an eloquent speaker and the world's media were open to him. But he wanted his message to be the example of his being. He wanted to teach without words, to transmit his wisdom, as, he believed, that wisdom had been transmitted to him, directly from the heart of the Sun.

Having circled North America, he borrowed a yacht from Joseph Fairfield's grandson and sailed across the Atlantic for his tour of Europe - the first time, incidentally, that he had ever left America - apart from travelling through the inner planets of the solar system, that is. I followed him on the news sites: standing in Rome, Barcelona, Prague, on the steps of the Parthenon, on the peak of the Jungfrau in the Alps, in the courtyard of the World Justice Assembly in The Hague, in front of the Eiffel Tower, in front of the Kremlin.

Then he came to England to visit me in my Somerset home. It was good to see him in the flesh once again. We talked of the past and of the future, but mostly we talked of living in the present. We'd worked together on perhaps the most ambitious project mankind had ever undertaken. We'd been travelling companions on the ultimate space flight. And now we communed on a level that I have rarely known with another being.

After a few days, I decided to show him something of my neighbourhood, our local slice of green and pleasant land. We took a walk to the coast and then along the famous footpath that completely circumambulates mainland Britain.

One day we found ourselves upon a cliff-top near a red and white painted lighthouse. I shall refrain from elaborating upon the precise location of this lighthouse, just as my father, in writing "*Tales of Kaph*" refrained from ascribing the individual stories to anyone but himself. The anonymity of this particular lighthouse shall be preserved.

A well-placed bench on the cliff edge provided an ideal perch from which to observe the display of the setting Sun, enacted with customary perfection. We watched in silence. Sunsets make words redundant.

An elderly couple were standing nearby, similarly rapt. Once the Sun had disappeared, I turned my gaze from the western horizon and saw them, smiled and raised a hand in greeting.

The man raised his hand in acknowledgement and the pair strolled off, arm in arm, towards the door of the lighthouse.

"You live there?" I shouted across to the couple.

"We do indeed," replied the man, "and we often come out to watch if the sunset promises to be good."

"We've taken your favourite seat," I said, rising to my feet.

"That's all right. We believe it to be the best placed sunset watching bench in Britain. We're happy to share it with others who obviously appreciate the spectacle."

Dancing Mountain was on his feet, too. "Thank you," he said. "It's a seat worth sharing."

Of course, they just stared, wide-eyed, at the figure of Dancing Mountain, the last colours of the sunset sky still dancing across the photocells of his artfo jacket.

The woman pointed at him, spluttering out her words. "You're... you're that chap we've seen... On the news... Walking... Whatseecalled?"

"Dancing Mountain," the big man stated, offering a polite bow. "And this is my good friend Doc."

"Pleased indeed to me you," said the elderly man, stepping forward and offering his hand to us both. "We've been following your travels on the news. My name's Pooter. Matthew Pooter."

We shook hands. The man exuded bonhomie, I thought.

"And this is my partner, Cathy Hardy. No relation, I might add."

"No relation to whom?" I asked.

"To either Catherine Earnshaw or Thomas Hardy."

"Catherine Earnshaw of Wuthering Heights?"

"No relation at all," he repeated.

"But she's a fictional character, isn't she?"

"So is Charles Pooter, but I've been asked, so many times, if I'm related to him that I'm beginning to think he really was real, and perhaps a distant forebear. Or perhaps I'm a fictional character, too - the fictional great-great-grandson of the famous Charles Pooter, star of 'Diary of a Nobody'.And my Cathy's always saying that my behaviour and my attitudes are just like his. I don't know what she means by that, I'm sure."

"I'm not with you, sir," said Dancing Mountain who was almost certainly not acquainted with the English classic.

"Sorry," said Mr Pooter. "Just my little joke. I once worked with a scientist called Dr Charlotte Darwin and she always appended 'no relation' when stating her name."

"Pay no notice," said Cathy Hardy. "He always has a glass or two of port before sunset and it always makes him a bit squiffy."

"Nonsense, m'dear," replied Mr Pooter. "But I see you gentlemen are travelling types," he added, glancing at our backpacks on the ground by the bench. "Where are you spending the night?"

"We'll find a flat bit of grass somewhere on these cliff-tops," said Dancing Mountain. "We have a tent and all the necessaries."

"Perhaps a hot drink before you retire?" ventured Cathy, invitingly.

"Or even - ahem - a glass of port?" added Mr Pooter, indicating the door to the lighthouse.

"Most civil of you," I said. "We happily accept."

The lighthouse was everything one would expect of such a noble structure: a cylindrical tower built of massive blocks of stone, maybe forty feet high, immaculately painted on the outside in wide red and white bands. At the summit, the light still sent its warning to passing ships - once fuelled by wood, then gas, now electricity, automatically ignited and extinguished, taking its signal from the Sun. Lighthouse keepers became redundant years ago. Those lighthouses that retained living quarters for their keepers had mostly been sold off as private residences: a home of guaranteed panoramic views, exposed but well insulated, carrying a few hundred years of romantic baggage.

This one had four levels, a single room on each. A stout wooden door gave access to an entrance hall-cum-storeroom-cum-kitchen. The first floor was a circular living room, the second a bedroom plus bathroom. The top floor, of course, housed the light.

A spiral stone staircase connected the rooms. Up this we were led to the living room, sparsely but comfortably furnished: two armchairs, a wooden table and two chairs, a small bookcase and a chest of drawers against the wall. A wood-burning stove provided heat for the entire home. Most notable about this room were the four windows, facing the four cardinal points, tall, narrow, wide-silled and offering wonderful views of both land and sea. We stood a-while at the west facing window to gaze upon the final colours of the sunset.

Cathy insisted that we guests should take the armchairs, while she and Mr Pooter perched on the wooden dining chairs. A bottle of port sat upon the table, next to a single glass. After asking our preferences, Cathy fetched three more glasses from the chest of drawers and Mr Pooter filled them.

"To lighthouses and their welcoming residents," said Dancing Mountain, raising his glass, and we all did likewise, our glasses meeting for a quick clink at the exact centre-point of the room.

"So, how did you come by such a home?" I asked.

"We've always loved lighthouses," said Cathy. "When this one came on the market, we couldn't resist. It's small, as lighthouses go, but perfect for an old couple like us."

"My father was a lighthouse keeper," said Matthew Pooter.

"And so was mine," said Cathy.

"A remarkable coincidence," said Dancing Mountain.

"We prefer to call it a synchronicity," said Matthew Pooter. "It was the destiny of both of us, one might say, to spend our final years in a lighthouse. The path of that destiny was a series of synchronicities."

"My father was a great lover of synchronicities," I said. "He wrote that once you start to experience them, you see them everywhere. All moments, all people, all places are connected and flow in the single dance that we call time. A synchronicity is a glimpse of the beauty of that dance, a potent correspondence between an inner and an outer event."

"Indeed so," said Matthew Pooter, adding enigmatically, "But where lies the boundary between inner and outer?"

We all looked at him and he returned the gaze of each of us in turn - long, lingering gazes that seemed to be full of love and awareness.

"There is no boundary," he quietly answered his own question.

And all four of us gazed in turn at each other, and the energy within that circular lighthouse room seemed to take a quantum leap to a higher level.

We were silent for what seemed like many minutes. It was me who broke that silence.

"My father once said that each synchronicity is the start of a new story."

"Let's hope it's a story with a happy ending," said Matthew Pooter, a man who, now in his eighties or nineties I would guess, had perhaps found a happy ending to his own story.

"It's not for us to say," said Dancing Mountain, "whether the end of the story be happy or sad. Nor, indeed, exactly where one story ends and another begins."

"The story of life," I said, following his drift, "has no ending. It just goes on forever changing."

"You're right, Doc," said Dancing Mountain. "This old Earth of ours just keeps on changing, and for all our wit, our ingenuity, our technology, our selfish greed, our thoughtless pollution, our cruel abuse, our absurd arrogance, we're all nothing more than ripples on the surface, alive for our brief span, then gone. Meanwhile, the Earth and the Sun live on."

We all stared at the wood-burning stove, a black cylinder beside the wall, its transparent door revealing the glowing embers of driftwood from the beach, and in the light of that ancient sunshine we each remembered our own stories: stories full of ups and downs, of successes and failings, of synchronicities and so-called accidents: stories that had led us all to this place, this moment.

At length, the deep voice of Dancing Mountain broke into our reveries. “So, you strike me as a spiritual man, Mr Pooter. May I ask what religion, if any, you follow?”

“You may ask, and I will respond,” said Matthew Pooter. “And you are right to separate the words spiritual and religion. I follow no particular religion. In my time, I have examined many and, although I see good things in them all, I have found none that resonates wholeheartedly with my heart and mind. I’ll say nothing against all those religions that are so deeply cherished by so many millions. It’s just that they’re not for me.

“But as for spirit - I see it everywhere: here, behind the eyes of the four of us, here in this cosy room, out there upon the cliffs, out over the endless sea, the setting Sun, the starry night sky - all is spirit.”

“Well said,” said Dancing Mountain. “We share the same vision, I believe.”

Matthew smiled. “We share the same spirit, I believe. And that same spirit, for each of us, lies at the very centre of everything. I know you to be a space scientist, Mr Mountain. No doubt you may point to some remote black hole as the centre of our galaxy, our Sun as a trivial blip of light circling round it. I see things differently. From my personal, subjective point of view, the singularity of the galaxy is right here, and all that other stuff radiates outwards, slowly revolving, increasing in insignificance in proportion to its distance from this precise centre point. Your scientific, so-called objective viewpoint is, I believe, a fiction. There is no such thing as an objective view of the Universe, because to have such a view, one would have to stand outside the Universe, and that is impossible. We each have our subjective view of things, and that plonks us firmly at the very centre.

"So that's my spirituality, Mr Mountain. It starts right here. His Majesty the King is not the most important person in the country. I am. Jesus Christ is not the supreme human being. I am. God is not a distant, separate entity, overseeing the whole works from some celestial vantage point. He is right here, looking through the eyes of this ageing, decrepit and rather pathetic specimen of humanity called Matthew Pooter!"

He gave us all a beaming smile and sipped his port.

"I like your spirituality, Matthew," replied Dancing Mountain. "Yes, I was once a space scientist, and, yes, I once imagined a near infinite Universe with our tiny planet and our even tinier lives as nothing more than passing specks of dust in the grand scheme of things. But Doc and I, we've been to the heart of the Sun. And things look very different from there. You're right. The heart of the Sun is within each of us."

"We are each the sole heir of the whole world," I quoted.

"Thomas Traherne," said Cathy.

"You know of him?"

"Of course," said Matthew. "You never enjoy the world aright till the sea itself floweth in your veins, till you are clothed with the heavens and crowned with the stars. That, succinctly put, is our spirituality."

"And you live happy lives, I can see that," said Dancing Mountain.

"We do our best," said Matthew. "Over eighty years of doing just that have convinced me of the simplicity of happy living. The matter is clear. To be kind, to be aware, to be patient and to be humble. These are the qualities that, I believe, encapsulate 'The Good Life'. Kindness, Awareness, Patience and Humility - gathered together in the acronym KAPH."

Dancing Mountain looked at me. We shared a moment's wonder.

"My aim in life," continued Matthew, "is to manifest these qualities as often as possible, which really means as often as I remember. And so I do, although often I err, slipping into unkindness, unawareness, impatience and egotism. Not to worry. If I continue to do my best, then hopefully my best will continue to get better."

With that, he picked up his glass from the table. "I raise a glass of port to KAPH. This shall be my sacrament."

Once again, we all clinked our glasses together at the exact centre-point of the circular room. I was so astounded by the coincidence of coming upon another KAPH devotee in this remote coastal outpost of England, that I was at a loss for words. Dancing Mountain was also content to savour the moment in silence. Besides, our host, Mr Pooter, having taken centre stage, was enjoying the limelight.

"Cathy and I have lived in this lighthouse for thirty years or more," he continued. "We've grown old together here. It is likely that we were both conceived in a lighthouse and it is our hope that, when our time comes, we shall die within these sturdy walls."

Dancing Mountain and I both nodded and smiled. Words like those need no verbal response.

"We go little out into the world, these days," continued Matthew, "but men and women of the world come to us, from time to time, and we are happy to see them. Travellers, like yourselves, are always welcome."

His warm gaze enfolded us and we felt welcome indeed.

"You remind me, sir," he continued, addressing me, "of one such traveller we entertained, oh, many years ago - perhaps twenty or more. Something in your face, your bearing, your manner and gestures brings up his image in my mind's eye. His name, strangely, was that same acronym I just mentioned. He called himself Kaph."

Yes, my heart skipped many a beat, my eyes widened, a flush of excitement spread like a breaking wave over my whole body and my attention became riveted to the moment. Yet I said nothing in reply. The spell woven by Matthew's words was too precious and too fragile to risk disturbing.

"Kaph," repeated Matthew, and Cathy was nodding."I asked him, somewhat puzzled, 'Just Kaph?''Kaph the writer of tales,' he replied, 'Kaph the walker, the listener, the sunset watcher.'

"He stayed with us for several days, making a considerable impression on us, it must be said. Like you, Mr Mountain - or so we have heard tell of you - this Kaph carried no money but paid for what hospitality he received with story-telling or poetry. When he left us, he gave us a poem he had written, right here at this very table, immaculately scribed with a quill pen upon a piece of old vellum. We kept it, of course, framed it and look to it often. Even now it sits upon the sill of our east facing window."

He turned to indicate the window, and Cathy, who was the more sprightly of the two, reached for it and handed it to Matthew who passed it to me.

"Our eyes are weak in this twilight," he said. "Perhaps you would care to read it to us all."

I held the frame for a few moments, but my hands were shaking, my eyes were watered over and my emotions too turbulent to be able to focus on the hand written words. I passed it to Dancing Mountain whose deep, clear voice seemed more appropriate to this extraordinary occasion.

He began reading at once, slowly and softly, as the last colours of the setting Sun seeped into the western window and the wood-burning stove infused a warm glow into the round room...

"When all fine words are spoken, when all bold deeds are done,
when the outflows of our egos have dried up
and the last strains of garble and gossip have faded into silence,
when all things clutched are discarded, all grasping relaxed,
all pride humbled, all opinions tossed to the wind

Then we stand free, as open and vulnerable beings,
as migrant visitors to this world,
as empty souls replete with experience,
as gloriously glowing vacancies,
holes through which life is pouring in never-ending stream.

We are each the Holy Grail, the Christ, the Buddha,
each the centre and the circumference,
each the light, the seer and the seen,
each the source and the expression of That Which Is.
Each one of us the crown of creation.

When all fine words are spoken
Let us be silent
Let us be.

*

Now let us consider the world and all its wonders.
Let us unleash the muse, open hearts to the wisdom of intuition.
Let us savour the sights and sounds, the scents and tastes,
the touches and tingles on and within the skin,
the thoughts and feelings, the laughs and cries,
the stillness and silence that underlies the pageant,
the Being, the Awareness, the Bliss: all this we are.
Let us sit in the centre of it all.
Let us dance and sing, love and converse.
Let us be."

THE END

Acknowledgments

With thanks to friends and fellow writers who were the first readers of most of these stories and whose advice and criticisms were greatly appreciated: Wes White, Graham Morton, Chris Merritt, Caroline Tapfield, Anna Young and, especially, Johanna van Fessem.

Literary acknowledgments are due to Hermann Hesse, Jorge Luis Borges, John Fowles, P. G. Wodehouse, Walt Whitman, Thomas Traherne, Douglas Harding, Paul Kantner, Robin Williamson, Roger Waters, Van Morrison and Bob Dylan - plus, no doubt, numerous others.

Notes on the stories

1. The Heart of the Sun: The first draft of this can be dated back to the first year of the Twenty-first Century. Since then, it has gradually evolved. I still believe that its central idea might well be true.

2. The Last Five Minutes: This story was also written in the early years of the century, and I am pleased to have published it before the centenary of the events it describes. Yes, I know that many others have attempted to portray the same circumstances but it is a scene that deserves to be revisited by every generation of writers.

Although I have lived in Somerset for more than thirty-five years, I must apologise for inaccuracies in the dialect.

3. Shadow Walking: Winner of the 2010 Weston-super-Mare short story competition and first published in the competition anthology, "Shadows". Johanna and I walked the entire length of the St Michael Line, from Lowestoft to Lands End, in 2004.

4. The Tower: No doubt inspired by the work of Jorge Louis Borges, one of my favourite short story writers.

5. Pooter II: Okay, so Matthew Pooter is my fantasy alter ego and I love to see the world through his eyes and speak through his mouth. I have written an entire novel in his first person voice, which may one day see the light of day.

6. The Colour of Trees: First published in "My Weekly" magazine in 2007. A whimsical tale, but I like it.

7. Tales of Kaph II: Maybe it's a bit preachy and low on action, but I regard this as a pretty good expression of my personal spiritual philosophy. After the first "Tales of Kaph" was published, several people asked me how they could join the "Society of Kaph".

8. The Value of Money: Another whimsical tale. The first person character featured in another of my unpublished novels. Perceptive readers might identify this unnamed youth as the narrator of "Dictionary" in "Tales of Kaph".

9. The Dancing of the Lord of Weir: A fairy-tale-type story, based on the wonderful Robin Williamson song.

10. Pooh Sticks at the TIE Club AGM: A silly story written after Johanna and I walked the length of the River Wye in 2010, playing pooh-sticks at every bridge we crossed. Pooh-sticks is the ideal sport for idlers.

11. The Executioner's Paradox: Another silly story based on a delightfully absurd logical paradox.

12. Diverse Antecedents: Probably involves too many characters for a short story, and it needs to be read slowly and carefully, but I am particularly fond of it.

13. A Curious Elliptical Interlude: Curious indeed. At the end of the monthly meetings of our small writing group, we often choose a word by jabbing a finger onto a randomly opened page of the Concise Oxford Dictionary. This word may suggest inspiration for a piece of writing. I always enjoy this exercise, which has provided the initial impetus for a few stories in this book. In this case, the chosen word was "ellipse".

14. Whim's Tale: Best regarded as a fable about modern life.

15. Mr Perkins gets it right: Any similarity between characters and incidents in this story and events pertaining to Somerset County Council's attempt to close some of its libraries in 2011 is purely coincidental! I was happy to revive the characters of Ralph Perkins and Irene Firth.

16. A Tale of Misfortune: Strangely, this was the story least liked by the preliminary readers of this book, but it is one of my favourites. I await further comments upon it.

17. The Walker: Another story written many years ago that retains its relevance.

18. The Departure of the Cryptomancer: I was pleased to revive the character of Felix Sunheart.

19. Pooter Again: This and the following two "Epilogue" stories revisit some former characters and ideas. Although light-hearted, they are vehicles for the central "message" that I am trying to convey throughout all the stories. Much of this story was composed on Brean Beach and Down, where it is set, in 2013.

20. Epilogue I: Return from the Heart of the Sun: Of course I had to return to the opening tale and consider what happened next.

21. Epilogue II: The Sun of Kaph: This one just happened, some time after the first draft of the book was complete. It's one of my favourites and brings the book, I think, to a satisfying close.